A REAL KISS

"Thank you for saving my life," Casity murmured as she watched him bind strips of her petticoats around her swollen leg.

He reached for the branch he had gathered to serve as a splint. "Be thankful you aren't a horse," he said. "I might have had to shoot you."

When he had finished, he sank down beside her on the blanket, as if he belonged there. "Hey, mister," Casity snapped, "I appreciate what you've done for me, but if you think you and I . . . are going to . . ."

"There's one blanket between us," he said. "If I wanted to ravish you, I would have. All I want is a decent night's sleep."

"You don't find me attractive?" Casity asked. "Are you going to lie there and tell me that if I—and this is purely hypothetical, of course—offered you a kiss of gratitude, you would turn your back on me and go to sleep?"

Shaler rolled sideways, watching her luminous blue eyes widen as his lips moved closer. "Offer me a kiss of gratitude, princess. And then go the hell to sleep."

Casity moved closer and let her lips brush his.

Shaler frowned. "What was *that*?"

Was he making fun of her? "A kiss, of course."

He chuckled. "Not where I come from, it isn't."

Casity felt herself sinking into a cloud as his lips met hers and their bodies meshed tightly together, as if they were sharing the same skin . . .

FORBIDDEN KISS

GINA ROBBINS

ZEBRA BOOKS
KENSINGTON PUBLISHING CORP.

ZEBRA BOOKS are published by

Kensington Publishing Corp.
850 Third Avenue
New York, NY 10022

First Printing: December, 1995

Printed in the United States of America

This book is dedicated to my husband, Ed, and our three children, Kurt, Jill, and Christie, with much love . . .

One

Ogallala, Nebraska
1876

Casity Crockett instinctively ducked away from the whistling bullets that zinged down the main street, then plastered herself against the brick wall of the bank from which she had just emerged. With an air of resignation, she watched the passel of trail-dusty cowboys thunder through town—whooping, hollering, and startling the horses tied to hitching posts along the street.

Casity had heard the report earlier in the afternoon that another herd of longhorns from Texas had been driven into the stock pens. Along with the herd came a brigade of rowdy hombres anxious to celebrate the trail's end in the wildest fashion imaginable.

When Clint Lake, the town marshal, buzzed past her, Casity stared after him, wondering why he hadn't tired of these shenanigans and accepted a job in a more civilized town than Ogallala.

Clint turned abruptly, his dark brows furrowing in concern. "Are you all right, Casity? I'd escort you back home, but as you can see—"

"I'll be fine," she assured him.

"I'd feel better knowing you were safely tucked away," Clint insisted.

Casity offered an appreciative smile. Ever since Clint had assumed the duties of marshal six months earlier, she had known he had developed a certain fondness for her. She had always been polite but reserved in his presence, but there was no mistaking his interest.

Most of the men with whom Casity came in contact were reckless trail hands and shrewd gamblers. After several near-brushes with calamity, she had become extremely cautious. In her estimation, men lived a day-to-day existence, treating women as if they had only been created to pleasure their lust. Casity had suffered enough leering smiles, wolfish whistles, and lurid propositions the past few years to turn her into a cynic at the ripe old age of twenty!

Thus far, the only man in town to whom she bothered to give the time of day was Clint Lake. That was not to say she encouraged his attention, but neither had she rejected him. She supposed that if she ever felt the inclination toward romantic involvement, Clint would be her first and only choice. He was courteous and respectful, and even a mite reserved around her . . .

When a stray bullet plunged into the water trough beside the boardwalk, Casity found herself engulfed by powerful arms and propelled back inside the bank. Her wide blue eyes caught a glimpse of Clint's face only a few inches above hers. They were suddenly sharing the kind of familiarity she had never experienced with a man.

Clint was hard-pressed not to take those dewy pink lips under his, as he had dreamed of doing since he first laid eyes on this auburn-haired beauty. But he had been taught to treat a lady with the utmost respect and courtesy. Still, there were times—like now, especially now—when he was sorely tempted to steal a kiss to determine if Casity Crockett tasted as good as she looked. However, noble reserve and another barrage of pistol fire brought Clint to his senses. With tremendous effort, he set Casity away from him and cautiously tucked her behind the door.

"Stay out of sight until the wild bunch blows through town to drink their fill at their favorite watering holes," Clint instructed as he drew his pistols and pivoted toward the street. "I don't want anything to happen to you, Casity."

Once the cloud of dust rolled past and the bark of pistols resounded in the distance, Casity sped out the door and headed toward her uncle's dry goods store. The blaring shots mingled with the wailing whistle of the train, which was due to arrive within the next few minutes. From all indications, it would be a hectic night. The town marshal would have his hands full corralling the drunken horde.

No one would be able to sleep a wink, Casity mused as she scurried down the boardwalk. How she detested the spring and fall cattle drives that left the town overrun with unruly heathens!

In the twilight, Casity surveyed the swarming hooligans intent on announcing their approach with blazing pistols, assuring the citizens of Ogallala that Texas had arrived. They came to shoot the place up, drink themselves blind, and make complete nuisances of themselves.

Very soon, tinkling piano music would fill the air and the calico queens would have a heyday entertaining the whiskey-bound cowboys licking their lips in anticipation of an endless night of rotgut, gambling, women, and song . . .

Suddenly two of the obnoxious trail hands reversed direction to clamber onto the boardwalk atop their wild-eyed steeds. Casity found herself nearly trampled by the horses and looking into the hungry stares of two lusty men who smelled worse than their mounts. Casity swore neither man nor beast had bathed since their departure from Texas!

"Where've you been all my life, honey?" Ned Johnson drawled in what Casity assumed was his most provocative tone.

She wasn't impressed; in fact, she was highly offended. Their intense survey of her body got her hackles up in a hurry. "Excuse me," she said, flashing the stubble-faced ruffian a glance that could have frozen kerosene. "Kindly let me pass, sir."

"Ain't too friendly are you, honey?" Russel Bassett chuckled as his gaze continued to wander over Casity's physique.

"I am not anyone's *honey*," she snapped, tossing her auburn curls. "Now remove your horses from my path this instant! You're supposed to be Texans, not barbarians."

The train whistle broke the strained silence as the two men stared at Casity like starved sharks. Ah, what she wouldn't have given for a big stick! She would have pounded some manners into these rude, offensive heathens whose stench was making her eyes water. Not only did they stink to high heaven but they were physically unappealing as well. The taller of the two had hatchet-like features, close-set black eyes, and limp, stringy brown hair. The other man was built like a tree stump. His face reminded Casity of rising dough and his ruddy complexion was one solid freckle.

Since the human barricades refused to remove themselves from her path, Casity detoured into the street and then stepped back onto the boardwalk to continue on her way. Tiring of their game, the two men clattered off down the street to blow a few more holes in the wispy clouds.

Casity cursed the fact that her uncle had settled in such a raucous town. If she had any sense, she would pack her belongings and strike out on her own, putting as much distance as possible between herself and this plague of pesky Texas cowpokes. But she didn't have the heart to leave her uncle—her only living relative.

Aunt Hilda had gone to her reward the previous year, and Casity knew all too well how devastating it was to lose loved ones. She had remained with Uncle Daniel for moral support, just as he had come for her when her parents had died in the typhus epidemic eight years earlier. If not for Daniel's kindness and generosity, Casity would have wound up in an orphanage or on her own at the tender age of twelve. She owed Daniel a great deal. To desert him while he was still grieving over Hilda would be most ungrateful. Since she and Daniel were the last of the Crocketts she supposed they should stick together, but sometimes . . .

Casity flinched when a stray bullet ricocheted off the supporting beam of the print shop, missing her head by mere inches. *Men!* she fumed as she buzzed on her way. They were such an uncivilized lot. She wouldn't give a hundred dollars for the whole herd of them.

Amid the uproarious laughter, thundering horses, and flying bullets, Casity made her way down the alley to the Crocketts' living quarters at the back of the dry goods store. A sigh of relief escaped her lips when she stepped inside, but her relief was short-lived. She heard growling voices wafting from the front of the store. She tiptoed through the parlor to eavesdrop on the conversation between two men and her uncle.

"I'll gladly furnish you all the traveling provisions

you need when you can pay for it," Daniel was saying in a firm tone. "Until then, these sacks remain here."

"Now hold on, old man. You ain't in any position to make demands."

Casity poked her head around the corner to see the very same men who had harassed her on the boardwalk. She certainly didn't blame her uncle for refusing to offer credit to these scraggly scoundrels. More than likely, they wouldn't be back to pay for their supplies.

It wouldn't be the first time some trail hand skipped town with goods after he had squandered his wages on harlots and hard liquor. Daniel would have been bankrupt years ago if he extended credit to these Texas sidewinders. They were renegades and outlaws for the most part. If railheads and cattle towns like Ogallala were fortunate, these scalawags would shoot each other before they harmed innocent victims. But all too often, a decent citizen wound up biting the bullet.

"We're taking the supplies, old man." Ned Johnson's hatchet-like features turned to stone as he whipped out his pistol.

When Daniel stretched out his hand to be sure the heaping sack remained where it was, Casity's blue eyes widened in alarm and an audible gasp escaped her lips. Ned Johnson misinterpreted Daniel's gesture as an attack, and the unexpected sound of Casity's voice caused him to react reflexively. The pistol exploded and Casity watched in stunned horror as her uncle pitched backward on the floor.

With pistols cocked and ready, both men wheeled around to see Casity standing in the doorway.

"It's the same prissy bitch we saw on the street," Ned scowled. "Get her."

Panic-stricken, she lurched around to take cover. She was the only witness to a senseless murder, and the two snarling renegades had that look about them—a look that spelled certain death! Her survival instincts hard at work, Casity sprinted off before either man could get a clear shot at her.

"It's us or her," Ned growled as he rushed toward the back of the store. "If she wags that sassy tongue of hers, we'll be swinging from a rope."

Fear tightened Casity's throat as she barreled through the parlor to the back door. Behind her, she could hear the scrabbling of boots and the men's obscene curses. Blood-pumping terror spurted through her as she dashed outside. Darkness had descended on the riotous cowtown. The shot that killed her uncle had mingled with the constant random gunfire. Casity's only chance of survival was to disappear into the darkness.

Cursing her skirt, Casity zigzagged down the alley, dodging trash cans and shadows, knowing only a miracle could save her. She could still hear muffled curses and the exploding pistols aimed in her general direction. She was sure to suffer the same fate as her uncle, she thought hysterically.

Only when both men paused to reload their revolvers was there a remote chance of escape. Like an uncoiling spring, she bounded down the alley. Even the sound of the train's whistle couldn't drown out the hammering of her own frantic pulse against her eardrums.

"You ain't going anywhere, bitch. You're going to end up just like the old man," Ned sneered. "And if you run for help, we'll send your guardian angel to hell right along with you!"

The way Casity saw it, her only hope was to buy herself a train ticket. Although she had deposited the day's earnings in the bank, she had kept her own wages. The train would be her salvation. Once she had decided how to deal with this tragic affair, she would double back to Ogallala . . . if she managed to get out of town alive.

Another shot whizzed past her head, causing her to shudder and offer up another hasty prayer.

"Argh!"

When Ned Johnson stumbled over the crates strewn about the darkened alley, Casity took advantage of the distraction to dart between the pastry and printing shops. The train whistle beckoned her once more, but the depot was another block away. She could hear the rumbling locomotive creaking on its tracks. Damn it all, she was going to miss the train! It had already gathered its west-bound passengers and was rolling on its way, leaving her at the mercy of two murderers hot on her heels!

Casity dashed across the crowded street, veering around a mob of trail hands who were trying to decide which watering hole to visit first. Her anxious gaze focused on the lantern dangling in the window of the caboose. There would be no time to purchase a ticket at the depot, only time to race after the train and throw herself onto the back platform. Nor would there be time to grieve her uncle's passing. She would have to save her mourning until later—if there was a *later*.

Clutching the hem of her skirt, Casity jogged past another throng of foul-smelling men. If she was lucky, her pursuers might not realize she had jumped on the train until after they had torn the town upside down looking for her.

Casity could think of a few friends she might have called upon for assistance, but the idea of siccing those two ruthless devils on a defenseless acquaintance was unthinkable. Clint Lake would have come to her rescue, but Casity didn't have the faintest notion of where he was at the moment. He had more than enough trouble trying to keep a lid on this rowdy town. Later, she would notify Clint of the details surrounding her uncle's death and her hasty departure. *If* she escaped this disaster alive!

Gasping for breath, Casity raced alongside the track. She stretched out her hand toward the railing of the caboose as the train gathered steam and speed. A cry of despair wobbled in her throat when she saw the platform of the caboose inch farther away from her fingertips.

In a last-ditch effort, Casity threw herself toward the railing. Her shaking fingers clamped around the metal. Without the slightest concern for modesty, Casity flung her bare leg over the rail and half-collapsed on the teetering platform. Safe at last. Praise the Lord, safe at last . . .

"What's going on here?"

Casity's thick lashes swept up to see two booted feet and a massive chest above her. The train attendant surveyed the scene in the lanternlight that splayed through the door of the caboose.

"You okay, miss?" Bernard Stokes questioned.

The concern in Bernard's voice was sweet music to Casity's ears. "I nearly missed the train," she croaked as she gathered her knees beneath her. "There wasn't even time to purchase my ticket."

Two brawny arms reached out to hoist her to her feet. "Well, don't worry about that, missy. The conductor will gladly take your money. We have plenty of extra seats."

Casity cast an apprehensive glance over her shoulder and grimaced when she spied the shadows lurking in the distance. She had the unshakable feeling that her would-be assassins had seen her bound onto the train and would be following her.

"Come along, missy," Bernard insisted. "We'll get you settled in."

Still dazed from her terrifying experience and her uncle's tragic death, Casity allowed herself to be shuffled into the caboose. It was on the tip of her tongue to explain the horrifying events, but one look at the elderly attendant warned Casity that this man would inevitably get himself killed if he tried to protect her. She had heard Ned's venomous threat and she had no doubt that he meant what he said. No, her only recourse was to lie low until she could find a lawman capable of holding his own against those two heartless murderers.

"You just wait here," Bernard instructed with a comforting smile. "I'll climb over to the second-class passenger car and tell the conductor we have a late arrival. When the train pulls into the next whistle stop, you can take a seat. In the meantime, use one of the bunks to rest."

Casity nodded mutely as she watched the bulky man lumber out the door to pull himself atop the train. Judging from the noxious fumes permeating the caboose, several cattle cars had been coupled directly in front of them. But Casity preferred the smell of cattle to the stench of death . . .

A sob caught in her throat when the horrifying event exploded in her mind's eye. Now that the danger had passed—temporarily at least—Casity felt the full impact of her loss. An empty ache filled the cavity where her heart had been. A flood of emotions overwhelmed her and guilt hammered at her conscience. If she hadn't startled those two heathens her uncle might still be alive. It was her fault. *Her fault!* Because of her slip at that critical moment, she was left alone in the world. The torment she had experienced when she lost her parents and her aunt swamped her, increasing with rapid intensity. It seemed everyone she had ever loved had been stripped from her life. Now she was the last of her breed—with a death threat on her head!

Through a mist of tears, Casity stared at the swaying lantern as it cast dancing shadows on the walls. She promised herself, there and then, that she would never allow herself to care so much for another living soul again. One more traumatic loss would truly and surely destroy her. She was already feeling like a person on a train bound for nowhere, with no hope of a future . . .

Casity squeezed her eyes shut and cursed the snarling faces that appeared before her. Damn those murdering bastards! They had taken the life of a good and decent man in exchange for their rotten supplies! Daniel Crockett's life was worth a good deal more than that! But what could one expect from those uncivilized barbarians? They were men—despicable one and all! Clint Lake was the only man whom Casity had ever allowed near her. She had even kept him at an arm's length, just in case he turned out to be as rotten as the rest of his gender.

Guilt, grief, and bitterness burgeoned inside Casity as she flung herself on the cot to release another surge of hot tears. Someday, somehow, she would hunt down those murdering barbarians and give them their comeuppance. There were too many unsolved crimes in Ogallala as it was, too many deaths. Avenging Daniel Crockett's death would become her personal crusade. Those two butchers would pay with their lives!

With that vengeful thought, Casity cried herself to sleep, only to be awakened by a horrifying nightmare. Despite her fierce need for revenge, one thought echoed through her mind: she couldn't become the hunter because she was still the prey.

To what extent would her uncle's assassins be willing to go to locate and exterminate her? Casity shuddered to think of it. They would be tracking her—she knew that as well as she knew her own name. And they wouldn't give up until they had accomplished the dastardly deed.

If she had any sense, she would keep a low profile on the train. If she could hold out long enough to gather her wits and devise the best way to proceed, she might be able to begin *her* search for *them*. Then, she would have the element of surprise on her side. Her emotions were running much too high at the moment. She had to give herself ample time to cope with her loss and consider the most appropriate action.

Casity settled back on the cot to regenerate her strength and spirit. No matter what she had to do, no matter how long it took, she would avenge Daniel's death. She had nothing left in this cruel world and no one to depend upon but herself. Revenge and bitterness would have to satisfy this hollow ache that engulfed her. From this day forward, she would live for her mission—justice. She had nothing else . . . and she may not even have that if those two merciless scoundrels caught up with her before she had time to turn their vile deeds back upon them!

Two

Deadwood, Dakota Territory

"You did *what?*" Shaler McCain bit down on the end of his cigar and nearly swallowed half of it as he stared incredulously at the wiry red-haired man who lounged in his chair with his broken leg elevated in front of him.

"I sent off for a mail-order bride," Tweed Cramer repeated as he gnawed on the corncob pipe clamped between his teeth.

"That's what I thought you said." Shaler shook his raven head and muttered something Tweed didn't particularly want to hear.

Probing amber eyes zeroed in on the older man. Tweed looked like a rather silly king sprawled on his throne, surrounded by meager necessities. Their mountain cabin was barely large enough to accommodate the two of them. There were only three rooms, constructed of rough-hewn logs that allowed drafty ventilation—summer and winter. Hell's fire, where would they stash a woman?

"Well, hell! What's a-matter with havin' a wife?" Tweed questioned indignantly. "I'll be laid up for a few weeks and there's chores galore to be done around here. It ain't unnatural for a man to get hisself a wife, you know. It happens all the time. Since we struck gold, I can afford to have one if'n I want one."

"If you have a wife, she'll want to know exactly where you're going when you leave and where you've been when you get back," Shaler predicted. "And if you come stumbling in half-drunk with a strand of hair on the sleeve of your shirt, you had better make damned sure you have a horse to match!"

Tweed harumphed and settled himself more comfortably in his chair.

"And just what kind of wife are you going to get by placing ads in newspapers?" Shaler plunged on without giving Tweed the chance to respond. "Most likely, you'll be saddled with some pathetic looking she-male who only hankers for protection and security. All women really want from men is their money and you damned well know it!"

"And all men want from women are warm bodies and a chief cook and bottle washer," Tweed pointed out. "Men get what they want and so do the women. Seems to me, it ain't such a bad bargain. A man don't even have thoughts about women 'til he's at least thirty-five. A'fore that, he's just got urges. Now that I'm forty-two years old, I can see the practical purpose of havin' a woman around—permanent-like."

Shaler rolled his eyes ceilingward with an exasperated sigh. "Tweed, you've had some crazed notions in the past, but this time you've surpassed yourself. Why in the world did you order a bride without consulting me first?"

Tweed stared at the brawny giant who had plunked down in the chair across from him to puff on his cigar until he had surrounded himself in a cloud of smoke. "You're my adopted son, remember? I don't have to get yer permission for nothin'. And hell, look at this place." His bulky arm made an expansive sweep of the interior of their cabin. "I've been laid up with this broke leg and you're comin' and goin' all the time. Maybe I want a female to keep me company and clean this pigsty up." A wry grin pursed his lips, exposing the gap between his front teeth. "I've given you lots of things the last twenty years, Shay. But I ain't never given you a stepmama. Maybe it's time you had one."

The remark brought Shaler back to his feet to pace the floorboards. It was true that this crusty mountain man had taken him in after his parents and younger brother had been killed in an Indian massacre in Colorado. Tweed had provided for Shaler and taught him everything he needed to know about surviving in the wilderness. Shaler had everything he wanted right now. The *last* thing he needed was a fussy stepmother underfoot! Tweed must have suffered brain damage, along with his broken leg, when he tumbled down the hill. He definitely wasn't thinking straight when he impulsively ordered a bride, intending to take whatever he could get—which undoubtedly wouldn't be much!

"If you've been feeling the need for feminine companionship, you should have said so," Shaler grumbled. "I would have gladly loaded you up and hauled you into Deadwood's 'Badland' district to the dance halls and brothels. You could have had as many females as you wanted, as often as you wanted them."

Tweed puffed on his pipe and gave his bushy red head a negative shake. "I want a proper wife, not a whore."

"Same difference," Shaler said dismissively. "Dealing with a mail-order bride will be trickier than braiding a mule's tail. We've got things to do in Deadwood and you damned well know it. You're the one who made these arrangements. Now you're trying to complicate matters by dragging in some damned female!"

Tweed's whiskered chin tilted to a stubborn angle. "The deed's done and my bride will be arrivin' next week. I'm tellin' you now so you'll have time to adjust to the idea of a stepmama."

Shaler cursed under his breath and vowed *never* to adjust to such an insane idea as long as he lived!

"And since I've got a broke leg, I'll stay here with our claim while you trot down to Deadwood to pick up my bride."

"Hell's fire, Tweed, this is—"

Tweed flung up a pudgy hand, demanding silence. "You worry too much, Shay. Havin' a woman around ain't gonna ruin yer life. It was pert'near ruined when I found you in that snowy mountain pass, hidin' under a boulder that wasn't much bigger'n you was. If I'd have stumbled onto you five minutes later, you wouldn't be here a-tall. You owe me yer life. I'm askin' a small favor in return for all I've done for you. Go pick the woman up at the stage depot, be polite as you know how, and accept her. It's the least you can do."

Shaler opened his mouth with another objection, then decided it was a waste of breath. Tweed had that determined look about him. Nothing was going to change his mind, except perhaps the blow of a sledgehammer. Still scowling over the news about Tweed's bride, Shaler stalked outside to stare off into the distance.

The faintest hint of a smile pursed his lips as he surveyed the panoramic landscape of the Black Hills and pondered an encouraging thought. This wilderness was man's country—it was survival of the fittest around here. Any civilized female would take one look at Deadwood and this cabin and hightail it back to the conveniences of society. Since Tweed wouldn't be at the stage depot to meet his bride, Shaler would have time to discourage the woman from following through with this ridiculous marriage. And he wasn't going to be polite and courteous about it, either! Why, when he was finished with that gold-digging bit of fluff who couldn't find her own man, she'd be damned good and ready to leave the territory!

Shaler could picture his stepmother now. She would be as wide as a barrel, ugly as original sin, and as desirable as a wet mop. Shaler would actually be doing Tweed a favor by sending her back in the direction she had come.

Grinning devilishly, Shaler ambled through the clump of aspens and spruces to dip up a pail of fresh water from the spring below the mine shaft. Yes sirree, by the time he finished with his former-future stepmother, she'd be begging him to buy her a stage ticket.

Imagine a woman underfoot! He had dealt with a conniving female at the impressionable age of nineteen and the experience had cured him for life. Women couldn't be trusted. They were necessary evils to satisfy a man's basic urges, but no self-respecting, self-sufficient man needed a woman around all the damned time!

And love? Bah! There wasn't such a thing. Marriage only supplied basic necessities for husbands and wives. Even at the age of ten Shaler had been aware that his parents shared no deep-abiding affection. They simply occupied the same space in the Colorado mountain valley, and they begot two children to propagate the species because that was expected. The marriage had nothing to do with love and everything to do with convenience. Shaler's father provided shelter, protection, and food. His mother prepared the meals, raised her two sons, and tended their home. His parents had tolerated each other and that was about the extent of it.

Shaler scooped up the bucket of water and reassured himself that his intervention was his moral obligation. He had to save his father from disaster. When the arrangements fell through—and Shaler would make sure they did—Tweed would drop this foolish notion of matrimony and concentrate on their original purpose for staking a claim in the Black Hills. They had plans and none of them included having some plump, waspish female whining all the damned time. A woman in a man's bed on occasion was one thing, but a bride in his cabin day in and day out was quite another matter entirely! Shaler simply wouldn't have it. A stepmother? Hell's fire, Tweed had lost his ever-loving mind!

When the west-bound train paused at a water station, Casity was escorted to the second-class passenger car. It had taken most of her cash to purchase a ticket to Cheyenne, Wyoming, leaving barely enough for food and some new clothes.

The recent tragedy was too fresh in her mind to think past arriving at the first sizable community on the rail line and eluding the two men who followed her. Casity didn't know what she was going to do about living expenses while she laid low, other than find some type of employment that would conceal her from the vulturous eyes of her would-be assassins.

After the conductor had shown Casity to a vacant seat at the front of the car, she sank down beside a young woman who looked to be about her own age. While the bubbly blonde chatted with her male companion, Casity squirmed to find a comfortable position on the bench seat. She wasn't in the mood for conversation, or for the attentions of a group of male passengers who surrounded her. Since she'd had her fill of those of the male persuasion the previous night, she wasn't the least bit receptive to admiring glances.

Although Casity didn't consider herself a raving beauty, one look in the mirror assured her that she wasn't what one could call *homely*. Her bosom was too full to escape notice, her waist too trim, and her hips too curvy. Since all men noticed an appealing body and an attractive face, she'd been cursed for life and forced to tolerate lusty glances and rude propositions.

Casity fended off several potential suitors with a

chilling glare and then glanced out the window to watch the sun make its ascent into the sky. Lord, she felt so empty and dead inside. Nothing seemed to matter much anymore. She was simply existing, nurturing a vengeance and wallowing in grief. Casity didn't want to accept the fact that she had lost her uncle forever. She couldn't think of even one reason why she should return to Ogallala when it held such terrible memories.

Not all that many people would miss her, except maybe Clint Lake, who had been trying to work up the nerve to court her for six months. Most of Casity's female acquaintances were envious of her good looks and jealous of the male attention she received, even when she didn't care to receive it.

Lord, what a terrible cynic she had become! Well, she had good reason. She had nothing but tortured dreams to haunt her and two vicious men hunting her.

"Where are you headed?"

A female voice filtered through Casity's bitter musings. She glanced over to see the slightly overweight blonde smiling curiously. "West," Casity replied evasively.

The blonde giggled in response. "Aren't we all? Priscilla Lambert is my name. I was on my way to Deadwood, Dakota, until I met Nate." Her fingers glided over her male companion's hand, giving it an affectionate squeeze. "I had resigned myself to a life with a man who could afford to care for me. But that was before I met Nate on the train from Omaha. That's my home . . . or at least it was."

Casity stole a quick glance at the fashionably-dressed man beside Priscilla. He looked to be a gambler from the cut of his clothes and the softness of his hands. If Nate whoever-he-was was Priscilla's dream come true, there was no accounting for the poor girl's taste.

It also seemed to Casity that Priscilla was the kind of person who never had much of anything pertinent to say, but always felt compelled to say something anyway. She was already droning on about Nate's quick mind, dashing looks, and marvelous plans for a rosy future when they reached San Francisco.

If Casity had been a betting woman, she would have wagered that Priscilla was being taken for the ride of her life and that she would soon be discarded when Nate's wandering eye settled on another gullible female. The poor girl had so many stars in her eyes she couldn't see Nate for what he was.

"Anyway . . . if I hadn't responded to the ad for a mail-order bride, I would never have met Nate," Priscilla prattled on.

When Priscilla glanced adoringly at Nate, Casity nearly gagged. No one would ever catch *her* worshipping a man!

Priscilla chewed her lip thoughtfully. "I do feel bad about disappointing the miner I was supposed to marry in Deadwood, and about spending the money he sent for my wedding gown."

Not bad enough, obviously, Casity thought to herself. No doubt Priscilla had darling Nate to thank for convincing her to spend the miner's money.

"My intended husband paid for my ticket, my expenses, and wardrobe and all, but I don't want him to think of me as ungrateful." Her speculative gaze focused on Casity's fetching features. "You wouldn't be headed to Deadwood, by any chance, would you? I would feel much better if someone could deliver my apologies in person."

"Deadwood?" Casity stared blankly at the blonde. *Deadwood?* Is that the kind of place a woman on the run would go when her would-be assassins were breathing down her neck? Why, she could wind up *dead* in Deadwood!

"I've been told that since gold has been discovered,

money flows like wine in the Black Hills. I also heard tell that there's such a scarcity of decent women in mining camps that females are treated like royalty. I even heard one tale of a dance hall queen who auctioned herself off to the highest bidder for a full month—sharing his home and whatever else. It doesn't sound as if a woman would have difficulty scratching out a living in a mining town." Priscilla giggled in an annoying high-pitched tone. "If I had accepted Tweed's offer, I would probably have an overblown impression of my importance in Deadwood."

"Tweed?"

My former fiancé." Priscilla fished the letter from her purse, along with the stagecoach ticket from Cheyenne to Deadwood. "Tweed Cramer sounds like a likable sort of fellow, judging by his note. But I cannot imagine that he could be half the man Nate is. So why take that risk?"

Casity peered around Priscilla's shoulder to study dear darling Nate. In her estimation, neither Nate nor Tweed seemed like prizes. Nate was obviously a silver-tongued gambler who lured naive females and helped them spend their money. Tweed Cramer was probably a pathetic excuse of a man who was so desperate for female companionship that he was willing to take any type of bride he could get—sight unseen. And sight unseen would probably be to his best advantage, Casity speculated. She could just imagine what this Tweed character looked like and how he behaved. Being a man, he couldn't have much going for him.

"Of course, I don't know where you're headed or for what purpose, but this stage ticket is yours if you would kindly locate Tweed Cramer and extend my sincere apologies." Priscilla held up the ticket and graced Casity with a hopeful smile.

"Deadwood?" Casity repeated stupidly.

Was there truly such a place where men were so overwhelmed by the sight of a respectable woman that they treated her like a queen? And what sort of job could she acquire in a mining town that wouldn't force her to resort to the humiliating professions of calico queens and soiled doves? She would starve first!

Come to think of it, she did have a great deal of practice in store management after working for her uncle. Perhaps she could find gainful employment in the mining town. After all, she had learned to deal with the rougher elements of society in a cowtown. Could a mining community be any worse? And if those two murderers didn't realize she had changed modes of transportation, she just might be able to elude them. Maybe she could lose herself in the Black Hills for a few weeks. The idea was tempting.

"What did you say your name was?" Priscilla persisted.

"I didn't."

Priscilla studied Casity's wry smile which cut becoming dimples in her cheeks. Returning the grin, she laid the stage ticket and accompanying letter in Casity's lap. "If there's some particular reason why you prefer not to disclose your name, perhaps you might even wish to be Priscilla Lambert for the next leg of your journey to . . . Deadwood perhaps?"

And perhaps Priscilla did belong with Nate what's-his-name, Casity decided. The blonde was shrewd— Casity would give her that.

Priscilla gestured toward the ticket and smiled impishly. "If you have no need for the ticket, then you can pass it along to someone else. My only stipulation is that you, or the bearer of this letter, explain my change of plans to Tweed. Surely he will forgive me, knowing I found true love en route."

True love? Now there was a contradiction in terms

if Casity ever heard one. No man would ever be true, and love was only an illusion that caused nothing but agony for those who dared to care. As for herself, she would never allow anyone close enough to feel the pain of loss again.

"And who knows," Priscilla added as she adjusted the plumed bonnet she had purchased with part of Tweed's money. "You may take one look at Tweed and decide you might like to become his mail-order bride."

Casity had no aspirations, now or ever, of being anybody's bride—period!

When the train whistle signaled their stop at Julesberg's roundhouse for breakfast, Casity waited until all the other passengers had trooped down the aisle before she rose to her feet. If she pinched her pennies she could afford a meal to compensate for the one she had missed the previous night. But hungry though she was, she wasn't about to go dashing off the train and take the risk of being intercepted by her would-be killers.

Deadwood, Dakota? Casity reflected on what Priscilla had told her. Well, maybe if she got desperate she would make the journey. But surely Cheyenne, Wyoming, would be far enough away from those who sought to dispose of her and large enough for her to lose herself in the crowd . . .

A horrified gasp escaped Casity's lips when she glanced out the window to see two scraggly men studying each passenger who stepped from the platform. She recoiled before Ned Johnson and Russel Bassett noticed her. My God! They must have run their horses into the ground to catch up with her. Curse the train's schedule for waylaying at every podunk whistle stop and piddling tank town between Ogallala and Cheyenne. She might have been better off if she had stolen a horse.

Casity ducked under the windows and moved toward the rear of the passenger car. When she heard the clat-

ter of boots on the front landing, she surged through
the back door and practically leaped over the railing
to the freight car. In desperation, she closeted herself
with the excess luggage and oversized trunks stacked
in the compartment, then scrambled between the piles
of luggage and dived behind the largest trunk. When
the door swung open, Casity didn't dare draw a breath
for fear of being noticed.

"She's gotta be here somewhere," Ned Johnson said
as he surveyed the shadowed recesses. "I swore I saw
her chasing after the train in Ogallala. The conductor
said he remembered seeing a female who matched the
description I gave him."

"Maybe she bought a ticket in the first-class passenger
car," Russel speculated. "We haven't checked it yet."

"I think we should buy a ticket and search all the
cars while we're en route to Cheyenne," Ned suggested.
"I'm not giving up until I get my hands on that bitch."

Casity gulped hard after the voices died away. Although she would have liked nothing better than to
locate a sheriff or bounty hunter to shoot those murderers, she doubted she would live long enough to see
justice served. Her only chance was to hide out until
they gave up their search.

When Casity's stomach protested the missing of another meal, she sank down behind the trunk and
chewed on her fingernails. Curse her rotten luck! She
had hoped to have a head start on her would-be assassins. Now they were riding the very same train with
her! What she needed was a disguise.

Pursuing that thought, Casity pried open a nearby
trunk and rummaged through it to find a set of boy's
clothes. At least they would make it more difficult for
her would-be killers to spot her.

She decided she'd rather starve to death than be
shot down in cold blood.

Three

Casity endured the next leg of her journey like a martyr. There was no comfort to be found while wedged in the corner of the freight car like a piece of luggage. When the train whistle announced their arrival at the next stop, Casity zigzagged through the maze of crates and trunks to step onto the platform. Garbed in the breeches, shirt, and hat to conceal her identity, she made a beeline toward the back of the roundhouse. She had counted on the fact that Priscilla would make use of the ladies' room at the back of the building. Casity hoped to intercept Priscilla because she needed a favor—a big one!

When Priscilla breezed through the door to freshen up, she balked at the sight of the "lad" lingering in the corner.

"You're in the wrong place, young man," Priscilla scolded. "The men's accommodations are—"

When Casity removed her hat, allowing her auburn curls to cascade down her back, Priscilla blinked like a startled owl. "So there you are. I wondered what had become of you. Why are you dressed in that getup? Has it anything to do with why you withheld your name? What kind of business are you in anyway?"

The blonde seemed intrigued. Priscilla was shrewd *and* inquisitive, Casity concluded.

"I've decided it's in my best interest to travel to

Deadwood and do you the favor of informing Tweed Cramer that you will not arrive as planned," Casity said quietly. "In return for being the bearer of disappointing news, I ask a favor of you."

Priscilla nodded agreeably. She obviously itched to be a part of the intrigue.

"I prefer that you pretend not to know me."

"I hardly feel that I do," Priscilla whispered. "You haven't taken me into your confidence, even after I practically spilled my life story. But I'm sure that's partially because of my runaway tongue."

A faint smile pursed Casity's lips as she surveyed the bubbly blonde. Even though Priscilla was prone to incessant chatter, she was a personable sort. "You'll be much safer if you plead ignorance if anyone poses questions about me."

Priscilla frowned warily. "Have you committed some heinous crime? Good gad! I befriended you and now you're telling me—"

Casity waved Priscilla off before she plunged into another vocal tirade. "A vicious crime has been committed, it's true. I was the only eyewitness. The two murderers are trying to dispose of me so I can't identify them."

"Oh, my . . ." Priscilla chirped.

Casity gnawed on her lip, chastising herself for revealing too much to a talkative female who may or may not be able to keep her mouth shut. Her only recourse was to scare Priscilla speechless.

"If the murderers suspect that you or Nate have the slightest knowledge of what I just told you, then you both could be in grave danger. These men have killed once and they're desperate enough to kill again in order to protect their vile secret. If anyone should ask, say nothing except that I mentioned traveling to Denver."

Priscilla nodded grimly. "I don't think I wish to know more than I already do, even if my curiosity *is* killing me."

"I assure you that you don't want to know much more," Casity said gravely. "Better to die from curiosity than an assassin's bullet."

Casity eased open the back door to make sure the coast was clear before she turned back to a wide-eyed Priscilla. "One word of advice. Never expect any man to be the answer to solve your problems or fulfill your dreams, Priscilla. I don't think there's a man on earth who can be trusted completely. I know two in particular who can't be trusted at all."

"If you're referring to Nate—" Priscilla hastily defended, only to be interrupted by Casity's bitter laughter.

"Only time will tell how dependable a gambler can be. You're *gambling* on his loyalty to you . . . and so is he, I'll wager. Take nothing for granted, Priscilla, and be sure you keep some options available. In a man's world, a woman has to rely upon herself if she wants to survive."

When the door creaked shut, Priscilla stared at it pensively. "My, what a strange woman! Paranoid, I suspect," she mused aloud.

Although Priscilla was prone to talk to herself as well as anyone else who cared to listen, she clamped her mouth shut the instant she sailed out the door and saw two scraggly-looking men lingering in the hall. Suspicion instantly clouded Priscilla's mind, after her peculiar conversation with whoever-she-was.

"One of the passengers mentioned you might know something about the woman sitting beside you earlier this morning," Ned Johnson said without preamble. "Do you know where she is?"

Priscilla valiantly mustered her composure and

forced a smile. These two scalawags definitely didn't look like the type with whom a decent woman would associate—not of her own free will!

"I'm afraid there isn't much to tell," she replied in an even tone that concealed her uneasiness—she hoped! "I don't know her name." Priscilla feigned a pensive frown, striving for just the right effect. Having achieved it, she congratulated herself on her theatrical ability and continued, "However, she did mention something about traveling to Denver. But I must confess that I did most of the talking, though that isn't unusual. I'm quite often guilty of that. My father used to say I was ever so fond of listening to the sound of my own voice. My mother claimed I couldn't formulate a single thought without sharing it with the rest of the world. But truly, I do enjoy conversation. It seems ever so much better than silence—"

When the two men rudely dismissed her and turned away, Priscilla stifled an impish grin. For once her nonstop babbling had been a blessing rather than a curse.

"The favor is repaid," she murmured softly to the lingering image of the mysterious auburn-haired woman in men's clothes. "And good luck to you, wherever you are. Judging by those two heathens, you're going to need all the luck you can get!"

With a confident tilt of her chin, Priscilla soared off to rejoin Nate. But since Casity's predictions about the two evil-looking men held true, Priscilla began to have misgivings about males in general, and Nate in particular. Perhaps she should heed the mysterious woman's advice.

"I think we should get married in Cheyenne," Priscilla declared as she and Nate boarded the train.

Nate missed a step on his way to the platform and very nearly fell on his face. "What brought that on?"

"It *was* marriage you had in mind when you talked

about a bright future for us, wasn't it?" Priscilla eyed him warily when he shifted from one foot to the other without meeting her direct gaze. "Well? Wasn't it?" When Nate hesitated again, Priscilla tapped her foot and crossed her arms over her ample bosom. "If I'm nothing more than the time you're killing you had better tell me now, Nate Higgins!"

Since Priscilla blocked the steps to the platform, forcing the other passengers to mill around her, she took advantage of her audience. "These good people are waiting, Nate, and so am I. Are we getting married or aren't we?"

"Well, I—" Nate tugged at his cravat which suddenly seemed to be strangling him.

Again, Priscilla tapped her foot and glared him down. "Yes or no, Nate."

"I'll marry her if you don't want her, though why you wouldn't want a lovely lady like this I cannot imagine," came a deep voice from the middle of the crowd.

Priscilla glanced around to see a tall, lanky man elbowing his way toward her. She quickly sized him up, finding him reasonably attractive, neat, clean-shaven, and seemingly sincere. She again reminded herself of the advice she had received in the ladies' room. Here was one of those possible options to which the mysterious auburn-haired woman had referred. If Priscilla were smart—and she prided herself in thinking she was—she would seize the opportunity.

She stared at Nate's soft hands before focusing on her would-be suitor's callused ones. He looked to be the type who had no aversion to hard work. The longer Priscilla studied the young man with liquid green eyes, the more she realized what a mistake she had almost made with Nate. Of course, she could always opt to travel to Deadwood to take Tweed Cramer's offer. But this sincere-looking young man was here and Tweed was miles away. Besides that, she had given her stage ticket to a woman who needed an escape, and Priscilla had spent most of the traveling money Tweed had sent—with a great deal of help from Nate, come to think of it!

"What's your name, sir?" Priscilla inquired.

"Oh, for God's sake, Priscilla, you can't be serious about this," Nate muttered.

Well, that certainly indicated Nate's feelings toward her, didn't it? He hadn't declared his affection or intentions. He scoffed at her impulsive actions—which he had been part of. Well, to hell with Nate Higgins! She was betting *against* this gambler, just as the mysterious woman had advised her to do.

Flashing her prospective suitor a beaming smile, Priscilla descended the steps to curl her hand around his muscled forearm.

Jacob peered down at the pert blonde and smiled admiringly. "You're the prettiest thing I ever saw. I noticed you when I stepped on board at Ogallala. But since you were with him, I . . . well . . ." He patted her hand in a most gentlemanly fashion. "The name is Jacob Warner. I own a ranch west of Cheyenne and I traveled to Ogallala to buy replacement cattle for the ones I lost in the blizzard last winter."

The longer Jacob talked, the more certain Priscilla became that this impulsive courtship would be more to her advantage. Jacob delighted in conversation as much as she did and he was more physically appealing than Nate.

"I think we're going to get along just fine," Priscilla proclaimed as she sank down on the bench seat beside Jacob.

"So do I, Priscilla, so do I," Jacob agreed wholeheartedly.

Priscilla smiled in satisfaction. She honestly couldn't

believe her luck. It only served to prove that life was full of surprises—some of them good. She could only hope the mysterious blue-eyed woman with the melancholy smile would also be blessed with a stroke of good luck.

From the look and sound of things the young woman could certainly use her share—and then some. Priscilla shuddered to think how she would react if she had witnessed a murder and was being chased. No sirree, she wasn't going to change her mind and romp off with Nate or anyone else. Cheyenne, Wyoming, was as far down the rails as she was going to go. Jacob Warner was offering security and commitment and perhaps even love . . . in time. Until then, Priscilla vowed to settle for the good deal she'd gotten!

Employing every precaution, Casity tiptoed out the door of the freight car and hit the ground running. Within minutes of reaching the bustling city of Cheyenne, she lost herself in the crowd. Thus far, she hadn't seen hide nor hair of her pursuers and she planned to keep it that way. If she were lucky, Priscilla had been able to point those two scoundrels in the wrong direction, giving Casity time to purchase a new gown and present her ticket at the stage depot.

Although Casity took the risk of being caught in a most embarrassing situation, she undressed in the alley behind a stack of empty crates. A few minutes later, she emerged in her tattered gown and made her way to a shop stocked with fashionable dresses.

Hesitantly, Casity handed over all the money she could spare for her necessary purchases and scuttled back into the alley for another quick change. Then, keeping a low profile, she scurried down the street toward the stage depot. Her gaze constantly darted from side to side, keeping a sharp lookout for the two men.

Having presented her ticket to the stage agent, she gathered up a discarded newspaper and hid behind it, just in case her assailants showed up. After sitting on pins and needles for an hour, she heard the agent request the passengers to board the stage for Deadwood. Breathing an enormous sigh of relief, Casity clambered into the coach beside a buxom female who required more than half the seat to make herself comfortable. Two middle-aged men sat across from them, smiling in masculine appreciation and rattling on about how they were going to strike it rich in the mining camps of Dakota. When the stage bustled on its way, Casity found herself bombarded with questions, none of which she answered directly. A shrug here and there sufficed for the first few hours of the journey north.

"You married?" Tobias Turner inquired as he helped Casity down from the coach several hours later.

"No." Casity surveyed the modest stage station that served their evening meal. God, she was near starvation!

"Would you like to be?" Tobias quickened his pace to match Casity's hurried strides.

Casity was oblivious to everything except the tantalizing aroma of baked bread and beans.

"I said . . . would you like to be?" Tobias persisted when he received no response.

Casity frowned. "Would I like to be what?" She was so distracted by the thought of food that she hadn't paid Tobias the slightest bit of attention.

"Married," he prompted with a hopeful grin.

Casity tore her eyes away from her meal to assess the stubble-faced prospector. He was as tall and lean as a fence post. Now was the time to assure this nuisance of a man that she had no intention whatsoever of engaging in conversation or anything else. He and his even skinnier friend had badgered her quite enough already. She simply wanted to be left alone. Tobias Turner and Willis Fritz may as well know, here and now, that she wasn't the least bit interested in anything either of them had to offer.

"Mister Turner, there are many things I desire from life, but marriage is not even on the list," she said with blunt candor. "You may be looking for a wife, but I'm not searching for a husband."

The declaration worked superbly. Tobias crept over to his chair and wilted beside Willis, whose eyes had fallen to his plate. The only time either man opened his mouth was to shovel food down his gullet—and both did so in a most repulsive fashion, Casity noted. She tried to ignore the sound of chomping teeth and smacking lips and concentrate solely on her meal.

Damn, maybe she should have remained in disguise to avoid the attention of these two clowns. But Casity wasn't certain she could have fooled even these imbeciles at close range. Her only option was to remain as aloof as possible to discourage them. After what she had endured the past few days, surely she could tolerate these two prospectors, *if* they kept their distance.

Although Casity felt more sociable after her ravenous hunger had been appeased, she still kept to herself during the long hours of traveling. The stage driver and guard had informed their passengers that they would be traveling during the night in hopes of avoiding Indian and outlaw attack. It seemed the Sioux and Cheyenne were stirred up about the influx of white people into their sacred land and they had been attacking with alarming regularity. To compound that problem, thieves were preying on stages, stealing gold shipments and frisking passengers for cash and jewels.

Casity decided that any outlaw who went to the trouble of robbing this particular stage and its passengers was wasting his time. She had depleted her money supply and she had no jewels on her person. The other passengers' finances seemed to be as strained as hers.

Casity frowned at her thoughts. It amazed her that she had become so conditioned to danger and hardened by the events that had led her to this stage to Deadwood. After her uncle's death and her madcap flight, she had accepted her fate with grim resignation and spent her time calculating her next move to elude her pursuers rather than simply being scared to death. She had been living on the edge so long that dealing with danger had become second nature. An encounter with thieves or Indians seemed like just another obstacle. And besides, Casity had already suffered the worst luck anyone rightfully ought to have, having lost her only relative and being chased by murderers.

What else could possibly go wrong in her life . . . ?

"Hell's fire," Shaler McCain muttered as he plucked up another chunk of gold from the *arrastra* and studied it in the bright sunlight.

"Now what's a-matter?" Tweed glanced from the crude mining device, which sifted from rock, to his disgruntled son.

Shaler glared at his father, who was basking in the sunshine to give his broken leg another of its many rests. "You bought one helluva claim. Not only have we found color and dug out enough ore to keep us operating for months, but we're rich to boot."

"Hell, I've been lucky all my life," Tweed declared.

"I just seem to stumble onto good fortune. We'll just have to buy another claim that doesn't turn out to be a mother lode. I always did wonder what it would be like to be stinking rich. I guess I'm gonna find out." His green eyes narrowed on the chunk of gold Shaler clutched in his fist. "Are you absolutely certain we're sittin' on an honest-to-goodness strike?"

Shaler nodded. "We've got enough pure ore in this load to start our own mint."

"Don't look so sour about it," Tweed chuckled. "We'll make other arrangements to be sure our scheme works properly."

Tweed was silent for a long moment while he watched Shaler toss the priceless nuggets in a bucket as if they were repulsive to the touch. It did seem that the deeper they dug, the better the ore. The supply didn't show any sign of dwindling, but striking it rich hadn't done a damned thing for Shaler's foul disposition. For a week, he had been as unsociable as a wounded lion.

"You ain't still mad 'cause I ordered a bride, are you?" When Shaler didn't dignify the question with an answer, Tweed nodded thoughtfully. "That has to be it. Nobody would scowl about a handful of gold nuggets unless somethin' else was botherin' him."

"Hell yes, I'm mad!" Shaler exploded after trying to keep the peace for seven days. The more he'd thought about Tweed's insane impulsiveness the more it annoyed him. "Thus far, you've allocated your share of the gold for your bride-to-be's spending spree in town. If she learns we struck paydirt, she'll be ordering fancy furniture from Europe and all sorts of unnecessary paraphernalia. I'll be the one who'll have to tote all her extravagances up here on the backs of mules. Before you know it, there will be lacy bedspreads and frilly curtains. You won't be able to see out and you know how you hate that hemmed-in feeling, Tweed."

"Yer jealous."

Shaler tossed another nugget in the pail and rounded on Tweed. "Of what, for God's sake?"

"Yer accustomed to havin' all my attention and now yer afraid my new wife's gonna crowd you out."

Shaler flung the older man a withering glance. "I'm not a damned kid who feels threatened by a stepmother."

"Then what's got you riled?"

"We have an express purpose for being here," Shaler said pointedly.

"So you keep remindin' me every other minute. But what's that got to do with my bride?"

"She'll be in the way!" Shaler all but yelled at his father.

Tweed levered himself off the blanket, grabbed his cane, and limped back to the cabin. "She ain't gonna be in *my* way," he said with great certainty. "Now get yerself washed up. The rabbit stew should be ready by now."

"Rabbit stew *again?*" Shaler complained. "That makes four days in a row."

"Well, no other game has wandered by while I've been sittin' out among them trees. It ain't as if I can go sneakin' up on much of anythin' in my condition. I hope to hell my new bride enjoys laborin' over a hot stove. I'm gettin' tired of my own cookin', and I'm damned sure sick of yers!"

After Tweed had scaled the steps with as much agility as a man with a bum leg could manage, he hobbled back around to face Shaler. "This is the day yer supposed to fetch my bride, in case you forgot."

As if he could forget! Like a man condemned to the gallows, Shaler had been dreading this day and count-

ing the minutes of freedom he would have left if that
shrew of a bride was determined to rule this roost!

"After lunch, you ride into Deadwood and fetch Priscilla Lambert for me. The stage should arrive late this
afternoon. Get her a room at the best hotel and let her
shop to her heart's content in the mornin'," Tweed
instructed. "And make double damn sure she feels welcome. You hear me, Shay?"

"I hear," Shaler grumbled. "And so will *she*. I hope
you realize you'll have to stop cursing when your bride
arrives. She'll probably insist that you shave those
wooly whiskers and give up your pipe as well. Proper
women are fussy about things like that. She'll make a
new man out of you, even if you don't have complaints
about the old one."

Tweed wasn't fooled for a second. He knew Shaler
was fiercely opposed to any kind of change. "I'll tell
you somethin', Shay. It wouldn't hurt you none to
clean up yer act a little neither! We could both do
with a few social graces. Yer new stepmama might
make a better man of you, too. And considerin' the
way you've been behavin' the past week, there's plenty
of room for improvement."

Shaler muttered under his breath as he stalked back
to the stream to wash away the dirt and sweat. With
any luck at all, his *new stepmama* would turn tail and
run after Shaler greeted her as rudely as possible. He
wasn't cutting her any slack, that's for sure!

The heartless gold digger! She probably planned to
hoard as much money as she could get her greedy
hands on and then trot back to civilization. Tweed
would be crushed and Shaler would have to restrain
himself from saying, "I told you so." Damn women
everywhere! They were all worth their weight in
trouble.

Well, this manipulative harridan would have to get

past Shaler McCain first! And he could be mighty mean and nasty when he felt like it. This time he was going to be mean and nasty for a damned good cause: to save Tweed from a fate worse than death—matrimonial torture. Yes indeed, Shaler would send Priscilla Lambert packing the instant she arrived. She had made a long trip for nothing because there was no way in hell that Shaler was going to let her get within ten feet of Tweed!

Four

Mentally plotting his encounter with Tweed's mail-order bride, Shaler zigzagged through the clumps of aspens, spruces, and pines to reach Deadwood Gulch. Because of its location in the steep-walled valley, the town of three thousand inhabitants had only one main street. The community reminded Shaler of a bustling ant den. Deadwood was not the kind of town in which a decent, self-respecting female would choose to spend her life, though a few did. Why? Shaler couldn't imagine.

The town had followed the natural order of progression, just as all mining and cowtowns had in the West. While prospectors scurried through the Black Hills to sift gold dust, a flood of undesirables arrived upon the scene. They weren't as intent on panning *gold* as they were on panning the *miners*. In Shaler's opinion, mining camps created a food chain in which one group fed on another.

The fact that Deadwood had already developed a reputation as a wild and rowdy town would work to Shaler's advantage, and to Priscilla Lambert's disadvantage. This community was crawling with drunken prospectors down on their luck, wily pickpockets, shifty-eyed gamblers, and shrewd swindlers making a killing off men who wound up in the wrong place at the wrong time. Yes indeed, Deadwood had a lot of growing up to do before it could become respectable.

Effortlessly, Shaler swung from the saddle and made sure his pouch of gold was tucked deep in the pocket of his buckskin vest. Although he had honed his ability to defend himself over the years, learning from one of the famed masters of the six-shooter, he still felt uncomfortable carrying around so much gold— more gold than he had planned on finding in the shaft in Bonanza Gulch, that was for sure!

Hell's fire, what did he need with gold anyway? He was a man of simple tastes who'd been raised in the Rockies and lived for challenges. In the wilderness, staying alive was all the occupation a man needed, and he often had to work very hard at it.

In this rowdy mining town, a man found himself pitted against the voracious greed of mankind. Carrying a pouch of gold in Deadwood was an invitation to trouble. Gold was the devil's currency. It brought out the worst in men and lured the most unsavory individuals on the planet—including and *especially* those of the female persuasion.

For damned certain, Shaler wasn't going to inform Priscilla Lambert that her husband-to-be had become stinking rich. The sooner he met that husband-hunter and read her the riot act, the sooner she would be on her way. Then he'd tell Tweed that his mail-order bride had developed a severe case of cold feet, and that would be the end of this ridiculous farce!

Shaler growled in disgust when he saw a drunken miner stumble out of a saloon and toss several gold nuggets into the street, just for the amusement of watching a half-dozen starved prospectors dive into the dirt to retrieve them. The lust for gold was distasteful. It served to remind Shaler that he was more at home in the Rockies where his closest neighbors walked on four legs and fought over a morsel of food rather than a pile of glittering rock.

Although Shaler never made it a practice to start a fight, he never walked away from one, either. And furthermore, he didn't approve of one man taking unfair advantage of another. When one of the scrambling prospectors lit into his competition with fists and feet, Shaler felt compelled to intervene. One old-timer was about to be broken to bits by a man half his age, just for the gold nugget he clutched in his fist.

The old man was wheezing and gasping by the time Shaler plunged into the melee. With one thrust of his meaty fist, Shaler sent the old-timer's vicious attacker skidding in the dirt and the brawl was over as quickly as it began. Men scrambled out of Shaler's reach before he beat them black and blue with blows that carried enough wallop to fell a grizzly bear.

It wasn't the first time Shaler had broken up a senseless fight in the street. Since his arrival two months earlier, he had earned a reputation that gave him all the space he needed, plus a few extra yards for good measure.

Shaler supposed his size and stature gave him the necessary edge. As Tweed constantly reminded him, Shaler was as big as a polar bear and twice as mean when he got his dander up. But he didn't do so often because he had learned to control his temper, as well as his other urges.

In his estimation, it was a rare man who could maintain his self-control while making his way through an insane world. And they called this *civilization*? Shaler scoffed cynically at the caliber of individuals who inhabited Deadwood. He had met mountain lions who were less vicious and more predictable!

True, Shaler had been forced to kill a few worthless individuals the past few years. The ones he had launched into the hereafter had been well-deserving of their fate. They had also left Shaler no other choice. Yet, he preferred to be remembered for his restraint, not his skills of self-defense. After all, if a man didn't have control of himself, just what the hell did he have?

When Shaler wheeled back toward the stage depot, he was well aware of the hush that had fallen over the crowd. Even a few drunkards had sobered up after watching him pound some manners into the vicious miner.

Shaler had just set foot in the stage depot, focusing his concentration on his upcoming encounter with his former-future stepmother, when the ticket agent groaned aloud. A curious frown ruffled Shaler's dark brow as he watched the disgruntled agent reread the message he had just received.

"God have mercy," the agent sighed in dismay. His gaze circled the office as he made the grim announcement to the waiting passengers. "I just received a report that George Custer, and his Seventh Cavalry were massacred at Little Big Horn River. Crazy Horse, Gall, Rain-in-the-Face, and Low Dog combined their forces of three thousand warriors to swarm Custer. George's brother Tom, his nephew Henry Reed, and his brother-in-law James Calhoun all died in the battle. Of the two hundred soldiers involved, there were no survivors."

Shaler grimaced at the shocking news. "I suspect we'll see even more Indian uprisings after that."

"I expect so," the agent agreed. "We'll have to increase the number of guards on the stages to protect the passengers. Those cocky Indians won't show us any mercy now."

Shaler had no time to mull over Custer's fatal disaster. Alarmed yelps and frantic shouts heralded the approach of a rider who was waving his arms like a windmill as he raced toward the stage depot.

"The stage has been attacked!" the miner squawked. "Injuns! Three of 'em!"

For a half-second, Shaler hesitated, wondering if this wasn't just the kind of discouragement Priscilla Lambert needed to send her skedaddling back home where she belonged. A confrontation with renegades would scare the living daylights out of Tweed's mail-order bride. Unfortunately, Shaler would have to live with his nagging conscience if Priscilla Lambert met her Waterloo on the road to Deadwood and he made no attempt to rescue her.

In a single bound, Shaler leaped to his steed and took off like a discharging cannonball. If things progressed from bad to worse, he would have a legitimate excuse for not bringing the woman home. And in this neck of the woods, things had an uncanny knack of turning from *worse* to *worst* in a hurry!

Casity braced herself against the window as the stagecoach careened around a horseshoe bend, kicking up a cloud of choking dust. Overhead, she could hear the guard blasting away at the Indians who had appeared out of nowhere to give chase. Arrows whizzed past the window and Casity instinctively ducked, just as she had become conditioned to doing in Ogallala during cattle season.

Her eardrums nearly shattered when the plump female beside her started screaming bloody murder. The two prospectors on the opposite seat were fumbling with their pistols and doing nothing helpful in this harrowing crisis—one of so many Casity had faced of late. As unskilled as these two clowns appeared to be, they were more likely to shoot the occupants of the coach than to wound an Indian!

"Here, give me that," Casity muttered after Tobias finally wormed the pistol out of the band of his breeches.

Crouching on her knees, Casity gripped the revolver in both hands, closed one eye, and took aim as best she could. When the coach hit a deep rut and bounced on its springs, her shot went astray and hit a tree branch. Damn!

Amid the thunder of hooves and the creak of the coach, Casity could hear the war whoops growing louder with each passing second. Lately, it seemed somebody was always chasing after her. *This*, Casity realized, was the *something else* that could go wrong in her life. She had escaped her uncle's murderers, only to die in a stagecoach . . .

All thoughts scattered like leaves in a cyclone when the wobbling coach skidded on loose rock, sending the occupants tumbling helter-skelter. Casity knew disaster was about to strike again when the off-balanced coach tilted to a precarious angle. All four passengers slammed against the door, sending the coach crashing onto its side.

Casity was the most fortunate victim of the wreck because she landed on top of the pile. Beneath her was the oversized woman of forty or thereabouts. And beneath the woman—who was screaming at the top of her lungs about the prospect of being raped, scalped, and murdered—were the two scrawny men. Casity had to struggle to pull herself up to the side door which lay atop the overturned coach. Somehow or other, she had to lever herself up and pry the rotund matron out before she squished the two men flat as flounders. But it served those two gawking clowns right, thought Casity.

At the moment they both had all the woman they could handle.

When the frightened horses finally came to a halt, Casity shoved her shoulder against the jammed door latch. After three unsuccessful attempts she managed to prop the door open and scan her surroundings. The Indians had disappeared as quickly as they had arrived. It seemed they enjoyed the fiendish thrill of scaring the wits out of stage occupants.

Casity glanced toward the driver and guard, who had been ejected from their perch when the coach overturned in the dirt. Both men were scrabbling on their knees to retrieve their weapons in case of another attack. The female was still screaming hysterically while Tobias and Willis wailed in agony, sure every bone was broken.

Bracing her hands against the door facing, Casity strained to hoist herself out of the stagecoach. After mopping the unruly auburn curls from her face, she coiled atop the coach and reached back inside to heave the plump matron to her feet. Suddenly the sound of thrashing hooves drowned out the older woman's squeals, and Casity twisted around a moment too late to save herself from another catastrophe.

Three bare-chested braves whizzed past the coach. They had obviously been lying low until some fool—namely Casity—climbed out of the stage. They descended on her like a swarm of hornets.

The air left her lungs violently when the nearest warrior snaked out a bronzed arm to jerk her off the upturned stage. For one unnerving moment Casity was left dangling in midair while the steed pelted down the path. Before Casity could gather her wits and wiggle free, the Indian brave shoved her facedown and left her in a jackknifed position while he thundered off.

Casity knew it was all over when she heard the fat

lady burst into a chorus of "Amazing Grace." Although Casity had outfoxed her uncle's killers, she had been unable to escape the wrath of renegade Indians. This was the beginning of what looked to be a very bad end!

The stage driver had informed her early on that the Black Hills were holy ground to the Sioux and Cheyenne. Their Great Spirit descended into the mountain valleys to speak with the tribal chiefs, telling them of the rainbow-colored stones scattered through the mountains.

According to the Indian legends, the bravest warriors would see the shining stones after death, and the experience would prepare their eyes for the splendors which awaited them in the Happy Hunting Ground. Although it was said that the spirits allowed the Indians to hunt in the sacred mountains, there was no sacrifice great enough to save them if they dared to remain within the holy hills indefinitely. Obviously the Indians didn't take kindly to whites tramping through their Great Spirit's territory, either, and Casity was about to be punished for it.

Sending up a hasty prayer that if death came to her, it would be quick and merciful, she clung to the saddle blanket. She waited, hoping to see a break in the timber so she could launch herself backward and run for her life.

For a brief moment, Casity wondered if whites would be permitted to view the rainbow stones embedded in the Black Hills. No, she decided as she watched the trees fly past her at phenomenal speed. Indian legends probably only applied to their own kind. She wouldn't be fortunate enough to witness the marvels of the Indian spiritual world. The only luck she'd had of late was bad . . .

* * *

It wasn't difficult for Shaler to locate the ill-fated stagecoach. A trembling female voice resounded through the V-shaped valley. Within minutes, Shaler and the two stage attendants who had accompanied him descended down the path to see the driver and guard limping toward the overturned coach.

Shaler crouched on the saddle to step atop the stage. Despite the seriousness of the situation he almost laughed out loud when he peered down at the wide-hipped female sprawled in a pile of calico and petticoats, arms outspread and feet braced on the seats. Her mouth was shaped like a capital "O" and her eardrum-shattering screeches reverberated through the coach, drowning out the agonized groans of the men who were trapped beneath her.

So this was Tweed's mail-order bride, Shaler presumed. Judging by her size, he predicted the woman could sit down on Tweed and squash him as flat as a shadow if he dared to refuse to do her bidding. Well, the old goat deserved just such a bride, Shaler thought spitefully. This loud-mouthed, overgrown female would teach Tweed a few lessons he would not soon forget! Tweed would be the one ready to hightail it out of town before the wedding, not the other way around!

Dropping to his knees, Shaler stuck his head and arm inside the coach to lend the squawking female a hand. When she hoisted herself upward, Shaler very nearly toppled down onto her. Steadying himself, he latched onto a pudgy hand and gave a mighty heave-ho. Finally, the woman popped out of the cramped space like an oversized cork from a narrow-necked bottle. She was still belting out sounds that could make the hair on the back of a man's neck stand straight up.

Shaler stared at the rotund matron, picturing her as his stepmother. He shuddered. He hated to ask, but he had to know. "Are you Priscilla Lambert?"

"No," the driver answered for the still-squealing matron. Clutching his wounded arm, he gestured toward the path that led south. "Those renegades kidnapped the other poor girl riding the stage. That's probably the one you're looking for."

Shaler leaped back to his saddle. He wasn't sure if he was disappointed or relieved to know the pudgy female he had met wasn't his stepmother-to-be. At any rate, Priscilla Lambert wasn't safe in Deadwood *yet*. And considering her predicament, she might never be!

Leaving the other men to repair the damaged coach and revive the two male passengers, Shaler nudged his steed into its swiftest gait. The sorrel gelding responded while Shaler slid his revolver from its holster and prepared himself for anything.

Having dealt with various hostile Indian tribes in the Rockies, Shaler knew his foe preferred stealth and the element of surprise. They could be lying in wait for him or simply riding hell-for-leather, gloating over capturing a white woman. One never knew when dealing with cunning Indians.

After several minutes of thrashing through the brush, Shaler sighted the three riders. He fired two quick shots above their heads, hoping to persuade the warriors to drop their captive and save themselves. Thus far, no lives had been lost—white or red. Shaler preferred to keep it that way. If he was forced to kill one of the braves, it would only add fuel to the feud between Indians and whites.

For the life of him, Shaler couldn't figure out why he was sticking his neck out to save a woman he didn't care to meet. He had yet to lay eyes on her and already she had caused him a peck of trouble. Typical woman, he thought sourly. What else could a man expect from the female of the species?

* * *

The instant Casity heard the bark of a pistol and felt her captor flinch, she took full advantage. When the brave swiveled his head to locate his pursuer, Casity shoved her knees into the steed's flank, causing it to leap sideways. The startled horse kicked up its heels, and she pushed herself backward while the warrior tried to maintain his seat.

Although Casity's ingenious escape-attempt proved successful, she landed with a thud and back-somersaulted down the steep slope. She yelped as she slammed into rocks and trees like a boulder on a downhill roll. It was impossible to dodge oncoming objects when she couldn't see where she was going.

A dull moan rose in her throat when her head collided with a rock. The world went black in less than a heartbeat. Like a rag doll, Casity cartwheeled the rest of the way down the incline to land faceup in the creek. But she wasn't aware of the cool water that soothed her scrapes and bruises. For all she knew, she—like the lineage of Crocketts before her—was lost and gone forever.

Suddenly, Casity was hovering in a world of peaceful silence, devoid of pain and memories. It was the first peace and quiet she had enjoyed in more than a week. But as bad luck would have it, Casity wasn't conscious of her long-awaited solitude. She wasn't conscious—period!

Five

Shaler had seen the woman roll off the cliff like a windblown tumbleweed, disappearing from sight. To his relief, the three Sioux braves never broke stride, leaving their captive. Shaler pulled his winded steed to a halt and dismounted near where Priscilla Lambert was last seen alive. Cautiously, he sidestepped down the wild tumble of rocks, trees, and underbrush, forcing his reluctant steed to follow or risk having its head pulled off at the shoulders.

Halfway down the hill, Shaler spied the tattered mass of calico and petticoats. Priscilla was sprawled in the creek, her head covered by her skirts. One leg was twisted at an unnatural angle. The other one was extended and partially concealed by clinging pantaloons that had suffered irreparable damage during her fall. From the look of things, Priscilla herself had suffered irreparable damage as well. If she wasn't dead, it would surprise the hell out of Shaler. She had taken a terrible spill that could easily have broken her neck, and every other bone as well.

Shaler pronounced his future stepmother dead before he reached her mangled body. She hadn't moved a muscle since he first spotted her several minutes earlier.

Squatting down on his haunches, Shaler slowly outstretched the woman's injured leg and then reached up to pull the damp skirt away from her face. His jaw dropped off its hinges when he found himself gazing down at the stunningly lovely, auburn-haired nymph who looked to be only twenty if she was a day. Hell's fire! This was to have been his stepmama? This was Tweed's mail-order bride? Incredible!

Mesmerized, Shaler surveyed her flawless complexion while water rippled over her chin, leaving only her lips and her pert nose exposed to air. If the creek had been running an inch deeper she would have drowned, provided she wasn't dead already.

A thick fringe of black lashes lay upon her creamy cheeks like fairy's wings. Her heart-shaped lips turned upward at the corners, even when she wasn't smiling, and she definitely had nothing to smile about right now! Her features were so perfect, so delicate, that Shaler couldn't pry his eyes away from her.

This bewitching siren—who had a shapely body to match her enchanting face and who could have been every man's fantasy—was Tweed's mail-order bride? She was gorgeous by anyone's standards and Shaler had set his standards exceedingly high.

There *had* to be something wrong with her, some repulsive flaw. Perhaps she had a voice like that human gong Shaler had pulled from the overturned stagecoach. Or maybe she had a witchy disposition. Visually, however, Priscilla was absolutely perfect. Beyond that, Shaler couldn't say for certain. If this preposterous marriage did take place, Tweed would be the most envied man in Deadwood Gulch. Why, men would swarm the cabin just to get a look at this dazzling beauty. Shaler and Tweed could make a fortune selling tickets for mere glimpses of her! Shaler couldn't believe Tweed Cramer's astonishing good fortune.

"I'm questioning the luck of the man who chased after his contrary mule and tumbled onto a vein of gold?" Shaler scoffed at himself as his fingertips skimmed over the sleeping beauty's unresponsive lips.

It was true that Tweed had suffered a broken leg in the fall, but the fortune he had discovered had made him feel considerably better.

Shaler gave himself a mental slap for letting his mind wander. His first order of business was to pull this beauty from the creek bed and attempt to revive her. He could do all his speculating and pondering later.

Just as Shaler leaned down to scoop Casity up, she roused to consciousness. Her vision was too blurred to realize it was her rescuer who had grabbed hold of her rather than one of her Indian captors. Her self-preservation instincts came to life in a half-second. She thrashed wildly in an attempt to roll away and scramble to safety. But within a moment, a wave of nausea crashed over her and darkness circled like a looming vulture . . .

"Oooofff!" Shaler grunted uncomfortably when a flying elbow caught him in the belly. He had overextended himself to retrieve the woman, and when she unexpectedly knocked him off balance, gravity got the better of him. With a squawk, Shaler landed right in the creek, pressing Casity deeper into the mud.

Dripping wet, Shaler straddled her and hurriedly lifted her head from the water. This time the woman didn't rouse; she was dead to the world. After Shaler scooped her up to lay her on the ground, he sank back to marvel at her beauty all over again. She truly was a sight to behold, even when she looked her worst.

Although he never considered himself a ladies' man, he had been in the company of a few attractive females in his time. None, however, could begin to compare to this half-drowned mermaid.

A thousand questions leaped to mind. Why would she come to Deadwood of her own free will? Why did she prefer to marry a man sight unseen when she could have had her pick of the crop? Did the possibility of gold lure her into mail-order wedlock?

Shaler's probing eyes made a thorough sweep of five-feet-three-inches of luscious body attached to that beguiling face. *This,* he decided, would be the most dangerous kind of female on the planet. She could distract a man from her true nature. She was undoubtedly like Kitty LeRoy—Deadwood's notorious calico queen—who called a great deal of attention to herself with her gypsylike attire.

Although Kitty was a real beauty, with her thick curly brown hair and appealing figure, she had already been through five husbands. She packed several revolvers and a dozen bowie knives to defend herself against trouble. Hell's fire, men were the ones who needed to defend themselves against *her,* Shaler thought sourly. More men had been killed fighting *over* her or *with* her than all the other women in the Black Hills combined.

Most folks had lost track of who had killed the most men—Kitty or her discarded lovers. The woman had no heart, no conscience, and no inhibitions whatsoever. She had even disguised herself as a man on one occasion when one of her lovers—with whom she was furious— refused to draw on a woman. Being an excellent markswoman, Kitty had won the gunfight and her lover lost his life. But temperamental creature that she was, Kitty felt bad the moment the showdown was over and she sent for a clergyman to marry the two of them before her lover died.

Kitty's gambling house, known as the Mint, was her headquarters for luring her future husbands. Her most recent victim was a German prospector who had struck it rich the previous month. Kitty had managed to drain him of eight-thousand dollars before she drove him from her door and crowned him king of fools with a whiskey bottle.

No doubt Kitty and Priscilla were two of a kind—the curse of a man's life! Priscilla could be even deadlier than Kitty, Shaler predicted. There was a certain innocence about this female that intrigued a man and triggered his protective instincts. But Shaler was willing to bet the pouch of gold in his pocket that this woman was anything but innocent!

Well hell, he didn't have time to dawdle. The sun was sinking on the horizon, cloaking the hills in inky black shadows. The cool of night would settle on him and his unconscious charge, who was lying in her wet clothes, chilled to the bone. Shaler had to admit that the prospect of undressing this shapely goddess held devilish appeal. It was to his good fortune and for her own welfare, that he peeled the soggy garments away.

Rising to full stature, Shaler walked over to fish some clean clothes from his saddlebag. He and Priscilla would have to share the garments he had brought along for his overnight stay in Deadwood. She could use his shirt and he would wear the breeches—just as every man should do in every workable relationship with a woman.

Removing the damp gown and petticoats from Casity's delectable body turned out to be as torturous for Shaler as it was pleasurable. For the first few moments he felt guilty about ogling her delicious form. But after a minute he stopped feeling guilty and enjoyed the view of satiny skin and feminine curves.

Lord! She was the stuff masculine dreams were made of and Shaler was having one! In rapt fascination, he took inventory of all her assets. Every inch of her silky body was exquisite. His fingers itched to caress her, but Shaler forcefully restrained the impulse. It was a difficult challenge to look without touching.

Her curvaceous body seemed to beg for a man's touch. Another one of her lures, he thought cynically.

"Get hold of yourself, man," Shaler muttered aloud. "You're acting like a damned schoolboy!"

Having chided himself for his inappropriate thoughts, Shaler wrestled Casity into his oversized shirt. But even after he had turned her this way and that she still hadn't roused. He was hesitant to transport her to town before she regained consciousness and could tell him about her injuries. There was nothing to do but fasten himself into his dry breeches and wait until the dazed nymph awakened.

Leaving Casity sprawled on his saddle blanket, Shaler gathered wood for a fire and set out to hunt game. From the look of things he would be here a while. If he was lucky, those Indians would scurry out of the Black Hills before they offended their Great Spirit, who only permitted his people short jaunts onto sacred grounds.

An hour later, Shaler had a rabbit—rabbit again for the fifth day in a row!—roasting over the fire. However, his thoughts weren't on his monotonous diet. They focused on the auburn-haired beauty who still lay on the ground like a limp doll. The more Shaler pondered having this tempting young female as a stepmother the more agitated he became. Damn Tweed for ordering a bride and double damn her for accepting the offer! Shaler would probably be lusting after his own stepmother and be forced to move out of the cabin.

Shaler found himself wishing the plump matron he had encountered at the stage had been Priscilla. It was going to be difficult to stare at this bewitching female without reminding himself that he had seen every inch of her and envisioned touching her in ways that would have been improper if she were his stepmother. Shaler couldn't even face his father without feeling as if he'd betrayed Tweed. This female was already causing Shaler anguish and she definitely had to go. She could cause a new kind of conflict between him and his father.

When Casity's head rolled from side to side, spilling her curly auburn hair over her shoulder like a molten waterfall, Shaler eased down beside her. Before he realized it, his fingertips brushed over her cheeks and drifted over the goose egg that swelled on her temple. He wanted her to wake, and yet he didn't. Damn, was he becoming wishy-washy?

He had made a pact with himself a week earlier to be as rude and unpleasant as possible in order to send Priscilla packing. It was going to be difficult not to be sympathetic after her hair-raising abduction by renegade Indians and her subsequent fall down the side of a mountain. Yet, there were times when a man had to stand firm on his convictions. This woman had no place in Shaler's life, or in Tweed's.

Pain crashed through Casity's skull, hammering in rhythm with her pulse. She ached from her eyebrows to her ankles—every movement was a test of her ability to withstand pain. Disjointed fragments of remembered horrors danced through her foggy mind, tormenting her while she struggled toward reality.

Over and over again, she relived the harrowing incident that had sent her fleeing from Nebraska. When two sneering faces lunged at her, Casity flinched and tried to wriggle free, but hands like steel bands held her fast. Her eyes fluttered open to see a hazy shadow looming over her. She fought in earnest, thrashing like a wild creature.

"Easy, honey." Shaler sank down on Casity's belly to hold her in place. "I'm the one who saved your life. No need for you to try to relieve me of mine."

The deep, rich timbre of the man's voice worked

like a sedative. The hands and body that restrained her didn't bite into her with fierce pressure.

All the fight went out of Casity and she slumped back on the ground to exhale a ragged sigh. She was so tired of trying to be strong, tired of bearing the tremendous emotional burdens of the past two weeks. How she longed for Uncle Daniel's comforting arms and soothing voice to assure her it had only been a terrifying nightmare, that her life hadn't changed dramatically—again.

Hard as she tried, Casity couldn't contain the flood of tears that streamed down her cheeks. Her life had become an endurance contest and she was exhausted from the ordeal. Her head was killing her, her leg burned like fire, and the scratches on her arms and legs stung as if kerosene had been poured on them. She was starved to death and she didn't even know where she was, or with whom!

When the tears scalded Casity's cheeks like an erupting geyser, Shaler eased down cross-legged, unsure of what to say or do. He wasn't accustomed to a woman's tears and he wasn't certain if they were a ploy or true emotion. Whatever the reason, her tears made him decidedly uncomfortable. This lovely nymph looked so vulnerable and so damned tempting it was frustrating. Not only had Shaler seen her *physically* naked but *emotionally* naked as well.

When Casity rolled to her side and curled up into the fetal position, her leg screamed in agony, setting her off on another tearful tangent. Shaler was as distracted by her soul-shuddering sobs as he was by the tantalizing display of bare flesh that glowed like honey in the firelight. Her loose shirt rode high upon her thigh, barely covering the sensuous curve of her hip.

"Would you like something to eat?" he asked, feeling terribly inadequate. "I snared a rabbit. It should be cooked by now."

"Yes . . . I . . . would . . ."

Lord, this man probably thought she was the biggest baby on the continent. The thought made Casity cry all the harder.

Like an agile tiger, Shaler rolled to his feet to retrieve the cooked meat. Since he hadn't come prepared for a rescue mission, he was without plates, cups, and eating utensils. There was nothing else to do but serve hare-kabob-on-a-stick.

"Here. Maybe you'll feel better after you eat." Shaler hoped so. He wasn't coping any better than she was with her hysterics!

Casity wiped her eyes on her shirt sleeve and levered up to a sitting position to mop the tangled curls from her face. It was only then that she got a good look at the bare-chested stranger who squatted on his haunches, holding a facsimile of a lollipop. It was also at that moment that Casity realized the sleeve upon which she had wiped her eyes was a man's shirt and that her aching leg was bare to the thigh!

With a startled yelp, she recoiled, covering herself as best she could from the handsome stranger's roaming gaze. "What did you do to me!"

None of the things he had visualized doing, that was for damned sure!

"You fell in the creek," Shaler said as calmly as possible. "You were unconscious and soaked to the bone. I gave you the shirt off my back." Well, not exactly, but it sounded chivalrous. Considering the hysterical look on her face, he had to say something to calm her down. "But don't worry, I kept my eyes shut the whole time I was undressing you." *Liar! He never even dared to blink for fear he might miss something.*

The half-smile that tugged at the corner of his sensuous mouth gave him away. Casity flashed him that famous glare that had frozen a score of men in their tracks. For some reason she had lost her touch. It must have been her puffy eyes and the squiggles of tears that ruined the effect. This brawny giant with midnight hair and shoulders like a bull didn't even flinch. If anything, his smile grew wider and more roguish, displaying pearly white teeth and dimples that bracketed his mouth.

"Hey, don't worry about it," Shaler said with a shrug that made his muscles ripple.

Casity's traitorous gaze made a slow, thorough sweep of his physique, wishing she didn't find him so appealing when she was so irritated with him for disrobing her without her permission.

"I've seen lots of naked bodies before," he said, as if that made it all right.

"Certainly not mine!" Casity huffed.

"I have now." He couldn't help but tease her. "But if you've seen one body you've seen them all."

Another outright lie flew off his lips. No female in recent memory had a body to match this one. Her skin was like silk. She had a birthmark on her left hip that reminded Shaler of a tear drop and she had eyes as clear and blue as a Rocky Mountain stream. She was a fascinating creature.

Casity didn't know how to respond to Shaler's remark. She didn't know whether to be shocked or reassured. She had never found herself in such an awkward situation or involved in such an outrageous conversation with a man. This ruggedly handsome stranger was a totally new experience for Casity. He had seen her as no other man ever had—buck-naked and wailing like a banshee!

Attempting to muddle through as best she could, Casity reached for the rabbit lollipop, only to feel another searing pain shoot through her swollen leg. When she grimaced and grabbed her kneecap, steady hands glided over her clenched fingers, gently moving them out of his way to inspect her injury. The stranger's touch put her on immediate alert, and Casity instinctively withdrew into her own space to avoid the appealing scent that threatened to fog her senses.

A frustrated sigh tumbled from Shaler's lips. Putting his hands upon her—even for diagnostic purposes—was hard enough on him without her reacting so dramatically.

"Hell's fire, I'm not going to rape you. That's hardly my style," Shaler muttered. "If that had been my intention I would have done it long ago. Now just relax, princess. I want to determine if you suffered a sprain or a break."

"You fancy yourself as a doctor, too, I suppose," Casity remarked, recovering a portion of her customary spunk.

And it was about time, too! This attractive stranger didn't know the real Casity Crockett—yet.

Shaler's broad shoulders rose in another shrug that called even more attention to his arresting physique. "I've set a few broken bones and performed primitive surgery when necessity demanded it."

His hands moved expertly down her leg, inspecting her injured thigh and calf. His tender touch elicited sensations that had no business whatsoever attacking her at a moment like this! It was only because her emotions were in a tailspin, Casity thought reasonably. If she were her old self, she would have felt nothing at all for this darkly handsome stranger.

"Your leg isn't broken, but it's badly sprained," Shaler said. Hell's fire, he thought, touching her triggered the damnedest feelings inside him and they refused to go away. "The swelling has already begun around the knee joint. It should be chilled immediately.''

When Shaler ambled away, Casity's gaze lingered on the broad expanse of his back and trim hips until he became one of the swaying shadows of the night. My, what a magnificent specimen he was! He was lean and incredibly well contoured from the top of his head all the way down to his toes. Earthy sensuality seemed to pour out of that perfectly symmetrical, vibrantly masculine bundle of bronzed flesh and knotted muscle. He moved with an unconscious grace and elegance that was like poetry in motion.

Mmm . . . all that rippling muscle and male vitality definitely appealed to the feminine eye . . . Damn it, what was the matter with her? It wasn't like her to be intrigued by the sight of a man. No situation could be as potentially threatening as the one she presently found herself in! She was all alone in the forest with this rugged stranger who smelled like the whole outdoors. He mesmerized her when he moved with the agility of a jungle cat.

Muttering at the perverse wanderings of her mind, Casity snatched up the rabbit lollipop Shaler had stuck in the ground while he inspected her leg. She didn't realize how famished she was until her first bite. Then she attacked the juicy meat ravenously.

While Casity was devouring the food, Shaler was down at the creek—scowling, pacing, and cursing the air blue. He had vowed to be mean and nasty to Priscilla in hopes of putting her to flight. Thus far, he had been anything but! Her tears and vulnerability had gotten under his skin and he had been gentle and compassionate. That was hardly the kind of behavior likely to assure that gorgeous sprite that she wasn't welcome in Deadwood. This was to be his stepmama, after all. Imagine that! Well, Shaler sure as hell couldn't.

Yet, considering the near-calamity Priscilla Lambert had endured, he would give her a short grace period before he began his snarling. After all, he couldn't send her running back to civilization if she couldn't even walk, now could he? After she had a good night's sleep and he designed a splint to support her injured leg, Shaler would begin treating her according to his original plan.

Yes, he would be sociable and compassionate until morning. Then, he would cart her back to Deadwood, tell her what was what, and stuff her on the next stage.

He was going to forget how lovely and desirable Priscilla was. He was going to forget who she was and how he longed to . . .

The titillating thought put his body on a slow burn and left him aching in the most uncomfortable of places. With a disgusted scowl, Shaler peeled off his breeches and plunked down in midstream to cool off. He did not appreciate the lack of support he was receiving from his self-control. He had always taken it for granted—until now. But there was something about this particular female that aroused him in the most phenomenal ways. Although they were perfect strangers, he felt as if he had seen various facets of her personality that he doubted most of her male acquaintances were allowed to see.

Come morning, Shaler promised himself, he would begin his campaign to rout Priscilla Lambert from the Black Hills. First he had to get her back on her feet—and he couldn't do it while he was dawdling in midstream, trying to keep his male urges in check!

With that thought, Shaler waded ashore and stuffed himself back into his breeches. Gathering the discarded petticoats to use as cold compresses and bandages, he propelled himself toward camp. He was going to keep this relationship on a doctor-patient basis. He would tend her, soothe her, and touch her only when necessary. That shouldn't be all that difficult since she seemed leery of him. He could handle this situation just as he handled all others—coolly and efficiently. No problem . . .

Six

No problem . . . the words came back to haunt Shaler as he stepped into the clearing to survey the scene before him. The woman sat with her injured leg outstretched and her left leg curled in front of her. A wild cloud of auburn hair cascaded over her shoulders. The curly tendrils seemed to catch fire in the golden light and burn like the midday sun. She was devouring the roasted rabbit as if she hadn't eaten in days. She reminded Shaler of a child—so uninhibited, so unaware of her devastating beauty, and oblivious to her rapt audience of one.

Shaler had known many women in the usual circumstances—in bed. He never lingered longer in a woman's presence than the time it took to appease his needs. But he was forced into an entirely different situation when it came to this appealing sprite. He had seen her various moods, watched her dissolve into tears and then regather her feisty spirit. She was like an ever-changing kaleidoscope, and he marveled at the different facets of her personality. When he looked at this blue-eyed beauty, he saw far more than just a delectable body, more than just a bewitching face. There was a great depth of strength and vitality that even her near brush with disaster hadn't completely crumbled.

Still smiling at this intriguing nymph, Shaler ambled back to camp, making enough racket to announce his arrival. And again, he saw her retreat into herself, drawing the shell of cautious reserve back into place like protective armor.

"Could I have another helping of rabbit? It's delicious." Casity self-consciously tugged the oversized shirt back into some degree of decency.

Knowing this handsome stranger had seen her in the altogether left Casity feeling ill at ease in his presence. He had a distinct advantage over her, and she hated that. Casity never felt comfortable with a man unless she was in perfect control of the situation.

Shaler whittled off another chunk of meat with his knife and stuck it on her stick before settling down to satisfy his own hunger—the kind food could satisfy, anyway.

After Shaler finished his meal, he gathered his makeshift medical supplies and hunkered down beside Casity, who reflexively shrank back into her own space. The instant he put his hand on her thigh, she almost jumped out of her skin. Damnation, her reaction wasn't making this easier. When she flinched, he felt it all the way through his nerve endings. What affected her affected him. It was not a good thing to be so totally and completely aware of her! He had to stop this nonsense—it was making him crazy!

"I'm going to splint your leg," he forewarned her, his voice wobbling from the effects of the frustrated passion eating him alive. Shaler met her wary glance and concentrated on the upcoming task. "This is going to hurt, princess, no matter how gentle I try to be." Shaler handed her the stick from her rabbit lollipop. "Bite on this if you need to, but don't move. You jammed your knee when you fell and it's halfway out of its socket."

Casity braced her arms beside her. "Is this going to

hurt worse than tumbling down a hill, slamming into every obstacle along the way?"

He placed his left hand firmly around her thigh, feeling her fierce reaction to his touch. His right hand curled around her calf as he positioned himself at her feet. "I don't know exactly how bad this is going to hurt. You'll have to tell me when it's over—"

"Ouch . . . damn!" Casity shrieked around the stick she had clamped between her teeth. She sucked in her breath as fire shot down her injured leg. Perspiration beaded her brow and the world turned a fuzzy shade of gray. But Casity brazened it out, if only to prove to this stranger that she wasn't the emotionally unstable creature he thought she was. "That wasn't too bad—"

"I'm not finished yet." Shaler crouched above her and then uncoiled with lightning speed. He gave her twisted knee a quick, painful jerk that couldn't be avoided if it was to be set properly.

"Damnation!" Casity hissed. A wave of nausea rolled around her stomach as agony undulated through her. Her fingers instinctively clutched his, biting into his flesh, as if delivering pain would minimize her own misery.

Shaler watched the spasms of pain cross her face and the color seep from her cheeks. He also noted the mist of tears that clouded her eyes as she clenched her jaw in an attempt to bite back an agonized wail. She had held up admirably. Exceptionally well, Shaler amended. When he had set Tweed's broken leg, the older man had howled and squealed like a stuck pig for hours on end, swearing Shaler had pained him a-purpose for making his adopted son swallow castor oil when he was a young lad. But this mere wisp of a woman refused to allow Shaler to see her blubber again. She was going to bite back the tears, even if it killed her, and it looked as though it was about to.

"Done," Shaler announced as he reached for the strips of petticoats. "Now all we have to do is pack the joint and secure the splint. I'll brew a healing salve tomorrow."

Casity sagged back to the ground and heaved a shuddering sigh. Her stomach was undergoing a volcanic eruption, her pulse was hammering like a tom-tom, and her mouth was so dry she could have spit cotton. And her leg! God, it had felt better out of socket. A tear dribbled out of the corner of her eye and Casity turned away, hoping her handsome, self-appointed physician hadn't noticed.

He had. Those probing golden eyes missed nothing.

Tenderly, Shaler reached up to catch the tear drop on his forefinger. "If it makes you feel better, I think you're incredibly brave." He graced her with the kind of smile that could wilt a woman's resolve—if she let it.

"It doesn't help," Casity had to admit.

"I probably would have screamed my head off," Shaler confessed.

Her face turned toward his, mesmerized by the way the leaping flames of the campfire made his wavy hair shine like a raven's wing. The dim light framed the profile of his angular features, leaving Casity to marvel at the distinct lines in his face. The reflection in his tawny eyes fascinated her and she found her gaze roaming over his powerful shoulders to survey the massive breadth of his chest. She watched his knotted muscles flex and contract with his every movement before her eyes wandered down the rock-hard plane of his belly.

Casity cursed herself when her gaze dipped even lower. She tried to ignore the most perfectly structured male specimen she had ever laid eyes on, but mercy, there was a lot of him to ignore!

With a determined jerk, she brought her eyes upward to see that Shaler was watching her watch him. Her admiring gaze and wanton thoughts had betrayed her! That had never happened before. What kind of spell had this handsome rogue cast on her?

Shaler forced himself to reach for his improvised supplies. Feeling her all-consuming gaze had a profound effect on him. Well, he wasn't going to think about it, he vowed firmly. Sure as hell, his male needs would get the better of him if he did.

True, it had been over a month since he had . . . Well, it had been a month, that's all. A month wasn't such a long time compared to a man's lifetime. He could survive without sex for extended periods. Never mind that this was the greatest challenge his willpower had ever confronted and that he was losing this fight for self-control. But the battle wasn't over yet. He could rally his defenses if he put his mind to it. He was keeping this encounter completely respectable and proper. He could do it if he really tried!

"How far are we from Deadwood?" Casity asked for lack of anything better to say.

Lord-a-mercy, for a woman who had never had an aversion to silence she suddenly felt the need to say something, anything, to divert these wicked thoughts that filled her mind when she stared too long at this sinewy giant.

"We're about two miles away as the crow flies and five miles by horse," Shaler reported as he wrapped the damp cloth around her kneecap. "We'll break camp first thing in the morning."

Casity nodded. The thought of climbing onto a horse with her leg burning like hell on fire held no appeal. She was battered and bruised and every movement tested her threshold of pain.

"I didn't thank you for saving my life," she murmured as she watched him bind strips of her petticoat around her swollen leg.

"You're welcome."

Shaler concentrated on his task, wondering why his fingertips were so damned sensitive all of a sudden. Her skin was so incredibly soft—he knew he was using any excuse to touch her, no matter how innocent the gesture appeared to be. It was anything but innocent, he was ashamed to confess.

He reached for the branches he had gathered to serve as splints and bound them to her leg before making the final wrap. "This will feel awkward, but it will prevent unnecessary pressure on those tendons and joints until they mend."

"How long?" Casity questioned.

"A week, maybe two." When she groaned at the inconvenience, Shaler's lips curved into a teasing grin. "Be thankful you aren't a horse. I might have to shoot you."

And just how, Casity wondered, was she going to find employment in Deadwood if she could barely walk? There probably weren't all that many jobs available which required no physical exertion. Damn . . .

Her discouraged thoughts trailed off when Shaler sank down beside her on the saddle blanket, as if he belonged there. "Hold it right there, mister," Casity snapped. "I appreciate all you've done for me, but if you think you and I are going to, that we—"

Shaler cut her off with an explosive snort. He was more annoyed with himself than with Casity's protest. All his senses went on full alert the moment his body brushed against hers. That shouldn't have happened. He was in control . . . wasn't he?

"There's one blanket between us," Shaler reminded her reasonably. "My spare shirt and your gown are still wet, so they won't be worth a damn. I already told you that if I'd wanted to ravish you I would have. All I want is a decent night's sleep."

Casity peered over at the swarthy giant sprawled out beside her. "You don't find me attractive?" she heard herself ask and then wondered why. No doubt, the blow to her head had scrambled her brain.

"Yes, as a matter of fact I do," Shaler growled as if he resented the admission, which he certainly did. "But I want sleep, not sex"

Hell's fire, what an accomplished liar he was turning out to be!

"Do you mean to tell me that a man can actually sleep beside a woman without . . . er . . . well . . you know."

Casity's face flamed with embarrassment. Why was she so uninhibited in the presence of this stranger? It was very odd how one could be so completely candid when one could see the beginning and end of a brief acquaintance which would in no way effect the rest of one's life. It was like stepping outside of one's self in a place out of time. Very, *very* strange indeed.

It didn't help matters that Casity had been hounded by a kind of daring recklessness since her uncle's death. It was as if nothing mattered quite as much as it had before. The tragedy had also driven home the idea of her own mortality, reminding her that each day that she managed to elude her pursuers was precious and each encounter could very well be her last.

A deep peal of laughter rang in the night air, releasing the tension that hummed through Shaler's body. "Do you think all men are sex perverts?"

"Yes, and aren't they?" Casity inquired in all seriousness.

"You'll be shocked to learn that it is quite possible for a man to function rather well without . . . er . . . well . . . you know," he assured her, flinging her words back with a teasing grin that Casity found devastating.

Casity was posing questions she had always been afraid to ask until now. She couldn't imagine even having this conversation, especially with any of her other male acquaintances. At the mere mention of the topic, they would have been all over her like a rash.

Was it possible that there was actually one man in this hemisphere who could see a woman as a thinking, feeling creature and respect her individuality? Surely not. This stranger had to be using some sort of ploy.

Casity eyed Shaler skeptically. "Are you going to lie there and tell me that if I—and this is purely hypothetical, of course—offered you a kiss of gratitude for saving my life, that you would accept it without expecting more, that you would turn your back on me and go to sleep?"

They were treading on dangerous ground here. Shaler swore he felt the earth tremble at the mention of the possibility of tasting those rosy lips. He had never found himself in such a provocative conversation with a woman without actually doing something about it! But hey, he could be as totally objective as any female. And he had never walked away from a challenge, either. Testing his mettle had become a way of life in the mountains of Colorado. He could be as steady as a rock and would never be outdone by a mere wisp of a woman!

"I most certainly could settle for no more than a kiss of gratitude," he assured her confidently. "Hell's fire, princess, a kiss is just a kiss, with a beginning and an end."

"Is it?" Casity honestly didn't know. She was proud to say she had never offered a man a kiss, except for the pecks on the cheek she had given her father and uncle when she was a child. That didn't count in her book.

Shaler cocked his head to assess this inquisitive nymph from a different angle. Maybe she wasn't as worldly and experienced as he had assumed. Or perhaps she was only toying with him the way some women were prone to do. Shaler didn't give a flying fig for coquettish games. He was forthright and plain-spoken for the most part. If he wanted something he usually said so without making a big to-do about it.

Casity met his pensive gaze, wondering at the peculiar sensations his nearness evoked. This stranger could tempt and bedevil even the most cautious of women—of which she was certainly one. But he wasn't forceful or overly aggressive. He made her feel safe and protected. He also stirred her femininity as no man ever had. For once, she was permitted to enjoy her attraction to a man without feeling frightened or threatened.

Casity wondered how it would feel to tunnel her fingers through that crisp hair that covered his broad chest, to have his lips hovering upon hers . . .

"If I asked you to kiss me, would you do it?" Casity questioned out of the blue, surprising them both.

"No," Shaler turned his back and scowled. "So don't ask."

"I thought you said a kiss was just a—"

"Well, maybe I was wrong," he grumbled, tossing her a silencing glare. "Look, princess, let's just get some shut-eye, shall we? You're bruised and wounded and I'm . . . tired."

Sure he was. That's why his body was as taut as fence wire and he had to turn away to conceal his arousal.

Casity blinked when Shaler cushioned his head on his bent arm, closed his eyes, and ignored her. Why was he so huffy all of a sudden? She had only asked a few questions and suddenly he seemed annoyed.

Another thought crossed her mind and Casity

frowned suspiciously. "You aren't one of those men who prefer the company of *other* men?"

Shaler twisted around so quickly that the whirling draft tore the words off her tongue. "No, I am not!" he practically yelled at her. "Hell's fire, woman, do you always talk this much? Can't a man have a little peace and quiet around here?"

"Why are you so put out with me?" Casity questioned, bemused.

She had become extraordinarily comfortable around this handsome stranger who had proved himself to be a gentle and capable protector; so much, in fact, that it was insulting to have him make such a spectacular display of ignoring her. No other man had treated her as if she were a nuisance, and Casity didn't know how to react. She usually had to fend men off, but suddenly she had become the pursuer instead of the prey. It gave her an intriguing insight.

"I'm put out because you're asking annoying questions," Shaler muttered, glaring at her over his shoulder.

"If you ask me, you're making a big deal out of a kiss you assured me was no big deal."

Shaler rolled sideways, watching her luminous blue eyes widen as his head moved deliberately toward hers. His gaze focused on her parted lips, determined to put an end to her questions and satisfy his curiosity as well as hers. "Well fine, princess. One kiss of gratitude and then go the hell to sleep."

Casity closed the narrow space between them to kiss him full on the mouth. It was a quick but pleasant meeting of lips. "Thank you for saving my life. I'm most grateful."

Shaler frowned. "What was *that*?"

Was he making fun of her? "It was a kiss, of course." He chuckled. "Not where I come from, it wasn't."

"Then how is it done where you come from?"

"Like this . . ."

Casity was stunned by her involuntary response to his kiss. The touch of his lips was so light and tender it made her insides melt. She felt herself sinking as his body half-covered hers, heightening her awareness of him, dramatizing the difference between her soft skin and the hard, lean contours of his masculinity. His massive chest brushed provocatively against the taut peaks of her breasts and the muscled column of his leg glided over the exposed flesh of her thighs.

There was nothing aggressive or forceful about his embrace. He allowed her to test her response to him while he appraised his reaction to her. He took no more than she offered, and yet, the gentle pressure of his lips left her longing for more.

When Casity's hand slid up his forearm to settle on his chest, Shaler felt his heart slam into his ribs and stick there. Her inquisitive touch was like the flutter of a butterfly's wings—lightly teasing him until he instinctively moved closer to her hand, closer to her body, closer to the compelling fire that flickered through his bloodstream.

When he explored the soft recesses of her mouth with his probing tongue, she countered in like manner. When his hand lifted to caress her cheek, her fingertips investigated the line of his jaw. When he inched closer, so did she—until their bodies were meshed tightly together, as if they were sharing the same skin.

Shaler couldn't honestly remember being so stunned or devastated by a kiss. In fact, he couldn't even remember when his first kiss ended and the second and third ones began! He wanted to go on kissing her until he was forced to come up for air.

When Shaler finally found the will to withdraw, their gazes locked and he drowned in the rippling depths of sapphire blue. Shaler knew, right then and there, that the self-control he had too often taken for granted had evaporated in a puff of smoke. He couldn't remember feeling so vulnerable—or caring so little that he was.

The world suddenly shrank. Time ground to a halt. There was only here and now—no past, no future—only a sweet, forbidden fire that demanded to be fed.

"That's what kisses are like where I come from, princess," he said huskily. "Are you satisfied now?" *He* wasn't. God! The taste of her lingered on his lips and he wanted her so much his entire body ached!

Satisfied? No, Casity wasn't satisfied at all. Those tantalizing kisses hadn't appeased this craving inside her; they intensified it. She was aching for something she didn't understand. But then, nothing made sense to her, not this erotic night beneath a dome of twinkling stars, not these intense feelings of longing. Nothing!

Since she had awakened after her ordeal, she hadn't been herself. Casity didn't recognize the wanton woman she had suddenly become. He had kissed her and she felt as if she had come back to life.

A wry smile played about Shaler's lips. "For a woman who had a lot to say, you've certainly grown quiet," he noted.

"How did you do that?" she asked in amazement.

"Do what?"

"Kiss me until I couldn't think straight."

Casity studied the craggy face above her, hypnotized. Her index finger traced his lips, remembering the taste of him . . . craving more.

The narrow space that separated them seemed like miles. When his muscular body had been pressed to hers, she'd felt so secure, so content, so radiantly alive. Now there was nothing but emptiness.

Shaler groaned when her finger skimmed his lips and those thick-lashed blue eyes peered up at him. "Dangerous . . ." he whispered, more to himself than to her.

He knew he should move away, but *he couldn't*. Not when he had become so enchanted.

"Mmm . . . dangerous," Casity murmured in agreement.

Danger had become her constant companion of late, she reminded herself. Perhaps that was why she had become so reckless around this nameless stranger. All she really knew about him, was that he had saved her life . . . and that the touch of his lips was like a taste of heaven after two weeks of hell.

Suddenly, Casity wanted things she had never even considered until this moment. Was it so wrong to cast caution to the wind, to savor what little pleasure she could for one brief moment? Could it be so wrong to be attracted to a man whose kiss and caress felt so wonderfully right? Why shouldn't she enjoy this moment?

As instantaneously as metal being drawn to a magnet, Shaler felt his hand drifting over her thigh. His pulse pounded like a jackhammer at the feel of her silky flesh quivering beneath his exploring fingertips. He felt her helpless reaction, saw it in her eyes, and was starkly aware of the force of his own heated response. Blood pounded through him so hot and heavy that he could barely breathe.

He wanted to withdraw, but he couldn't make himself move. "Tell me to stop," Shaler murmured, his voice thick with passion.

"I—I . . . can't . . ." Casity admitted shakily. "I—"

Her breath stuck in her throat as his caresses wandered beneath her shirt to swirl over her belly and circle the peak of her breast. Casity felt hot chills tin-

gling up her spine. The newness of a man's hands
and lips gliding across her flesh caused a rush of desire to flood through her. His mouth and fingertips
were teaching her the art of passion—and left her wanting to learn more.

All the while Shaler explored her body his eyes
never left her face. He watched the play of emotion
across her features, felt himself drawn deeper into the
spell. His hands shook as he unbuttoned her shirt,
exposing her silky flesh to his appreciative gaze.

"You're lovely, exquisite . . ." Ever so slowly, his
head descended until his lips whispered over the
throbbing peaks he had unveiled in the moonlight.

It was as if he were allowing Casity all the time in
the world to stop him. And yet, there wasn't enough
air in her lungs to voice even one protest. Each masterful touch left her sighing in indescribable pleasure.

Every few seconds, Shaler raised his head and gazed
into her eyes, gauging her reaction, giving her one
last chance to stop what had already gone too far.
Casity was too paralyzed by the unexpected pleasure
to resist. His tender seduction had made her a captive
of her own awakening desire.

His hands and lips caressed her, evoking phenomenal sensations. Casity couldn't move away from his
skillful touch any more than she could command the
stars to disappear from the black velvet sky. His seduction was so slow and deliberate that each sensation
was heart-stopping.

His lips and teeth teased her breasts with such tender expertise that Casity instinctively arched toward
him. When he took each aching tip into his mouth
and tugged gently, she gasped in disbelief. She could
feel delicious heat spreading through her body as his
hands feathered over her belly and lingered there to
monitor her response. She held her breath while his

lips suckled at her breasts and his fingertips moved down to the ultrasensitive flesh of her thighs.

"Open for me," Shaler commanded as his hand tangled in the soft curls that shielded her femininity.

At his gentle insistence, she relaxed beneath his touch. She watched him with eyes like liquid sapphire, feeling warm flames pool deep inside her. When his palm settled between her legs and his fingertip caressed her, Casity clasped her hand self-consciously over his.

"I won't hurt you," he assured her huskily.

His lips came back to hers, his tongue thrusting gently into her mouth as his fingertip lightly probed her moist heat. The intrusion of his tongue and the penetration of his hand left Casity gasping.

"Please—!" Her voice became a quiet moan as he stroked her, teased her until bubbly sensations drenched her body, showering her with pleasure.

"I intend to please us both," Shaler whispered in husky promise.

When he nudged her legs farther apart with his elbow, she gave no thought to further protest. She was too beguiled by the tingling sensations assaulting her, too hungry to learn what other feelings awaited his gentle touch.

Shaler savored her lips and groaned at the silky heat surrounding his fingertip. His languid probing drew a moan of surrender and he shuddered when he felt her body returning his caresses. He longed to summon even more response from her, to enjoy her pleasure as if it were his own.

Shaler honestly couldn't fathom what had come over him. He had never taken so much time and satisfaction in exploring a female body, never wanted to become so lost in a woman. But this perfectly-formed angel compelled him to commit every satiny curve to memory. He wanted to touch her, to taste her, to pleasure her as much as caressing her pleasured him.

Each unhurried touch was like their first kiss—a startling revelation demanding to be fully savored. This kind of passion involved more than two bodies and basic instinct. This magical experience tugged at his heartstrings as nothing ever had before. It was like living a dream, feeling his most private fantasies unfold until he could no longer distinguish reality from illusion.

Casity could not contain the breathless moan that rose in her throat when the world slid out from under her. She was dangling in space, marooned in a universe of relentless sensation. She felt as if she were on fire, and each tender touch ignited more flame. His fingertips teased and aroused her to wild abandon, leaving her to wonder if she could survive the pleasure that intensified with every flick of his tongue and touch of his hands.

Shaler felt as if he were moving in slow motion, sensitized by each delicious taste and touch. Each moment seemed to expand and intensify until he was lost in infinite sensuality. Making love to this enchanting female demanded an emotional commitment from him that he had never offered a woman and had not intended to, even now. But this slow, sweet magic was amazingly satisfying. There was no rush, only languid delight. He wasn't *taking;* he was *sharing* each wondrous sensation that rippled through her supple body and became part of his. He wanted to heighten and prolong the pleasure, to cherish this unique experience that had never come before and may never come again . . .

"No . . . !" Casity choked on her breath when his fingertip unleashed wild shudders that pulsated in the core of her being and spread through every inch of her virginal body. The shimmering spasms left her aching for something more, something . . .

When Shaler's muscular body glided possessively over hers, Casity gave no conscious thought to denying him. She welcomed the velvety warmth that filled the empty ache inside her. Suddenly he was satisfying the monstrous craving that she feared nothing could satisfy. Her nails dug into the rigid tendons of his back as he became the living fire that consumed her. His hips moved, and she shuddered as he filled her completely. Casity closed her eyes and held onto him as if her very life depended on it.

Only for a brief instant did Casity experience pain before sheer pleasure flooded through her like a raging river. He set the cadence of passion and her body moved in perfect rhythm with his, meeting and matching each hard, driving thrust, aching to dissolve in the sweet fire she sensed awaited her.

His lips descended upon hers to capture her gasp of wonderment. Casity felt the dizzying crescendo build until splendor expanded and exploded, completely shattering her composure. A fiery rapture radiated through every fiber of her being, sizzling through every nerve ending.

When Shaler shuddered above her and clutched her to him to ride out the turbulent storm they had created on this cloudless night, Casity felt sweet release drenching her spent body. This was the wild bliss to counteract the nightmare that Casity's life had become.

A soft sigh of contentment tumbled from her lips when Shaler tenderly kissed her eyelids, her brows, and that sensitive spot at the base of her neck. Absently, she stroked his shoulder, marveling at the exquisite sensations that still engulfed her.

When Shaler eased down to cradle her in his arms,

she was exhausted, completely drained of emotion, of strength. If only she could dwell forever in this wondrous world . . .

Shaler was too mystified by what had transpired even to question what he should have been feeling and thinking. He only wanted to hold this auburn-haired beauty, to reflect upon each incredible sensation that had swept over him. He was drunk on the scent of her, on the feel of her silky body lying in his arms.

He and this lovely sprite fit together like two pieces of a puzzle. He couldn't move, didn't want to let go of the sweet splendor that holding her aroused in him. She slept so trustingly beside him, her head resting on his shoulder. He could feel her breath whispering in his ear, calling him back to paradise . . .

Ah, if this wasn't heaven, it was close enough for Shaler.

Seven

Just as dawn spilled through the canopy of trees to signal the beginning of another summer day, the thump of impatient hooves brought Shaler slowly awake. He was reluctant to withdraw from the soft warmth that warded off the chill of a mountain morning. With considerable effort he pried one heavily-lidded eye open to see his sorrel gelding staring at him from the other side of camp. That was *before* his gaze settled on the tangled auburn hair that cascaded over his shoulder . . .

Shaler suddenly remembered where he was and what he had done. Reality struck like a doubled fist to the jaw. Dear God! He had never known what a short walk it was from heaven to hell! He had betrayed his father's trust for one moment of ecstasy!

Shaler inched away, careful not to wake the sleeping beauty beside him. He couldn't face her yet because he couldn't even face himself! In all his thirty years he had never made such a fool of himself. Nor had he allowed anyone to do it for him—*especially* not a woman! Damnation, what had seemed so gloriously natural the previous night had become a disaster . . .

With a muffled groan Shaler spied the telltale stains on his saddle blanket. A virgin? A VIRGIN! He didn't want to believe it. She couldn't be! How could a dream so quickly become a nightmare?

Shaler made a beeline to the creek and let loose with a raft of curses. Damn that cunning little witch! She should have told him she was untouched. What game was she playing?

Had Priscilla Lambert come to Deadwood, planning to use Tweed as her meal ticket, and then decided to latch onto the first man who crossed her path?

No doubt Priscilla planned to look him up later and demand marriage to rectify the wrong. And fool that he'd been, he had fallen right into her trap!

All those unsettling questions she had posed the previous night had been nothing but a ruse. Too bad that conniving female hadn't known he was Tweed's son. Hell's fire, she hadn't even asked his name! Didn't that just about say it all?

By the time Shaler finished turning the incident over in his mind he was good and mad. Priscilla had *made* him betray Tweed—the generous, warm-hearted man who had taken Shaler in when he had nowhere to go. She had entrapped him for her own fiendish purposes.

Well, Shaler McCain was nobody's pawn, especially not a woman's! If little Miss Priscilla Lambert thought she had outfoxed him, she had damned well better think again. She was going to be on the first stagecoach out of Deadwood and that was that. Shaler wasn't about to take her home to Tweed. No way in hell!

After she realized Shaler wasn't going to "do the right thing by her"—if that was what she was expecting after their reckless night of passion—she wasn't going to become his stepmother, either. She couldn't spoil twenty years of friendship between him and Tweed because Tweed was never going to know what had happened. Shaler would take this secret to the grave, even if his conscience gave him hell for the rest of his miserable life!

"Well, what did you expect?" Shaler snarled at his reflection in the water. "She lured you in like a fish swallowing bait. But she damned sure isn't having the last laugh."

After Shaler had his one-sided conversation, he was in the perfect frame of mind to approach Miss Priscilla Lambert. Now she would discover just how mean and nasty he could be. And if she started up with those tears again, he wasn't letting them get to him. Vulnerable? Her? Ha!

Scowling furiously, Shaler lurched around and stomped back to camp. None too gently, he nudged the sleeping siren awake and reminded himself how much he despised her.

"Get up, princess. You're wasting daylight. You have a stage to catch, and I'm going to make double-damn sure you're on it!"

Shaler's booming voice and his abrupt nudge brought Casity awake with a start. She glanced up to see six-foot-two-inches and two hundred pounds of brawny muscle towering over her, glaring at her like black thunder. Gone was the compassion and tenderness of the previous night . . .

When Casity remembered the intimacy they had shared, reality hit her like a hard slap in the face. What had seemed so right and wondrous the previous night was glaringly wrong in the light of day. Casity, fool that she had been, had let her guard down completely after the harrowing incident that had left her bruised, battered, and hopelessly vulnerable. In an effort to forget the cruel nightmares of her past, she had lived only in the present, seeking whatever pleasure and comfort she could grasp without considering the future and its consequences.

From the harsh sound of his voice . . . Lord! She didn't even know the name of the man who had stolen her innocence and who was glaring at her as if the entire incident were all her fault. Casity had never behaved so foolishly in all her life. Now she would have to pay dearly for it.

This sinewy rake had obviously played a role for her benefit, assuring her he had no intention of seducing her. And she, being totally naive about the seductive techniques of rogues, had fallen for it. She had begun to trust him, and that was exactly what he had wanted all along. Once she was without her protective shield, he had taken advantage. All he had wanted was what every other man wanted from a woman—and she had let him! *Let him,* God have mercy on her wretched soul!

Shame flushed Casity's cheeks as she propped up on an elbow to face the looming lout. Until now, she had not considered how difficult it would be to endure the "morning after the night before." But apparently this charismatic stranger was accustomed to seducing women and then discarding them like damaged merchandise. It was probably just a game he liked to play.

He was not the same gentle man she was with the previous night, and by damn, she wasn't the same idiotic woman he had cleverly compromised, either! This rake was about to meet the *real* Casity Crockett. The woman who had fallen beneath his spell no longer existed.

When Casity struggled to sit upright and cover herself, Shaler saw all the signs of the strong-willed woman their encounter had only hinted at.

Well, that was fine with Shaler. He wasn't going to be stupid enough to fall prey to the scheming Priscilla Lambert again. He knew exactly what she was about and it wasn't going to work with him. His conscience wasn't bothering him in the least, he convinced himself. He hadn't *stolen* her virginity; she had *offered* it to him as part of the bait.

After Casity had gained her feet—without Shaler's assistance—his gaze narrowed ominously. "Let's get one thing straight right here and now, Priscilla Lambert—!" Shaler sneered hatefully.

When Casity opened her mouth to inform him that she was not the aforementioned lady, Shaler flung up his hand to demand silence.

"You didn't think I knew who you were or why you came to Deadwood, did you?" he asked with a sardonic smirk.

He still didn't know why she was here! Damn this cocky rake. He was full of assumptions. Nothing would have pleased Casity more than to cram her fist into that obnoxious smirk.

"Well, I know plenty about you, princess." His amber eyes raked her with mocking disdain. "You answered Tweed Cramer's ad in the newspaper, thinking you could take his money and then flit off to your next foolish victim."

"Are you Tweed Cramer?" Casity croaked when he finally allowed her time to speak.

Shaler snorted. "Not hardly, honey. I'm his son."

Casity blinked in disbelief. "How old is Tweed?"

"Forty-two, according to his calculations."

Casity studied him. Tweed's son looked to be at least thirty, if she was any judge of age. So how was it possible for Tweed to have a thirty-year-old son? And what kind of son would deflower his own father's intended bride? Casity suddenly despised this rapscallion more than ever.

The puzzled expression on Casity's features was one Shaler had noted plenty of times when folks tried to figure out the ages of father and son. "Tweed adopted me after my family was massacred by Blackfoot Indians," he explained, though why he bothered he didn't know. Habit, he supposed. "But that's no concern of yours. The point is, I won't have some scheming she-male as my stepmother! Your conduct last night proved you had no loyalty to your betrothed."

Casity flinched as if he had struck her. *Her* conduct? Had that rendezvous in the moonlight been a test? Obviously! Of all the dirty, rotten tricks! This deceitful scoundrel had tested his own father's betrothed! He thought *she* was despicable? He was far worse. This slimy snake had outsmarted himself. Casity wanted to tell him so, but he was ranting and raving.

"Tweed, the trusting and easy-going soul that he is, didn't realize what kind of deceptive female he might encounter in this ridiculous bargain," Shaler growled disdainfully. "But you showed your true colors last night, princess. You didn't even bother to ask my name because it didn't really matter to you, did it?" He didn't allow her time to respond. He simply plowed on—full steam ahead. "I was to be your insurance in case your mail-order marriage didn't work out. You thought you could come running to me and demand marriage after one passionate night. But if you think for one minute that I'm the least bit interested, you're wrong! Passion is passion and I could have gotten the same thing from anyone else."

His hateful gaze swept over her. "You knew perfectly well that Tweed wouldn't know whether he was getting a virgin, so you had nothing to fear if you did marry him. You may not have been an actual whore by profession, but you certainly proved that you're one by nature. You disgust me!"

Casity gasped in outrage. That bastard! If he thought she was Priscilla Lambert without bothering to ask her, then she would let this arrogant ogre think whatever he liked. He thought he could intimidate her, did he? No man got the better of Casity Crockett!

Out of pure orneriness, she should play out this charade and let this rascal stew in his own juice. Let him live with the fact that he had schemed to seduce his would-be stepmother. Why, he had twice as many sins to repent as she did! He had betrayed the trust of his father and plotted to export Tweed's would-be bride before they even had the chance to meet. He was a scoundrel of the worst sort, another nightmare she was forced to endure. He had no heart, no soul, and certainly no conscience! She despised him!

Shaler snatched up his vest and fished out the pouch of gold Tweed had given him. "This money is yours to purchase a decent set of clothes and buy a stage ticket to anywhere, plus enough to keep you until you find some gullible fool to marry you. But if you think I'm going to let you marry Tweed, you're dead wrong. I'll tell him what happened between us and he'll throw you out."

His harsh tone was worse than a slap in the face. "You make me sick!" Casity hissed angrily.

It didn't matter that she wasn't who he thought she was. Any man who would portray the Good Samaritan just to test and then deflower a woman so she wouldn't marry another man was detestable!

"I'm feeling a little nauseous myself," Shaler snapped back.

"I have despised several men in my life, but I never knew what hatred really was until I met you," Casity spluttered. "You set out to betray the father who took you as his own son, interfering in his plans and in his life. You're utterly ruthless and heartless. Perhaps *I* will be the one who tells Tweed what you did and why! Let *him* be the judge of who committed the gravest sin against him!"

Shaler hadn't expected to have his threat thrown back in his face. Obviously, he hadn't given this wily shrew full credit. She was sharp-witted and quite capable of defending herself after she had recovered from her near-brush with death. She had certainly buried the vulnerability he had seen the previous night. Or was all that vulnerability he *thought* he saw just another convincing part of her act? Hell's fire, was she trying to blackmail him? Well, he'd gladly pay to get rid of this sneaky vixen. He had more gold than he could spend in a lifetime anyway.

"All right, how much will it cost me to buy your silence and get you on a stage?" he demanded gruffly.

Casity glowered venomously at him. "There isn't enough money in the federal mint to buy me off!"

Not to be outdone, Shaler glowered right back. "Am I to understand that you can be *had* but you can't be *bought?*" he asked in a scathing tone. "How very odd, considering that, to *your* kind of woman, those two things usually go hand in hand."

For those two remarks, Casity could have shot him— he was going to pay supremely.

"I have every intention of telling Tweed that you're an ungrateful, traitorous son," Casity assured him snidely.

That would ruin this insufferable cad. She would make his life a living hell, just as he had done to her. Damn the man. He was just one more thing that had gone wrong in her life. She hated him!

Shaler stared at her in disapproval, his lips curled in a sneer. "And just how do you think you're going to get past me to Tweed?"

Casity employed the technique she had found quite useful in her previous dealings with obnoxious men. Like a striking snake, she gouged Shaler in the belly with her elbow. When he doubled over, she jabbed him in the jaw, causing him to bite his tongue. She hoped his tongue swelled up in his mouth and choked him!

"You little—"

Shaler's fingers curled, itching to put a stranglehold on her swanlike neck, but Casity didn't even flinch. Her chin tilted upward, practically daring him to assault her. Shaler suddenly felt as if he and this hellion were on a par physically. Her explosive temper seemed to compensate for the differences in their size.

"Go ahead," she encouraged him. "Add a few more bruises to lend credence to my testimony. When I tell Tweed you attacked me forcefully—and show him the bruises, he'll whip you within an inch of your miserable life!"

At that moment Shaler came as close to beating the tar out of a female as he ever wanted to come. He could almost hear Priscilla telling her version of the story to Tweed, in between buckets of crocodile tears. No doubt she would attribute every last bump and bruise to Shaler's rough handling and say she had fought valiantly to prevent being ravished. Shaler shuddered to think how low this female would stoop.

Difficult though it was, Shale clenched his fists and held them at his sides. "Name your price, Priscilla. I want you out of my life—*forever,*" he said with distinct menace. "I don't give a damn how much it costs me. I'll buy you a ticket to anyplace you want to go."

"I'd prefer that you bought yourself a ticket—straight to hell!" she blared.

He sneered, teeth bared. "No need to go where I've been for the last twelve hours."

After flashing him a glare hot enough to burn the iron off a skillet, Casity gathered what was left of her dignity and hobbled over to retrieve her gown and tattered pantaloons.

"I asked you a question and I demand an answer," Shaler boomed. *"How much?"*

While Casity shook out her gown and limped toward the underbrush to dress, she mulled over the infuriating incident. She wondered if it was possible to attach a monetary value to the loss of her respectability and the amount of humiliation she had endured. Not only had she lost her innocence to this wretched man, but he had destroyed the blossom of newly awakened femininity with the frost of his rejections. What price could a woman attach to having her life completely ruined?

Although it was true that Casity was extremely short on funds, this was still a matter of principle. This big bully's infuriating conduct had triggered her sense of ethics, and for that he was going to pay—through the nose!

"Answer me!" Shaler bellowed furiously.

Pivoting on her good leg, Casity flung the despicable lout a smirk. "I'm thinking it over. I'll let you know what I've decided after I've dressed." With that, she ducked into a clump of bushes.

Shaler cursed and swore and paced as he never had before. He had never had much respect for females, but he had even less now! That firebrand had turned him against all women. He would never trust a female any farther than he could throw her!

While Shaler was pacing furiously, Casity was calculating her next move. Her original purpose for traveling to Deadwood was to put time and distance between herself and her uncle's murderers and to inform Tweed that his postal-delivery bride had gotten lost in the mail. She needed a refuge, enough cash to sustain her, and a bounty hunter who could confront those ruthless murderers. Perhaps there was a way to repay that midnight-haired scoundrel for disgracing her, while she waited for the manhunt to begin. She could kill three birds with one stone—and one rotten bird in particular.

With a devilish smile Casity wriggled into her gown. Tweed's adopted son made her want to see just how mischievous and disagreeable she could be when she really tried. She wanted to see him squirm, force him to be polite to the woman he presumed to be his future stepmama. Under the pretense of requesting time to become acquainted with Tweed before marriage, Casity could lie low in Deadwood—and also give that tawny-eyed rogue the hell he deserved.

After all, she could pretend to be Priscilla if she wanted to. No one in Dakota Territory knew who she was. The letter from Tweed and the stage receipts were in Casity's purse, which was still in the stage. She had all the props to assume Priscilla's identity.

She would keep house for Tweed, just as she had for her uncle. After a week or so, when her leg had mended, Casity would announce that the marriage would not take place and she would find gainful employment. By then, that rapscallion would have worked himself into a tizzy. Serve him right, it would!

When Casity emerged from the underbrush, using a sturdy branch as her crutch, Shaler was ready and waiting. "Well? Have you decided upon a price?" he spat disrespectfully.

"I have," she confirmed as she sidestepped up the hill.

"Damn it, woman, where do you think you're going?"

"To Deadwood," she informed him without paying him the courtesy of glancing in his direction. "I have decided I can't be bought for any price."

Scowling furiously, Shaler scooped up his saddle and slapped it on his steed none too gently. By the time he reached the road, Casity was standing in the middle of it.

"Which way is Deadwood?" she questioned, unable to get her bearings.

Shaler fished into his saddlebag for a cigar, lit it, and surrounded himself in a cloud of smoke. As aggravated as he was, it was a wonder he didn't have smoke rolling out his ears!

"It's a damned shame you don't know the directions, princess," he smirked. Nothing would have pleased him more than for Priscilla to get herself lost.

"I know my directions well enough to know which creek you are going to be up when I'm finished with you," Casity countered, blue eyes blazing.

Since Shaler had refused to direct her toward Deadwood, Casity studied the location of the sun and then aimed herself in what she deduced to be a northwest direction. Her conclusion must have been correct because Shaler overtook her a moment later and continued on his way, letting Casity walk on her splinted leg while he trotted off on his steed. Not only was he cruel, but he was also inconsiderate. Casity expected as much, horrible man that he was!

Hell's fire, if Shaler had known how the previous night would turn out, he would have left Priscilla's knee out of its socket. She could have crawled to Deadwood for all he cared. With another growl, he nudged his gelding into a canter and left her choking in his dust.

Although Casity's leg was killing her, she maintained a slow but steady pace. Suddenly, the jingle of harnesses and the creak of a wagon jostled her from her spiteful musings. She limped around to flag down the driver who stamped on the brake the moment he saw her. When the bushy-haired prospector hopped down,

Casity recalled what Priscilla had told her about love-starved miners treating respectable females like heads of state. Thus far, she hadn't experienced any royal treatment. Quite the contrary, in fact. But thankfully, the miner—who lifted her onto the wagon seat and inquired about her comfort a half-dozen times during the first mile—seemed more the type Priscilla had described.

A gloating smile hovered on Casity's lips when the wagon rolled past Shaler, whose miniature conscience had finally gotten the better of him and compelled him to reverse directions to retrieve the lame lady in distress. He had obviously planned to let her limp along for a mile or so before making her beg for a ride. She really hadn't expected him to come back at all. It appeared he did have a shred of decency in him—though not much.

When the wagon rolled past, Casity glanced at the prospector, who was garbed in homespun clothes that could have used a good scrubbing. "Do you happen to know who that man is?" she inquired in a tone that revealed none of her irritation.

"Shaler McCain," the miner informed her. "He and his pa got a claim north of Deadwood in a place called Bonanza Gulch."

Well, at least now Casity had a name to attach to that polecat. After all the hateful things he had said, she had refused to ask Shaler his name out of pure contrariness.

She and Shaler McCain would meet again in Bonanza Gulch, she promised herself. Casity was already anticipating the encounter. By the time she was through with him, he would think twice before he tried to manipulate another woman!

Eight

Casity wasn't prepared for the enthusiastic reception that awaited her when she arrived in the bustling mining community at the base of Deadwood Gulch. News of her horrifying experience the previous afternoon had preceded her to town. Before she could inch off the wagon seat under her own power, a swarm of men surrounded her. When they noticed her splinted leg and the bump on her head, they were beside themselves with concern.

Priscilla Lambert was right after all, Casity decided. A woman could easily allow herself to be influenced by all the exaggerated courtesies extended to her the instant she hit town.

"I'm fine, really," she insisted after being asked about her welfare for the umpteenth time. "But I could use some food."

Casity found herself half-carried to the nearest restaurant where a dozen men offered to buy her meal in exchange for the pleasure of her company.

While Casity ate like a farmhand, Shaler stood like a sentinel, trying to second-guess her intentions. He muttered at the possessive feeling that hounded him when a raft of love-starved miners fussed and fawned over the lovely newcomer. He had no reason to feel responsible for, or protective of, her. She would probably become the bad dream from which he could never wake before she finally got out of his life. Perhaps she would take a fancy to one of her many suitors and Shaler could leave her in Deadwood. Nothing would make him happier.

It might be difficult to return to town and pretend he didn't know that hellion, but he could endure, especially if he never bothered to tell Tweed his mail-order bride had arrived. By the time Tweed was able to venture to town, Priscilla would probably be gone. Shaler could only hope!

Casity hobbled out of the restaurant an hour later, ignoring Shaler as if he were just another supporting beam that fronted the building. Shaler watched her propel herself toward the stage depot to retrieve her purse and satchel. Of course, her entourage of admirers followed like a queen's dutiful attendants. It was disgusting to watch grown men grovel.

Scowling, Shaler pushed away from the post and aimed himself toward the saloon. He could use a drink . . . or three. Maybe a little rotgut would cool his smoldering temper and ease the razor-sharp edge of guilt that sliced through him. He doubted it, but it was worth a try.

From the window that overlooked the main street, Reece Pendleton assessed the town's newest arrival. He had heard the report of the young woman who had been abducted by Indians. Apparently she had managed to escape in one piece. And what a lovely piece of fluff she was, too! Reece's gray eyes drifted over the shapely beauty, liking what he saw, eager to see much more.

"Reece?" Tim Brady prompted when the elegantly-garbed man became so distracted that he forgot what he was talking about. "You were saying . . . ?"

Reece pivoted around after Casity disappeared into the stage depot, trying to concentrate on the conversation. "I was saying that I have sent for two of my former acquaintances to assist in our business ventures. Ned Johnson and Russel Bassett are traveling up from Texas with a cattle herd. They should be here in a couple of weeks."

Puffing on his cheroot, Johnny Varnes eased back in his chair to study his business partner. "We could use a few more competent men. We lost three last week when they tried to persuade a group of miners to sell their claims to your company."

"I think you'll find Johnson and Bassett assets to our business." A devilish smile quirked Reece's lips. "Their strong-arm tactics can be very persuasive."

Reece had managed to earn the confidence of Deadwood's two gang bosses, who owned and operated several saloons and gambling houses. He had even convinced Johnny Varnes and Tim Brady to invest in the mining company. Thus far, the arrangements had worked superbly. Reece had employed Varnes's and Brady's henchmen to acquire the deeds to mines that had produced a considerable profit.

After promoting his mining project, Reece had persuaded outside investors to sink money into the company. He had been able to live in style, flaunting his money and power. With Brady and Varnes backing him, Reece had established himself faster than he had anticipated. Now, what he wanted, he took. And just recently he had a hankering to acquire the affections of the voluptuous female who had arrived in Deadwood. She seemed to have attracted considerable attention from every man she encountered. Reece was anxious to assess the newcomer at close range to determine if she was as stunning face-to-face as she was from his office above the Gold Nugget Saloon.

Tossing his thoughts aside, Reece focused his attention on his associates. "Have your saloon keepers given you any inside information about miners who have struck it rich lately?"

Johnny Varnes snorted explosively. "I've heard rumors, all right, but not about rich strikes. The miners are trying to form an alliance to hire a gunslinger to clean up the town and provide protection. I've also heard more reports that some stockholders are questioning your managerial abilities. They haven't been earning dividends on their investments and they want to know why."

A crafty grin tugged at the corner of Reece's thin mouth. "Can I help it if some of the mines they purchased played out without covering the expense of searching for ore? If a man gambles, he has to learn to accept losses."

"Just make sure you don't drain your stockholders to the point that they send some gunslinger up here to push us around," Tim advised. "I don't want some trigger-happy shootist waltzing in here. We're turning a tidy profit with our gaming halls, and I don't want anybody messing up the good deal we've got."

"We could always hire Broken-Nose Jack McCall to dispose of any gunslingers who might come around," Johnny Varnes suggested.

Reece's brows flattened over his narrowed gray eyes. "You mean that drunken gambler who had his face bashed in with the butt of a pistol?" He scoffed at the absurdity of enlisting McCall to do anything except mop saloon floors.

Johnny Varnes shrugged off Reece's skepticism. "It's true that the man's chief ambition is to earn enough money to keep from being sober for more than a few hours. But he'll do almost anything if you keep him supplied with free whiskey."

"We had him picking pockets in the saloons for a share of the profit," Tim added. "The bartender doctored the drinks of the men flashing gold dust. McCall relieved them of their cash while they were groggy."

Reece's face contorted in a distasteful frown. "I'd rather not have any association with that good-for-nothing drunkard unless absolutely necessary. You can use him as a petty thief if you wish, but I prefer to employ men who stay sober until they've carried out my orders."

"Well, I'm damned well not going to sit back and let some professional sharpshooter take over our town, even if I have to enlist McCall's services," Johnny insisted. "I've already heard that the miners have asked Shaler McCain to serve as town marshal since he has already broken up several fights. If he's as good with a pistol and shotgun as he is with his fists, he could cause us trouble. What we don't need is for the county sheriff and his men to start patrolling Deadwood."

Reece shrugged, unconcerned. "McCain doesn't strike me as the type who cares to pin on a badge to clean up this town. He likes to come and go as he pleases and he seems perfectly satisfied to work his claim and reap what little profit he can find. But if he does consider taking the job, we'll send out a few men to discourage him."

Tim grinned. "Men like Ned Johnson and Russel Bassett?"

"Exactly like Johnson and Bassett." Reece strode toward the door and paused to glance back at his associates. "If you'll excuse me, gentlemen, I have an errand to run."

"Does it have anything to do with whatever distracted you at the window?" Johnny razzed.

Reece broke into a wry smile, but he didn't elaborate. He wasn't about to let his associates know there was a new attraction in town. Reece preferred not to share his women until he had tired of them. He had never believed it wise for business associates to share the same pleasure. At the moment, the pleasure of Deadwood's new arrival was foremost on Reese's mind and he was anxious to make her acquaintance.

Casity had retrieved her purse and the small satchel containing one dress and the men's clothes she had worn to escape her pursuers. Clutching her meager belongings, she hobbled to the post office to send a letter to Clint Lake in Ogallala. She offered a brief account of the incident that forced her to flee, gave a detailed description of her uncle's murderers, and requested that Clint keep an eye on the dry goods store until she deemed it safe to return.

Clint was the only man Casity came anywhere close to entrusting with her secret. Thus far, he had proved himself a capable and responsible marshal—and friend. Now she wished she had encouraged a slight involvement with him, just so she would have known what to expect when she had the humiliating misfortune of dealing with Shaler McCain.

When Casity ventured back to the street, Shaler was nowhere in sight. That suited her just fine. Instead, another unfamiliar face greeted her with a charismatic smile. The fashionably-dressed gentleman dropped into an exaggerated bow and then offered Casity his arm. What he expected her to do with it, she wasn't sure. With men, a woman never knew for certain, she reminded herself cynically.

"Deadwood welcomes you with open arms, my dear," Reece purred in his most provocative tone. "Reece Pendleton at your service."

Casity was quick to note that the cavalcade of miners who had been following her had retreated a pace when Reece approached. She couldn't help but wonder why. This stout, blond-haired man, who had more mustache than upper lip, seemed to hold a position of power in the community. Judging by the cut of his clothes and his expensive jewelry, Casity surmised that Reece Pendleton was successful, even if she couldn't guess the nature of his business. Perhaps she could use his generosity to obtain employment after she had taught Shaler McCain the lesson he wouldn't soon forget.

"And you, of course, are Priscilla Lambert," Reece added with another charming smile.

Casity let the misconception ride like a chip on a roulette wheel. "I'm pleased to meet you, Mister Pendleton." Her tone was neither discourteous nor overly encouraging.

"Call me Reece," he insisted as he ushered her down the boardwalk. A frown crossed his brow when he noticed her limp. Until that moment he had been too preoccupied with more intriguing parts of her to pay much attention. "Are you in need of a physician, my dear? There's a man in town who boasts both veterinary and doctoring skills. Although he is not exactly certified, he might—"

Casity flung up a hand. "It's only a sprained knee which has already been attended, but thank you for your concern."

Reece glanced at the conglomeration still following after the arresting beauty like participants in a parade. "I wonder if we might find a place that allows us more privacy. I would very much like to become better acquainted . . . without distractions."

Casity just bet he did! Typical man. As if she didn't know what Reece Pendleton had on his one-track mind.

He was being as polite and respectful as Shaler McCain had been before he took what he wanted. Casity wasn't stupid enough to fall into another deceitful trap. She had learned her lesson all too well the first time!

"In the future perhaps." Casity practiced the policy of leaving her options open, just as she had advised the real Priscilla Lambert to do. "At the moment I have business to conduct in Bonanza Gulch with a man named Tweed Cramer."

His blond brows jackknifed. "May I be so bold as to ask what kind of business you have with Tweed?"

"Household duties," Casity hedged.

Reece nodded thoughtfully. "I heard Tweed had suffered a broken leg, but I didn't know he had sent away for assistance. I assumed Shaler would take up the slack."

A broken leg? So that explained why Tweed had sent his scheming son to meet his mail-order bride.

Reece leaned a mite closer than necessary and Casity had to force herself not to retreat. "I can offer you far less taxing duties, my dear, and at higher wages."

Couldn't he just! Casity wondered what type of services she would be expected to perform for this rake. As if she didn't know! "Thank you, Mister . . . Reece. I'll keep your offer in mind after Tweed is back on his feet. However, I have committed myself and I would be remiss if I ignored my new employer when he's in need."

"Then perhaps I could lend you my buggy." Reece indicated the shiny black carriage in front of the town's most fashionable hotel. "If there's anything else you need, don't hesitate to ask. I'm in suite number two and the door is always open."

When Reece had set Casity upon the plush carriage seat, he stepped back to assess the curvaceous beauty who was even more bewitching at close range than at a distance. He had tired of the paramours who catered to him for the costly trinkets he could provide. But here was a challenge that piqued his interest. He would give himself a couple of weeks to win her over—all in the proper manner, of course. But very soon, he would enjoy the pleasures of this enchanting female and take her to his bed . . .

Smiling like a hungry barracuda, Reece ambled back to his office. While he was awaiting this lovely siren's return, he would tend to some unfinished business and check on his order for the Blake jaw-crusher—a state-of-the-art mining device that could break down large chunks of ore at the rate of one hundred tons per day. The steam-powered machine had originally been developed in the East to produce ballast for ships and to break stones for use on highways and railroad beds.

The equipment was due to arrive within the week, and Reece made a note to send a few of his employees to Cheyenne to pick up the shipment. He had no intention of allowing some mining company in Colorado to swipe the device for its own use. If Ned Johnson and Russel Bassett had arrived in Cheyenne, Reece could send along the message with his men, instructing them to hire his new employees as extra guards.

If the Blake jaw-crusher proved as effective as he had been told, he could increase his profits tenfold. The *arrastra*, which most of the miners employed to separate ore, couldn't compete with the heavier equipment. Very soon, the prospectors would be forced to sell their claims and join Reece's work force. He was already well on his way to becoming the richest man in the territory and with the new machine in operation he could be making money hand over fist.

Now what woman would turn her back on such possible riches? Reece smiled shrewdly. Even the proper young beauty he had just met would be eating out of his hand when she learned that he could keep her in a manner of which she had only dreamed. Reece relished the idea of possessing the most stunning female in the territory. Deadwood's lovely new arrival was just what he needed to reinforce his position. She was an envied prize and he intended to have her by his side . . . and in his bed . . .

Shaler muttered sourly when he stepped from the Number Ten Saloon. He had intended to keep an eye on Priscilla, but she had vanished from sight. With any luck, some drunkard had made off with her, gloating over his good fortune. The poor man would regret tangling with that hellcat soon enough. Shaler certainly had.

Well, good riddance to Miss Priscilla Lambert. Shaler would gather needed supplies and head toward the cabin without giving Priscilla another thought. By the time he returned home he would have rehearsed the story he planned to tell Tweed. And if all went well, Tweed would never know his mail-order bride had come and gone. Although Tweed would never have the chance to thank his adopted son for sparing him the plague of Priscilla Lambert, they would both be a helluva lot better off without her!

Casity was certain she had stepped into a totally different world as she made her way along the bumpy path that wound through the Black Hills. These panoramic mountains had obviously gotten their name be-

cause of the dense pines that gave the craggy peaks
an inky black appearance, even when bathed in sunlight. When she stopped to ask directions at Lard Pail
Bill Raddick's mining camp, she was treated royally.
The prospectors practically stumbled over themselves
to get a close look at her. She was proposed to twice
and found herself bombarded by various other offers
which she politely declined.

One miner offered her a handful of gold dust if
she would simply sit down and converse with him for
a half-hour. A fish-eyed prospector offered the same
amount of gold for a fifteen-minute conversation on
any topic she chose. Casity had the feeling she could
have named her price and it would have been met.

No wonder Shaler thought he could buy her off
with a few gold nuggets. The men in these mining
camps thought in terms of gold for whatever they desired. If Casity wanted to earn money in Deadwood,
it would be a snap. All she had to do was smile sweetly
and chitchat for a couple of hours. Then, she could
afford to replace her meager wardrobe and begin saving money to hire a bounty hunter. Once she had
repaid Shaler McCain for his treachery, she would
concentrate her efforts on acquiring money for her
vendetta.

First she would seek her revenge on that amber-eyed
rogue, and then she would turn her vengeance on her
uncle's killers. All in due time, Casity promised herself. One day, the grief and heartache she had suffered
would be avenged. Only then could she go back to
living her life. But for now, she had two missions, both
of which would distract her from the bitter memories
that haunted her . . .

Casity's troubled thoughts evaporated when she
topped a hill and peered down into a spectacular valley bursting with colorful wildflowers and groves of

trees. A sparkling stream meandered through the sloping meadow where a mine shaft had been carved in the side of the hill. On the rise above the creek was a log cabin. A water-powered *arrastra* churned and clanked while a stocky, red-haired prospector propped himself against the mining device. Casity knew immediately that she had located Bonanza Gulch and Tweed Cramer. The prospector was nursing a broken leg and leaning heavily on his cane.

With an impish grin Casity urged her steed down the path. She couldn't wait to see the look on Shaler McCain's face when he returned home to find her settled in, as if she belonged there. She relished the thought of shoving Shaler's just desserts down his throat. She hoped he choked on them!

Tweed's good leg bent at the knee when a vision of pure loveliness floated from the buggy to limp toward him. "Priscilla?" he chirped like a sick cricket. "My Lord, girl, if you ain't the purtiest thing I ever did see, I don't know who is!" Remembering his manners, Tweed pulled the worn hat from his head and bowed politely. "It's a pleasure to meet you, Priscilla."

Casity stared at the ruddy-faced man with liquid green eyes and a reddish beard. Her spiteful resolutions crumbled. There was something very endearing about this man. He had a certain presence about him that was utterly compelling. Casity liked Tweed on sight, and that was quite an accomplishment, considering the fact that she shied away from most men.

He reminded her of Saint Nicholas and a leprechaun all rolled into one, with his engaging smile, round face, and thick chest. As badly as Casity wanted to get even with Shaler McCain, her conscience wouldn't allow her to deceive Tweed. He deserved her honesty and respect, even if his annoying son didn't.

"I'm sorry to disappoint you, Mister Cramer, but I am not Priscilla," she told him gently.

Tweed's perceptive gaze traveled over her shapely figure and then returned to her face. "No?"

"No." Casity heaved a weary sigh. "I'm afraid Priscilla isn't coming. When I chanced to meet her on the train to Cheyenne, she asked me to deliver a letter to you in person because she—" Casity paused to choose her words carefully. "Priscilla met a young man during her trip and she—" Damn, this wasn't easy!

"And she chose him over me," Tweed finished for her. "Well, I can't say that I blame her. I know I'm not much to look at and she never met me. I s'pose I would've been tempted to do the same thing if'n I was in her place."

Casity blinked in surprise. Shaler had said his father was easy-going and took adversity in stride. Apparently it was true. Tweed had shrugged off his disappointment without losing his temper or wallowing in self-pity.

"I'm truly sorry to be the bearer of bad news, Mister Cramer." She fished into her purse to retrieve the letter. "Perhaps Priscilla explained it better than I."

Hurriedly, Tweed read the apology and then tucked the letter in his pocket. "Well, Shay kept tellin' me it was a bad idea. I guess things worked out for the best . . . unless of course you'd like to take her place," he added with a teasing grin.

"Actually, your son thought I was Priscilla," Casity reported. "And he still thinks I am because he was too busy reading me the riot act to let me explain."

"That sounds like Shay. He always thinks he's right about everythin' and he wouldn't admit he was wrong on a bet." He frowned curiously before glancing up at the hill. "Where is that rascal anyway?"

"I haven't the faintest idea." Casity struggled to keep the irritation from seeping into her voice. "We parted on a most unfriendly note. According to him, if he never sees me again it will be all too soon."

"He refused to accompany you out here?" Tweed muttered under his breath. "I'm gonna have to teach that boy some manners. He knows better than that!"

"He—" Casity bit down on her tongue, surprised at her impulsive need to spill her soul to this kindly man with gentle green eyes. It wasn't like her to take anyone into her confidence. But after the horrible two weeks she had endured, she felt she had to tell someone or she would burst!

Tweed's gaze narrowed pensively while Casity marshaled her composure. "He *what?*" he prodded relentlessly.

Casity's shoulders rose in a shrug and she forced a smile. "Nothing. It doesn't matter. I came to deliver the message and I've accomplished my mission. It was nice to meet you, Mister Cramer." Wheeling about, Casity limped toward the carriage.

"Shay didn't have anything to do with that bum leg of yours, did he?" Tweed wanted to know as he hurriedly hobbled after her.

"No, he splinted it for me after I was abducted from the stage by Indians. I tumbled down the hill when I escaped," Casity explained as she struggled to pull herself into the carriage.

Before she could seat herself, Tweed grabbed her arm and slowly turned her to face him. "You said Shay read you the riot act when he thought you was Priscilla? I mean to have the details, girl. He interfered in my plans when it wasn't his place. I wanna know what he said to you."

Casity didn't want to rehash the painful incident that had left her emotionally shattered. "I've said too much already."

"No. You ain't hardly said nothin' yet." Determined, he steered Casity toward the cabin. "Now yer gonna come inside and sit yerself down and tell me what happened, and that's that."

"But I—" Casity wasn't allowed to protest as Tweed propelled her up the steps.

"We make a fine pair with our lame legs, don't we, girl?" Tweed chuckled as he reached for the doorknob. "What's yer name anyway?"

"Casity Crockett."

"Casity." Tweed nodded approvingly. "I like the sound of it. You ain't related to Davy Crockett by any chance, are you?"

"Not that I know of."

Casity paused in the doorway to survey the rustic cabin that boasted wide windows which let the sunshine in. The cottage had a quaint, inviting look with its homemade furniture and cozy fireplace. And although Casity knew she should head back to town before dark, she couldn't resist the chance to sink down in a soft chair and give her throbbing leg a rest.

"Would you like a brandy?" Tweed offered as he set the bottle and two glasses on the table.

"I don't drink." Casity eased into the padded rocker and sighed in relief.

"You don't?" Tweed grinned mischievously. "Well, it's 'bout time you started. You don't wanna wait 'til you get too old to handle it." He poured her a tall glass and thrust it at her. "Now drink up. It'll cure whatever ails you."

Tweed watched Casity stare at the tall glass of brandy in wary trepidation before she took a cautious sip and then wheezed at its fiery taste. "Take another sip," he encouraged her. "Each one gets better."

When Casity did as she was told, Tweed plunked down to pour himself a drink. Perhaps it was deceitful of him to force this lovely lass to loose her tongue with brandy, but Tweed had every intention of prying out the details of her confrontation with his well-meaning but infuriating son. Casity wasn't going anywhere until Tweed knew exactly what had happened!

And sure enough, the brandy took the edge off Casity's nerves and she revealed the conversation between her and Shaler while Tweed muttered and scowled to himself without interrupting. Casity did have the presence of mind not to divulge the intimate details of the night that shouldn't have happened. No amount of liquor could force her to admit that she had submitted to that miserable rake!

When Tweed inquired as to why she had come all the way to Deadwood to deliver Priscilla's letter, Casity clammed up and he could tell that inner turmoil was eating her alive. By the time Tweed was finished gleaning information—as only Tweed could—he knew her whole life story, the incidents surrounding her exodus to Deadwood as well as Shaler's attempt to send his future stepmother fleeing in tears.

Heaving an exasperated sigh, Tweed slumped back in his chair and swirled the amber liquid around in his glass. "I've decided that meddlin' son of mine needs to be taught a lesson. And yer gonna help me."

Casity was all too happy to conspire with Tweed, since she had entertained the same spiteful ideas herself. And besides, it was getting late and she had drunk enough brandy to make her drowsy. The thought of tramping back to town when she didn't have enough funds left to rent a room for the night wasn't the least bit appealing. In fact, Casity would have been perfectly content to curl up in her chair and sleep until dawn.

Tweed leaned forward to get her attention when her eyelids threatened to close. "Yer gonna pretend to be Priscilla, just as Shay already thinks you are," he instructed. "And after I've meted out plenty of punishment to Shay for stickin' his nose in places it don't belong, I'll tell him the truth. 'Til then, yer stayin' in Shay's room and he can damned well camp out on the floor."

When Casity nodded drowsily, more interested in a nap than revenge at the moment, Tweed grasped her hand and drew her to her feet. "You go lay down and rest up. I want you to be wide awake when that ornery son of mine shows up."

Casity's heavily-lidded eyes swept up to peer at the kindly man who had managed to pry a confession out of her. Despite the fact that Tweed and Shaler weren't blood relatives, they could both be very persuasive. Shaler had relied upon seduction to get what he wanted while Tweed used brandy. Tweed had proved to be an excellent listener who seemed genuinely interested and concerned about her plight. He was also more of a gentleman than his horrible, impossible, insufferable cad of a son.

"You're a nice man, Tweed," she told him sincerely.

"Does that mean you wanna marry me?" Tweed teased as he flipped back the quilt and gestured for her to lie down on Shaler's bed.

"And ruin your life?" Casity chortled sleepily as she stretched out on the soft feather bed. "According to Shaler, I'd be the kind of curse no magic spell could break."

"Damn that boy," Tweed grumbled as he eased the door shut. "I'm gonna turn that rascal every way but loose!"

And Tweed fully intended to do exactly that after hearing Casity's heart-wrenching tale. Shay had made life worse for Casity instead of better. Bullheaded as Shay was, he had leaped to all the wrong conclusions.

Well, by damn, Shay was going to pay dearly for being so rude and disrespectful to sweet Casity Crockett. If Shay had been a few years younger, Tweed would have seriously considered taking a strap to him. But since he wasn't, Tweed was going to torment the hell out of him in ways that could hurt worse than a whipping!

Nine

A wary frown puckered Shaler's brow when he topped the hill to see a shiny black buggy in front of the log cabin. The carriage could have belonged to only one of three people in Deadwood who delighted in flaunting the wealth acquired by feeding off hard-working miners—Pendleton, Brady, or Varnes. At the moment, Shaler wasn't in the mood to be civil to any of them. He hoped word hadn't gotten around that their claim in Bonanza Gulch had produced high-grade ore.

Knowing the way Pendleton and his partners operated, Shaler wondered if the mining entrepreneur had come to offer to buy their claim. If they refused to sell—and Shaler wasn't ready to sell just yet—Pendleton would send out some of his thugs to twist a few arms. That was the way that scoundrel did business.

After swinging down from his mount, Shaler breezed through the front door. When he spied their guest, he stopped dead in his tracks. There before him sat Tweed with a glass of brandy in his hand and a pillow propped under his broken leg. In the chair beside him sat the very last person Shaler wanted or expected to see! Priscilla Lambert was sipping a cup of tea and nursing her sprained knee. Hell's fire! Shaler thought sourly.

"What the devil happened to you?" Tweed demanded without bothering with a greeting. "I sent you into town to fetch my lovely bride-to-be and she had to make her way out here the best she could . . . and on a bum leg no less!"

Shaler said nothing. He had yet to recover his powers of speech.

"And wait 'til you hear about all her bad experiences." Tweed took a sip and shook his shaggy head. "Why, it's a wonder she survived."

Shaler was beginning to wish she hadn't!

"Is this to be my new stepson, Tweed honey?" Casity inquired in a sugary voice, just to annoy Shaler. Sure enough, it did. "He's a fine figure of a man." She studied him ponderously, relishing every moment of Shaler's awkward apprehension. "He looks stout and sturdy enough to tend all the chores we need to have done while we're recuperating."

Fury smoldered through Shaler's body when he noted the mischief in her eyes. He could see the handwriting on the wall all too clearly. This miserable little package had purposely lit out of Deadwood to reach the cabin first so she could feed Tweed a crock of lies. If Shaler dared to contest her tale, she would tell Tweed what had really happened on the road to Deadwood. Curse her ornery hide! When he got that scheming witch alone, he'd strangle the life out of her!

"I hope you took time to get supplies while you was in town," Tweed remarked before helping himself to another drink. "My betrothed was distressed to find so little in the way of staples. She's half-starved after her ordeal and there ain't much food around here." Tweed gestured toward the stove. "Why don't you rustle her up somethin' to eat, Shay. I would've done it myself but—" He rubbed his splinted leg. "You know I don't get around as good as I used to."

When Shaler wheeled away without a word to fetch the supplies he had bought in town, Tweed snorted. "Get over here and meet yer new stepmama-to-be, nice and proper-like."

It was with visible restraint that Shaler pivoted toward the mischievous imp who sat like a princess upon her throne. Devilish delight sparkled in her sapphire eyes as she outstretched her hand, leaving Shaler to wonder if she expected him to kiss it. He would have preferred to take a bite out of it!

"It's ever *sooo* nice to meet you, *sonny,*" Casity purred in a syrupy tone.

A grimace tightened Casity's lips when Shaler clamped hold of her hand, giving it a discreet but painful squeeze that pinched her fingers together as if they were locked in a vise.

"It's nice to meet you, too," Shaler replied in a parody of politeness.

When Shaler released her hand, Casity flexed her cramped fingers and mustered another sticky-sweet smile. "After you unload the supplies and prepare us something for supper, please put some fresh linens on my bed." When Shaler lurched around in an effort to conceal his mounting irritation, Casity grinned spitefully. "But don't worry about cleaning your belongings out of my room until tomorrow. I can manage to maneuver around them for tonight. And I've already decided on a new furniture arrangement to improve the looks of this cabin." She shrugged nonchalantly. "But that can wait until later this evening. And the rest of the chores can wait until morning . . . after you fix our breakfast and do the washing.

Shaler couldn't have made his disgust more obvious if he had whipped out his pistol and shot her. With his teeth clenched so tightly that he very nearly ground off the enamel, he stormed outside. But not before

Casity spoke to Tweed in a voice loud enough for Shaler to overhear her.

"Oh, dear, Tweed honey, I don't think your son likes me very much."

"He likes you fine, sweetie-pie," Tweed cooed.

"Perhaps you should tell him so. I don't think he knows it."

"It'll just take him time to adjust to havin' a step-mama," Tweed assured her in a tone that Shaler couldn't miss.

"I do hope we'll get along." Casity exhaled a theatrical sigh. "I'd be most chagrined if my stepson didn't like me. Then one or the other of us would have to go. And I do so like it here in the Black Hills . . . with you, Tweed honey."

Shaler fumed as he grabbed the bundle of supplies from his steed. That woman had grit and style and a very quick mind—a dangerous combination for a female. She planned to make his life a living hell. No question about it. Using her lame leg as an excuse, she would have him fetching and heeling like an obedient servant. And poor Tweed. He was blinded by her beauty and her radiant smiles; he'd let her get away with murder. The old goat was obviously so entranced by his good fortune that he didn't realize that Priscilla was playing him for every kind of fool.

Well, there was nothing for Shaler to do but make life more miserable for her than she was making it for him. Before Tweed could set a wedding date, Shaler would have to rout Priscilla from their lives. He would give her hell every time he got her alone. He would be sure that everything he did for her was only half-done, and never to her liking. And just wait until she sank her teeth into the meal he prepared for her! She'd surely insist on rousing from her throne and tending to the meals herself. Her portions would be so heavily salted and seasoned that it would require a gallon of water to wash them down . . .

"Oh, Shay?" Casity yoo-hooed as he clambered through the door with an armload of supplies. "Will you fetch me another cup of tea?"

To her wicked delight she noticed Shaler looked like a pack mule as he carried all the sacks and boxes. This jackass was getting what he deserved.

"How soon can we eat?" Casity questioned. "I'm famished! The meals at the stage station left a lot to be desired."

And so would her supper, Shaler vowed spitefully as he shot her a venomous look. He dumped the supplies beside the door and stalked toward her.

Casity extended her empty cup and batted her eyelashes with such intensity that Shaler swore he could feel a draft. "You're such a dear, Shay honey," she crooned. "Next week, when I'm back on my feet, I'll repay you for all your help and consideration. I promise."

Shaler snatched the tin cup from her hand and stamped toward the potbellied stove in the far corner of the main room. The tea kettle was still steaming. It had nothing on Shaler. Scowling to himself, he jerked the pot off the stove and splashed tea in her cup, scalding his hand in the process. A muted growl rolled from his lips as he shook the sting from his seared fingers and muttered several expletives that would have burned a lady's ears.

Casity bit back an impish giggle as she watched Shaler thrash around, attempting to conceal his anger and his pain. She was loving every minute.

Tweed was having the same difficulty containing his mirth. Since those long years ago when tragedy struck, Shaler had kept his emotions in cold storage. But since Casity had arrived upon the scene, he was having a

devil of a time keeping a rein on his temper. It did
Tweed's heart good to know this lovely lady was getting
under Shaler's skin.

"I ran some chunks of rock through the *arrastra* this
afternoon," Tweed said conversationally. "We're still
gettin' good color. When you have time, why don't
you go down to the mine shaft and gather up the dust
and nuggets I filtered out. We don't want no poachers
to come snoopin' around to steal our gold. I've been
hearin' reports from other miners that their claims
are bein' robbed when no one's around to keep an eye
on them."

"Have you had much success with your mining?"
Casity questioned Tweed.

"We get by," Shaler answered for his father. By
damn, this gold digger wasn't getting a dribble of dust
from them!

"Actually, we—"

Before Tweed made the foolish mistake of announcing to Priscilla that they had scads of gold stashed
around the cabin, Shaler interrupted him. *"We get by,"*
he repeated emphatically, flashing his father a silencing glare. "We can keep food on the table and clothes
on our backs. It's a living."

"And speaking of food on the table, how long before supper?" Casity wanted to know. "I need to wash
up."

"No need to wash yer hands." Tweed's eyelid
dropped into a playful wink. "Shay will make sure
the food is clean."

Casity giggled at the remark and then leaned over
to pat him fondly on the cheek. "You're such delightful company, sugar. I think we're going to get along
just fine." Maneuvering around the footstool, Casity
hoisted herself out of her chair. "But if you don't
mind, I think I'll wander down to the stream to

freshen up and take a look at your mining operation while Shay is cooking. I find this gold business quite fascinating."

"Whatever you wish, honey-lamb," Tweed purred.

You're such delightful company, sugar. Whatever you wish, honey-lamb, Shaler mimicked under his breath.

Hell's fire, this gushy mush was making Shaler nauseous! Priscilla had already wrapped Tweed around her finger. The old coot had taken such a shine to her that he'd obviously do anything to keep her happy.

That woman was bound to cause conflict between father and son. She would keep pushing and antagonizing Shaler until he came to the end of his patience. And if he dared to explode, she'd tell Tweed what had really happened between them. And by that time, Tweed would be so hopelessly enamored with this scheming beauty that he'd be outraged with his adopted son. Damn, Shaler was in one helluva fix.

When Casity hobbled outside, Tweed sighed heavily. "Lord-a-mighty, Shay, ain't she the sweetest, purtiest little thing you ever laid eyes on? I'd only dared to hope for a woman who could cook and clean and accommodate me when I was feelin' amorous. But what a grand bargain. I'll be the most envied man in the territory." Tweed grinned outrageously. "And the smile on my face each mornin' won't be for nothin', either . . ."

Shaler cringed at the thought of his father lying beside that gorgeous beauty—touching her, kissing her . . . Shaler looked at his father and swore to himself. He hated these feelings of betrayal. He despised the lingering sensations that assaulted him after the reckless night he had spent with that cunning shrew. Shaler had barely been able to live with himself after what he had done. It was getting worse by the minute! He couldn't

even look at Priscilla without remembering that she had
been naked and responsive in his arms.

The bittersweet memory of their night together was
like a knife through the heart. Shaler was disgusted
with her behavior and yet in spite of everything he
still desired her. He had the inescapable feeling he
was just beginning to discover what hell was like—
wanting a woman and hating himself for wanting her.
Having been physically involved with the female who had
every intention of becoming his stepmother was tearing
him to pieces, bit by agonizing bit!

"This isn't going to work," Shaler muttered as he
stashed the supplies in the kitchen cabinet. "In the
first place, Priscilla is more than twenty years younger
than you are, Tweed."

Tweed shrugged a thick shoulder. "She makes me
feel twenty years younger. Besides, I know lots of men
who marry women half their age."

"You sent for her to cook and clean and all she's
done is lounge around, dreaming up chores for me."

"Well, what do you expect?" Tweed huffed. "She
was in a stagecoach wreck and injured her leg."

So Priscilla had told Tweed the truth, or at least a
portion of it. Shaler wondered if she'd bothered with
the facts or conjured up some other tale to milk sym-
pathy from Tweed. Not that it would have mattered,
he thought disparagingly. Priscilla could have told
Tweed the sky fell in on her and he was so bewitched
he would have believed it.

"I know yer against this marriage, but it looks as if
it's gonna work out fine," Tweed assured Shaler confidently.

"Just don't forget to weigh the gold every night and
again in the morning," Shaler advised. "Your bride-
to-be may decide to grab all the money she can carry
and flit off to parts unknown. It wouldn't be the first

time a miner found himself fleeced by a conniving woman."

"Quit bein' so damned cynical," Tweed snorted. "It's plain to see that girl's honest and true blue."

Honest? Hardly. True blue? Ha! She had seduced Shaler without even knowing who he was, just for insurance. Damn that woman. She was tying him in knots with her treachery.

"Oh, by the way. I bought us another claim this mornin'," Tweed informed his grumbling son. "One of the prospectors over in Pine Gulch decided to sell out. He ain't had much luck, 'cept for a little placer gold he found in the shaft."

Shaler set his resentment aside and nodded agreeably. "I'll go take a look at the claim after I tend all the chores Her Highness has planned for me tomorrow."

"I think the claim will be perfect for what we want." Tweed broke into a wide grin that made his sea-green eyes sparkle in the lantern light. "Perfect . . . just like my bride-to-be. 'Cept for this broken leg, I seem to be havin' the most incredible streak of luck."

Shaler lurched back around to peel potatoes for supper, wishing he could skin that saucy female alive. He was having to fight like the devil to control his temper. This unjustifiable feeling of possessiveness kept stabbing at him when Tweed referred to that auburn-haired hellion as his bride-to-be. Shaler cursed this simmering frustration that tormented him each time he thought of the tangled web Priscilla had woven. Shaler was between the devil and the deep. If he told Tweed the truth now that he was so enthused about the idea of wedlock, it would cut him to the quick. There was simply no way for Shaler to explain his side of the story without leaving himself vulnerable to attack.

Although that blue-eyed sorceress had seduced him for her own evil purposes, Shaler couldn't plead that he'd been overpowered, now could he? After all, he had known exactly who Priscilla was from the moment he saw her. Tweed would never understand or forgive Shaler for what he had done. Hell's fire, Shaler couldn't even forgive himself!

The only way to handle this situation was to make Tweed think it was *his* idea to cancel the wedding. Shrewd little Priscilla Lambert couldn't use her secret against Shaler if Tweed was the one who dissolved the arrangement. Somehow or other, Shaler was going to have to devise a scheme . . . and he'd better be quick about it. Tweed was getting ready to make his mail-order bride his possession in every possible way!

Ten

Although Casity had been offered the most accommodating sleeping arrangements she had enjoyed in more than two weeks, her dreams were fitful. She attributed her inability to settle into a comfortable position to the short nap she had taken late in the afternoon and the spicy food Shaler had purposely fed her at supper. Shaler had taken the opportunity to get even with her after she had ordered him around as if he were her personal lackey.

Heaving a weary sigh, Casity flopped onto her side and squeezed her eyes shut—again. She'd count sheep, she decided. And she must have counted a flock of thousands before she finally relaxed enough for sleep to overtake her. But fragments of disjointed memories kept getting tangled up in her mind. She was reliving the terrible incident that had sent her fleeing from Nebraska. The jeering faces of her pursuers kept leaping out at her, leaving her thrashing in the sheets. Twice, she caught herself the instant before she toppled out of bed in her dazed attempt to escape the swirling specters that bounced back and forth between nightmare and reality.

Casity found it impossible to measure time while she was trapped between one bad dream and another. She awakened in a cold sweat and then drifted off

into a cloudy dimension in which snarling devils
pounced on her . . .

A muffled squawk erupted from her lips when she
was unable to catch herself before she dived headfirst
out of bed and landed with a thunk on the planked
floor. Her eyes popped open as she rolled over to stare
at the ceiling and untangle herself from the sheet.
Curse it, she didn't know why she had even bothered
to try to sleep. Now, she was more exhausted than
she'd been when she'd gone to bed!

When a strange shadow hovered in the doorway,
Casity instinctively recoiled. She groaned when she accidentally slammed her injured knee into the bed
frame, leaving her to wonder why she hadn't left her
splint on for protection. Before she could crawl onto
all fours and lever the weight off her tender leg, the
shadow descended upon her, engulfing her in powerful arms.

"Having bad dreams, princess?" Shaler dropped
her—none too gently—on what had once been *his* bed.

Casity stiffened at the feel and scent of the man
who was partially responsible for the wild dreams that
plagued her. "Yes, thanks to you and your heavy hand
on the salt and seasoning," she accused.

Shaler sank down on the edge of the bed where he
belonged. "If you don't like the way I cook, get up
off your throne and do it yourself, princess. After all,
that's one of the main reasons Tweed sent for a mail-
order bride," he reminded her flippantly.

Casity presented her back to the infuriating rapscallion who was doing his damnedest to make her stay
in Bonanza Gulch as unpleasant as possible. She supposed they were even. She had gone out of her way
to annoy him all evening and he had retaliated.

"You may leave now," Casity said curtly.

Shaler's jaw clenched at her haughty tone of voice.

His hands hovered around her neck, imagining his fingers as a choke necklace. "Funny, I was thinking of saying the same thing to you, princess."

He had taken to calling her "princess" and Casity had gotten very tired of that nickname already. She was also getting fed up with this big galoot's presence in her room and in her life! He had treated her abominably, leaping from one erroneous conjecture to another. And she was here to see that he paid for it!

"You can pull your best punches . . . but you won't rout me from this cabin," she assured him determinedly. "I'm immune to you."

Their eyes locked in a visual duel as potent as pistols at twenty paces.

"Are you truly immune to me?" There was a mocking purr in his voice as he leaned close to breathe down her neck, causing her to flinch at his suffocating nearness.

"Yes." She bared her teeth and growled, "Now crawl back on your pallet with the rest of the pests that slither across the cabin floor—"

Casity jerked away when his hand settled familiarly on her hip. Her eyes widened in alarm when Shaler shoved her over on her back and loomed over her.

He scowled down at her. "Don't ever forget whose bed you're sleeping in, princess. And remember, I could do whatever I wanted with you—"

"And if you dared to try, I'd call Tweed," she interrupted.

His taunting chuckle filled the narrow space between them. "As if Tweed could hear you, the way he snores. You would have that to look forward to if you married him—which you won't. I'll never let this ridiculous farce go that far."

Casity pressed the heels of her hands against his bare chest, trying to force him to give her room to breathe. She may as well have attempted to move a mountain. He didn't budge an inch.

"Damn you, Shay, leave me alone," Casity hissed in frustration.

"Not until you pack up and leave." He silently cursed his male body for reacting so spontaneously to her touch. He resented his fierce reaction to this feisty imp, especially when he despised everything about her.

"I'll *never* leave just because you *pressured* me into it." Casity's chin and jaw emphasized her determination. "I'll never give you the satisfaction—"

She gasped in alarm when his mouth took firm possession of hers, stripping her breath away. Her body tensed when his arm encircled her, pressing her against him. The scent and feel of his body lying familiarly against hers triggered unwanted memories of a night that *did not exist!* Casity fought the traitorous sensations that sizzled through her body. They served to remind her of the shameless way she had responded to this golden-eyed devil in a moment of madness. Curse his seductive hide. He wasn't going to repeat an encounter that never happened. She would not permit it . . .

When his kiss became tender and compelling, Casity wanted to scream in frustration. It would have been much easier to reject him if he had been rough and abusive. But no, not this rake. He knew how to make a woman's defenses collapse, how to make her forget the meaning of self-control. He forced her to take half the blame when she melted in his arms. Shaler McCain was truly a wizard of the worst sort. He was devilishly alluring and he knew it. He also knew just how to make a woman succumb, even against her will.

Shaler cursed himself up one side and down the other. He couldn't seem to remember his original motive for kissing this bewitching female. The irritation that flooded through him moments before burned away in the heat of desire. Although he felt as if he were betraying Tweed, he was driven by the overwhelming need to touch her, to retest his reactions to her, to get her out of his system once and for all . . .

Suddenly Shaler wasn't kissing and caressing her for spite, but for the pleasure of it. Hell's fire, why couldn't he keep his hands off this gorgeous woman? He knew what she was and why she was here. But that didn't stop him from wanting her beyond reason.

One touch and Shaler found himself transported back to that magical night, wishing he hadn't discovered the kind of things he had never known about the most potent kind of passion—the kind that could steal a man's sense of logic and leave him a prisoner of his own needs. He hated his spontaneous reaction to her, the hunger that consumed him every time he came within kissing distance of her. He knew she was poison and yet he couldn't wait to savor another taste of those lips, to caress her silky flesh and lose himself in the heady sensations that made time stand still.

When his hand tunneled beneath the sheet to glide up her thigh and swirl over her belly, Casity felt herself trembling in anticipation and torment. She couldn't let this delicious assault on her body and senses continue or she would humiliate herself all over again. If only Shaler hadn't awakened those slumbering needs and preyed on her vulnerability. If only she didn't find this rascal so physically appealing . . .

The feel of his lips whispering over her chemise caused a fleet of goose bumps to rise over her skin. Casity's breath lodged in her chest when he nipped and suckled at the throbbing peaks through the sheer fabric. And when his hands delved beneath the garment to caress her breasts, she felt the burning ache uncoil deep inside her, just as it had that fateful night when she had forgotten everything except the wondrous pleasures of his masterful touch.

Why did this frustrating man, who believed the worst about her, set off a chain of wild, compelling reactions inside her? Why was she so powerless to resist him? She had come here to repay him for treating her so disrespectfully, not to shame herself again!

That thought finally took root in her mind, giving Casity the will she needed to resist the pulse-jarring kisses and bone-melting caresses that had seized control of her body. When she twisted away, clutching the gaping chemise against her chest, Shaler withdrew to sit up on the edge of the bed.

A black scowl puckered his brow when his common sense returned. Damn it, he wasn't solving the problem; he was making it a dozen times worse! Priscilla Lambert was truly and surely the curse of his life. She had pitted father against son. Shaler had to get a firm grip on himself before he confronted this strong-willed female again. She could make him lose sight of his purpose faster than any woman alive!

Muttering to himself, Shaler rose to his feet and stalked back to the parlor, only to stumble over the chair Priscilla had insisted he rearrange to suit her tastes. She had set stumbling blocks in his life with her very presence. But by damn, he wasn't going to buckle to his basic desires again. She would probably use them against him in her crusade to marry Tweed and evict Shaler from his own cabin.

Still growling at his lack of control, and at that exasperating nymph who'd made herself at home in *his* bed, Shaler flopped facedown on his pallet . . . and groaned audibly. Lying facedown when a man was in a profound state of arousal was damned uncomfortable. Shaler shifted sideways, finding only minimal relief from the throbbing ache. Damn that woman—she made him ache all over.

Shaler wasn't able to sleep a wink. Between Tweed snoring up a storm in his bedroom and Priscilla tossing, turning, and moaning in the bed which had once belonged to him, the night had become a three-ring circus! Shaler had been aware of every creak of her bed, every whimpered word in her nightmares. Well, he hoped he was the reason for her bad dreams. It was his only consolation.

Casity didn't know how long she lay there lecturing herself about her wanton responses, but it seemed like a hundred years. Finally, she gave up trying to sleep and quietly eased from bed. As hard as she tried, she couldn't seem to forget that Shaler had slept where she slept, that this room was filled with his personal possessions. She had become one of his possessions when she had surrendered to him on a night she wished she could forget.

With that troubled thought, Casity braced her hands on the windowsill and stared up at the canopy of stars that winked down at her. She felt an impulsive need for fresh air to whisk away the masculine fragrance that clung to her. She had to escape the room that held that midnight-haired devil's ever-constant presence.

Without taking time to retrieve the leg brace that she had removed before bathing, Casity eased a hip onto the ledge and slipped outside. Balancing her weight on her good leg, she inhaled deeply and sighed. In the still of the night she heard the faint echo of scratching and clawing in the distance.

A muddled frown knitted her brow as she limped around the corner of the cabin to seek out the source of the muffled sounds. Barefoot, Casity hobbled between the clumps of aspens and pines, using the tree trunks for support until she reached the stream below the cabin. Her perceptive gaze focused on the shadowed entrance of the mine shaft that had been carved in the hillside. When Casity reached for the side of the *arrastra* to steady herself, the rudimentary mining device creaked on its frame and the chunks of rock near the end of the chute plunked into the tin pan Shaler had employed earlier that evening to separate the gold dust.

Casity froze to her spot, wishing her curiosity hadn't gotten the best of her. Whoever or whatever had made itself at home in the dark shaft had heard her approach. The noise had stopped.

Fool, Casity berated herself as she pivoted to retrace her steps. What had she planned to do if she met with trouble? Defend herself with her bare hands and feet?

The rustling in the bushes near the mouth of the tunnel prompted Casity to quicken her pace. She had only reached the grove of aspens when a bulky body slammed into her, tossing her into the grass. Before she could scream bloody murder, a grimy hand clamped over the lower portion of her face. Casity bit savagely at the fingers, provoking a pained yelp.

"LeRoy, get over here and help me with this wildcat," Buster Crane hissed as he removed his hands from Casity's teeth and shoved her head into the ground to prevent her from sending up a bloodcurdling scream.

LeRoy Penrod waddled forward as fast as his stumpy legs could carry him. In a flash, he produced the smelly handkerchief that he had tied around his sweaty neck. After he had made an improvised gag, LeRoy helped Buster restrain their squirming captive.

"Well, ain't we the lucky ones," Buster sniggered as his gaze wandered freely over Casity's skimpy attire.

"Not only did we scratch out a little gold, but it looks like we'll get to mix business with pleasure, too."

Casity tried to lash out with her foot when the two foul-smelling hooligans hoisted her up to tote her away. She inflicted more pain on herself than on the swindlers, who had sneaked into the gulch to rob from the claim. Her tender leg throbbed when she kicked LeRoy in the hip—the blow didn't even faze the sturdy scavenger, but it brought Casity excruciating agony.

"A feisty one she is, too." LeRoy latched onto Casity's left arm while Buster clutched at the other. "I like my women wormin' and squirmin' when I take 'em."

Casity strained with all her might when she realized these two scoundrels' disgusting intentions. She would ten times rather battle the traitorous sensations Shaler aroused in her than be subjected to the heartless abuse that these two men had in mind.

And things became progressively worse! There weren't two offensive-smelling scalawags robbing the shaft of its gold. There were three of them! The third man had been left to tend the horses, and it wasn't long before Casity realized why he had been assigned to that task. The raggedly dressed oaf, who was every bit as tall as Shaler and outweighed him by a ton, had the blankest expression on his face that Casity had ever seen.

It was obvious that Milo Pitt's largest commodity wasn't brains but brawn. It was his duty to make sure that the horses didn't escape while he awaited the return of his partners. Casity knew she didn't have a prayer when all three men closed in around her.

When Milo reached out with a huge hand to grope at her, Casity felt a wave of nausea. Milo grinned down at her, exposing his missing two front teeth.

"Me first," Milo demanded.

"Sure, sure, Milo, whatever you want," Buster reassured the big ape. "Just help us get her on a horse before somebody hears us and comes looking."

Casity cringed as she was lifted and deposited in the saddle. When Milo glided his callused hand over her bare leg, she instinctively kicked him in the chin—for all the good it did her. He never even blinked. As far as Casity could tell, the attack never even registered in that chunk of rock that served as his skull.

Eleven

Shaler strangled an angry growl as he watched the three poachers stuff their barely-clad captive on a horse. He scolded himself thoroughly for venturing out of the cabin without a weapon. After he had heard Casity's bed creak and realized she had sneaked out the window, he had decided to let her take her midnight stroll without following her. But the muffled sounds had put him on his feet—he had only taken time to don his boots before slipping outside. He knew better than to dash off without being prepared for anything, especially when this particular female was involved. Unfortunately, he had allowed thoughts of her to cloud his thinking.

Now here he was, crouched in the bushes without the shotgun or knife that could have made a world of difference. Shaler had half a mind to let these three hooligans tote that troublesome bundle off. It would save him plenty of anguish and frustration if he did. But knowing what these scalawags had in mind left a sour taste in Shaler's mouth.

No woman, no matter how annoying she was, deserved to be treated with such disrespect. This auburn-haired beauty had only known one man's touch, and Shaler had been more gentle and attentive with her than any woman he had ever taken in his arms. The fact that he was her first and only lover activated his possessive instincts. It was unwarranted, to be sure, considering her devious motives for being here. But still . . .

When a muffled shriek interrupted his thoughts, Shaler felt his entire body stiffen with apprehension. The big gorilla who had swung up in the saddle behind Priscilla was groping at her with fanatical fascination—like a child with a curious new toy. He had to do something—and quickly!

While the other two men scurried around to collect the gold they had chipped from the drift in the mine shaft, Shaler surveyed his surroundings and considered his options—of which there were damn few. His gaze rose to the overhanging limbs of the pine tree directly behind the horses. He rose from the bushes like a shadow and threaded through the trees. Grasping the branch above him, he negotiated through the limbs like an acrobat. Soundlessly, Shaler pulled himself onto one limb to reach for another. Without a weapon, he was left with only the element of surprise on his side.

The scuffling noises caused by the two men gathering chunks of ore in their gunny sacks concealed the sound of Shaler's approach as he maneuvered through the tree like a jungle cat. When LeRoy and Buster loaded their sacks behind their saddles, Shaler sank down on the limb, waiting for the most opportune moment.

Just as the two men stuffed their feet in the stirrups, Shaler leaped on them, forcing them off balance. Both men toppled to the ground and scrambled for their pistols. But quick as they were, they were too slow to overtake Shaler. He landed squarely on the back of the lead horse, causing it to rear in surprise.

In a flash, Shaler snatched the rifle that hung in its sheath beside the saddle horn. Using the weapon as a club, he hammered Milo on the back of the head before the slow-witted oaf had time to react. Problem was, Milo's head was as hard as granite. It took two forceful blows to faze him, and even that wasn't enough!

Shaler's weapon caused Milo to slam into Casity, forcing her facedown against the frightened steed. Out of the corner of her eye, she could see LeRoy and Buster slithering out from under the horse's hooves. Although Milo had bound her hands in front of her, Casity was able to grasp the bridle and turn her steed toward the two men who had yet to gain their feet.

LeRoy grunted painfully when Casity rammed her horse against him, knocking him back to the ground. Milo jerked upright in the saddle and twisted around to smash a meaty fist into Shaler's face. Casity jerked on the bridle, sending the horse prancing in a tight circle. Bodies flew in all directions as her horse collided with the riderless mount. The punch Milo had directed at Shaler struck the barrel of the rifle. Knuckles cracked and Milo howled like a wounded bear.

Although Shaler had been cursing Priscilla relentlessly, he was impressed by her quick reactions in dangerous situations. If she hadn't reined the steed around in time, he would have been forced to take the full brunt of Milo's powerful blow before warding off the attack of the two other men. Thanks to her clever tactic, Shaler had managed to crack Milo's knuckles before wheeling to club Buster over the head.

LeRoy, however, sprang to his feet, wielding the pistol he had retrieved . . . but he was unable to fire a shot before Shaler swung the rifle like a boom. The oncoming blow lifted LeRoy clean off the ground and sent him skidding in the grass.

While LeRoy was counting stars, Shaler devoted his attention to the oversized galoot who still had Casity trapped in front of him in the saddle. It had just occurred to Milo to use his captive as a shield. He looped his arm diagonally across her chest to brace her against him, practically daring Shaler to launch another attack.

There was one counter tactic Milo-the-slow had failed to consider while he sat there grinning in toothless triumph. The instant Shaler cocked his makeshift club to attack, Casity threw herself sideways. The butt of the rifle smeared Milo's smile all over his face and sent him teetering backward. The steed reared up when the excessive weight shifted to his rump. Like a boulder, Milo—who was still clutching Casity to him— somersaulted to the ground.

Casity was thankful the big brute hadn't landed on top of her—she would have been crushed. As it was, Milo's body broke *her* fall. The only pain she experienced was the wrenching of her already injured leg. Her shriek died beneath her gag as she instinctively clutched at her tender knee.

By the time Casity's cry was silenced, Shaler was looming over her like a bare-chested savage on the warpath. He twirled the rifle into firing position to get the drop on Milo. Swiftly, he reached out to yank Casity away from the stunned giant who'd had the wind knocked out of him. Then Shaler's hand snaked out to snatch the pistol from Milo's holster. He shoved the confiscated weapon into Casity's hands and stared grimly at her.

"If he moves, shoot him." Shaler spun around to disarm LeRoy, who'd been knocked flat a moment earlier. "Get up on your feet *now* or you'll never get up again."

Shaler's menacing growl prompted LeRoy to do as he was told. With his hands held high, he obediently wobbled over beside Milo.

Reclaiming the pistol from Casity, Shaler gestured toward the horses. "Fetch some rope, princess."

"You ain't gonna hang us, are you?" LeRoy croaked, frog-eyed. "Hell, all we did was dig a little gold from the shaft—"

Casity ripped the gag from her lips and added furiously, "And scared ten years off my life. Just shoot them, Shay. After what they intended to do to me, I want to draw blood—plenty of it!"

At the sound of Casity's spiteful tone, LeRoy gulped over the lump in his throat.

Shaler's lips quirked in a wry smile while he watched Casity storm toward her assailants. He had seen her temper the first time they'd clashed. But it was far more amusing when her fury wasn't directed at *him*. Now these three hooligans were the object of her wrath. And how true it was that the fires of hell couldn't hold a candle to a woman's fury. This wildcat was indeed a sight to behold!

Curses tumbled from Casity's lips as she limped over to slap LeRoy upside the head with her coil of rope. After wheeling around, she whacked Milo's bouldersized shoulder for good measure. "The next time you galoots go near a woman you'd better show her a little respect!" she fumed. "I'm sick and tired of having men behave like a bunch of despicable cretins. I hope—"

"Uh, princess, the idea was for you to bind these men to a tree," Shaler reminded her in between chuckles. "You can give them their forty lashes once you have a *captive* audience."

Casity lurched around to stalk toward Shaler. "*You* tie them up while *I* hold the rifle," she demanded in a huff. "If they resist, I want to be the one to blow them to smithereens." Of course, she really wouldn't have done anything of the kind, but better that these ogres thought she might, Casity figured.

"Don't give her that rifle!" LeRoy protested. "She's half-crazy. She'd fill us full of lead for looking at her the wrong way!"

"Then don't look at her the wrong way," Shaler advised with an ornery grin.

LeRoy didn't dare, nor did Milo. They were meek and submissive while Shaler bound each of them to his own personal tree.

"Put more rope on Milo," Casity instructed. "Big as he is, he'll burst loose."

"I'm perfectly capable of tying secure knots," Shaler grumbled. Hell's fire, what he didn't need was for this bossy female to tell him what to do and how to do it. "Don't worry about your friend Milo. The only way he'll get loose is if he takes the pine tree with him, roots and all."

That seemed to pacify Casity. She piped down, even though she monitored Shaler's every move to be sure he used enough rope. When Milo and LeRoy were securely staked in place, Shaler strode over to wrap Buster in another coil of rope. Buster hadn't yet roused to consciousness. He was still out cold when Shaler dragged him to his tree and lashed him to it.

While Casity stood balancing on her good leg, it occurred to her that Shaler had come to her rescue without a weapon. The man was truly amazing. He had attacked like a one-man posse. His complete absence of fear suggested that nothing frightened him anymore. Although Casity had her heart set on hating him, she couldn't help but admire his phenomenal skills. She wished she possessed half his knowledge of the art of self-defense.

The fact that Shaler had come to her rescue *at all* surprised her. This would have been the perfect opportunity to be rid of her for good. Why hadn't he let these three ogres cart her off?

When Shaler pulled the rifle from her hands, Casity peered at him inquisitively. "Why didn't you let them take me? That's what you really wanted."

Shaler muttered at the loaded question. Leave it to this curious sprite to ask. "I do want you out of here, but not at the risk of your life. I'm not *that* spiteful."

"Well, you could have fooled me," Casity replied with a smirk.

"The truth is that you caught me in a weak moment and I felt sorry for you," Shaler snapped back.

Casity thrust out her chin. "I don't want your pity. All I want is your apology for treating me so disrespectfully since the moment I met you!"

"And all I want is your gratitude for saving your lovely neck a second time, princess," Shaler growled. His gaze impulsively dropped to her barely-concealed breasts and the creamy flesh of her thighs and his body began to respond. "And why the hell can't you wear a long flannel nightgown like most females do? You should expect to be mauled if you run around in the middle of the night dressed like that."

Casity had completely forgotten about her attire. She must have looked a sight in her thigh-length chemise, her hair flying around her in wild tangles. The fact that this rake had called her attention to her indecent exposure irritated her all over again.

"Even if I were running around naked that's no excuse for men to take advantage. And it certainly wasn't my fault that these three clowns were out here robbing your gold mine when I was taking a walk," she added self-righteously.

One thick brow elevated as his intense gaze took in her curvaceous figure—again. "And just what prompted you to take a stroll at this hour? Something bothering you, princess? Like maybe your conscience? You weren't feeling guilty about luring me into your room under the pretense of having a bad dream, while your fiancé was snoring in the other room, were you?"

So he was back to needling her again, was he? Well, Casity could give as good as she got.

"I wasn't luring you anywhere, you arrogant ass. You might consider yourself God's gift to womankind, but I find you a bothersome bore, if you want to know. Your amorous display assured me that you have about as much common decency as these three morons. I intend to inform Tweed of your late-night visit to my room, and don't think I won't!"

Shaler took one step forward, his tawny eyes glittering dangerously in the moonlight. "Do it, princess, and see where it gets you," he challenged with a mocking smile. "Thus far, I've gone easy on you. But believe me, you don't want to get on my bad side. I can be very unpleasant when I feel like it."

Casity had seen the vicious side of his nature when he took on her captors single-handed. When battle broke out, Shaler McCain was definitely a force to be reckoned with. But she refused to be intimidated under any circumstances, especially by this raven-haired devil. She had made herself at home in Bonanza Gulch for the express purpose of watching Shaler fry in his own grease. He wasn't going to frighten her away, no matter what tactic he employed. She could take anything he dished out and serve it right back to him!

"And while we're on the subject, sonny boy," she smirked in a ridiculing tone that would have done Shaler proud—if she hadn't been using it on *him*. "Don't ruffle my feathers, either. Tweed happens to worship the ground I walk on, in case you haven't noticed. One word from me and you'll find yourself without a home to call your own. So don't push unless you plan to get shoved—*out.*"

Shaler took another step closer so that only a few inches separated them. Damn her gorgeous hide. He wanted to shake her . . or grab hold of her luscious body and kiss her to death. Shaler wasn't sure which. This female was frustrating him beyond words. He resented this gnawing hunger that simply staring at her aroused in him. He also resented her intrusion in his life—and the crosscurrent of emotions she set off inside him.

"You know something, princess? I'm beginning to have serious regrets about tonight's escapade. The next time somebody totes you off, I'll stand aside and let it happen."

Casity wheeled toward the cabin, but she had only taken one step before her injured knee buckled beneath her. If Shaler's hand hadn't shot out to steady her, she would have fallen flat on her face. To her surprise, he swept her up in his arms and carried her to the cabin.

"Don't say I never did anything for you," he muttered. "And next time you trounce off in the middle of the night, wear your splint."

The feel of his arms against her back and the underside of her legs was not a sensation Casity preferred to dwell upon. Each touch, no matter how harmless, triggered her awareness of this brawny giant. The brush of his chest against her arm stirred memories of another time and another place.

"Put me down," Casity bleated. "I'd rather crawl to the house than have you carry me."

Shaler would have preferred it himself. Even when he was perturbed with Priscilla, she still had the power to arouse him. Hell's fire, if he didn't get hold of himself he would wind up doing something crazy again.

"Fine, crawl if you wish," Shaler said as he set her

on the stoop. "Just don't trip over me and my pallet on your way to *my* bed."

When Shaler surged through the door ahead of her, he was greeted by Tweed's loud snoring. Hell's bells, Tweed could sleep through a cyclone! Shaler had found himself in the midst of a battle and Tweed had blissfully slept the night away, totally unaware that poachers were scurrying around in his front yard in an attempt to abscond with his gold and his mail-order bride. But then, Tweed had always been notorious for sleeping like a rock. When his head hit the pillow nothing disturbed his sleep.

Casity veered around Shaler's bulky form on the floor and hobbled to bed, careful not to put excessive pressure on her throbbing leg. An audible sigh tumbled from her lips as she eased beneath the sheet. Perhaps living at the cabin while she retaliated against Shaler wasn't one of her brighter ideas. True, she needed a place to stay until her injury healed. But her sprained knee was in worse condition than it had been the previous night—and so was she. Having that dark-haired rascal underfoot was torment, pure and simple. The mere sight of him put excessive strain on her temper and her blood pressure. She had to take a wide berth around him or else . . .

Casity refused to consider *or else*. All she wanted was a few hours' rest to revive her energy and spirit. She would face the next few days and endure the wisecracks Shaler flung at her. The hell he planned to give her wouldn't compare to the hell she planned to give him. In her opinion he hadn't suffered enough.

When Shaler finally realized his mistake, she hoped he felt all of two inches tall. She couldn't wait to see the look on his handsome face when his father told him that she wasn't Priscilla Lambert and that she never had any intention of marrying Tweed. Soon

Shaler McCain would discover just how wrong he could be. And considering the fact that Shaler hated being wrong about anything, his humiliation was sure to kill him. Casity hoped she was around when it did.

Yawning broadly, Tweed pulled his suspenders into place and hobbled from his bedroom. His bleary-eyed gaze swung to Casity, who sat at the table sipping her coffee while Shaler fried bacon and eggs.

"Mornin'," Tweed muttered as he levered himself into his chair.

When Tweed leaned over to give her a peck on the cheek, Shaler unintentionally stabbed the eggs, making them weep all over the skillet. What the sweet loving hell was wrong with him? Why couldn't he bear to watch another man—even his own father—touch Priscilla?

"Did you sleep well, honey-bunch?" Tweed inquired. He snapped his fingers, silently requesting Shaler to bring him a cup of coffee. "There's nothin' like a peaceful night's sleep to revive a body, is there?"

"Last night was anything but peaceful," Shaler contradicted as he sauntered across the room to set Tweed's coffee cup in front of him. "Three poachers were digging gold from the shaft while you snored your head off."

Tweed blinked in disbelief. "What?"

Hurriedly, he hoisted himself out of his chair and scurried to the spacious windows that fronted the cabin. Sure enough, there were three men tied so tightly to the trees that they couldn't move a muscle.

"Did they cause you much trouble?" he questioned curiously.

Shaler's broad shoulders rose in a shrug. "Not much."

Casity arched a delicate brow and marveled at his modest reply. Shaler seemed to take everything in stride, except her presence in his cabin. Everything she said and did seemed to rub him the wrong way.

"I'm taking those scavengers into Deadwood and file charges with Sheriff Brown this morning." Shaler scooped up the weeping eggs and dumped them on the plates. "I also need to purchase a new saddle blanket." He shot Casity a glance that made her squirm skittishly in her chair.

"What's a-matter with the old saddle blanket?" Tweed inquired.

Casity averted her gaze when penetrating golden eyes drilled into her. Leave it to that scamp to remind her of the saddle blanket—the one that bore evidence of her lost virginity. That insensitive polecat. He took every opportunity to remind her of her disgrace and shame.

"I just need a new blanket, that's all," Shaler replied and then silently congratulated himself for making this wily female flinch at the memory of what she had done. "Anything you want from town, Tweed?"

Tweed hobbled back to the table, following the tempting aroma of breakfast. "I don't need nothin' from town except for you to file our new claim." He glanced at Casity. "How 'bout you, sweetie-pie? Do you need somethin'?"

Casity's lashes swept up to see Shaler glaring at her from his position behind Tweed's chair. No doubt he was expecting her to ask for something extravagant to reinforce his low opinion of her.

"Well . . ." Casity chewed on her lip, wondering if she dared to make a request after Shaler had flung her such a homicidal glare.

"Anything you want, puddin'," Tweed encouraged

her. "Name it and it's yers. Shay will be glad to fetch it."

Shaler McCain would be nothing of the kind! This little gold digger was setting Tweed up, practically making him beg her to voice her whim. It would be an expensive one, too, he predicted.

"If you're sure it wouldn't be too much trouble, there is something I would like," Casity murmured without meeting Shaler's reproachful glower.

He was still standing behind Tweed's chair, pantomiming the gesture of having one's throat cut with a dagger. The silent threat assured her that he would make her pay dearly if she requested an expensive purchase.

"It won't be too much trouble," Tweed assured her.

Shaler's glittering amber gaze bored into her like a worm into an apple.

"I would like to have a long flannel nightgown." She stifled an impish smile when Shaler did a double take, bewildered by her modest request.

"Is that all?" Tweed's shoulder slumped in disappointment. "Yer too frugal, sugar. Surely you can think of somethin' besides that."

"That's all I want." Casity stared at Shaler over the rim of her coffee cup. "Actually my needs are few and my tastes are simple."

Weren't they just! Shaler silently smirked. In a few days, after she had drawn Tweed completely beneath her spell, she would ask for the moon and the old codger would probably try to fly off to fetch it for her, broken leg and all.

"Any particular color?" Shaler inquired.

"Whi—" Casity clamped down on her tongue so quickly that she nearly bit it in two. She would never feel comfortable wearing white again, thanks to this heartless rake.

For a half-second, Shaler almost felt sorry for her—
almost. He knew what she had intended to say before
she bit down on the word. The thought of their reckless
night together was working on her miniature-sized conscience—as well it should. After all, she had lured him
in, just as she was trying to lure Tweed now.

"Any color will suffice," Casity murmured, staring
at her plate.

After gulping down his meal in two bites, Shaler
grabbed his pistols and marched out the door to tend
his errand.

"Don't worry about us," Tweed called when Shaler
breezed off. "We'll be here discussin' our weddin'
plans."

Shaler's back went rigid as stone and he broke stride
before composing himself to continue on his way.

Casity's shoulders sagged in relief, grateful for a
few hours' reprieve. Tweed would divert her attention
from the brawny giant who preyed so heavily on her
thoughts and her emotions. Thank the Lord for
Tweed!

"Now then." Tweed leaned back in his chair to
stretch out his splinted leg. "I want you to tell me
'bout the incident with them poachers. Shay ain't
much for details."

Casity shrugged nonchalantly. "Like he said, not
much happened."

If Shaler wasn't going to elaborate, then she wasn't,
either. In fact, she preferred to forget that the incident—and other unnerving incidents of recent weeks—
everhappened.

Tweed studied Casity for a moment. He had the inescapable feeling that much more had happened than
he'd been told, but he didn't press her. Instead, he
speculated on the discreet glances that had been skip-
ping back and forth between Shaler and this enchant

ing beauty. Tweed was no fool. He had felt the electrifying tension in the room the instant he walked in. He couldn't help but wonder if there wasn't more going on between his son and this vivacious nymph than just a cold war.

Shaler always made a habit of keeping his own counsel. He only told Tweed what he wanted his father to know, and no more. And Casity wasn't one bit better about revealing her innermost thoughts. It had taken several glasses of brandy to prompt her to relate the tragic trials of her past. Even then, Tweed wasn't sure he had heard the entire story.

"Casity, I know this ain't none of my business, but—"

Tweed's probing stare warned Casity that he intended to delve deeper into the secrets of her soul than she preferred. "Let's go for a walk, Tweed." Casity surged out of her chair to clear the table.

She had no intention, however, of washing the dishes. She was going to leave them for Shaler because he hated the thought of lowering himself to such menial tasks and she delighted in watching him do domestic chores.

"This is such a lovely valley and such a fine morning, don't you think?" she inquired as she limped toward the door.

When Casity sailed outside on her bum leg, Tweed discarded the question he wasn't even sure he should ask. "It is a fine mornin'," he agreed as he trailed after her.

"Thank you." She outstretched her hand so they could assist each other down the steps.

"For what?"

"For not asking." She gave his hand a fond squeeze and smiled gratefully. "And for giving me a place to stay when I had nowhere to go. But I think it would be best if I—"

"Nonsense," Tweed cut her off. "I like having you here and here you will stay until I've decided that son o' mine has paid proper penance. Now I don't wanna hear any more talk about leavin'. It ruins my good disposition."

Hand in hand, Casity and Tweed limped down the hill. Ah, it was good to take time to enjoy their beautiful surroundings, Casity thought as they ambled toward the stream. For the past two weeks, she had no time for anything except the strenuous task of staying alive. With Shaler out from underfoot for the day, she could relax and enjoy the company of the man who had become a substitute for the father and uncle she had lost. It was nice to have at least one trusted friend in this world, Casity mused as she inhaled the fragrance of the bouquet of wildflowers Tweed picked for her. One friend was ever so much better than having no friends at all . . .

Twelve

Casity slept better than she had in two weeks, except for that night when she and Shaler had . . . Forcefully, she shoved the thought of a night that *didn't happen* out of her mind. Her feelings for that midnight-haired rake grew out of revenge, nothing more. She planned to enjoy Tweed's company while she bided her time until Shaler paid his well-deserved retribution.

With each passing day, Casity found herself growing fonder of Tweed. He was a lovable character and had a knack for making her feel at home. He filled her head with interesting tales of his experiences in the mountains of Colorado and New Mexico where he had hunted and trapped to make a living for himself and the boy he had saved from an Indian massacre. He also informed her that James Butler Hickok, better known these days as Wild Bill, had lived with them for three years while he was trying his luck at trapping. From Tweed, Casity had learned all about Wild Bill's younger days when he had worked as a scout who guided wagon trains to California.

There was a natural warmth about Tweed that made Casity drop her guard, even though past experiences bade her to be wary of men on general principle. But Tweed was different. He was the exception to the rules she made regarding men. It truly was a shame that Priscilla Lambert had opted to head to California with

Nate the gambler. Casity hoped the young woman had come to her senses in time to see the error of her ways. Priscilla could have found happiness with Tweed Cramer, even if he *was* twice her age.

As for Casity, she wasn't sure she ever wanted to marry or become deeply involved with a man. Her bittersweet encounter with Shaler had only made her more cynical about liaisons—especially the kind in which a woman did all the giving and a man did all the taking.

The friction between Casity and Shaler had grown considerably worse after he returned from his overnight stay in Deadwood. He had spitefully purchased a red flannel gown and Casity hadn't missed its insulting insinuation. If it had been Shaler's intention to make her feel cheap and unwanted, he had been successful. And to further annoy her, he implied that he had cavorted with women who named their price—which he had paid. Casity assured herself that his suggestive remark had only inspired anger, not jealousy. She didn't care how many women he had seduced while he was in Deadwood, as long as she wasn't one of them!

Unfortunately, her mind had trouble convincing her body that she never again wanted to experience the splendor of Shaler's skillful touch. Casity didn't want to think about the feel of his sinewy arms around her, the taste of his kisses, the tingling caress of his fingertips . . .

"Too bad you can't clean up your conscience as easily as you wash your clothes," Shaler smirked as he watched Casity scrub her blue calico gown in the stream. "And aren't you a long way from your throne, Your Highness?"

Casity flinched at the mocking voice that nipped at her from out of nowhere. "You shouldn't sneak up on a person like that," she scolded without glancing in his direction.

"And how is it possible to sneak up on a sneak?"

Casity half-turned to flash him a scathing glare. "It seems to me that the pot is calling the kettle black. You asked for this."

"*I* asked for it?" Shaler hooted sarcastically. "Princess, you're the one who set me up for blackmail. And for the past few days, you've had me tending you and Tweed as if I were your damned servant! 'Fetch a cup of tea, will you, *please?*' " he mimicked. " 'Move the bed'—the very one that once belonged to *me*, by the way—'over there, *please*. Draw my bath water for me, *please*. You're such a good *boy*, Shay.' " He snorted loudly and glared at her. "Hell's fire, you treat me as if I were your dutiful dog!"

Casity rinsed out her dress and laid it over a nearby branch to dry before hobbling around to confront Shaler face-to-face. It was the first time in four days that she had been with him without Tweed as a buffer. Unwillingly, her gaze wandered over the buckskin clothes that fit him like a second skin, displaying his muscular physique to its best advantage. He was a magnificent creature. Too bad she hated him.

"It was I who fell into your vicious trap," she contradicted. "And if you provoke me, I'll see to it that Tweed knows the full story of the stagecoach raid— with all its incriminating details."

When Shaler took a step closer, Casity tilted her chin defiantly. "If you dare to touch me, I'll scream my head off. Tweed will come to my aid and I'll tell him you tried to attack me, lusty beast that you are."

With extreme effort, Shaler remained calm, looming over Casity like a thundercloud, without snatching her up and shaking her until her teeth rattled, which was what he really wanted to do.

"I've washed my last dish and moved my last stick of furniture for you, princess," he growled. "And I'll tell you something else—if you don't pack up and get out—"

"You'll *what*? Throw me out?" Her fiery blue eyes raked over him with disdain. "I don't honestly know where you find the gall to keep up this pretense in front of your father. Any man who would do what you did to your father's betrothed doesn't deserve to live under the same roof with him. Tweed is one of the kindest, warmest men I've ever met. That's quite a compliment, considering I detest most men with a vengeance!"

"You certainly didn't seem to hate *me* the night we—"

Casity struck like a coiled rattlesnake, leaving her handprint on Shaler's bronzed cheek. He didn't even flinch, curse him! Her physical attack seemed to have no more effect on him than the bite of a pesky gnat.

"—The night we made love beneath the stars," he continued, just to infuriate her—which it most certainly did.

When she attempted to strike again, Shaler caught her arm in midair, frustrating her even more.

"I wasn't myself that night," Casity spluttered in defense. "I—"

"Oh really? Then who *were* you, princess?" Shaler released her arm as if touching her repulsed him.

Casity was so irritated and humiliated that the truth very nearly flew off her tongue before she could bite back the words. Luckily, she gathered her composure in the nick of time and matched him glare for glare.

"I hate you, Shaler McCain," she gritted out between clenched teeth. "You're the most cruel, insulting man I've ever met."

"The feeling is mutual. And if you think I'll permit

you to marry my father, you're a bigger fool than I first thought."

Casity wasn't about to give him the satisfaction of telling him she had no interest in marrying anybody. Let him boil in his own broth until she announced her departure. Let him serve her those salty meals and ridicule her every chance he got. Let him fill her bathtub with cold water. She could endure. She could tolerate anything after all she'd been through. She wasn't leaving until she was damned good and ready.

"Tweed said he wanted you to take him over to see the new claim he bought," Casity informed him, quickly changing the subject before they clashed—again.

"And what will you be doing while you're left unattended in the cabin?" Shaler wanted to know. "Searching for pouches of gold?"

"I have no need to steal gold from Tweed. He gave me a pouch this morning and urged me to go into town to purchase anything I desired."

Shaler scowled at the news. "I suppose you plan to gallivant around town with the man who loaned you his carriage. Who did you bedazzle with that smile of yours? Pendleton, Varnes, or Brady?"

"It was Reece Pendleton, if you must know. He offered me employment if my arrangements with Tweed didn't work out."

"I'll bet he did," Shaler snorted. "You'd spend all your time on your back, if I know him."

Casity had tried to keep a lid on her temper, but Shaler's rude comment caused her to blow her top. She cocked her arm to strike but to her dismay, he caught her hand again. This time he used it to yank her against him. His free hand clamped onto the back of her neck, tipping her head back to meet his furious gaze.

"I let you slap me once," he hissed into her livid

features. "But you'll never get away with it again, princess."

"Let me go!"

Casity was shocked by the instantaneous reaction of her body. The remembered sensations inspired by more intimate moments assaulted her and she cursed her infuriating lack of control.

"I said let me go!"

Casity panicked when unwanted memories sent warm tingles rippling through her. She gasped in panic when she noticed the glitter in his golden eyes, the ever so slight inclination of his head. He was going to kiss her, damn him! She didn't want another tormenting memory!

"Don't you dare, Shay," Casity muttered the instant before his sensuous mouth rolled over hers.

Shaler cursed himself soundly when he felt the soft texture of her lips beneath his. He didn't want to kiss her, he tried to convince himself. He wanted to strangle her. But the moment he tugged her into his arms, an uncontrollable hunger gnawed at him. He had spent the past few days assuring himself that he never wanted to get this close to her again. She was an evil curse.

This was the woman Tweed had decided to marry, for God's sake! And yet, Shaler couldn't look at her without remembering the wild, sweet intimacies they had shared, the splendor he had discovered in her arms. He hated what she had done to him *then* and he hated what she was doing to him *now*. She had complicated his life to such frustrating extremes that she haunted his dreams. Because of her he had been forced to sleep on the floor, knowing she was in his bed, knowing she might wind up being his stepmother—of all things! But as much as he despised this blue-eyed nymph, his body ached for the delicious pleasure they had shared that reckless night beneath the starry summer sky . . .

Against his will, Shaler found himself transported back in time, experiencing the same mindless sensations that had once overwhelmed him. He felt himself drowning in the kiss, dissolving against her delectable body, absorbing her as if she were a vital, missing part of him.

After just one taste and touch, Shaler couldn't get enough. He wanted to recapture every fantastic moment, to feel her silky curves beneath his fingertips, to forget everything except the dizzying rapture he never realized existed until this conniving beauty had used her sweet innocence to captivate him.

Casity was appalled at her eager response to his kiss. Lord, one would have thought she was a harlot the way she melted in his arms. Her protest had evaporated into a puff of steam. She could feel herself yielding when he stole her breath away and then generously returned it in another tender kiss. His hands flowed over her hips, guiding her intimately against the contours of his body, holding her to him as he had done on that night out of time. A burning ache sizzled in the core of her being, dissolving her will to resist.

His mouth was like liquid heat and her body instinctively greeted his, as if their time apart had fanned the flames of passion, increasing this maddening hunger that refused to go away. Her senses were so saturated with the scent and feel of him that Casity arched against his body and kissed him back before she even realized it!

What was there about this infuriating man that made her forget who and where she was? He could make time stand still. It was as if he had stripped away all her protection, exposing vulnerabilities she never knew she had until he came into her life. He preyed on her desires like a poison. He drew her into his spell like a wizard, making his will her own.

When his hand swirled over her ribs to caress the taut tips of her breasts, she cursed herself ten times over. And when his lips trailed down her throat to flick at the throbbing peaks that he had exposed with his skillful caresses, she swore she was burning alive!

How could she be so furious with this scoundrel one moment and so hungry for him the next? Not only did she react violently to the sting of his words but she was also incredibly sensitive to his touch. She was far too aware of Shaler—that was the problem, Casity decided just before her injured knee buckled beneath her. The unexplainable mysteries of biological attraction were hard at work, plotting against her. Nothing Shaler said or did escaped her notice, even when she was trying so hard to ignore the man—and the memories they had made in the moonlight. He insulted her and it cut her to the bone. He touched her and her body caught fire.

Casity had constantly reassured herself that the only reason Shaler had been able to crack her shell and steal her innocence was because she had been dazed, injured, and completely vulnerable. Now she had no excuse whatsoever. This impossible man made her contradict herself all over the place. He left her feeling wild and reckless and astounded by her own body's responses. He made her want things she didn't need. He made her feel . . . alive . . . uninhibited . . . even when she didn't want to be.

When Shaler's thigh insinuated itself between her legs and he lifted her to him, Casity struggled for a breath that wasn't thick with the scent of him, but her lungs were filled with his masculine fragrance.

Her hands tunneled through the lacings of his doehide shirt to caress his chest, to feel his heartbeat matching her own. Her lips opened when his probing tongue sought entrance to the moist recesses of her mouth and her body quivered when he fit her against the bold evidence of his desire.

Had she no shame? No willpower? How could she want this man who had used her as if she were his private whore and then ridiculed and tormented her?

Shaler couldn't believe the intensity of need that swamped and buffeted him. As desire burned through him, he couldn't seem to get close enough—fast enough—to the source of pleasure that engulfed his mind and body. He resented the restrictive garments between them, resented the complete loss of self-control. Hell's fire, this woman could turn him into a walking hypocrite so fast it made his head spin. He detested her wily scheme to bewitch his father and yet he craved her like a starving man. He constantly battled guilt and passion, haunted by a fierce need that defied his control.

The decisive stamp of hooves and the impatient snort of his steed brought Shaler back to his senses—and not a second too soon! Obviously, the sorrel gelding had more brains than Shaler.

Inhaling a steadying breath, he set Casity away from him and forced himself to retreat a step before the pull of her body drew him back.

"Damn you, woman," Shaler rasped. "You're twisting me in knots. Why won't you go away and leave me in peace?" His amber eyes flamed down at her, his jaw clenched in frustration and restraint. "I swear, when I get near you, I cannot imagine what else hell can possibly have to teach me that I haven't already learned from wanting you so much and knowing I can't have you . . ."

When Shaler lurched around to snatch up his steed's reins and stalk toward the cabin, Casity clutched the

nearest tree for support. She took several deep breaths
and fought for composure. She felt betrayed by her
body and abandoned by her common sense. Shaler
thought *he* had been cursed by the tortures of hell, did
he? He didn't know the half of it!

Dear Lord, how could a physical attraction become
so potent that it took control over her mind? How
could she claim to despise a man that she wanted until
she fairly shook, remembering the pleasures he had
taught her? Ah, hell must be an internal battle that
tore the soul apart!

With trembling fingers, Casity fastened her gown
and tried to breathe normally. Considering her reaction to Shaler, she would have to take great pains to
make sure they never found themselves alone together
again. Casity simply couldn't trust herself. Each time
he dared to touch her, she felt herself teetering on
the border of shameless abandon.

There would be no more kissing or touching, Casity
promised herself faithfully. She would take a wide
berth around that tawny-eyed rogue from this day forward and stick to Tweed like glue until she returned
to Deadwood. Tweed was her salvation, her only defense against her own desires.

Clinging to that reassuring thought, Casity stretched
out her injured leg and hunkered down to scrub her
flannel nightgown in the stream. She wasn't walking
back to the cabin until she had herself under absolute
control.

It took a while . . .

When Shaler had returned earlier in the afternoon
from Pine Gulch, after inspecting the claim Tweed
had purchased sight unseen, he had been in a foul
mood. Now, he was in an even worse frame of mind.

Confronting the devil's own temptation beside the stream and losing his self-control had been the last straw. How much longer could his conscience and sense of guilt restrain him from succumbing to the demands of desire? This battle between mind and body was tearing him in two!

The instant Shaler sailed through the door, his narrowed gaze settled on Tweed and he vented his frustration. "Can't you do anything wrong?" Shaler muttered at his father.

Tweed frowned at the strange accusation. "What the devil are you talkin' about?"

"I'm referring to the claim you bought in Pine Gulch." Shaler lit his cheroot and puffed vigorously. "I swear, you've got the Midas touch. That mine is full of productive drifts. I set off an explosion to widen the shaft. And sure as hell, I hit a rich vein. That's twice, Tweed. The whole idea here was to find a mine that wasn't worth the paper the deed was written on!"

"Well, damn," Tweed grumbled. "I didn't think that claim would be much of a producer. Nobody else has had much luck in Pine Gulch."

"Nobody else has your kind of luck," Shaler amended crankily. "Since you've managed to strike high grade ore not *once* but *twice*, I took it upon myself to buy another claim to suit our purpose."

"Don't tell me you struck gold, too?" Tweed chuckled.

"No, I don't have your brand of luck." All the luck Shaler seemed to be having was the bad luck that went by the name of Priscilla Lambert! "The claim I bought in Mule's Ear Gulch hasn't shown any signs of profitable veins. What you touch turns to gold. But what I touch turns to rock."

"I'll get my hat and we'll ride over to look at it," Tweed suggested.

Although Shaler wasn't enthusiastic about leaving that scheming female alone with so much gold stashed around the cabin, he definitely needed to put some distance between them so he could cool off. It hadn't helped a helluva lot that he had avoided her the past few days—absence just added more fuel to the blaze. Shaler had dared to get within two feet of her and had caught fire—again. What was there about that woman that triggered so much emotion? Shaler honestly wondered how much he could endure before he . . .

"You ready?" Tweed inquired when Shaler simply stood there, staring at the far wall, seeing the image of auburn hair and sapphire eyes.

Shaler puffed on his cigar, eager to replace the taste of those kisses with the bite of tobacco. It wasn't helping.

"I'm ready," he assured his father.

Ready to pull out his hair! Shaler couldn't stand much more torment before his composure cracked. If something didn't give—and quickly—he wasn't sure he wanted to be held accountable for his actions.

And what really infuriated Shaler was that he had attempted to forget one woman by turning to another in Deadwood. Big mistake! The instant Shaler wrapped his arms around the shapely calico queen, it had been all wrong. Imagine that! It was downright scary to realize he had become a man of such discriminate tastes. Two weeks earlier any woman would have satisfied him. Now the very last woman he *wanted* was the one he most *desired!* He had been cruelly cursed.

Tweed surveyed Shaler's claim that overlooked the trickling creek in Mule's Ear Gulch. His gaze drifted to the mine shaft that Samuel Heaston had blasted out of the side of solid rock.

"Samuel said he hadn't found much color, except in placers in the creek," Shaler reported to his father. "He did some crevicing in the shaft and there looks to be some quartz deposits scattered around. I think this mine should serve our purpose. It has definite possibilities, especially since all the water rights are attached to the claim."

Tweed hobbled over to the entrance of the shaft and peered inside. "Old Samuel sure as hell didn't believe in blastin' out a very big hole to crawl through, did he?"

Shaler stared at the narrow stone passage and grinned. Tweed had always been leery of cramped spaces, such as shafts, caves, and tunnels. He had made certain their cabin in Bonanza Gulch boasted plenty of windows to let the outside world in.

"Do you want me to blast a bigger tunnel?" Shaler teased. "I know how scared you are of enclosed spaces."

"I ain't scared of nothin'," Tweed snapped. "But I think you oughta set off a small explosion in the interior so we can salt the rock. It'll make the mine more attractive to our buyer when we sell it." His brows drew together like two fuzzy caterpillars over his green eyes. "Have you come up with the right additives for saltin' this mine yet?"

"I haven't had time to check the ore sources under a microscope, but I will before we do the salting," Shaler assured him.

Tweed hobbled away from the stone-lined passage to survey the meandering stream. "Yes sirree, I think this claim is gonna suit our purpose just fine. We'll have our intended buyer right where we want him." His gaze discreetly darted to Shaler to gauge his reaction to the upcoming remark. "Thus far, I've been too preoccupied with my bride-to-be to spend much time thinkin' about our claims."

The sensitive subject put a scowl on Shaler's face. "Haven't you gotten tired of that sticky-sweet smile of hers yet?" he grumbled. "For all your expectations about cooking and cleaning, I'm beginning to wonder if she's ever worked a day in her life. I've been doing all the work and she's been doing all the bossing!"

"She's got a sprained knee, for Pete's sake," Tweed said in her defense. "Besides, I don't want her to wear herself out before the weddin' and honeymoon."

Shaler flinched as if he'd been stabbed. Honeymoon? He didn't want to think about that. It was bad enough that he lay awake every night, wanting that blue-eyed nymph beyond reason and hating himself for it. His conflicting emotions were eating him alive. He felt guilty for coveting his father's betrothed and furious with himself for letting that cunning female back him into a corner.

"I can't decide what date to pick for the weddin'," Tweed went on as he limped back to the buggy they had borrowed from Casity. "I'd rather not have this splint hamperin' me on our honeymoon. But I dunno if I can wait another three weeks to marry that girl and have her cuddled up beside me."

If Tweed didn't cease painting those vivid verbal pictures, Shaler was sure he'd explode with frustration. "I don't want you to marry her," he declared vehemently. "She's only using you. Mark my words, Tweed, you'll regret it."

Tweed heaved himself onto the carriage seat and lifted his stiff leg into place. "I'm gonna tell you this just once more, Shay, and I never wanna have this conversation again. I'm entitled to a wife if'n I want one and can afford to keep one—which I do and I can. Nothin' you can say will change my mind."

Shaler sank onto the seat and took up the reins. His attempt to convince Tweed that his ladylove was all wrong for him was an utter failure. That left Shaler with one of two options, neither of which would endear him to his father. But it was better for Tweed to be furious for a month than sorry for the rest of his life.

Beginning this very evening, Shaler intended to find a way to rout that auburn-haired troublemaker from the cabin. He had become more aware of her with each passing hour, more befuddled by his own irrationality. Priscilla Lambert had to go, by hook or by crook!

Pondering that thought, Shaler aimed the buggy toward the cabin. He was going to force that woman out of Tweed's life, for his own good. She belonged with a man like Reece Pendleton, curse her manipulative hide! As far as Shaler was concerned those two deserved each other!

Thirteen

When Tweed suggested that Casity accompany Shaler to Deadwood to do their errands, Casity immediately balked. "I'd prefer to wait until you can go into town with me," she insisted, turning pleading eyes to Tweed.

"That's mighty sweet of you, honey, but the trip is too long for me while I'm on the mend. My leg is already achin' something awful after ridin' out to survey the new claim. Yer gettin' around purty good. You don't have to wear yer splint at all," he noted as he placed a heaping sack of gold nuggets in her hand. "I need more time to recuperate. In the meantime, I want you to go to town to buy some fancy dresses. And while yer there, pick out some curtains and other accessories for the cabin. This place needs a woman's touch."

This place needs the woman gone! Shaler silently amended. And if things worked out according to plan, Priscilla wouldn't be making the return trip. This was his opportunity to shove her out of the way for good. Snide remarks hadn't worked worth a damn. Now he'd escalate his efforts to get her out of his life!

"Tweed, I have no need for more clothes," Casity tried to object. "And I—"

Tweed flung up a stubby hand to silence her protest. "Nonsense, sugar. I want you to have all the things a woman needs." He half-turned to glance at his adopted son. "Most women would be whinin' and beggin' for comforts and luxuries, but not my sweet bride-to-be. Ain't she somethin', Shay?"

"Yeah, she's something, all right," Shaler muttered as he clamped hold of Casity and practically dragged her out the door. "I'll be sure to see that she gets exactly what she deserves."

Casity didn't like the sound of his remark! He seemed a little *too* anxious to be on their way.

After Shaler tied his steed behind the carriage, he bustled Casity onto the seat, leaving her staring beseechingly at Tweed. "Please don't make me go. I'd rather stay here with you."

"No need to fret, puddin'," Tweed reassured her. "Shay will take good care of you. Now buy yerself somethin' purty to wear for me, ya hear?"

When Tweed blew Casity a kiss, Shaler snapped the reins over the horse's back. The buggy lurched forward, flinging Casity against the back of the seat. Her legs flew up in front of her and she had to grab Shaler's forearm to keep from somersaulting out of the carriage.

"You beast," she hissed as she righted herself. "You did that on purpose."

Shaler's unrepentant smile made his eyes twinkle. "At least you're smart enough to know it."

"So that's what you're planning," Casity accused. "That's just what I thought."

"*What* is just what you thought?"

"I'm going to have an accident en route to town, aren't I? First it was whiplash. What next? A nasty fall from the buggy at high speed?"

Shaler smiled mischievously. "One never knows what hand Fate will deal, does one? I guess that's why we call those unexpected occurrences *accidents*."

Casity anchored her fingers around the edge of her

seat while Shaler popped the reins again, sending the
steed into a reckless clip around a horseshoe bend.
She had already had one nerve wracking ride in the
stagecoach and wasn't anxious to endure another!

"Slow this thing down!" she blustered furiously.

Shaler stamped on the brake, catapulting Casity forward. If she hadn't caught herself, she would have been
thrown onto the horse's back and trampled under its
hooves.

While Casity was pulling herself back onto the seat,
Shaler inched nearer. Before she could notice, his arm
snaked around her waist. She found herself flat on
her back, pressed to the seat beneath Shaler.

"Let me up, you big ape!" she fumed.

Shaler ignored her and shifted so that his body half-
covered hers. "I've been thinking it over." His head
moved purposely toward hers. "Since Tweed is bound
and determined to marry you, I don't see why I
shouldn't enjoy a few fringe benefits. There's no need
for me to travel all the way to Deadwood for feminine
attention. Of course, I'll pay you. While Tweed is out
tending chores at the mines, you can be nice to me.
And knowing how passionate you can be, I'm sure you
can keep both of us satisfied."

Casity braced her hands on his chest to hold him at
bay. "You're a despicable fool," she muttered. "Since
lust is your constant state of being, you should be used
to it by now. I'm not a handy outlet for physical release!
And don't think I won't tell Tweed about your disgusting proposition because I most certainly will!"

"No, you won't," Shaler contradicted. Despite her
attempt to keep him at arm's length, his lips feathered over her flushed cheek. "Every time I touch you
I can feel your body responding. You're just as addicted to this as I am. You're the kind of woman who
enjoys cuckolding one man and toying with another.

You haven't told Tweed what went on between us behind his back yet and you never will."

"Get away from me!" Casity screeched as his mouth descended on hers, silencing any further protest.

She wormed and squirmed, but to no avail. Shaler's weight easily held her in place. Casity did all she could, vowing to feel absolutely nothing but repulsion. She would lie there like a slab of stone, offering no encouragement or response whatsoever. When this amber-eyed devil tired of his game he would release her, knowing she had enough willpower to resist him.

A wry smile pursed Shaler's lips when he felt Casity stiffen beneath him. "Do you honestly believe you can pretend indifference, princess?"

"You can kiss me 'til the sun goes down, Shaler McCain, and I'll still be indifferent," she declared defiantly.

"Is that so?" His thick brows rose at the challenge.

"You might as well plant a kiss on yonder rock."

Shaler's lips hovered a few inches from her mouth. "Even rocks have been known to melt, princess, and so will you, I'll wager . . ."

"Not for you, Devil McCain. Never again!" she vowed fiercely.

Shaler promised himself that he would make her enjoy her defeat. He was determined to break this hellion's spirit once and for all—before she broke his! He would make her beg for his touch. When they reached Deadwood, she would be too mortified to accompany him back to the cabin. This scheme was foolproof, he thought proudly. She'd be afraid to return to Bonanza Gulch because she'd realize at long last that she was no match for him.

"I do hope you don't plan to waste a great deal of my time with some futile experiment," Casity flung at him. "I don't want to miss lunch—"

Casity swallowed her breath when his hands began to wander. She mustered her willpower and counted to ten—backwards—twice. "There, you see? You're having no effect whatsoever."

His lips flitted over her like a hummingbird. His tongue stabbed sensuously into her mouth before he nipped lightly at her bottom lip. His thumb slid over her chin to monitor her pulse as he smiled against her lush mouth.

"Still nothing, princess?" he whispered in amusement.

"Nothing," she lied for spite . . . and for her pride.

"I've lost my touch then?"

His thumb glided across her collarbone. The buttons of her gown seemed to dissolve beneath his deft ministrations. Casity flinched at the tender but unexpected touch of his forefinger skimming the pebbled crest of her breast.

His brow arched as he took the hardened tip between his fingers and tenderly plucked until her back involuntarily arched and a helpless sigh tumbled free. "Your sweet body doesn't lie, princess," he whispered as he bent his raven head to capture the dusky bud. "Admit it. Whatever is between us is *definitely not* indifference."

"I don't want to want you . . ." Casity rasped, as if speaking the words could make it so.

"Nor I you," Shaler admitted huskily. "But the wanting is there, princess, like a fire that continues to feed its own flames . . ."

Shaler suddenly lost sight of his original purpose. He hadn't intended to react to the feel of her luscious body melting like summer rain beneath his all-too-sensitive fingertips. This was to have been a strategic maneuver. He had only intended to prove that she was no match for him.

But when he lost himself in those petal-soft lips,

that was all the reason he needed to kiss her. Rediscovering every responsive point on her curvaceous body was reward aplenty. Shaler's hands had developed a will of their own. They moved beneath Casity's tattered petticoats, longing to touch her even more familiarly than he had that first night. And, all too late, he realized his obsessive longing had sneaked up to swallow him alive.

Casity's breath came in ragged spurts when his butterfly caresses ascended up her leg to swirl over the soft flesh of her inner thighs. She could feel her defenses eroding, feel those forbidden sensations streaking through her like lightning. Her heart froze when his fingertips glided higher—touching, teasing, tormenting. When his lips whispered over the tips of her breasts, Casity lost the will to fight.

She was a discredit to her gender! A weak, spineless creature ruled by desire instead of logic. Despite everything, Shaler could still twist her insides into hot, aching knots, making her want him with every fiber of her being. She had spouted her defiance at this infuriating man who was making her retract her words, one shivering response at a time. When was she ever going to learn that she had met her match in Shaler McCain? She had tried to spite him and reject him, but she always fell victim to his charms. She was a hopeless cause, fighting an impossible battle.

Shaler levered Casity into a half-reclined position on the seat and knelt between her legs, his hands refusing to remain still for even a moment. The taste of her fragrant skin was on his lips, fogging his senses. He ached to explore every inch of this beguiling siren, to appease this maddening need that spurred him on mercilessly.

While he suckled at her breasts, his hand splayed across her satiny hip, pushing the fabric of her pantaloons out of his way. His fingertips drifted along the quivering flesh of her thigh and he heard her breathless gasp when he cupped the delta of curls that guarded the sweet secrets he had once discovered in a forbidden dream. His fingertip glided into the silvery heat of desire he had called from her, eliciting another moan. Mesmerized, he watched her head tilt back and her lashes flutter shut as he traced the sultry folds and felt the warm rain of her response luring him deeper.

Shaler felt his manhood grow hard when her body contracted around his fingertip. Fire splintered through him when pleasure coiled inside her and her breath broke on a ragged sigh. He knew he would never be satisfied until she was his again—completely. He needed to watch her grow faint with rapture and follow her into mindless ecstasy. He yearned to hear his name on her lips in whispered cries of hopeless abandon.

"No! Please . . . No!" Casity choked out when a fireburst of sensations overshadowed the nagging voices of pride and conscience.

Shaler gloried in the sensual spasms that drenched her body, felt her nails biting into his shoulders as he parted her thighs to fully explore the soft, molten core of femininity.

"I want to touch you everywhere, to taste you . . . to claim you in ways I've never dared before . . ." he murmured achingly.

His mouth moved over her and the thrust of his tongue began the uncontainable responses he longed to share with her. Shaler felt the convulsive sensations rock her body and vibrate through him until every nerve and muscle was knotted in need. A quiet groan rumbled in Shaler's chest as his fingertips and tongue ignited yet another sweet explosion that rippled through her body into his. What she felt, he felt, and the incredible intimacy they had shared with no others drove him over the brink.

The silky heat of her response was on his lips, his fingertips. Her fists bit into the muscles of his arms and she held onto him as he shifted her once again to pleasure her with secret intimacies he had never wanted to offer any other woman. It was as if he were living through each explosive sensation.

"Shay, no—!" Casity gasped in wild disbelief, when unbearable pleasure shivered through her.

"Yes, princess," he whispered, spellbound. "I want to give you the sun and feel you give it back to me—"

When she cried out his name hoarsely, Shaler knew he was hopelessly lost. He no longer cared about the consequences, no longer cared that he had seduced her in broad daylight, and on the seat of a borrowed buggy. He was quaking with needs so profound that nothing except pleasuring her and taking absolute possession of this bewitching beauty could satisfy him.

Shaler hated feeling so completely out of control, but when he gazed up into that exquisite face that reflected the wild passion he had called from her, self-control abandoned him. He was clutching at the buttons of his breeches, hungry to feel the warm heat of her response folding around him like liquid silk, engulfing him.

Perhaps it was true that restraint cleansed the soul and soothed the troubled conscience, but it was definitely hell on a man's body! Shaler had kept his distance longer than he could stand. He was a man who had battled addiction—and lost. Nothing seemed as necessary and urgent as this gigantic need that crashed through him like thunder.

Savoring and devouring this lovely imp in the most intimate of ways had only intensified his craving. To feel himself gliding into that silken fire was the only truth his mind and body could understand.

When he guided her thighs apart with his knees and moved toward her, Shaler saw the haunted expression in her sapphire eyes. He knew he was seeing the reflection of his own tormented feelings as his body settled deep within hers. They both resented this fierce attraction to each other. Yet, they could no more stop the onrush of forbidden passion than they could change the course of the tides.

When the wild, sweet fire that raged between them blazed hotter, Shaler felt himself sizzling in passion's raging flame. He clutched Casity to him, tearing every last thought from his mind. He drove into her, caught up in needs as ancient and instinctive as time itself. The breathless rhythm of their passion demanded all his strength and emotion. He couldn't stop himself from wanting her—wildly, desperately, completely. He couldn't let her go without losing a part of himself!

That dizzying thought didn't have time to take root before the world burst in a kaleidoscope of radiant colors. Shudders of ecstasy undulated through him. One aftershock after another riddled his spent body as he clung to Casity, gasping for breath, afraid to release her for fear he would be flung into infinity.

This devastating passion had been exactly like the first time, only better—or worse, depending on one's perspective. Hell's fire, his addiction for this auburn-haired nymph had become as tangible as the feel of her trembling body molded intimately to his. If he didn't get her out of his blood and out of his life—immediately—He was going to be a man so possessed that every thought, every emotion would depend on her. He would be doomed to disaster!

Shaler had met a few men in his time who had become so captivated that their very world revolved around a woman. The poor wretches lived and breathed for those soft, feminine creatures. Shaler recalled that one time a decade earlier he had been on the verge of that kind of idiocy himself. But, in the nick of time, he had realized the light of his life was a heartless sorceress who was using him as a stud while she enjoyed the luxuries provided by her wealthy, elderly husband.

And now history was trying to repeat itself! Shaler had become obsessed by his soon-to-be-stepmother. He couldn't let that happen! He couldn't live with himself if it did. He was already being tortured by so much guilt and desire that he was torn apart inside. Before long he wouldn't even be the master of his soul!

When Shaler opened his eyes and realized where he was and what he had done, it tormented and mortified him. He hadn't even bothered to remove all their clothes in his haste. Although Priscilla was definitely a conniving female, she didn't deserve to be seduced on the seat of a borrowed buggy in broad daylight. Had he lost all his good sense?

Shaler didn't see how Priscilla could hate him more than he hated himself at this moment. Yes, he had intended to drive her away from Bonanza Gulch, but not by ravishing her like a starved tiger! Didn't he have one shred of decency or willpower left? He couldn't say *no* to this bewitching enchantress. He had no shame!

A horrified gasp escaped Casity's lips when reality hit her. Lord, the things she had let him do! She had lost all sense of personal pride—and in a buggy beside the road, of all places!

Her gown rode high on her hips and her breasts were bare. And worse, she had practically clawed Shaler's shirt off him in her efforts to touch him as intimately as he had touched her. She had allowed her desires to rule her, refusing to consider the consequences while this blinding passion ran its course.

Casity had to put some distance between them or she would never be able to live with herself. Sometimes she wished Uncle Daniel's murderers had caught up with her and put her out of her misery. Her life had been a shambles since that terrible night!

Despite Casity's attempt to maintain her composure, it cracked like eggshells. Tears dripped down her cheeks as she clutched her gown to cover herself and struggled to sit upright. She couldn't stop crying, even after she had sworn up and down that this horrible man would never see her blubbering again.

This would have been the perfect opportunity for Shaler to ridicule this tangle-haired beauty, but he didn't have the heart. Instead, he fastened himself into his clothes, retrieved the reins, to put the steed into a trot. His gaze focused on the rocky path while he chewed himself up one side and down the other.

"You have your wish," Casity choked out a half-mile later. "I'm not going back to Bonanza Gulch. Tell Tweed whatever you like. I don't care . . ." She drew a ragged breath and blinked back the infuriating tears. "It might also please you to know you've turned me against men to such a degree that I'm swearing off them for the rest of my life!"

Shaler squeezed his eyes shut and viciously cursed himself. "I—"

"Don't say one word, damn you." Casity blinked back another rush of emotion. "I don't care if I'm penniless and starving, I wouldn't come crawling back to you or your father. There will be no bribes, no blackmail. I want nothing from either of you—"

Her words trailed off into a shuddering sob. Shaler sat stiffly beside her. He and Tweed were finally free of this witch. That was what he wanted, wasn't it? Then why did he feel like such an abominable ass? Damnation, nothing had gone according to his plans. He felt sick to his soul.

"Here." Casity grabbed his right hand and stuffed the pouch of gold nuggets into it. "I'm sure your whores expect payment for their services." She muffled a sniff and forced herself to continue. "But I don't want your money or Tweed's. You taught me a lesson that can't be bought for any price. I want nothing to remind me that I ever knew you! I hate you!"

With that, Casity dissolved into a torrent of tears.

Shaler had believed that he could handle any situation, but this one had him stymied. There were times, he decided, when saying nothing was the best a man could do. Besides, he could almost feel the hatred and contempt emanating from this nymph's petite body. She looked so fragile and vulnerable that if he said anything he was afraid she'd disintegrate before his very eyes.

Hell's fire, revenge was such a destructive emotion. Shaler had been intent on defeating this strong-minded female. Now that he had, he felt nothing but more guilt and regret. Who the hell said revenge was sweet? Vengeance only showed a man how low he could stoop—and Shaler didn't like the way it made him feel. Even a snake had a better view than Shaler did at the moment! He was a discredit to his name, an ungrateful son, a heartless bastard who deserved every curse Priscilla Lambert hurled at him.

The instant Shaler pulled the carriage to a halt in town, Casity climbed down and limped across the boardwalk. Heaving a deep sigh, Shaler hopped to the ground and headed toward Reece Pendleton's office. Without bothering with the amenities, he informed Reece that the borrowed carriage had been returned.

"I also have a claim I've decided to sell," Shaler added. "Are you interested?"

Reece eased back in his chair. "I might be. Where's the mine?"

"Mule's Ear Gulch. The water rights go with it."

"Why are you selling?" Reece questioned curiously.

"We don't have the time or equipment to mine the claim properly," Shaler explained. "We can barely keep up with the one near our cabin. Now that Tweed has a broken leg, he can't manage much traveling."

"I'll ride out and look at the mine in a few days," Reece offered. "If it looks to have possibilities, I'll buy the claim."

"Fair enough." Shaler spun on his heel to exit as abruptly as he had entered.

"Oh, by the way, has Miss Lambert completed her obligations to Tweed?" Reece queried interestedly. "She told me he was to be her employer while he was on the mend."

Shaler frowned at Reece's expectant expression. It seemed Priscilla had left herself another option, in case her marriage and her attempt to blackmail Shaler fell through. No wonder she had decided to abandon Bonanza Gulch! She probably planned to turn her attention to Reece. And what did Shaler care if she did?

Shaler's thoughts trailed off when one of Reece's hired men burst through the door, grinning in amusement.

"Boss, you gotta see this! Remember that pretty piece of fluff who arrived in town last week? Well, she's back. She called a crowd of men out of the saloons and put herself up for auction to the highest bidder!"

"What?" Shaler hooted in disbelief.

"She claims she'll cook and clean and care for whoever takes the bid. She's selling herself out for hire for two weeks."

Shaler was out the door and gone before Reece's employee could catch his breath. To Shaler's stunned amazement, Casity stood atop a crate, a swarm of men around her. Shaler would have stormed over to yank her off her pedestal, but he was afraid he'd incite a riot.

This was all his fault, he thought sickly. He had humiliated this woman to such an extreme that she had plunged over the edge. Hell's fire, he couldn't even make a bid to save her from this ridiculous auction. She would reject him, even if he offered her five hundred dollars in gold. God, what a mess!

"And all arrangements will be null and void if the highest bidder refuses to behave like a perfect gentleman," Casity stipulated as she addressed the large crowd.

As if there was a perfect gentleman anywhere on the planet, Casity thought cynically. But it didn't matter, not anymore. Nothing did. No one could humiliate her more than Shaler McCain already had. If she could deal with that devilish scoundrel then she could deal with anyone! Thanks to Shaler she was beyond caring. She merely existed, endured and survived.

When her gaze settled on Shaler, who towered over the rest of the crowd, anguish cut through her like a double-edged sword. Casity couldn't bear to look at him because the very sight of him provoked too many bittersweet memories.

"I'll give fifty dollars for two weeks," someone spoke up.

"I'll give one hundred," came another eager bid.

"One twenty-five."

"One *thousand* dollars . . ."

A hush fell over the crowd. The men turned in synchronized rhythm to see Reece Pendleton swaggering forward to collect his prize.

"*One thousand dollars,*" he repeated as he reached up

to lift Casity down beside him. "The entertainment is over, gentlemen. The lady is coming with me."

When Reece propelled her toward his office above the Gold Nugget Saloon, Casity looked the other way when she passed shoulder-to-shoulder beside Shaler. She knew she had lived up to his low estimation of her, but she didn't give a damn what he thought. Her behavior had been totally irrational and impulsive.

Casity had been desperate for funds and a place to stay while she recovered from her humiliating ordeal. She only knew she had to be sure Shaler would never come near her again, not for any reason. Now that she'd be paid one thousand dollars for two week's work, she could hire a bounty hunter and see to it that her uncle's killers were punished. After that, Casity didn't care what happened to her. She was leaving Deadwood, never to return. That should make that dark-haired devil happy!

With a triumphant smile, Reece escorted Casity up the steps to his office. He had been surprised to find this lovely lady on the auction block, but he was delighted with his new prize. She was well worth the price to have her all to himself for two weeks. Of course, he had no intention of obeying her hands-off policy; with some gentle coaxing, he was sure she'd succumb. Reece could be a very persuasive man when he wanted to be. After all, he had convinced dozens of stockholders to invest in his mining company, hadn't he?

"When this town simmers down, we're going to find you the most fashionable gowns Deadwood has to offer. All charged to my account, of course," Reece insisted.

"That isn't necessary," Casity said dully.

"Perhaps not, my dear, but you bring out the generous side of my nature." He reached out to trace the delicate curve of her cheek. "Your beauty should be enhanced by fine clothing. And I want to show you off."

If Reece wanted her to scrub floors and wash windows in expensive gowns, that was fine with Casity. It was his money, after all. But if he thought for one second that he could buy her affection, he was sorely mistaken. Casity was offering herself as a housekeeper and companion and that was the beginning and end of it. Never again would she allow herself to be manipulated into another compromising position. If Reece came near her, Casity would close her eyes and visualize Shaler's handsome face. She would remember her shame.

Reece's light touch against her cheek couldn't stir a smidgen of feeling within her—not repulsion, not pleasure, nothing. Casity was immune to him. Only one man could crack her defenses, but she would never let that particular man close enough to humiliate her again. After dealing with Shaler McCain, men like Reece Pendleton would be mere stepping-stones, not stumbling blocks in this nightmarish misadventure she referred to as her life!

"After we've made the purchases, my sweet, we'll enjoy the best meal money can buy," Reece promised.

Casity nodded mutely after he dropped the heavy pouch of gold in her hand and shepherded her toward the door. Reece could tempt her with gowns and meals, but that wasn't going to change their bargain. He bought himself a maid and companion for a fortnight, not a willing lover.

Casity cursed the haunting image that floated in her mind as she ambled down the boardwalk, battling another flood of tears. She hated him because he had made her hate herself. He had stolen the very life from her. She was aching to the roots of her soul because she couldn't resist that amber-eyed devil who brought her both agony and ecstasy. Curse him! And curse her for letting him break her spirit!

Fourteen

Shaler strode into the Bella Union Saloon to drown his misery in a bottle of whiskey. He scolded himself for feeling responsible for Priscilla's rash actions. She had certainly livened up Deadwood with her outrageous auction! The town was buzzing and the incident was beating Shaler's conscience black and blue. He tried to assure himself that she had only gotten what she deserved. But deep down inside, Shaler knew he had treated Priscilla Lambert in ways no man should treat another human being, woman or no.

Shaler closed his eyes and swallowed a jigger of whiskey in one gulp. It didn't numb his guilty conscience or ease his troubled thoughts. He could still visualize those shiny tears that boiled down her cheeks.

Knowing she was at Reece Pendleton's mercy, while in her present state of mind, tore Shaler up inside. He shouldn't have cared what became of her, but he *did* care, too much for his own good.

"Shaler McCain? Is that you?"

Shaler pivoted away from the bar toward the oddly familiar voice. His eyes widened in surprise when he spied the strikingly handsome face beneath a black pancake hat. James Butler Hickok sat alone at a corner table in his customary manner—his back to the wall. It had been fifteen years since Shaler had crossed paths with the man who had become a legend in the cowtowns of Kansas and in the Buntline Wild West Show that toured the East. Since those early days when Shaler, Tweed, and James had roamed the mountains of Colorado and New Mexico together, James had been nicknamed "Wild Bill" and his reputation as a pistolero had spread far and wide.

James had been a young man of twenty the first time Shaler had met him. After guiding a wagon train to the California gold fields, James had returned to Denver to work as a hunter and trapper in the Rockies. That was where Tweed and Shaler had met him for the first time. For the next three years James had shared their cabin as they traveled through the rugged mountain passes, living off the land, honing survival skills against man and beast. James was only three years younger than Tweed and both men had cared for and instructed their half-grown ward, who had learned all he could from them.

When James had been mauled by a bear at Raton Pass, Shaler and Tweed had nursed him back to health. James still carried the grizzly's scars on his shoulders and chest—he had very nearly been scalped by the swat of those deadly claws. Since James had needed time to recuperate, he had accepted a job as a stock-tender at the Overland Stage Company at East Rock Creek Station in Nebraska Territory.

That was the last time Shaler had seen the muscularly built, blond-haired shootist. Although Shaler had read reports about James's incredible skill with his ivory-handled revolvers, he had seen the sharpshooter in action years earlier and had profited by the instruction James had given him. In fact, Shaler had become James's protege during their three years together. Everything Shaler knew about handling weapons he had learned from the master himself.

When the Civil War erupted, James had enlisted

and served as a scout and occasionally as a spy for the Union forces. James—or "Wild Bill," as he had come to be known thereafter—had turned his talents to marshaling in the riotous cowtowns of Hays City and Abilene, Kansas, after the war ended.

"Good Lord, boy!" James chuckled as he sized up the brawny man who ambled toward him. "You grew considerably since the last time I saw you." He unfolded his six-foot-one-inch frame from the chair and measured himself against Shaler. "You grew up *a lot!*"

"I was only thirteen the first time you saw me," Shaler reminded him as he clasped James's hand, giving it a fond squeeze. "And what the devil are you doing in Deadwood?"

James dropped back into his seat and pulled out the vacant chair beside him so that neither of them had to turn their backs on the other occupants of the saloon. "After I got tired of entertaining the Easterners with the Wild West Show, I guided several miners to Dakota when Custer claimed there was gold in the hills." James shook his blond head and sighed ruefully. "Custer should have resigned his commission in the army and took to mining. His luck really ran out when he confronted Crazy Horse and his warriors."

"The crushing defeat against the army has all the tribes stirred up," Shaler reported bleakly. "Three renegades attacked one of the stages en route to Deadwood a few weeks ago. There were other raids up by Jackass Gulch and Sweet Betsy Gulch a few days earlier. Between the Indian uprisings and the robberies by Big Nose George and his outlaw gang, Dakota has become a trouble spot." He scrutinized James for a long moment. "Are you planning to tame this place down?"

James gave his head a shake. "I've had my fill of marshaling. I thought I'd try my hand at mining. Might as well." He shrugged lackadaisically. "I've done everything else at least once in my life. I even got married four months ago."

"You?" Shaler croaked like a sick bullfrog.

"Me," James affirmed. "But the civilized life just wasn't my style. Agnes went off to visit her relatives and I agreed to bring a train of prospectors to Dakota. When I made the return trip to Cheyenne, I met up with Colorado Charley and we decided to do some prospecting together. Maybe after a month or two I'll be ready to try settling down again."

"And in the meantime, you can expect to be hounded about pinning on a badge to clean up Dead-wood," Shaler predicted. "I've already been approached by the miners three times myself. But I have other business here."

James eyed his handsome friend speculatively. "Are you still as fast on the draw as you used to be when you were just a kid?"

Shaler shrugged, grinned, and sipped his drink. "I'm adequate."

"Adequate?" James chuckled at Shaler's modesty. "You were faster than greased lightning after I taught you to handle a six-shooter." A curious frown creased his brow as he scrutinized Shaler. "Just what brought you to Deadwood, if not mining?"

Shaler lifted his glass to his lips and smiled wryly over the rim. "Why don't you come back to the cabin and surprise Tweed and we'll discuss the matter in private."

James's blue eyes widened. "Tweed is here, too?"

"He's here," Shaler confirmed. "He's nursing the broken leg he suffered chasing his runaway mule down the ravine. He stumbled over some exposed tree roots and discovered a rich vein of gold at the base of the tree where he lay howling in pain."

Laughter exploded from James. "Struck it rich by

accident, did he? That sounds like Tweed." After James polished off his drink, he rose to full stature. "I'm anxious to see that old buzzard again. He razzed me unmercifully when I met with that unsociable grizzly in Raton Pass. Now's my chance to repay him."

Renewing his acquaintance with James Butler Hickok was just the diversion Shaler needed to take his mind off Priscilla. He had even managed *not* to think about her for a whole quarter of an hour. But he found himself paying penance when he and James parted company to collect their horses before meeting at the edge of town. Shaler had just swung into the saddle when Priscilla emerged from the dry goods store, laden with packages—compliments of Reece Pendleton, no doubt.

Shaler could see her retreat farther into herself at the sight of him. But he felt compelled to speak, even if she despised the sound of his voice and the bitter memories that his presence evoked.

"Don't do this, princess. You'll regret it. Reece Pendleton will only bring you trouble," Shaler warned softly.

Her chin jutted out and her blue eyes sparked fire. "Don't tell me what to do, damn you. And don't talk to me about trouble and regret. I have regretted the day I met you and each day since. Don't ever come near me again. I want to forget I ever knew you!"

On the wings of that bitter remark, Casity scurried off without waiting for Reece to emerge from the store. She bit back the sob that bubbled in her throat.

Casity hadn't been able to put much distance between them before Shaler noticed her tears. With a heavy heart and a nagging conscience, he reined his sorrel gelding toward the outskirts of town to meet Hickok. It was high time he concentrated on his purpose for traveling to Deadwood. He had scads of arrangements to make. With Hickok's help, perhaps he could set his trap and catch the rat he had been sent to Dakota to snare.

Tweed stumbled back against the wall and plopped into his chair when James Butler Hickok ambled inside the cabin as if he owned the place.

"What in tarnation are you doin' here?" Tweed hooted incredulously.

"Broke your leg, did you, Tweed?" James snickered as he sauntered inside to tower over his old friend. "Let me have a look at it." He hunkered down to inspect the splints that encased Tweed's right leg. "You aren't as surefooted as you used to be, it seems. You're getting old, my friend. Shaler should have put you out to pasture years ago."

"I ain't much older than you are." Tweed scowled while James inspected the leg with wicked glee. "I'm just more mature than some folks near my age who waltz in, tryin' to scare a body half to death!"

James's expression sobered as he outstretched his hand. "It's good to see a friendly face. Nowadays, wherever I go, there's always some cocky young gunslinger eager to challenge me to better his reputation."

"You shoulda stuck with huntin' and trappin' like I told you," Tweed declared.

"You're the one who said I should find another occupation since I couldn't wrestle a grizzly without getting chewed to pieces," James reminded him.

"Did I say that?" Tweed's broad grin displayed the gap between his teeth.

"You most certainly did," James confirmed.

"Well, I didn't mean for you to disappear for fifteen years!" Tweed gestured toward the empty chair beside him. "Sit yerself down and tell me if all them rumors

I've heard about you are true. Shay can fix us some supper while we're—'' His voice drifted off when he glanced at the doorway. "Where is she?"

Shaler shifted uneasily from one foot to the other. He had hoped Hickok's arrival would make Tweed forget his missing bride-to-be. No such luck. Shaler wasn't looking forward to giving an account of Priscilla's disappearance. Tweed was going to be irritated, sure as hell.

"She stayed in town," Shaler mumbled as he closed the door behind him.

"What for?" Tweed asked impatiently.

"She *who?*" James interjected curiously.

"Tweed's mail-order bride," Shaler muttered. "The old fool sent off for a female to fuss over him in his dotage, but he wound up with a woman he couldn't handle, even on a day when he had two good legs under him."

For the moment, Hickok was forgotten. Tweed focused his penetrating glare on his adopted son. "You ran her off, didn't you? You've been tryin' to get rid of her since she showed up."

"Well, damn it, it was for your own good," Shaler blurted. "You don't need a wife and you never have. Just ask James what he thinks of wedlock. He tied the matrimonial knot four months ago and here he is in Dakota, panning for gold. Some men aren't cut out to be husbands. James is one and he freely admits to it. You're another one, Tweed!"

Tweed glanced at Hickok, who had sprawled back in his chair to listen to the rapid-fire exchange. "Yer married?" he chirped in astonishment.

"Sort of."

"What the hell do you mean *sort of?*" Tweed persisted. "Either a man is or he ain't. Now which is it?"

James's shoulder rose in a nonchalant shrug. "Some

men just have too much tumbleweed in their blood to settle down. I tried the life of leisure for as long as I could. But a few months of high society at a time is all I can manage. Agnes understands my need to roam. She knows I'll be back after I've answered the call of the wild."

"And what's the story on this Calamity Jane character I've been hearin' about who's been chasin' after you all these years?" Tweed quizzed.

James's blue eyes twinkled as he glanced at Shaler and then at Tweed. "As for Jane, she's always been crazy about me. There are some women a man just can't shake, no matter how hard he tries. She followed me to Deadwood, even after she found out I was married."

"It seems there are some men who just don't have enough brains to keep a good woman when they find one." Tweed aimed the remark at Shaler, along with a fuming glare. "It only goes to prove that every jackass prides hisself in thinkin' he's got horse sense!"

Shaler scowled after the insult. "For chrissakes, Tweed, she's gone and she isn't coming back. Priscilla and I had . . . words . . . on the way to town." That wasn't all they'd had, but Shaler wasn't about to elaborate. He felt bad enough as it was. "Priscilla decided to stay in town and she auctioned herself off to the highest bidder for two weeks of domestic duties and female companionship—of the most respectable kind," he felt compelled to reassure Tweed before he exploded like a keg of blasting powder. "Reece Pendleton paid a thousand dollars for the pleasure of her company."

"*SHE DID WHAT?*" Tweed bugled in astonishment. Like a cannonball, he burst out of his chair and stamped toward Shaler, brandishing his cane like a lethal weapon. "And what did *you* do to upset her so much that she'd do something as crazy as that?"

Shaler grimaced when Tweed looked as if he meant to strike him about the face and body with his cane. It couldn't have hurt Shaler more than the bites his conscience had been taking out of him, that was for sure. Shaler had expected Tweed to be upset, but not *this* upset!

"Answer me!" Tweed bellowed impatiently. "What did you say to her to send her tumblin' off the deep end?"

"Tell him," James encouraged. He crossed his arms over his chest and grinned while Tweed made stabbing gestures with his improvised sword. "You've certainly aroused my curiosity."

Shaler expelled an enormous sigh and sidestepped to avoid the blow that was headed his way. "I told Priscilla I would never allow this ridiculous marriage to take place because she was only using Tweed to get security and his wealth. Then I—" Shaler wisely chose to back away from his furious father. "—I told her that since she planned to trade her body for security she may as well pleasure the both of us like a common wh—"

"Damn you, Shay!" Tweed exploded. "How could you be so cruel and insultin'? I raised you better than that!"

Although Shaler did have the decency to look ashamed of what he had said and done, Tweed came at him like a cavalryman answering the signal to charge. Shaler agilely dodged the slash of the cane that was meant to knock some sense into him. Even if Tweed was positively livid and threatened to beat the stuffing out of him, Shaler was glad he had gotten the unpleasant incident off his chest. It was weighing him down like an anchor. True, Shaler regretted his actions and harsh words. But hell's fire, he had only done what was necessary. After all, he had done it for Tweed's own good!

After Tweed had wielded his makeshift sword and missed his target repeatedly, he aborted his attempt to beat his idiotic son black and blue. "Sit down over there and listen to me, you moron," he fumed. "I'm gonna enjoy the hell out of tellin' you what an ass you made of yerself." His green eyes narrowed into angry slits. "And you better listen good, too. We're gonna have a long talk that'll teach you not to stick yer nose in somebody else's business."

Tweed's annoyed gaze focused on Hickok, who had burst out in a snicker after watching Tweed chase Shaler around the room like a madman. "And you keep yer trap shut, James. By the time I get through, you'll think Shay's the lowest form of life on this earth!"

When Hickok wiped the grin off his face, Tweed took a deep breath, causing the lacings of his buckskin shirt to strain across his chest. "More than two weeks ago, I sent Shay to fetch my mail-order bride, bein' as how I had a bum leg. I gave him a fist full of nuggets to purchase anything her heart desired in hopes of makin' her life here more tolerable. But Shay didn't tote her back as I requested.

"I glanced up the hill one day to see a woman approachin' in a buggy—all by herself. 'Where's my son?' I asked myself. I sent him on a simple mission and he gets lost? Is this the same man who can pick his way through the wilderness with his eyes closed? Not damned likely, I assured myself."

His reproachful glare hammered into Shaler, who squirmed in his chair as if he were sitting on a cactus. "So there I stand, propped on my cane, siftin' gold dust from the *assarata*, waitin' for this beauty to rein her buggy to a halt. And down she steps on her injured leg to introduce herself. O' course, I'm thinkin' all my fantasies have come true because my mail-order bride is an angel sent straight from heaven. But the angel ain't meant for me, it seems. Instead, she hands me a letter from Priscilla Lambert who had second thoughts about travelin' to Dakota to marry a man she never met."

Shaler's mouth dropped open like a pelican's and his vocal cords collapsed in his throat.

" 'You ain't Priscilla?' I says to her. 'No,' she answers most politely. 'Well, would you like to be?' I asked her flat-out."

Shaler sank a little deeper in his chair and groaned.

"Sit up and pay close attention, Shay," Tweed demanded with fire in his eyes. "I ain't even half-done with this tale and you don't feel near as bad as yer gonna feel when I get through!"

Having scolded his son in the manner he so richly deserved, Tweed continued. "I could tell there was somethin' botherin' the purty little lady so I pressed her to tell me what it was since she seemed on the verge of tears. I offered her a glass of brandy to calm her nerves and a shoulder to lean on instead of accusin' her of everythin' in the book like some people I know." He glared at his son. "Next time, Shay, it would be wise for you to remember that *suspicion* ain't *proof! Ask* next time instead of *assumin'!*"

Tweed then proceeded with his explanation. "It turns out the little lady's name is Casity Crockett. She'd been havin' the worst round of bad luck—it took three glasses of brandy to pry the information outta her because she's too independent to even consider relyin' on anyone but herself."

Tweed dropped into the chair beside the table and poured himself a drink to cool his temper and lubricate his vocal cords. "She told me her parents came down with typhus when she was only twelve. Since there was nobody else to care for them, Casity tried to nurse them herself. And when they passed on, she believed she'd failed them and that it was *her* fault they'd died."

Tweed shook his head sadly and continued, but not before flinging his son another disapproving glance. "Casity's aunt and uncle came to fetch her from the farm where she grew up and they took her in as their own child. When her aunt died last year, Casity suffered yet another devastatin' loss. And as if that wasn't enough, she witnessed her uncle's murder in Ogallala, Nebraska, where the two of them owned a dry goods store. The two scoundrels who killed her uncle—her only livin' relative, by the way—chased after her to shut her up permanent-like. But what's infinitely worse is that she feels responsible for her uncle's death because her gasp of terror set off the chain reaction that caused the shootin'. She feels she's as much to blame as if she actually pulled the trigger!"

Tweed was right. Shaler was feeling worse by the second. This grim tale was tying his emotions in knots!

"Casity managed to jump a train bound for Cheyenne and that's where she met up with Priscilla, who had fallen under the spell of a silver-tongued gambler. Priscilla gave Casity the stage ticket and the letter to deliver to me. The only reason the poor girl showed up in Deadwood a-tall was because her life was in grave danger. Them two murderers were hot on her heels and she'd already dodged plenty of bullets with her name on 'em."

"Good Lord," Hickok murmured compassionately. "It's a wonder she didn't lie down and give up."

"She might've if'n she didn't have such incredible resilience and spunk," Tweed agreed. "But Casity

Crockett is made of sturdy stuff. Or at least she was until my charmin' ass of a son confronted her."

He paused to fling Shaler a glare that cut to the quick—and deeper. "Besides bein' chased by two killers who'd come up with a cattle drive from Texas, Casity was abducted from the stage by renegade Indians. And then along comes my exceptionally bright boy who didn't even bother to ask the lady if she was Priscilla Lambert. Oh no, he was too smart to waste his valuable time with insignificant questions! He rescued Casity, bandaged her injured leg, and then tried to buy her off with the sack of gold I sent along with him for her weddin' gifts. He lambasted her for tryin' to swindle me and threatened her if she dared to get anywhere close to me!"

Tweed shook his wiry red head and glowered at Shaler in disgust. "This is the thanks I get for raisin' you like my own flesh and blood, for feedin' you and carin' for you and teachin' you to be a man." He sighed deeply and plowed on. "Casity told me how rude you was to her, but she didn't ask for nothin' from me in the way of compensation. I insisted that she stay at the cabin to recuperate from her injury. I also told her I wanted to play along with the charade since you thought she was somebody else without botherin' to find out for sure. After what she told me, I was ready to let you stew in yer own juice for awhile, Shay. You made her so furious with yer threats and yer high-handed manner that she wasn't about to tell you the truth and I didn't blame her one damned bit!"

"God have mercy," Shaler mumbled dispiritedly. He wanted to crawl into a hole and die of shame and regret.

"If the Lord shows you any mercy, He's a better sport than I am," Tweed snorted disdainfully. "You've been holdin' a grudge against all women since that piece of fluff in Denver broke yer heart at a tender age. You *assumed* Casity was Priscilla and you *assumed* she was after my money, just because she committed the unpardonable sin of bein' born a woman."

Tweed muttered under his breath and flashed Shaler another disparaging glance. "Now you've tossed Casity in Reece Pendleton's lap. I wouldn't wish such things on my worst enemy and I sure as hell wouldn't wish that on a woman who has nowhere to go and no one to turn to for assistance. I was gonna let her stay as long as she liked so she could lie low. I'd grown damned fond of her, in fact. If I couldn't have a wife, I thought I'd enjoy some female companionship for awhile."

"I'm sorry," Shaler quietly apologized.

"You ain't nearly sorry enough to suit me!" Tweed snapped brusquely. "You ain't got as much conscience as a buffalo in a stampede. A sorrier excuse for a son I've never met, either! I don't rightly know if I tried to teach you proper manners too fast or if you just learned too damned slow, but if you feel like a heel after what you did, you sure as hell oughta! And the next time I fall off a cliff and break my other leg, I s'pect you'll just trample all over me instead of helpin' me up! All of a sudden you've turned out to be the kind of man who'd offer a drownin' victim a canteen of water!"

"Hell's fire, Tweed, I said I was sorry!" Shaler grumbled in frustration. "What do you want me to do to prove it?"

"Throw yerself headfirst off a mountain," Tweed spitefully suggested. "That oughta convince me yer sincere."

"Maybe you ought to make him crawl back to Miss Crockett on his hands and knees and apologize all over himself," Hickok inserted.

"Oh, Shay will do that all right," Tweed readily affirmed. "As soon as we have the mine in Mule's Ear Gulch salted and ready for Reece Pendleton's arrival, Shay is gonna pay Casity a visit. Even if she can't stand the sight of him, he's gonna make damned sure she listens to his apology." His gaze drilled into Shaler. "You hear me, boy?"

Who couldn't? Tweed's words were ricocheting off the rafters. Shaler felt awful. Tweed had always said that what a man did during the day he had to sleep with that night. And considering the torment Shaler had heaped on Casity, he doubted he would sleep at all for several nights to come! Now that he realized how honest Casity's intentions had been until he'd started hurling cruel accusations at her, it made him nauseous.

He couldn't blame her for reacting to him the way she had. She was contrary and high-spirited enough to balk at his harsh demands. She had been vulnerable and tormented by her past and he had taken her virginity and then ridiculed her. She had been reaching out for comfort and compassion to ease her burden and he had seduced her before jumping down her throat and treating her like the dirt beneath his feet. He had trounced on her feelings, wounded her pride, and attempted to buy her off. No wonder she despised him so thoroughly. She had a thousand excellent reasons for hating him and Shaler had a few hundred himself!

"First thing in the mornin' we're gonna head over to that new mine in Mule's Ear Gulch and get it ready to sell. And you better not botch this scheme up as royally as you did with Casity Crockett or I'll skin you alive," Tweed threatened venomously. "Casity deserved to have the last laugh and, by damn, she'll have it in due time. Yer gonna make that girl come back here so I can keep an eye on her. And she ain't leavin' this cabin until you manage to get back into her good graces neither! I don't care how mean and nasty she is to you, Shay. Yer gonna take everythin' she dishes out."

"She won't come back because she can't stand the sight of me," Shaler informed Tweed.

"Well, I wonder why!" he snorted derisively. "But whether she can stand you or not don't make no difference. You've got hell to pay and yer payin' it. If'n she wants to use you as her scapegoat then you'll become her whippin' boy. If she wants to walk all over you then you'll wear her footprints on yer back. Yer gonna be so nice to her that she won't be able to muster any more reasons to hate you. Yer gonna kill her with kindness if'n that's what it takes to repay all the hurt you heaped on her."

Shaler would have preferred to walk barefoot through hell's inferno. Facing Casity now that he knew the truth was going to be the hardest task he had ever undertaken.

Heaving an exasperated sigh, Tweed hobbled over to whack Shaler on the shoulder with the blunt end of his cane to relieve the rest of his frustration. "Now get outta my favorite chair and rustle up some supper. Me and James got a lot of catchin' up to do."

Shaler meekly did as he was told. And all the while he cursed himself but good. But after a few hours, the old curses lost their sting and he had to invent a few new ones to hurl at himself. Hell's fire, how was he going to get within ten feet of that lovely firebrand without inciting her wrath? Shaler figured he had about as much chance of gaining Casity Crockett's forgiveness as a fish had of swimming across Death Valley!

Fifteen

Casity stood in the middle of Reece Pendleton's luxurious suite while he circled around her, viewing one of his elegant purchases from every possible angle. Two weeks earlier, Casity would have resented such behavior in a man. Reece was studying her and her blue satin gown and matching plumed hat as if he were a prospective buyer examining a piece of horseflesh. But now that Casity had her pride and spirit stripped from her—courtesy of Shaler McCain—she had lost her panache and her vitality. She may as well have been a mannequin on display because she was no more than an empty shell.

Seeing Shaler was the only thing that could excite any emotion inside her. Because of that heartless devil she had lost contact with the only friend she had. Tweed had proven himself kind, caring, and considerate and she had looked upon him as a substitute for her father and uncle. He had respected the limits of their friendship and had demanded no more than her companionship. He had even agreed to play along to watch Shaler squirm like the worm he was . . .

"You look enchanting, my dear," Reece murmured as he swaggered around to face Casity. His index finger drifted over her cheek to trace the curve of her lips. "You and I are going to enjoy the pleasure of each other's company for the next few weeks."

No, she was going to *tolerate* his company, Casity silently amended. After Shaler's treachery, the thought of having a man touch her so familiarly left her feeling like a block of ice. Reece could be as charming and debonair as he pleased and she would allow him to think his gallantry was impressing her, if that's what he wanted. But he couldn't burrow his way into this shriveled cavity that had once held a heart, no matter what he did.

"Come along, sweetheart," Reece purred as he laid his hand on the small of her back to guide her toward the door. "I want to show you off to all my acquaintances. I'll be the envy of Deadwood."

Typical male, thought Casity. Men always delighted in latching onto a feminine trinket to flaunt in front of their friends. They cared nothing for a woman's true feelings as long as she did as she was told.

Well, just wait until these two weeks were over. Casity would be free of all obligation to any man! No one would ever use her for any purpose again. She was going to find a refuge in some remote valley and live like a hermit! And if any man dared to encroach upon her privacy she would frighten him away with a sawed-off shotgun—as soon as she learned how to use one!

Harboring that spiteful thought, Casity permitted Reece to escort her down the stairs and onto the street. Because of her outrageous behavior two days earlier, she found herself the object of a great deal of attention. Men hovered around her as if they were paying their respects to royalty. She had been every kind of fool to pit herself against Shaler McCain. She had lost more than she could ever hope to gain.

When Shaler set the long fuse inside the mine shaft in Mule's Ear Gulch, James Hickok frowned bemusedly. "What the devil are you doing? I thought you said you were going to sell this claim. So why bother opening it up?"

The earth shook and dust belched out of the tunnel. James stepped back a few paces to escape the fog rolling toward him.

"Have you ever heard of saltin' a borrasca?" Tweed quizzed.

Hickok gave his blond head a negative shake.

"And you came up here to pan gold?" Tweed smirked. "Yer gonna have to do some quick learnin' if'n yer gonna become a respectable miner."

"Luckily, I have an expert to teach me," James grunted sarcastically. "You always did claim to be an authority on just about everything, Tweed."

Shaler bit back a smile while Tweed and James practiced the playful camaraderie they had enjoyed in the old days. Listening to the two men razz each other brought back memories. James had come into Shaler's life at a time when he was trying to recover from the loss of his family. He had felt alone and disoriented and depressed. Nothing had mattered . . .

A sigh of torment escaped from his lips when he stumbled onto that thought. He knew exactly how Casity must have felt the night he had rescued her from the Indians. She, like he, had wanted to find something to hold onto in her anguish. She had been reaching out for strength, support, and solace. He had responded by deflowering her and then bombarding her with threats and insults. And to make matters worse, he had sent her a *red* flannel nightgown to imply what he thought of her. Not only that, but Shaler put on a spectacular display of discarding the saddle blanket upon which they had made love, carelessly tossing the symbolic object aside as if the loss of her innocence was insignificant to him. God, he had de-

moralized Casity and she hadn't deserved one ounce
of his ridicule!

Casity had been forced to leave everything she
owned behind to escape her pursuers in hopes of saving her life. She had no funds, except the bribe money
he had offered to get her out of Tweed's life. Shaler
was dreadfully sorry for being so cruel and merciless.
What an insensitive cad he had been! Damn it, she
should have told him the truth instead of limping off
without an explanation. He would have listened if she
had given him a chance . . . wouldn't he?

"Now pay attention, James," Tweed commanded.
"I'm only gonna tell you this once. A borrasca is an
unproductive mine. If you salt it with samples of rich
ore, you can attract foolish buyers to take it off yer
hands."

"That's illegal," James pointed out.

"Sure as hell is," Tweed agreed with a scampish grin.
"But if'n you wanna catch a sly fox, you gotta set a
cunnin' trap. The fox we got in mind is too wily to be
fooled by simple trickery. Some folks plant gold salts
in their claims before tryin' to sell them—"

"You mean the gold salt medication used to relieve
kidney complaints for those who imbibe too much
whiskey?" James questioned curiously.

"One and the same," Shaler confirmed. "Some of
the shrewder prospectors use a shotgun to salt hard-
rock mines. By splattering the face of a drift with car-
tridges filled with gold you can make it look as though
there's a rich vein deep in the shaft."

"The blastin' powder Shay used to set off this explosion contained gold dust from Bonanza Gulch and
Pine Gulch," Tweed explained, leaning against his
mule to rest his stiff leg. "In a matter of seconds, we
enriched the low-grade ore from this mine to make it
look profitable to a buyer. We'll also plant soluble gold

chloride in the new cracks to raise the assay value. Our prospective buyer can take samples from anywhere he chooses and he'll still think he's gettin' his hands on a rich strike."

"If I buy a claim, how will I know if I've been hornswoggled like the poor fella you're planning to swindle?" James queried.

"It's damned hard to be sure you haven't been cheated," Tweed admitted. "That's why me and Shay are gonna help you check out yer claim before you buy. And if you see rich ore just layin' around on the floor of the shaft, you can bet it's been planted. Even the laziest prospector in the world would've bent over to pick it up on his way out. But there's some fools who fall for them cheap tricks."

When the cloud of dust that filled the shaft finally settled, Shaler, Tweed, and James ventured inside. Tweed, of course, brought up the rear of the procession so he could remain close to the mouth of the cavern since he had an aversion to close spaces. After Shaler had poured gold chloride in the cracks to give the illusion of productive ore deep within the drift, the threesome trooped back outside.

"Are you going to tell me who and why you're planning to bamboozle an innocent man?" James inquired as he propped himself against a rock.

"Innocent?" Tweed sniffed caustically. "If he was innocent we wouldn't be settin' the pigeon up. Sometimes a con artist deserves a taste of his own medicine. Reece Pendleton used some of the same tactics to lure prospective stockholders into his minin' corporation. One of his investors is a friend of mine from Denver. The old goat struck it rich in the Rockies, but that wasn't enough for him. He invested fifteen thousand dollars in Pendleton's Mining Company and thus far he ain't received a penny in dividends. Accordin' to

Pendleton, the mine Amos Grant purchased required a helluva lot of excavation, which means new machinery and lots of manual labor. Pendleton told Amos Grant that his profit was eaten up in necessary expenses."

"The way Tweed and I have it figured, Pendleton is draining his investors for money and putting their names on low-grade claims. He keeps the highly productive mines for himself," Shaler explained. "Several of his stockholders have taken him to court but without success. He always presents contracts which specify low-grade mines for his investors as evidence in his cases. Never once has he been found guilty of fraud."

"And the only way to recover the bad investment is to hoodwink Pendleton into spending thousands on a bad producer," Tweed added.

"So when is this pigeon supposed to inspect this mine?" James questioned with a wry grin.

"At the end of the week," Shaler informed him with a devilish smile. "When Pendleton takes his samples to the assayer, he'll think he's happened onto a bonanza. The money he pays us for the claim will reimburse Amos Grant for his losses and force Pendleton to sink even more money into locating the mother lode that he believes is buried in this pile of rock."

"Even Pendleton's own personal assayer won't be able to tell the difference between saltin' and a pure vein," Tweed confided merrily. "Shay put all of our samples under a microscope to be sure there were no traces of suspicious ingredients that might cause the assayer to question the potential in Mule's Ear Gulch. Pendleton won't know he's been had until after he's sunk a fortune into this dry gulch." Tweed paused to light his corncob pipe and then grinned all over again. "And you know what they say, James. Pigs get fat, but hogs get slaughtered. My friend Amos Grant asked me and Shay to come to Dakota to take Reece Pendleton to market for making a hog of hisself in the minin' business.''

"Pendleton will be furious when he discovers you set him up," James warned.

Tweed shrugged a thick shoulder and puffed on his pipe. "He can be as furious as he wants, but there won't be a damned thing he can do about it, just like there wasn't nothin' Amos could legally do to get his money back."

James's blue eyes darted from one long-time friend's face to the other's. "You better watch your backs," he advised solemnly. "Desperate men have desperate ways."

"I ain't worried," Tweed assured him confidently. "Shay can handle an assortment of weapons as good as you can. If Pendleton tries to draw down on Shay, he'll wish the hell he hadn't!"

"Maybe," James murmured quietly. "But all the same, you better expect the unexpected . . ."

Tim Brady drummed his fingers on the desk, impatiently awaiting Johnny Varnes's arrival in their office in the back of Bella Union Saloon. Tim had also tried to contact Reece, but the man was so busy courting his newly acquired lady friend that he couldn't find the time to attend the meeting.

A muddled frown puckered Johnny's brows when he breezed into the office and noted the sour expression on Tim's face. "You look like you've been sucking on a lemon," he smirked at his partner.

"May as well have been," Tim said as he slouched back in his chair behind the desk. "I just heard some unsettling news. One of the bartenders said he thought he recognized Wild Bill Hickok sitting at a corner table a few days ago. He was shooting the breeze with Shaler McCain and they left together.''

"How sure was the bartender?" Johnny asked apprehensively.

Tim's shoulder dropped in a noncommittal shrug. "The bartender reported seeing a man with shoulder-length blond hair, sitting with his back to the wall, just like Hickok always does."

"Damn." Johnny sank into his chair and stroked his mustache pensively. "I thought we'd seen the last of Hickok after he ran us out of Abilene. Sheriff Brown isn't much of a threat because he can't handle a six-shooter, but Hickok is another matter entirely. If the miners talk him into pinning on a marshal's badge, he'll come looking for us, sure as hell."

"We'll have to make sure Reece watches his step with the mining company," Tim mused aloud. "McCain and Hickok could be up to something."

Johnny nodded grimly. "I think we ought to call in Broken-Nose McCall and convince him to get rid of Hickok for us. If we wait around until Reece's gunslingers arrive from Texas it might be too late.

"I wonder what the hell happened to Johnson and Bassett. They should have been here by now. And Reece is no help at all these days," Johnny added irritably. "He's so bewitched by that pretty female that he only lets her out of his sight for a few minutes at a time."

"So I've noticed," Tim snorted. "He flaunts her like a new diamond ring. I haven't even been able to tell him about Hickok's arrival."

"I think we should haul McCall in here right now and start working on him without consulting Reece," Johnny advised. "It'll take a few days and several bottles of whiskey to convince him to square off against Hickok. We'll have to get him used to the idea."

"Do you know where McCall is?"

"The last time I saw him he was sweeping gold granules into a dust pan in the saloon, hoping to scrape enough together to buy a bottle of rotgut," Johnny reported.

"With any luck, he's still sober enough to talk to. Go see if you can round him up," Tim requested, "I'll try to make contact with Reece, if I can pry him away from that wench he's been sniffing after."

Johnny Varnes bounded out of his chair as if propelled by a spring. When he located Broken-Nose Jack McCall two hours later, the drunken gambler was lying in one of the bordellos in the "Badlands," snoring like a freight train. From the look of McCall, Johnny speculated it would take a full day to dry the besotted oaf out enough for him to even remember having a conversation. As was his custom, McCall would be riproaring drunk for at least a day. Recovering from his hangover would require at least another full day.

Since there had been no more sightings of the man fitting Wild Bill Hickok's description, Varnes and Brady breathed a little easier. If Hickok really had ventured back to Deadwood after leading a pack train of miners north the previous month, he must have just been passing through. That was fine and dandy with Johnny Varnes and Tim Brady. Hickok had run them out of Abilene six years earlier and if they never laid eyes on that pistol-packing lawman again that would make them more than happy!

Sixteen

Casity breathed a sigh of relief when Reece announced he had to meet with some of his business associates. For the past four days, she had felt suffocated by Reece's constant attention. He followed her around like a puppy, escorting her to breakfast, lunch, and dinner. He encouraged her to learn to play all the card games he enjoyed.

She had heard the tales of Poker Alice Ivers, who had come to Dakota after the death of her husband to seek her amusement in gambling dens. Alice had taken to smoking cigars, packing pistols, and dealing cards with the best of men. And, of course, there was Belle Siddons, who operated a casino in Deadwood and had changed her name to Madame Vestal after having been a Confederate spy. But Casity had no intention of taking to gambling to support herself, no matter how bad things got.

Heaving a tired sigh, Casity sank into the tub to enjoy her long-awaited solitude. She had bolted her bedroom door, just in case Reece "accidentally" walked in earlier than she expected. Although Casity had artfully dodged his amorous embraces and managed to keep their relationship as impersonal as possible, she knew what Reece wanted from her ultimately. She was no longer a naive fool, after all. Shaler McCain had taught her well . . .

Casity strangled on her breath when the red velvet drapes that bracketed the opened window rippled as if touched by an invisible hand. Her eyes widened in alarm when she noticed a pair of dusty boots protruding from the hem of the curtains.

Wildly, she glanced toward the door, calculating how much time she would need to grab her towel, leap from the tub, unlock the door, and escape.

"You!" Casity spluttered when she got her first glimpse of the intruder.

Shaler untangled himself from the drapes and sauntered across the elaborately furnished room. He had trailed Casity like a shadow throughout the day, but Reece had stuck to her like a flea to a dog. When Shaler saw Reece ambling down the boardwalk without Casity, he had shinnied up the supporting beam beside the alley and crept along the hotel balcony. There his footsteps had halted. Owl-eyed, he had watched this goddess disrobe and sink into her bath. The scene reminded Shaler of the night he had first encountered this enchanting beauty. He had peeled off her soggy clothes and savored every luscious curve, just as he had been doing this evening.

Damn, he couldn't even look at her without remembering the intimacies they had shared. It was like a haunting dream. For that one magical night, there had been no misunderstandings, no harsh words between them. They had simply responded to each other, hopelessly lost in a magical universe of unrivaled passion . . .

"What do you want?" Casity snapped as she sank deeper into the tub to cover herself in bubbles.

"I came to apologize," Shaler said calmly.

"Apology accepted. Now *GET OUT!*" she hissed, blue eyes blazing.

The faintest hint of a smile curled Shaler's lips as he watched Casity attempt to shield herself from his gaze. He hadn't realized how much he had missed their verbal sparring, though he hadn't forgotten the passion that still burned through him like wildfire. He felt a helluva lot less guilty about his fierce attraction after he learned this bewitching imp wasn't Tweed's mail-order bride. Now he wasn't so busy resenting Casity's scheming ploy. Indeed, he was far more fascinated with the woman herself. And there was plenty of woman to appreciate, Shaler noted as his eyes wandered over every inch of exposed flesh.

"You haven't even asked me what I'm apologizing for," Shaler prompted when he finally forced his gaze back to her face.

"It doesn't matter," she muttered. "Considering the density of the male mind I've learned not to ask questions." Her arm shot toward the window. "All I want is for you to go out the same way you came in—NOW!"

Curse the man! Why wouldn't he go away and leave her alone? How much longer did he intend to torment her?

"I completely misjudged you," Shaler admitted as he squatted down beside the tub. His forefinger trailed over the droplets that glittered like diamonds on her arm, wishing he could caress her as freely as the water that glided over her.

When Casity flinched as if she had been scorched, Shaler smiled wryly. She may have despised him, and with good reason, but his touch still stirred her, just as the light caress aroused him. The old familiar spark was still there, smoldering beneath Casity's contempt.

"Tweed told me the whole story," he murmured softly. "And you'll be delighted to know he raked me over the coals for leaping to so many idiotic conclusions."

Casity braced herself, refusing to respond to that seductive baritone voice and disarming smile. Perhaps this rascal thought a few words of apology would make things right. Well, he was wrong! He had hurt her more than he could possibly imagine. He had demolished her self-respect, her willpower, and her pride. She knew why he had come—to take what he had taken twice before. If he wanted sexual satisfaction then he could damned well search for it elsewhere! He was *not* finding it with her—ever again!

"Tweed wants you to come back to Bonanza Gulch," Shaler murmured as his fingertips drifted over her bent knee. "He misses you . . . and so do I."

Casity found it impossible to sink any deeper into the bath water to escape his erotic touch. She was trapped. Each lingering caress caused fire to sizzle through her nerve endings and the tepid water couldn't begin to cool it. Damn the man—he knew she was vulnerable and he enjoyed watching her fight the unwanted sensations that coursed through her body.

"Come out of the sea, little mermaid," Shaler whispered as his head moved steadily toward her trembling lips. "It's time for you and me to begin again—"

"No!" Casity bleated, dodging his oncoming kiss. "Go away and leave me alone. I despise you, Shaler McCain, and I will 'til I die!"

To her relief, Shaler straightened his brawny frame to tower over her. He was leaving, thank the Lord . . . ! Casity's eyes bulged from their sockets when Shaler peeled off his buckskin shirt and tossed it aside.

A gasp burst from her lips when he slowly unfastened the buttons on his trim-fitting breeches. "What the blazes do you think you're doing?" she croaked.

He grinned roguishly. "If you won't come out of the water then you leave me no choice but to come in after you."

All five of Casity's senses went on full alert when Shaler tucked his thumbs inside the band of his breeches and glided them down his hips. He stripped off every last article of clothing while Casity gaped at him in unwilling appreciation and disbelief. The last thing she wanted was to be distracted by such a magnificent sight. He obviously found devilish pleasure in watching her willpower crumble . . .

Her thoughts stalled completely when Shaler sank into the tub to face her. Her composure came unraveled when his legs glided around hers to make room for himself in a bath that was barely big enough for one. Casity sat like a rock, trying to tell herself she felt nothing but irritation. Marshaling her floundering defenses, she reached out her hand in a last-ditch effort to rout Shaler from her room—and from her life!

"All right, Shay, you win." She grasped his wandering hand in hers and pumped it as if she were drawing water from a well. "I forgive you for misjudging my intentions. I don't hate you anymore. I simply don't like you. Now will you *please* leave."

The peace-treaty handshake was a miscalculation on Casity's part. Shaler used her arm as a tow rope to pull her toward him—and when his arms encircled her to sit her on his lap, Casity knew she was lost. The depressing fact was that she had never been able to resist this rascal. He was an addiction. Each time he touched her, he brought her body to life.

"I truly am sorry for the pain I've caused you," Shaler whispered against the swanlike column of her throat. "In my need to protect Tweed, I hurt you." His lips feathered over her collarbone, leaving her quaking in his arms. "I confess that I am much too cynical where women are concerned. I was burned once a long time ago and I never forgave the lady for trouncing my heart. I suppose skeptics always have a tendency to believe the worst after they've been betrayed. It wasn't fair to judge all other women by one

216 *Gina Robins*

woman's behavior." His hand curled beneath Casity'
chin, forcing her to meet his steady gaze. "Teach m
to trust again, to believe. I want what we shared tha
first night, Miss Casity Crockett . . ."

Casity's breath caught in her throat when Shaler'
kisses trailed over her shoulder to the valley betwee
her breasts and then skimmed each throbbing peak
She was every kind of fool to let herself be persuaded
to set her bitterness aside. But his touch was magic
It wove a web of tantalizing sensations that numbed
her brain and sensitized every nerve in her body. In
stinctively, she arched toward him, feeling the wildl
familiar tingles of pleasure that had been her downfal
on that magical night an eternity ago. Shaler had
sparked those wondrous memories with his gentle ex
pertise. His hands and lips explored her body as the
had that first night, worshipping her as if she were a
priceless treasure.

Over and over again his kisses and caresses teased
aroused, and satisfied all her needs that fed upon each
other until passion exploded inside her like a coil o
living flame. Her trembling body was putty in the
hands of a master craftsman. He dissolved her bone
and turned her flesh to steam. He kissed her, breath
ing new fire into her. He whispered of the pleasure
she gave him and he made her believe she was more
than just the object of his passion.

Shaler felt Casity's luscious body melt against him
in hopeless surrender. He was going to enjoy her—
thoroughly and completely. He would revel in the splen
dorous sensations she aroused in him. There would be
no regret, no sense of guilt. She stirred him and he
stirred her and that was all that mattered. He still had
miles to go to gain her trust and convince her that he
was truly sorry for treating her so disrespectfully. Bu
for now, they would forget the agony they had caused

Wish You Were Here?

You can be, every month, with Zebra Historical Romance Novels.

YOU'RE GOING TO LOVE GETTING
4 FREE BOOKS

These books worth almost $20, are yours without cost or obligation
when you fill out and mail this certificate.
*(If the certificate is missing below, write to: Zebra Home Subscription Service, Inc.,
120 Brighton Road, P.O. Box 5214, Clifton, New Jersey 07015-5214*

4 FREE BOOKS!

Yes! Please send me 4 Zebra Historical Romances without cost or obligation. I understand that each month thereafter I will be able to preview 4 new Zebra Historical Romances FREE for 10 days. Then, if I should decide to keep them, I will pay the money-saving preferred publisher's price of just $4.00 each...a total of $16. That's almost $4 less than the publisher's price, and there is no additional charge for shipping and handling. I may return any shipment within 10 days and owe nothing, and I may cancel this subscription at any time. The 4 FREE books will be mine to keep in any case.

Name _____

Address_____ Apt. _____

City_____ State_____ Zip_____

Telephone ( )_____

Signature _____   LF1195
(If under 18, parent or guardian must sign.)

Terms, offer and prices subject to change without notice. Subscription subject to acceptance by Zebra Books. Zebra Books reserves the right to reject any order or cancel any subscription.

ZEBRA HOME SUBSCRIPTION SERVICE, INC.

120 BRIGHTON ROAD

P.O. BOX 5214

CLIFTON, NEW JERSEY 07015-5214

ach other and surrender to those sweet fires of summer that blazed so hot against the night.

When Shaler came to his knees and scooped Casity
into his arms to step out of the tub, she voiced no protest. Her blue eyes locked with his. He could detect the
wariness that still lingered there, despite their need for
each other. He was determined to chase her fears away,
to make her feel needed and protected and desired.

With dedicated gentleness, Shaler laid Casity in the
middle of the bed. His gaze wandered over her, marveling at her perfection. He adored looking at her,
touching her, making her respond to him.

When Shaler stretched out beside her and reached
for her, Casity stilled his hands. Her eyes wandered
over the broad expanse of his shoulders and her free
hand drifted over the dark hair that covered his chest.
Casity had never dared to touch a man the way she
longed to touch this handsome giant. She yearned to
possess the same power over his body that he held over
hers. She wanted to explore every inch of him until
she knew him better than she knew herself, until she
made him melt beneath her touch as helplessly as she
had always melted beneath his.

Odd, wasn't it, that her wounded pride demanded
some sort of consolation, even in the midst of passion.
By making him as vulnerable to her as she had been
to him, Casity was sure it would ease her pain. She
supposed it was true that she wanted to share the company misery loved so well. And she had definitely been
miserable in the knowledge that she was no match for
this rogue. She wanted to control him, to make him
move like a puppet that danced to her commands.
And perhaps, by completely destroying his defenses,
she might somehow regain her own.

And yet, when her hands and lips set out on a journey of discovery, Casity realized she didn't really want

to prove anything to anybody. She was captivated by
the feel of his flesh and muscle beneath her fingertips

Shaler McCain was an incredibly fascinating man
who reminded her of a panther. To touch him was to
take possession of this remarkable mass of energy, to
tame a wild creature who knew no man as master.

She marveled at the way the muscles of his belly
relaxed beneath her hands and lips, reveled in his low
purr of pleasure when she touched him. Shaler's re
sponses gave her a newfound sense of power and con
fidence. She employed the same bone-melting
techniques on him that he had used on her. And when
feminine curiosity got the better of her, she invented
her own unique ways to seduce and torment him until
he gasped for breath.

Feeling boldly reckless, Casity brushed her finger
tips over his muscled thighs and explored the velvet
length of him. Her hand enfolded him and her light
kisses savored him in ways she had never even consid
ered touching him before. She tasted him, absorbed
his strength, inhaled his alluring scent.

Shaler couldn't believe he had allowed this inquisi
tive nymph free license to his body! He had never
granted any other woman such privileges. He had al
ways been the one to initiate passion. But the instant
Casity's hands and lips moved over him, he became
powerless to stop her from doing whatever she desired
to do, as many times as she wanted to do it. It had
been his intention to soothe away the anger and hurt
he had caused her. Instead, she had made him his
willing slave, teaching him things he had never known
about desire, though he had arrogantly assumed he
knew all there was for a man to know.

"Lord, Cas, do you know what you're doing to me?"
Shaler breathed raggedly when her kisses and caresses

ent another wave of indescribable pleasure cresting
through him.

He hoped to hell she knew what she was doing to
him because he didn't! He couldn't even think straight.

His throaty voice and the glitter in his eyes put a
saucy smile on Casity's lips. It seemed Shaler was finally beginning to understand how helpless she had
felt when he seduced her, how tormented she had
been by the needs that consumed her.

"Do I pleasure you, Shay?" she purred as her
tongue measured the throbbing length of him.

"Too much." He gasped and then groaned aloud
when she touched him in the most intimate ways imaginable. "Come here, damn you, before I explode with
the need of you . . . !"

Casity ignored his demand. She had just begun to
discover all the sensitive places he liked to be touched.
Her hands and lips surged and receded like a rolling
surf caressing a seashore. Her fingertips drifted along
the hard staff of his desire and her kisses followed before she took him into her mouth and gently suckled,
feeling his entire body respond to her erotic explora-
tions.

"Enough," Shaler groaned in delicious torment.

"Not nearly enough," she whispered against his pulsating manhood.

Casity derived the most phenomenal sense of satisfaction in learning the feel of each plane and contour
of his body. She wanted to see each wave of pleasure
roll over him, watch him battle for control and admit
defeat. For once, Casity vowed, she would take him to
the brink of sanity and he would know all too well
how he had tormented her with his erotic caresses.
Only then would Shaler truly and fully understand
why she had been so haunted by her own lack of
willpower. Only when she had conquered him in the

same way could they meet on common ground and
put the turmoil of the past behind them.

"If it's your intent to kill me with divine torture
you've succeeded," Shaler assured her shakily. "Is thi
my comeuppance, sweet witch? Must I die of the wan
of you to compensate for all the anguish you suffere
because of me?"

Now he understood the full extent of her own su
render, Casity realized. She had made Shaler wan
her beyond bearing, beyond all rhyme and reason
Now they were soul mates soaring in that rapturou
dimension bound by no past, present, or future.

When Casity uncurled above him to caress hi
swarthy, masculine body with her own, she knew tha
at long last, she had made this giant vulnerable to th
deep-seated emotion inside him. He was beyond ca
ing. Nothing mattered except the wild, insane need t
satisfy the monstrous ache that consumed his body an
soul.

When Casity came to him, his needs suddenly be
came her own. She felt herself shudder uncontrollabl
when he became her greatest strength and, ironicall
her greatest weakness. The sensations that echoed ou
of his powerful body and rippled through hers mad
it impossible to tell where his pleasure ended and he
began. It was as if they were of the same flesh, sharin
the same frantic heartbeat.

What began as tender, deliberate seduction becam
a wild, fervent union of heart, body, and soul. Casit
could feel herself gliding in motionless flight, orbitin
the stars to bask in their warmth. Feminine reserv
abandoned her as she answered Shaler's demandin
thrusts and clung to him as if he were the only stabl
force in a universe of whirling sensation. Casity didn
stop to ask herself why it had been so important tha
Shaler understand how she felt each time he took cor

ol of her mind and body. She didn't pause to consider
hy she felt so vulnerable to him and to no other. All
e knew was that she was soaring higher and higher,
scovering an entirely new dimension of passion.

Spasms of ecstasy pulsated through her body as
aler clutched her to him so tightly that she could
o longer breathe and didn't care if she did. In fact,
e couldn't imagine why she needed air when she
d upon his strength as if it were her own. When
other tidal wave of rapture bombarded her, Casity
came engulfed in sweet, paralyzing sensations. It
as as if every thought and feeling she had ever ex-
erienced converged upon her and then expanded in-
de her—burgeoning, blossoming until it touched every
er of her being.

"Shay?" A cry of wonder escaped her lips when her
dy shuddered convulsively against his—again and
ain.

Shaler felt the last fiery surge of mindless desire
ain from his body, depleting every ounce of energy
d strength. Sweet mercy, what had come over him?
e couldn't even draw a breath—he knew he was prob-
ly crushing Casity and he couldn't even move away to
ve her the slightest relief.

For several moments, Shaler struggled to regain his
rength, but the theory that mind could conquer body
dn't hold true when a man had no mind left! This
manded all a man had to give—and then some.

Shaler had just begun to feel his sanity and energy
turn when he heard a rattle on the other side of the
droom door. Casity's wild-eyed gaze locked with his
r a frantic moment. Instant panic claimed them both
hen they realized they were about to have an unex-
cted guest.

Seventeen

Like a rocket, Shaler shot off the bed to collect h
scattered clothing. His eyes focused on the twistir
door knob. When he heard the creak of hinges, l
knew he didn't have time to dress or even climb o
the window. In desperation, he dived under the be
clutching his clothes.

Although Shaler would have preferred to allc
Reece Pendleton to know this lovely sprite was his pr
vate possession, he couldn't take the risk of infuriatir
this particular man just yet. The timing wasn't rigl
Reece was due to inspect the claim site in Mule's E
Gulch in a few days. Shaler couldn't risk having tl
mining entrepreneur back out now that the trap hะ
been set.

Irritation boiled inside Casity as she watched Shal
slink under her bed. Obviously he didn't think enou
of her to confront Reece. Nothing had changed b
tween them, she realized. She was still just the pla
Shaler came for physical release.

Her aggravation doubled when the lock gave way
the key Reece kept for just such situations. He ha
seen to it that she had no privacy whatsoever. Did l
think the mere possession of a key gave him the rig
to intrude on her privacy without permission? Ha
he left her alone hoping he could return to find h

in a vulnerable position, making it easy for him to take what he wanted?

Clutching the sheet beneath her chin, Casity waited until Reece appeared in the doorway. His gaze swept down her barely concealed form, taking it all in at a single glance. This was apparently the moment Reece had been hoping for, judging by the rakish grin that captured his fair features. He had deliberately backed her into a compromising situation and he looked more than eager to take advantage of that fact.

Like a strutting stag, Reece pranced across the room to tower over Casity. He ached to tangle his fingers in the silky auburn tendrils, to tilt her lips to his kiss. He yearned to peel away the sheet and compare his speculations about her body to reality. With that in mind, Reece sank down on the edge of the bed and braced his hand beside her shoulder.

Shaler scooted away when the mattress sagged with Reece's weight, a scowl on his face. What the hell was he going to do if Reece decided to force himself on Casity? Leap up stark naked to defend her? Hell's fire, if he was forced to reveal himself, Reece wouldn't go near the mine in Mule's Ear Gulch. All of his careful plotting would be for naught!

"Have I told you lately how lovely you are?" Reece whispered as he leaned down to press a kiss to her lips. "You take my breath away . . ."

Not entirely, Shaler thought sourly. This rake still had enough breath to flatter Casity and try to buckle her defenses.

Casity flashed him a look that warned him he was on thin ice. "I hope you remember the limitations of our agreement," she said firmly.

"I thought I could abide by your restrictions," Reece replied in a ragged voice. His gaze fell to the breasts concealed by nothing more than the sheet. "But you're quite a temptation for any man, despite his noble intentions."

Noble intentions, my eye! Shaler scoffed silently. Any man who constantly referred to his *noble* intentions was concealing *ignoble* intentions.

"I think you'd better leave, Reece," Casity advised with another meaningful glance.

"I think I'd better stay." His head hovered just above hers, thirsting for another intoxicating taste. "I think perhaps you're teasing me, little nymph. Why else would you be lying abed so early in the evening, wearing nothing but a sheet?"

Casity's eyes flashed blue fire. "I thought I could do as I pleased behind a locked door, but obviously my privacy extends only as far as you allow it since you have the key."

A reproachful frown gathered on her brow. "Let me make this perfectly clear. My body is not part of this bargain and it never shall be. I am not so devious as to tease a man into my bed. If I wish him to be there then I will come right out and tell him so. Only when a man has earned my respect and affection will I offer to share passion with him. I will not make love *to* him, I will only make love *with* him, as love was meant to be!"

Well, that wasn't exactly true, Casity reminded herself. She had ignored that idealistic philosophy when dealing with Shaler. But Reece didn't know that. And Shaler—weasel that he was—didn't seem to be all that eager to pop out from under the bed to make his presence known!

Reece hesitated a moment, trying to decide if a tumble in bed, even by force, was worth the cost of losing this delicious bundle. He had spent more than four days catering to her in an attempt to buy her affection. But this feisty imp was extremely strong-willed. Well,

I'm waiting no longer, Reece decided. He was taking what he wanted. The bargain be damned!

An outraged screech erupted from Casity when his hand trespassed on private territory. Her arm shot upward, catching him on the cheek, smashing his nose against his mustache. Casity would have given most anything if she could have grabbed hold of the pistol Shaler kept in his holster.

"I'm warning you, Reece, if you don't keep a respectable distance, I'll be forced to shoot you like the scoundrel you are."

Shaler took the cue, just as Casity hoped he would when she scooted toward the far side of the bed and dangled her arm over the edge. The revolver magically appeared in her hand, Reece recoiled in astonishment when Casity aimed the pistol at the private parts of his anatomy.

"You have one second to decide if you want to remain a man or become a eunuch," she hissed convincingly.

Scowling, Reece gathered his feet beneath him and stalked across the room. After putting a hand on the doorknob, he pivoted to glower at Casity.

"You've made a crucial mistake," he growled ominously. "I'm a powerful man in Deadwood, with dozens of employees at my command. You may find yourself attacked some moonless night. Your beauty might escape you forever."

"And if I am horribly disfigured, I'll know who to bring charges against, won't I?" Casity retaliated boldly.

A sinister smile tightened Reece's lips, so much so that his mouth disappeared beneath his thick mustache. "It will be difficult for a corpse to press charges, my dear," he assured her before he opened the door and slammed it behind him.

As if propelled by a cannon, Casity flew out of bed
to gather her belongings. By the time Shaler wormed
out of his hiding place, Casity had donned her chemise and pantaloons. With swift efficiency, Shaler
dressed and helped Casity fasten herself into her calico gown. Without uttering a sound that might alert
Reece, Shaler snatched Casity's bulging satchel up off
the floor and stuffed them through the window. Clasp-
ing her hand in his, Shaler tiptoed across the balcony
and swung a long leg over the railing to make his
descent. When Casity balked, Shaler swiveled around
to stare at her bemusedly.

A faint smile replaced his curious frown when Casity
contorted her body to stare warily at their intended
escape route. From all indication, she was leery of dangling by her hands before finding a foothold on the
supporting beam.

Casity Crockett afraid of heights? He could have
sworn this firebrand was afraid of nothing, not even
the devil himself! Considering all she had endured
the past month, one would have thought she wouldn't
have blinked an eyelash at a few acrobatic maneuvers
to escape her latest calamity.

Shaler leaned over to drop a kiss to her lips which
were frozen in a grimace. "Easy as pie, princess," he
whispered in assurance.

"Maybe for you," Casity took a second look at their
precarious route. "Why don't you try it in a dress and
see how well you manage? If you don't break your
neck, I'll be right behind you."

It wasn't helping matters that distant lightning
streaked across the western sky, alternately illuminating their escape route and plunging it into darkness.
Fierce gusts of wind swirled around Casity and she
feared she would be blown off the balcony—if she
didn't slip and fall first!

Shaler grabbed her by the shoulders and turned her around while he sat perched on the railing. In a matter of seconds, he had tucked the back hem of her skirt between her legs and fastened it around her waist so that she looked as if she were wearing baggy breeches. Using the lacing from his buckskin shirt, he tied an improvised belt around her waist to secure the excessive fabric.

"Any more excuses, princess?" he teased as he surveyed his imaginative creation.

Casity steadied herself against the strong blast of wind and glanced apprehensively over the railing before she forced out her reluctant admission. "Only one. I'm afraid of heights."

Shaler diverted her attention to the window through which they had come. "You have a choice. You can go back to your room and take your chances with Reece or you can climb down the beam with me."

"Those are my only two options?" Casity muttered sourly.

"Afraid so—"

Before Shaler finished the last word, his arm snaked around her waist to send her circling on the outside of the railing. Since Casity was dragging her feet, Shaler was left with no choice but to force her over the railing. He purposely mashed her face against his shoulder so that her cry of alarm would be muffled in his shirt. Casity sank her claws into the planks of the floor on the balcony when Shaler left her hanging. While he whispered encouragement and instruction, she jabbed her feet hither and yon, trying to find a foothold. Once she managed to secure her foot, she sank downward until she could wrap herself around the beam. When she gathered enough courage to slide down the beam, she plunged like a rock. Her feet hit the edge of the boardwalk, knocking her off balance.

She landed with a thud in the alley and struggled to catch her breath.

In extreme irritation, she watched, Shaler glide down the beam like a monkey making his way through jungle vines. It made her wonder how many windows Shaler had sneaked out of while he was carousing!

After Casity picked herself up off the ground, she wheeled toward the street. Before she had taken two steps, Shaler latched onto her wrist to swing her around to face him.

"Where the hell do you think you're going?"

"To rent a room for the night, of course," she replied crisply.

"*No*, you're coming with me," Shaler contradicted.

"*No*, I am not," she informed him in no uncertain terms. "Just because I *forgave* you for treating me so horribly doesn't mean I intend to *forget* what you said and did. And why would I want to go traipsing off with a man who didn't even have the courage to come out from under the bed to confront that scoundrel?"

Shaler scoffed. "I was damned if I did and damned if I didn't," he growled at her. "Knowing you, you would have been outraged if anyone in Deadwood knew we are lovers, even Reece Pendleton. Now you're mad because I *didn't* expose myself. I couldn't have won for losing. I never could with you. That's been the problem since the day we met!"

Casity knew he was right. She would have been infuriated one way or the other. She had been annoyed that Shaler hadn't come to her rescue and yet she would have been humiliated if he had made his presence known. Reece would have taken his vengeance out on both of them rather than just her. But why Casity felt the need to protect someone who needed no protection whatsoever she could not imagine!

Shaler clutched her hand and led her down the alley to retrieve his horse. "Do you know what your problem is, princess?"

"No, but I'm sure you plan to tell me," she sniffed sarcastically.

"You have a chip on your shoulder the size of Pike's Peak. You *assumed* I was too much of a coward to confront Reece."

"Well, weren't you?" Casity challenged as he dragged her along at a hurried pace.

Shaler rounded on her so quickly that she slammed into him head-on. "No, I'm not," he defended indignantly. "I happen to have an excellent reason for avoiding a confrontation with Reece just now. It has nothing to do with fearing him and everything to do with the reason Tweed and I came to Deadwood in the first place. And if you can calm down for a minute I'll explain it to you."

Casity blinked in surprise. "You didn't come to the Black Hills to search for gold and ravish every available female who crossed your path?"

"Good Lord, woman, credit me with at least some decency!"

"Don't talk to me about decency!" Casity cried in frustration. "You've taken advantage of me at the most vulnerable moments in my life. You have beaten my pride and self-respect black and blue a dozen times and then you had the gall to come crawling back with a few words of apology before you took what you wanted—again! Decent? You don't even know the meaning of the word!"

Damn, this was without a doubt the sassiest female he had ever come across. She was more of a cynic than he was.

Without preamble, Shaler scooped Casity off the ground and deposited her on his mount. Before she could gouge the steed and take off—which she looked as if she was about to do—Shaler grabbed the reins. When he had swung up behind her, he hooked an arm around her waist to make sure she didn't run off the way she had when she had been abducted by the Indian raiding party.

"I don't want to go back to Bonanza Gulch," Casity spluttered stubbornly. "I'm staying in Deadwood so I can get as far away from you as possible."

"Tweed sent me here to bring you back and back you go," he breathed down her neck. "Now, do you want to know what Tweed and I are really doing in the Black Hills or not?"

"Not," Casity snapped in defiance.

It was obvious that this spitfire was even more stubborn and contrary than she was curious, Shaler mused with a wry smile. Now why didn't that surprise him?

"I just want to be left alone! I would prefer to find a remote canyon and put as much distance between myself and all men as I can—including and especially you, Shaler McCain!" she repeated emphatically, just in case he hadn't gotten the point the first time.

"Fine, you can have our cabin and the claim for nothing when we get through with it," Shaler growled at the back of her head. "But until we are through with the cabin and can deed it over to you, I want you out of the way so you won't get into more trouble. And now, Madam Attilla, if you can refrain from shooting your mouth off for a few minutes, I'll tell you why I couldn't risk confronting Reece for a few more days."

Casity didn't know why she was so put out with this golden-eyed rapscallion; when she was with him she was overly defensive and everything he said seemed to set her off. He was beginning to matter too much to her and that worried her—a lot! God help her if she made the foolish mistake of falling in love with a man who obviously didn't want a permanent involvement. If he had, he would have been married long before now, she reckoned.

She was *never* going to fall in love with this handsome devil and that was all there was to it, Casity assured herself fiercely. Where had that idiotic notion come from anyway? That was the last thing she needed on top of everything else. Her purpose for being here was to lie low and hire a gunslinger to hunt her uncle's murderers down.

"Reece Pendleton teamed up with two swindlers by the names of Tim Brady and Johnny Varnes when he first came to Deadwood," Shaler explained before Casity could dream up another excuse to drag him into a debate that inevitably ended in a shouting match.

This spitfire was notorious for luring him into arguments before he even realized he was there, but he wasn't going to let it happen again! "Brady and Varnes have been known to drug and rob the patrons of their saloons and force them to sell their claims to Pendleton when he sees a chance to make money off them."

Shaler urged his sorrel gelding into a trot and followed the winding path illuminated by the flashes of lightning that pierced the churning thunderstorm. "Brady and Varnes used their strong-arm tactics to take control of several of the town's saloons and dance halls. The threesome joined forces, hoping to bleed the prospectors and mining investors every way imaginable. For the past few months Pendleton has been using his henchmen to persuade prospectors who refused to sell to him. He has also drained his stockholders and used their cash for his expenses without paying dividends. One of his disgruntled investors is an old friend of Tweed's who settled in Denver. Amos Grant didn't think it wise to make the trip himself for fear of arousing Pendleton's suspicion and prompting him to cover his tracks. That's why Tweed and I have posed as prospectors and have set Pendleton up."

"You're a private investigator?" Casity twisted around to peer incredulously at Shaler.

"At the moment, yes," Shaler informed her. "It would be more accurate to say Tweed volunteered me to do a favor for his friend. Amos and Tweed came west together to hunt and trap, but Amos came down with a severe case of gold fever during the Pike's Peak Rush. He was fortunate enough to find a rich claim and hold onto it. Since he made his fortune in mining, Pendleton convinced him to invest in the Black Hills strike. Amos didn't take kindly to being swindled so Tweed and I devised a scheme to give Pendleton a taste of his own medicine while putting him out of business."

"And how do you intend to do that?" Casity questioned.

"We had originally planned to salt the claim in Bonanza Gulch and sell it to Pendleton for a hundred times its value. But as luck would have it, Tweed stumbled onto a rich vein instead."

Casity couldn't contain her amusement. "Tweed struck it rich by mistake?"

"He's always been a lucky scamp," Shaler assured her. "He sent word back to Amos that he would be glad to reimburse the losses with the gold he unintentionally discovered. But Amos wanted Pendleton put out of business, not Tweed's charity. It was the principle that infuriated Amos. When the mine in Bonanza Gulch became a good producer, Tweed bought another one in Pine Gulch—sight unseen. But sure as hell, the second mine was loaded with ore so *I* bought the one in Mule's Ear Gulch because I don't have Tweed's incredible luck."

"I wondered why the two of you were buying claims
ght and left," Casity said.

"Finally, we found one that was totally worthless,"
haler went on. "Since you left the cabin, we've spent
ur time planting tracers of gold to convince Pendle-
n that he has a potentially productive mine to equal
e Homestake Mine, which has been paying thou-
nds of dollars monthly. Pendleton is supposed to
spect our claim in a few days. That's why I couldn't
elp you fend Pendleton off."

Casity was beginning to realize she was as guilty of
aping to conclusions as Shaler had been. She also
minded herself that if Shaler hadn't been under her
ed when Reece attempted to seduce her, she would
ave had no weapon at her disposal.

"If you and Tweed came to Deadwood to put Pendle-
n out of business and recover Amos Grant's invest-
ent, why did Tweed send for a mail-order bride?"

Shaler reined his steed down the trail toward Bo-
anza Gulch. "After Tweed broke his leg and acciden-
lly discovered gold, he decided he could afford a
ife to care for him. I think Tweed was following
mos's example. As soon as Amos struck it rich, he
ent wife-hunting. Personally, I thought the idea was
idiculous and that Tweed had cracked his skull dur-
g his fall. But Tweed got impulsive and sent off the
ewspapers ads without consulting me."

"And so naturally, you intercepted his bride and
ent her packing. How considerate of you to decide
hat was best for him," Casity smirked caustically.

"Well, hell's fire, I didn't like the idea of a marriage
f convenience to some unknown female who was
oking to latch onto my father for mercenary reasons.
Women only want security."

"They do not!" Casity erupted in protest. "Men are

the ones who want only one thing from the opposit
sex. They're cold-blooded and opportunistic!"

"Like hell they are!" Shaler countered. "Don't yo
think a man would like to be loved, needed, and re
spected for *who* he is, not what he can provide? Jus
once, I'd like to hear a woman say 'I love you.' Perioc
End of sentence. But most females have to start mak
ing demands. Their love comes with strings attached
They either want a man to pleasure them while the
cling to the purse strings of some other fool who ca
supply them with money or they want a lifelong com
mitment for security. Women drain men of their spiri
and freedom and still demand more."

"Of all the ridiculous . . . oh!" Casity spluttered
"Well, for your information, Shaler, women are no
where near as deceptive and manipulative as men. Jus
once *I* would like to hear a man say, 'I love you.' Perioc
End of sentence. Instead they whisper in that oh-so
persuasive tone 'I love you. I want you.' And when thei
appetites have been temporarily satisfied, they go mer
rily on to lure other unsuspecting females into thei
clutches."

"Now wait just a damn minute." Shaler twiste
Casity around to face him, leaving his steed to find it
own way to the cabin. "Have *I* sought out some othe
female to satisfy me since the first time we made love?

"I don't know. Have you sought out other women?
Casity quizzed him. "You insinuated that you ha
when you stayed overnight in Deadwood."

"No, I didn't," he assured her. "And it certainl
wasn't because I didn't have plenty of opportunity."

"So why didn't you?"

Shaler opened his mouth to respond, but he didn
honestly know the answer to the unexpected question
All he knew was that the body in his arms had be

longed to the wrong woman and nothing had felt right. And so he had turned away.

"Hell's fire, I don't know. Why did you refuse to cooperate with the highest bidder at that stupid auction?" he questioned.

"Because I—"

Casity slammed her mouth shut so fast she nearly clipped off her tongue with her teeth. The hasty answer that very nearly leaped off her lips hadn't set well with her at all. The humiliating fact was that, even though this raven-haired rascal had treated her shamefully, she was powerfully attracted to him. He was the only man who had the power to hurt her because she cared too much about him.

"I just didn't, that's all," she finished lamely.

Shaler curled his hand beneath her chin when she refused to look at him, bringing her face back to his. "Was it because of me?"

Casity slapped his hand away and stared at the lightning flashes outlining the distant mountain peaks. "Yes," she replied. "But it was only because you taught me a lesson I'll never forget."

He flashed her a rakish grin. "Is that the real reason, princess? Or was it because you're falling in love with me?"

"Don't be ridiculous," she snapped, itching to claw that cocky expression off his handsome features. "I have no intention of falling in love—ever. My uncle saw to it that I was properly educated and capable of handling business as well as any man. I can take care of myself and provide my own security. Fall in love with you? Never!"

Lord, Casity Crockett was a little spitfire when she got her dander up. She thought she could waltz through life without a man to protect her. And just where would she be now if he hadn't come along to

save her after she'd been abducted by Indians and kidnapped by poachers? And what sort of spot would she
have been in this very night if he hadn't handed her
his pistol to hold Reece Pendleton at bay? With her
good looks and fiery spirit she would always be pursued
by a raft of suitors. And now that she'd made an enemy
of Reece Pendleton she was flirting with danger—
again.

Before Shaler could fling more arguments in her
face, his sorrel gelding—to which he'd been paying no
attentionwhatsoever—decided to leap over the creek instead of wading through it. Shaler and Casity were both
caught unaware when the steed launched itself through
the air. Shaler was unable to clutch at the saddle horn
because Casity was in front of him. All he managed to
latch onto before the muscular steed's momentum flung
him backward was Casity's thigh. The unintended grope
caused Casity to yelp in surprise, and, in turn, her yelp
startled the steed.

Shaler felt the force of gravity tugging at him as the
frightened horse hit the steep creek bank on all fours.
The jolt sent Shaler cartwheeling sideways.

Another alarmed screech came from Casity when
she felt herself being dragged from the saddle by
Shaler's hand, which was still around her thigh. When
thunder boomed and lightning danced from cloud to
cloud, the wild-eyed steed bolted sideways and scrambled up the embankment. Casity and Shaler, however,
were lying in a pile—onebodyparthopelesslyentangled
with another . . .

Eighteen

A pained grunt erupted from Shaler when Casity plopped on his belly, forcing out the air that hadn't been knocked out of him by the unexpected fall. When he did manage to take a breath, he flashed Casity a wry smile. She was still sprawled half on, half off of him. Her face was only a few inches from his and the temptation to erase the distance and taste her honeyed lips was very nearly overwhelming. Shaler mustered his self-control and forcefully stifled the impulse.

"And here you claimed you hadn't fallen in love with me," he teased.

"I fell *with* you but not in love," Casity amended as she struggled to sit up without putting excessive pressure on her injured knee. "Had I known you were so clumsy on a horse I—"

Shaler grasped her forearm, bringing her back down on top of him, enjoying the feel of her full breasts against his chest. "It only goes to prove what happens when we become too involved in our arguments. We took that spill because of it."

His fingertips attempted to erase the defensive frown from her lips. "A truce, princess," he murmured as the flashes of lightning spotlighted her features, giving her a supernatural quality that fascinated him. "For once, I would like to know what it would

have been like if you and I had met under different
circumstances . . ."

The huskiness of his voice was doing crazy things
to Casity's pulse. The glow in his eyes hypnotized her.
And for a moment, she let herself ponder the possibilities if things *had* begun differently. She wondered
how she would have reacted if Shaler had continued
to treat her the same way he had on that magical night
when she first met him—before he came at her with
both barrels blazing.

When his hands glided up her hips to settle on her
waist, Casity felt her resolve melting. Shaler McCain,
it seemed, could be disarmingly charming when he
put his mind to it. His lopsided smile was impossible
to ignore, as was his lingering caress that reminded
her of more intimate moments. And when he was being playfully attentive, as he was now, he was downright adorable. The brief flashes of lighting made his
eyes sparkle like gold nuggets and Casity couldn't have
moved if her life depended on it.

The instant she resigned herself and leaned down
to seal their truce with a kiss, Shaler hooked his arm
around her and brought both of them to their feet.
Casity blinked in disbelief when Shaler bypassed what
might have become another impetuous interlude if
things had worked out the way they usually did when
she got within two feet of him.

"Now that we're afoot and probably won't be able
to outrun the storm anyway, I have something I want
to show you," Shaler said as he drew her up the steep
embankment.

They walked along the creek for several minutes
before he paused at the end of a fallen timber that
formed an improvised bridge across the ravine where
the stream widened into a natural pool. When Shaler
hopped onto the log and stretched his arms out for

balance, Casity watched him trip along the bridge like
an acrobat, exhibiting the kind of masculine grace that
had caught her attention the first time she saw him.
He made the precarious trek across the creek look
easy, just as he had done when he slid down the supporting beam of the hotel.

Casity eyed the log dubiously, noting that part of
the bark had rotted away, leaving slick wood beneath
it. While Shaler made use of the streaking lightning
to guide him to the opposite side of the log, Casity
wondered if she could make the feat look so simple
and graceful.

After Shaler hopped to the ground, he motioned
for her to follow in his footsteps. "Easy as pie, princess," he encouraged her.

"That's what you said on the balcony," Casity reminded him. "I nearly suffered a heart seizure when
you tossed me over the railing and left me dangling."

Shaler grinned wryly at her. "You really are going
to have to do something about your fear of heights.
If you keep this up, you'll have me thinking your fear
of falling in love with me has spilled over into every
facet of your life. Come on, chicken . . ."

Casity's head snapped up and her eyes flashed. "I
am *not* a chicken and I am *not* falling in love with
you," she assured him smartly.

Shaler propped himself against a tree and crossed
his arms and legs in front of him. "Oh yeah? Then
why don't you come over here and tell me that face-
to-face, chicken . . ."

Casity instinctively picked up the gauntlet and
stepped upon the log. Since Shaler had tied her skirt
around her, she didn't have to fear tripping on her
gown and plunging into the water below. Carefully,
she balanced on one foot and then the other to remove
her slippers and then hurled them at Shaler, making

him chuckle as he ducked away from the oncoming missiles.

Taking a determined breath, Casity waited until the lightning lit up the narrow path across the stream. After taking one cautious step, she heard Shaler imitating the sounds of a cackling chicken. The ornery rapscallion! He seemed intent on goading her. But strange as it seemed, Casity was lured forward by the deep, rich sounds of his laughter and drawn to the muscular silhouette poised beside the tree.

Things were progressing well until she was halfway across the improvised bridge, using her extended arms for balance. But then a peal of thunder cracked and Casity instinctively ducked. Her foot slid on the loose bark and she flapped her arms like a bird. Casity congratulated herself when she managed to hold her position . . . until that mischievous rascal at the other end of the log started grinning like a Cheshire cat.

"Shay, don't you even think it!" Casity yelped when he grasped the end of the log.

"Think what, princess?" he asked in mock innocence.

When Shaler jostled the log, Casity squealed in alarm. Her gaze dropped to the silvery pool beneath her. "You polecat! When I get my hands on you I'll strangle you for this!"

Her threat was a waste of breath. Shaler braced his legs and rolled the log sideways, forcing Casity to scramble to keep her balance. Despite her frantic efforts, she swan-dived off the timber and splashed in the pond below.

Shaler's uproarious laughter was the first thing she heard when she burst to the surface, gasping for breath. Ten to one, that ornery rake intended to laugh himself sick watching her flounder. Well, he'd be in for one whale of a surprise if he thought she was going to swim to him!

Still snickering, Shaler waited for her to swim toward him.

"I—"

Shaler watched Casity poke her head above the water to voice only one word before she thrashed and sank into the silvery depths.

"CAN'T—"

Down she went a second time, amid flailing arms and flying drops of water.

"SWIM—!" she croaked before sinking the third time.

The amusement Shaler had been enjoying died into shocked disbelief. When Casity didn't resurface after what Shaler considered to be an abnormally long time, he hastily pulled off his boots and leaped from the embankment. Hell's fire! He had only meant to have a little fun! He hadn't meant to drown her!

Frantic, Shaler groped in the water, trying to locate Casity's limp body at the bottom of the pool. After holding his breath until his lungs nearly burst, he resurfaced and dived back into the inky depths to begin his rescue attempt all over again. After three unsuccessful dives, Shaler burst to the surface, choking for breath. To his astonishment, he heard a giggle drift across the pool.

There sat Casity, her gown clinging like a second skin. She had obviously swum ashore while he was madly clawing at the stream bed. He had been so intent on his mission that he didn't notice she had sunk down beside the reeds to watch him dip and dive frantically.

"That was a rotten trick," Shaler scolded as he treaded water in mid-pond. "You scared the pants off me, princess."

"Did I? As I saw it, one rotten trick deserved another. That should teach you not to try to outsmart a woman."

"Is that so?" Shaler said as he glided ashore.

"Yes, that's so," Casity replied confidently.

When she inclined her head to monitor Shaler's approach, her hauteur dissolved into wary trepidation. Realizing he was up to no good—again, Casity scrambled to her feet. Shaler had that look about him, indicating that their fun and games were far from over.

With a squawk, Casity lurched around to scurry up the steep slope before Shaler did what he looked as if he meant to do—pluck her up and heave her right smack into the pond. Casity had only taken one step when Shaler lunged, latching onto her elbow. With a quick jerk, he sent her tumbling back into his waiting arms.

His amber eyes twinkled down at her as Shaler pivoted toward the creek. "I concede that I have occasionally been outsmarted by you, princess, but never outmuscled. Say you're sorry, or I'll toss you back in the pond."

"I'm not the least bit sorry and I'll tell Tweed on you!" Casity threatened between giggles. "Now put me dawn, you big brute."

Shaler's expression conveyed mock horror at the possibility of being taken to task by his father. But within a moment, he was grinning wickedly at her again. "I've always made it a practice to throw the *little* fish back . . ."

And with that, he launched her through the air into the stream. When Casity resurfaced, Shaler chuckled with delight. "And by all means, don't forget to tell Tweed I threw you in not once but twice, *tattletale!*"

Although Casity probably should have come ashore madder than a wet hen, she couldn't find fault with the boyish side of Shaler's personality. He had made her giggle like a child, after weeks of anguish.

Since his steed had dumped them both on the ground, Casity had forgiven and forgotten the previous conflicts between them. Shaler had treated her to one harmless adventure after another—teasing her, laughing at her and with her. Casity couldn't recall feeling quite so at ease with any other man. Although she had condemned Shaler a dozen times in the past, he had introduced her to a variety of extraordinary experiences. Reluctant though she was to admit it, she did cherish those blissful moments in his arms, even if her conscience nagged her about it later. She also relished this playful interlude that had brought laughter and simple pleasure back into her life.

When Shaler leaned out to offer her a hand, Casity stared warily at it, wondering if he was entertaining the thought of dousing her again. "If you're planning to dunk me I may as well stay where I am and save myself from having to swim ashore again."

Shaler surveyed the wet tangle of hair that framed her face and noted the expectant expression in her eyes. Dunking her had been the substitute for what he had really wanted to do since the moment his steed had dumped her on top of him. But in order to prove to this lovely cynic that a man could see a woman as more than a sex object, he had restrained himself.

Another streak of lightning seared the sky, followed by the drumroll of thunder. The storm was closing in on them and the last place Shaler wanted to be was in the stream. He had once seen a deer standing in midstream when a bolt of lightning speared through the heavens. The unpleasant memory prompted Shaler to grab Casity's hand and hoist her to her feet.

"No more pranks," he promised as he propelled her up the embankment.

"What were you planning to show me?" Casity asked as she curled her hand around his arm to pull herself up the cliff that overlooked the pool.

"I do have a destination in mind," Shaler assured her.

Shepherding her along beside him, he led her a stone's throw away from the fallen log and then veered around the edge of the terrain.

Casity pulled up short and gasped in amazement when Mother Nature's light show illuminated the plunging canyon below them. It was as if the world had dropped off the edge of the towering granite ridge, plummeting hundreds of feet to the fertile valley and silver stream below.

"According to the legends, this is the place where the Great Spirit stood to voice his wishes to the tribal chiefs," Shaler said as he leaned back against the granite wall and drew Casity against him. He gestured toward the darting spears of lightning that slashed across the valley. "The Great Spirit's voice can be heard for miles from here. The Cheyenne think this is a shrine. They believe they are allowed to venture into the holy hills to gather tepee poles and to hunt. But if they stay indefinitely, the *wakan* will strike them down."

Shaler didn't have to explain to her what the *wakan* spirit was. It was made clear by the eerie display of cloud-to-ground strikes that were being hurled into the valley. Indeed, there seemed to be something supernatural about this barren butte that rose above the pines and aspens. When lightning struck, one could see across the valley to the cascade of foothills in the distance . . .

When thunder boomed and the cool breeze warned that the storm was only a few miles away, Casity shivered in her wet clothes. Shaler's arms reflexively cuddled her against him before he turned so that his back shielded her from the fierce blasts of cold air.

"I think the Great Spirit is perturbed," Casity murmured as Shaler guided her around to the protected side of the mountain.

"At *me*, no doubt," Shaler replied. "I've offended the Great Spirit by believing the worst about you. I truly am sorry, princess."

Shaler had uttered those words earlier that evening, but Casity had been too aggravated and defensive to be convinced of his sincerity. Now, weaving along the wind-blown path of this magnificent summit, she honestly believed he regretted his cruelty. His attitude toward her had changed dramatically since he had crept into the hotel suite. He was playful, kind, and compassionate and treated her as his equal.

When the sky seemed to explode and thunder rumbled, Casity instinctively drew closer to Shaler. She felt the deep sound of his laughter reverberating through his chest as he curled a brawny arm around her waist and pulled her closer.

"Scared of storms, too?" he teased.

"No, only of loud noises. They remind me of pistols that can take a life in less than a heartbeat," Casity replied.

It dampened her spirits when she actually thought of that haunting sound that had taken her uncle away.

As if he had read her troubled thoughts, Shaler gave her a compassionate squeeze. "For me, it's the absolute silence that triggers the most painful memories," he confessed, wondering why he felt compelled to share that innermost secret with her. "That unnerving kind of silence just before a disaster is one I'll never forget. It's been more than twenty years since the massacre, but I've never forgotten the sound of that deathly silence."

Shaler shook himself loose from the memories of his childhood tragedy and quickened his pace as raindrops pelted the trees above them. He hadn't intended to tarry so long beside the creek before showing Casity the spectacular view from the butte, but neither had he been able to tear himself away from the stream and their playful antics. It was still a long ride to Bonanza Gulch and he had yet to round up his steed. Shaler's only recourse was to find shelter and outwait the storm. Outwaiting it with Casity was extra incentive not to rush back to the cabin in the wind and rain. Shaler was in no hurry. This night of playful camaraderie had surprised and delighted him, as had this bewitching woman with eyes as clear and blue as the morning sky.

Nineteen

Moving swiftly around the area where he and Tweed had camped when they reached the Black Hills, Shaler headed for the overhanging cliff that would provide protection from the storm. The wind hissed through the trees, warning Shaler he had waited until the last possible minute to seek shelter. He had just ducked beneath the overhang when the sky opened and huge raindrops cascaded down like a waterfall.

Peeling off his damp shirt, Shaler spread the garment on the rock floor and sank down onto it. He pulled Casity in front of him, letting her use his body like a cushion against the stone. An odd sensation threaded through him as they sat cozily nestled together, listening to the rain, the thunder, and the wailing winds unleashing their fury only a few yards away. Shaler felt strangely content, as if that elusive *something* that had been missing from his life had just appeared, as if he had momentarily grasped a magical feeling that transcended the physical boundaries of his existence.

"Cas?"

"Yes?"

Her voice was so quiet he could barely hear it over Mother Nature's cacophony of rain, thunder, and wind.

"Tell me true, princess, do you believe there really

is such a thing as love?" Shaler inquired, surprising Casity and even himself.

She half-twisted to study his angular features illuminated by brief shafts of white light. "I don't know, do you?"

"I asked you first," he reminded her with a light chuckle.

Casity settled back against his chest and rested her elbows on his thighs, satisfied to be where she was, despite the inclement weather. "Before I could believe in love, I suppose I would have to define it."

"And how does one go about defining an emotion that defies definition?"

"It seems to me that one has to understand what love *isn't* before one can determine what love *is*," she declared philosophically.

Another rumble of laughter rose from his chest, and Casity felt the echo of his amusement vibrating through her body as if his mirth were her own.

"I had no idea you were so analytical. A sure sign of a great mind, or so Tweed says."

The unexpected compliment brought a smile to her lips. Compliments from this particular source were certainly few and far between. Casity supposed that a man as self-reliant as Shaler McCain was extremely difficult to impress since he judged everyone by his own high standards. "Why, thank you, kind sir.

Shaler's thick brows furrowed over his squint. "You're hedging, princess. We were discussing love, as I recall. Don't think you can sidetrack me so easily."

"And just because you say I have a good mind, don't think I'm going to *let* you *let* me flounder through this philosophical discussion all by myself," Casity countered saucily. "You've been around more than I have, after all."

"Around what? Around more mountains? Yes, I've

certainly done that . . . ooofff!" His breath rushed out
when Casity playfully poked him in the belly.

"I expect you know your way *around* the female anatomy as well as a practicing physician," she predicted.
"You've probably forgotten more about romantic involvement than I'll ever learn. Calling upon all your
vast experience, do you believe that passion signifies
love?"

"No," he answered honestly.

"So you're saying sexual attraction is simply that,"
she paraphrased.

"I'm saying nothing of the kind." Shaler wondered
how the hell *he* had gotten on the firing line when *he*
was the one who had posed the questions about love
to *her!* Why had he allowed her to turn the tables on
him?

"So what *are* you saying, Shaler—Socrates—
McCain?" she ribbed him.

"Say, whose dumb idea was it to discuss love anyway?" he grunted sourly.

"Yours," Casity replied with a giggle.

"And you *let* me instigate such a discussion?" Shaler
tugged on a long strand of auburn hair, tipping her
face up to his. "That doesn't speak highly of that great
mind of yours, Casity—Plato—Crockett . . ."

His voice trailed off when their storm shelter lit up
like fireworks on the Fourth of July, illuminating her
face. Shaler had been doing a damned good job of
sitting there with Casity and not doing one thing
about it . . . until this moment. He hadn't touched
her, and he hadn't intended to, just to prove her
wrong about the supposed one-track male mind. But
hell's fire, it was difficult to ignore her for hours on
end. A man had his breaking point, after all. Shaler
had reached his—and then some!

Maybe Casity was right, though Shaler would prefer

not to admit any such thing. Maybe the male makeup
did center around lust. And if Shaler was thinking
lusty thoughts, it was all her fault! She was too appealing for her own good, and for his. To see her was to
want her and suddenly Shaler wanted her in the worst
way, even if he *had* made wild, sweet love to her only
hours before. With Casity, once was never enough. Satisfaction was only a momentary thing.

Casity gazed up into the ruggedly handsome face
poised above hers, listening to the sounds of her own
laughter fading into silence. And suddenly it was
strangely quiet in their rock pavilion. The storm had
rolled across the mountain, leaving a peaceful calm
in its wake.

It was *too* peaceful. Casity could hear forbidden
thoughts whisper through her mind, triggering familiar yearnings. Shaler had shown an intriguing part of
his personality to her this evening and she was re-
evaluating her opinion of him. That was not a good
thing because the more she liked him, the more vulnerable she became. And she had been way too vulnerable with Shaler McCain to begin with!

When their eyes met, Casity was hit by the shocking
realization that she wanted to feel his lips over hers.
Their previous topic of conversation left her wondering what it would be like to love this fascinating man
of many moods, to have him return her affection.
Would he be as considerate and attentive as he had
been that first night? Would he treat her with the
same respect and yet lighthearted playfulness he had
exhibited this evening . . . ?

Casity watched his head move slowly toward hers,
felt the warm, heady taste of his kiss spreading
through her like fire. His tongue traced her lips before
parting them to explore the soft recesses within. Casity
yielded to the faint pressure of his mouth, to the lan-

guid feel of his body lying all too familiarly against hers. She could feel his instant arousal while he cradled her between his legs and supported her as if he were a chair she was sinking into.

His expertise was devastating and Casity found herself wishing the kiss could go on forever—like the splendid view overlooking the Black Hills. She felt as if she were gliding over that panoramic valley, lifted by the wind . . .

And all too soon she was drifting back to earth.

Shaler lifted his head to stare down at Casity while she lay half reclined against him. "Was that another of the many mistakes I've made with you, princess?" he questioned huskily.

"It depends on your purpose," Casity answered, her own voice a soft purr. "What were you trying to accomplish?"

His index finger traced the curve of her lips as his pulse sped faster through his bloodstream. "By keeping my distance, I had intended to prove to you that I could be with you without wanting you desperately. But I never could keep away from you. Kissing you always becomes a purpose unto itself," he admitted. "I only hope that kissing you pleasures you half as much as it does me because I'm about to do it again . . . and again . . ."

There was a wealth of meaning in his remark. Casity felt her heart melt when Shaler confessed that he longed to show respect for her and that he wanted to give pleasure as well as take it. Shaler couldn't know how much it meant for him to be sensitive to her needs.

When Shaler tipped her face up to his, Casity shared the pleasure that spilled through her and offered the tantalizing sensations back to him as unselfishly as he had bestowed them on her.

His kiss was so deep and penetrating that it drew the very breath from her soul. Her body was no longer her own. It ached to become a part of his, to recapture those wondrous moments that defied description.

It seemed she and Shaler had come full circle to return to that first night that she had stubbornly insisted on referring to as a space out of time. Shaler was warm and tender and generous and she was eager and responsive. The sight and feel of him sent her senses reeling. Again, just as before, the past and future faded and Casity became entrapped in an eternal present. Her arms glided up his chest, feeling his muscles flex and relax beneath her gentle touch. When he braced his weight on his elbow to lever them into a reclining position on the pallet, Casity inched ever closer, relishing the feel of his body, offering promises of the ecstasy to come.

With the faintest hint of a smile he peered down at her. "It stopped raining."

"So it has," Casity observed without taking her eyes off him.

"I could go fetch my horse," he offered.

"Yes, you could."

"We could be back at the cabin in less than two hours."

"That's true."

Shaler had given Casity every possible opportunity to reject the hunger in his eyes. She hadn't said she wanted him but neither had she made a move to untangle herself from his embrace.

"Cas, I feel like loving you again," he told her in a voice thick with passion.

"What's stopping you?" Her luminous eyes locked with his and he very nearly groaned aloud with desire.

"I want your permission, princess," he said simply but eloquently.

Her permission? This man—who had bent her onto the carriage seat and made her want him while she hated herself for surrendering, the same man who had swaggered into her hotel suite to park himself in her bath before seducing her under protest—wanted her permission? Why? He had never needed it before. Why was he being so utterly considerate and impossibly charming? How was she supposed to resist him when he was the epitome of gentlemanly attentiveness? Shaler intrigued her with this new dimension of his personality.

"I can't say *I desire you* or *I want you*—" Shaler whispered as his lips trailed over her cheek to trace the elegant line of her jaw. "—Because that would confirm your low opinion of men. So what does a man say when he feels such fierce need for the incredibly lovely woman in his arms? That she arouses him beyond bearing? That mere words cannot convey the way she makes him feel inside when she's part of him and he's part of her?"

Casity was hopelessly lost! This darkly handsome rogue was making every effort to change her point of view, to redeem himself in her eyes. At that moment, Casity was prepared to forgive him everything!

"I want to experience those special intimacies you mentioned to Reece earlier tonight," he murmured as his fingers loosed the stays on the back of her gown. He brushed his lips over her cool skin, sending goose bumps skittering over her sensitized flesh. "I don't want to make love *to* you, princess. I want to make love *with* you. And who knows? Maybe we'll both discover what love *is* . . ."

Casity could not deny him. Nor could she restrain the urge to draw his head back to hers and answer with a kiss. When his arms tightened around her and

she felt his body tremble, Casity closed her eyes and
yielded in total abandon.

"Teach me to please you, princess. It's no longer
enough that I want you, but I want you to want me,
too," Shaler murmured. "Does this arouse you—?"

Casity's breath left her chest when his forefinger
drew lazy circles on her belly and then scaled the aching peaks of her breasts.

"Or do you prefer to be touched like this—?"

His lips skimmed the ultrasensitive tips before his
tongue flicked out to tease the dusky crests.

"Or this perhaps—?"

His free hand splayed across her ribs to push her
gown down to her hips. His hand drifted slowly over
her lower abdomen and curled around her inner
thighs. Casity gasped audibly as he brought all her
senses to life with his exquisite fondling.

"Do you want more or less of my touch, princess?
Your wish is my command . . ."

When his lips feathered over her belly and moved
lower still, Casity lost the ability to speak. A wild rush
of passion sizzled through her, making her body
quiver convulsively as he teased her to the limits of
sanity.

"I want you to feel that same maddening sense of
helplessness you caused in me earlier tonight," Shaler
whispered as his kisses retraced their scintillating path
across her pliant flesh. "You made me your mindless
possession and stripped away every ounce of my
strength. Now I want all of you, princess. I want to
touch every living, breathing part of you, as if your
body and soul were my own."

Casity forgot to breathe when his warm lips brushed
over her thigh and his hands parted her legs. His fingertips curled around her inner thigh and delved into
the moist heat of her. The slow penetration sent a

cascade of sensation tumbling through her—cresting, ebbing, and rising again with each languid stroke.

Her heated response to his intimate fondling burned all but one thought from Shaler's mind: he wanted Casity in every conceivable way, wanted to touch her very essence and feel her soft flesh coiling around his fingertips, his lips. He wanted to taste the warm, scented rain of passion, to experience each secret sensation that rippled through the very core of her being.

When his lips grazed the lush petals of femininity, he felt her tremble with pleasure. When he teased her with his tongue, he felt the deep spasms consume her and, in turn, consume him until her pleasure had become his own. He dared more than he had ever dared before, inventing new ways to draw every possible sensation from her quivering body until each response converged and expanded. He could feel her uncoiling beneath his mouth and fingertips, assuring him that she wanted him beyond bearing. Only then did he crouch above her, offering himself to satisfy the ardent need he had created in her.

When Shaler wrapped his arms around her waist and drew her beneath him, Casity's hands enfolded him, stroked him, guided the hot, velvet length of him without an iota of self-consciousness. Her lashes fluttered up to peer into those sparkling amber eyes that burned with the intensity of the summer sun. And when Shaler lowered his body to hers, burying himself deep within her, Casity felt glorious pleasure spreading through every muscle and nerve.

Spasms of ineffable ecstasy throbbed through her as Shaler drove into her. Casity was oblivious to the rocks beneath her—it was as if she were floating on a cushion of air. She was spiraling into the clouds—

dipping, diving, soaring into eternity . . . and beyond . . .

Shaler felt the white-hot surge of desire explode inside him. Indescribable pleasure claimed his mind and body. He responded with a wild, breathless urgency that set the frantic cadence of passion. He was a man possessed, driven by the shuddering impulses that rocketed through him. When he was in Casity's arms, splendor engulfed him to such fantastic extremes that he swore dying would have been easier than bearing this maddening, desperate brand of sensual ecstasy.

When Shaler suddenly clutched her to him and groaned deep in his throat, Casity felt the rapture pulsating through him and into her. Her hand slid up the lean, hard columns of his thighs to scale his ribs before settling on his powerful shoulders. A soft sigh escaped her as she held him to her without feeling the guilt and shame that usually descended upon her when sanity returned after their lovemaking.

Tonight Casity knew what it might be like if she loved this magnificent man and he loved her in return. It would be paradise—and she would have no regrets whatsoever. And perhaps, in his own unique way, Shaler was trying to reach out to her, to investigate the possibility of love—something they'd both been too cynical and cautious to consider until now.

A pack of howling coyotes broke the peaceful silence. Casity reluctantly released Shaler when he braced his arms and eased away, leaving her feeling cold and strangely empty inside. His lips came back to hers in a brief kiss which Casity eagerly returned.

"Making love *with* you," he whispered. "Mmmm, I like that best of all . . ."

Like a graceful cougar, Shaler rose to his feet and donned his breeches in one effortless motion. "I'll go fetch my horse. Keep your eyes and ears open for unwelcome visitors. Four-legged predators have a tendency to venture out after a summer rain."

With that word of warning Shaler disappeared like an Indian warrior—without so much as a sound. Dreamily, Casity got back into her wet clothes. She giggled when she recalled the frantic expression on Shaler's face when he thought she was about to sink into the pond. His expression had been worth the dunking she'd taken. And when he made wild, sweet love with her, brewing their own storm in the mountains . . .

Casity sighed deeply as she remembered the pleasurable sensations. Lord, after this incredible interlude with Shaler as the playful, exceptionally attentive lover, Casity wasn't sure she wanted to return to reality. She preferred this mountain paradise . . .

The yelp of coyotes echoed around the canyon rim and an owl hooted somewhere in the near distance. Then a twig snapped, amplified by the stillness following the storm. Casity tensed when she heard a low, threatening growl reverberating beneath the overhanging ceiling of stone. She shrieked in terror when a bulky form pounced from her blind side. Casity twisted around and flung up her arm to ward off the attack. Her arm froze in midair and she blinked in disbelief when Shaler's hearty laughter rang in the darkness.

"Gotcha!" he snickered as he wrapped her in a bear hug and swung her in a dizzying circle.

"You ornery scamp!" Casity pounded her fist on his chest in reprisal, but the sparkle in her eyes and her accompanying giggle ruined the whole effect. "You set me up on purpose, didn't you?"

Shaler nuzzled his forehead against hers before

dropping a light kiss to her lips. "I never did claim to be your Prince Charming, princess," he chuckled.

While they weaved their way back to the trodden path, Casity asked herself when she had spent such a delightful evening and found herself in such amusing company. She was sorry to say that she couldn't recall another night with another companion that compared to this one. How ironic that Shaler provided the worst—and also the best—times she'd ever had.

Perhaps she could put the past behind her now and make a new beginning with Shaler, just as he had requested when he came to fetch her from Pendleton's suite. Tonight, he had seemed very sincere. She had let her guard down completely when he whispered of his desire to make a fresh start.

Casity sighed appreciatively as she watched dawn spill over the mountain slopes, bathing the world in a rainbow of translucent pastels. Sunlight glistened like diamonds on the damp grass and leaves, adding brilliance to the peaceful valley where the log cabin was nestled in the pines.

Although Casity was anxious to see Tweed again, she was reluctant to leave the wonderland she and Shaler had shared. Shaler did care for her in his own way and she was helplessly attracted to him. He hadn't said those exact words but he had implied that she meant something special to him. It was in his touch, his smile, in that husky baritone voice . . .

When the cabin door flew open, Casity broke into a smile at the sight of the thick-chested, red-haired man who hobbled outside on his splint and cane.

"I'm glad you're back, hon," Tweed enthused as he scuttled to lift her from the saddle.

Casity found herself engulfed in a hug that nearly squeezed the life out of her. While Shaler reined toward the shed to feed and unsaddle his sorrel gelding, Tweed shepherded Casity up the steps.

"I was hopin' that damnfool son o' mine could convince you to return. I swore I'd skin him alive if he didn't apologize and make amends. I also told him he'd better find a way to return to yer good graces, no matter what he had to do. I coulda shot him when I learned how rude and insultin' he'd been the day you two rode off to town together."

Casity felt as if a knife had pierced her heart. So it was only because of Tweed's demands that Shaler had come to her at all, was it? Tweed had insisted that Shaler find a way to redeem himself and that scoundrel had convinced her he was sincere. That magical interlude had been nothing more than a carefully plotted scheme, just like the one Shaler had designed for Reece Pendleton. Damn that man! He had only intended to pacify his father and quench his passion at the same time. He and his ridiculous declaration that men were honorable creatures! That was an outrageous contradiction in terms.

Shaler had duped her by turning on his devilish charm and she had fallen for it like a romantic fool! Shaler was probably down at the shed, unsaddling his horse and laughing himself sick! That bastard cared nothing about her, not really. He had been putting on an act for her benefit. Despite what he had wanted her to believe, she was still just a convenience. All those softly uttered words were just another illusion!

Well, curse his hide. Casity was sorely wishing she'd shot Reece Pendleton where he sat and *then* blown Shaler to smithereens while she had the chance. She had been twice betrayed by that seductive rake. But, by damned, Shaler McCain wasn't going to humiliate her ever again! Because of his treachery and deceit there were so many nights in her life that *did not* exist it was making her crazy. This reckless affair was officially over, here and now!

The instant Tweed and Shaler had snared that swindling Reece Pendleton, Casity would be as good as gone. And if she found some man who attracted her interest maybe she'd use *him* to take care of *her* sensual needs. Never again would she be lured under that golden-eyed devil's spell and let herself believe he wanted more than just the pleasures of a woman's body. And the next time she did something as rash as selling herself to the highest bidder she'd give her body into the bargain, just to prove to Shaler McCain that he meant nothing special to her, either! Fall in love with him? Never! Not after he had mortified her—again! Damn him! And damn her for being so gullible!

Twenty

With a somber frown Tim Brady guided Jack McCall into his office and stuffed the inebriated gambler into the nearest chair. Jack tried to focus his bloodshot eyes on the man who had propelled him out of his room where he had intended to sleep off his most recent bender. But it was damned near impossible to see straight when his eyes were level full of liquor.

Johnny Varnes stared quizzically at his partner before he turned his gaze to the drunken excuse of a man who slouched in his chair. "Now, what's going on?"

"Hickok's back," Tim confirmed grimly. "I saw him myself. He was headed toward The Mint. Several miners gathered around him, asking him to put on a badge and clean up the town. The prospectors are all in a stew after one of their friends got worked over when he refused to sell his productive claim to Pendleton."

"Did Hickok commit himself?" Johnny asked worriedly.

"He *claims* he just came to the Black Hills to pan for gold," Tim reported sarcastically. "I don't believe it."

"Hickok's in town?" Jack McCall stirred like an overturned beetle attempting to upright itself. "Wild Bill Hickok?"

"Yeah, and we want you to get rid of him," Johnny

leaned his forearms on the desk to stare at the besotted gambler. "I thought you told us you had an axe to grind with Hickok. Didn't he gun down your brother in Kansas?"

"Damn sure did, the son-of-a-bitch," Jack said, slurring his words.

"You're good with a pistol," Tim inferred. "You could have your revenge on Hickok and do us a favor if you disposed of him. Any man who bested Hickok would be famous overnight, not just in Deadwood but all over the country."

Johnny Varnes got up from his chair and ambled around the desk to stare down at McCall. "We'll pay you a hundred dollars to take on Hickok, plus all the free whiskey you can drink for as long as you're in town," he offered.

Jack rubbed his bristly chin and considered the offer. "Maybe," he mumbled. "But not now. The time ain't right and I ain't sober."

"As if that's a regular occurrence," Tim muttered half under his breath.

"Nope." Jack hoisted himself out of the chair and staggered toward the door. "One of these days I'll take on Hickok, but it won't be now."

"Your brother will never rest in peace until you avenge his death," Johnny called after him. "Think about that, Jack. You're as tough as Hickok is. Maybe even tougher."

"I said . . . not yet," Jack mumbled.

When Jack wobbled on his way, Johnny glanced back at Tim. "We'll keep working on him. If we keep reminding him of his brother and bolster his confidence, he might come around."

"Well, he sure as hell better come around before Hickok decides to put on a badge and run us out of Dakota the same way he chased us out of Kansas!" Tim growled. "I don't relish looking down the barrel of his sawed-off shotgun again. We've got too much at stake here, especially after we joined up with Pendleton."

"That's a fact," Johnny affirmed. "I won't rest easy until I know for sure what Hickok is doing here and get him out of the way. Tomorrow night I'll drag Jack out of his stupor and haul him back to the office. If we talk to him long enough and often enough, he'll come around. In the meantime, we'll have one of our men keep a close eye on Hickok."

"Wild Bill Hickok is in Deadwood?" Casity chirped when Tweed mentioned the famed shootist.

Tweed eyed Casity warily. "Now, you listen to me, girl. Don't go gettin' any ideas about havin' James hunt down yer uncle's killers. James got out of the marshalin' business for good reason. He's made too many enemies of the wrong kind of people. He's thirty-nine years old and spent plenty of years solvin' everybody else's problems because they weren't fast enough on the draw to do it themselves. James took off his badge and he ain't got no hankerin' to put it back on again. All he wants is some peace and quiet. He and Shay looked over a potential claim and James bought into it with another old friend of his. James went into town get supplies for his new occupation of prospectin' and he's built a cabin in Lard Pail Billy Raddick's minin' camp, and that's that."

Casity didn't argue the point. She intended to wait until Tweed and Shaler rode off to meet Pendleton at Mule's Ear Gulch. When they were out from underfoot, she would set off for Lard Pail Billy Raddick's camp and let Hickok decide if he wanted the job or not. Casity had a thousand dollars in gold—compliments of Reece Pendleton—to offer Wild Bill Hickok.

Every speck of gold dust was his if he agreed to accept her proposition. This was the opportunity Casity had hoped for. A man with Wild Bill Hickok's reputation wouldn't have an ounce of trouble trailing her uncle's murderers.

After Tweed hobbled out the door to fetch his mule, Shaler pivoted to stare pensively at Casity. It disturbed him that she had been so remote since he'd brought her back to the cabin for her protection and for his peace of mind. She was utterly charming to Tweed, who fussed over her as if she were the daughter he never had. But each time Shaler got within ten feet of her, she shied away.

What bee did she have in her bonnet now? Shaler wondered. After the night of the storm, Shaler thought he and Casity were on the friendliest of terms. But she had stepped inside the cabin and *wham!* Suddenly it was as if a door had slammed in Shaler's face. It was as if everything they had said and done the night of the storm had never happened!

Why did he care that she was avoiding him? They had made no promises to each other, after all. If Casity had her way, she'd probably have nothing more to do with him.

If he had any sense he would ignore her instead of feeling hurt by her behavior. But the fact was, that blue-eyed siren was on his mind constantly, and he wasn't accustomed to being so preoccupied by a woman.

Shaler had had a helluva time forcing himself to sprawl out on his pallet on the floor the past few nights while Casity was in his bed. One would have thought it had been weeks instead of days since he had touched her. Hell's fire, he had even relished the thought of simply sleeping beside her in bed. Now was that crazy? Of course it was! That female had obviously tampered with his sanity.

In the past, Shaler had only wanted a woman in his bed for the usual reason. Damnation, it wasn't even winter and he couldn't even use the excuse of needing to cuddle up to a warm body to avoid the evening chill! It was the second of August, for heaven's sake, and it was as hot as hell in the Black Hills! So why did he have this compelling need to hold her, to make wild, sweet love to her until she drained every ounce of his strength—again?

"Shay, are you comin' or not?" Tweed hollered impatiently. "Pendleton will be at the mine before we are if'n you don't shake a leg. And speakin' of legs, mine is painin' me something awful, sittin' on this sway-backed mule in this heat. Let's go!"

When Shaler hesitated another moment, Casity wheeled away to scrub the breakfast dishes. It wasn't a good thing to spend too much time staring into those spellbinding amber eyes. The sight of this man could still trigger emotions she preferred to avoid. Shaler had taken advantage of her ridiculous weakness for him four times and that was four times too many! He didn't love her and she didn't love him and this ill-fated affair was over. That's the way Casity wanted it . . . didn't she? Well, didn't she? Of course she did. Falling prey to his attentions was like coming down with an affliction, but she would recover, she assured herself confidently. And very soon he would walk out of her life and return to his favorite haunts in Colorado. She would be relieved when he was gone . . .

"Cas?"

Her body pulled as taut as a harp string when that low, caressing voice rolled over her. Curse it, why did he have to use that tone with her? It inspired memories of moments that should never have happened.

"What?" She refused to meet his probing stare.

"Shay! Let's go! We ain't got all day!" Tweed yelled.

Shaler heaved a sigh and pivoted on his heel. "Never mind. I'd better go before Tweed throws another conniption."

Truth was, Shaler didn't even know what he had wanted to say to Casity, but he felt the need to say something. An odd feeling of doom had crept over him while he watched her turn back to her chores and dismiss him as if he were already gone. Shaler had never claimed to be clairvoyant, but he couldn't shake the uneasy premonition that rippled through him.

"God, it's hot out here," Tweed grumbled as he mopped the perspiration from his brow. "There ain't a breath of air in these hills. It must be at least a hundred in the shade. I'm steamin' like a clam." He nudged his mule down the path, thankful for the faint breeze that motion stirred. "I'll be glad to hightail it back to the Rockies. I never was cut out for this weather."

The thought of leaving Casity in Deadwood and him heading for Colorado put another damper on Shaler's spirits. Damn it all, what was wrong with him? That blue-eyed siren had somehow managed to get under his skin without him realizing it. The next thing he knew he'd be asking her to come to Colorado. As if she would even accept! Not likely, Shaler assured himself. Considering her standoffishness and resentment of the passion they'd shared, Casity would jump down his throat if he dared to invite her.

Shaler quickly recalled the remark Casity had made a few days earlier. She had agreed to forgive him for the terrible way he had treated her while he was laboring under his misconceptions, but she wasn't planning to forget the turmoil he had caused her. It would be best for both of them if they simply went their own ways and put their stormy affair behind them . . .

"Why are you so quiet all of a sudden?" Tweed asked.

When Shaler ignored the question, Tweed squinted back at the cabin with a wry smile. He had noticed how Shaler's gaze had followed Casity's every movement since she'd returned from Deadwood. Tweed had also caught Shaler staring at her closed bedroom door a dozen times.

Tweed's stony gaze settled on Shaler like a boulder. "Is there somethin' goin' on between you and Cas that I should know about?" he questioned point-blank.

"Nope," Shaler replied without glancing in his father's direction.

Tweed cocked his head to one side. "Okay, Shay, let me put it to you this way. Is there somethin' goin' on that you *don't want* me to know about?"

"What the hell is this? The Western version of the Spanish Inquisition?" Shaler muttered irritably.

"No, this is yer dear old daddy askin' if there's a chance of him becomin' a grandpa before his next birthday," Tweed said with his usual candor.

Shaler winced as if he'd been snakebit. "I—"

"Don't you lie to me, boy." Tweed snatched up his cane and reached over to whack Shaler on the shoulder. "At the time, I wondered why Casity was so anxious to get away from here that she sold herself at auction. What else did you do to her besides threaten her if she dared to come back? You admitted yourself that you threatened to take advantage of her if she stayed here. By damn, if you forced yourself on—" The very thought caused Tweed to mutter a string of muffled oaths. " 'Curse it, you better not have touched that girl. She ain't no harlot from the Badlands. She's a respectable lady!"

"Pipe down, Tweed," Shaler hissed. "You don't

need to announce our arrival in the gulch a mile before we get there."

"Don't change the subject. Did you or didn't you
compromise that poor girl after all the hell she's been
through?"

If there was one thing that could be said about Tweed
Cramer, it was that he was a persistent old coot. He
had the kind of curiosity that was fatal. When Tweed
wanted answers he probed and dug and pried until he
got what he wanted.

"And for God's sake, don't you *dare* tell me it happened the first night you spent together in the wilds
after she sprained her knee and escaped them Indians!" Tweed's green eyes glowed like hot pokers. "Was
that the first of many times you took advantage of
her?" When Shaler refused to answer, Tweed blurted,
"Well? Was it?"

Shaler heaved an audible sigh. "I thought you said
you didn't want me to tell you it happened the first
night."

Tweed vented his anger on its source by smacking
Shaler on the shoulder again. Shaler reined his steed
farther away from his father before he suffered another painful slash from the cane. That didn't discourage Tweed, who was at the height of his fury.
Hissing and sputtering, he chased Shaler down the
hill, brandishing his cane like a sword. He was infuriated that his slow-moving mule couldn't keep pace
with Shaler's long-legged sorrel.

The instant Tweed spied Pendleton's buggy beside
the creek, he lowered his voice and his cane. But he
was still simmering when he dismounted.

"This conversation ain't nowhere near over," Tweed
vowed stormily. "It's only bein' postponed." His irritation with Shaler couldn't have been more evident.
"I wish to hell I woulda tanned yer backside good and

proper when you was a kid. Maybe you wouldn't have turned out to be such a disgrace." With an exasperated sigh he limped toward the tunnel. "Deflowerin' decent ladies. Good Lord, I never heard the like and I certainly never expected it from you!"

With visible effort, Tweed set his irritation aside and peered inside the shaft. "Is that you, Pendleton?"

Reece glanced toward the echoing sound to see Tweed's bulky frame silhouetted by sunlight. "I thought I'd have a look around while I was waiting."

A triumphant smile pursed his lips. From what Reece could determine, the shaft lay close to a pure vein of gold. The existence of quartz embedded in the rock and the glittering dust in the drift suggested promising prospects. Reece hadn't seen such prime indications since he had attempted to buy the Homestake Mine, which had yielded five thousand dollars during its first few months of production, even while using primitive mining procedures. But George Hearst, the San Francisco entrepreneur who had set up his headquarters at the gold sites in Lead, Dakota, had outbid Reece and bought the property.

"Now don't think we don't know this is a good mine," Tweed called into the shaft. "The only reason we decided to sell it was because it's a long ride from our cabin. With this broke leg of mine, we can't keep up with the extra claim. But me and my son ain't greedy men. Our original claim pays the expenses and gives us ample spendin' money."

Reece ambled out of the tunnel with his lantern. "The mine shows possibilities," he agreed, though not enthusiastically enough to tempt Tweed and Shaler to raise their price. "But it will take heavy equipment to process the ore, plus a sizable labor crew. It'll be expensive to operate."

"True enough," Shaler replied as he moseyed up

beside Pendleton. "I don't claim to be an expert, bu
I've taken samples of ore to the assayer's office and i
looks good."

"How much are you asking for the claim?" Reece
queried as nonchalantly as possible.

Tweed rubbed his whiskered chin and pretended to
ponder the question. "Well, the Homestake Mine and
Golden Terra sold for one hundred and five thousand
dollars. O 'course, this ain't as good of a claim, but
think it should be worth at least thirty thousand dol
lars, don't you, Shay?"

"Thirty thou—" Reece swallowed his tongue and i
was a moment before his vocal apparatus began to func
tion properly. "I won't have any cash flow left to mine
this shaft if I spend thirty thousand."

"Well, I reckon we can contact George Hearst up
in Lead and see what he thinks the claim is worth,"
Tweed replied.

Reece grumbled under his breath. The last thing
he wanted was to loose another bonanza to his com
petition in Lead! "I'll take it, provided my assayer ap
proves these samples."

"Take all the samples you want," Shaler offered gen
erously. "I'll be in town within a few days and I'll deed
the claim over to you, if you decide to buy—*in cash.*"

"Cash?" Reece squawked. If he paid cash, it would
deplete his expense account and he would be forced
to take a loan at the bank so he could hire labor and
begin digging. He would have to cinch his belt for a
few weeks and he hadn't done that in over a year!

"Cash," Tweed affirmed with a firm set of his jaw

"Oh, very well," Reece muttered. "If I buy the claim
you'll be paid in full when you sign the deed."

While Reece scurried around taking samples from
various locations in the shaft and from the creek
Shaler bit back a sly smile. He'd love to see the look

on this scoundrel's face when the rocks hauled out turned up nothing but more rock. Reece Pendleton would be bankrupt by summer's end. In the meantime, he'd sweat it out—literally and figuratively. That was exactly what this conniving rascal deserved after he'd swindled so many investors and muscled defenseless prospectors out of their claims.

After Reece clambered back into his buggy and sped down the path, Tweed shouted in triumph. "Reece Pendleton can kiss his fancy clothes and swank hotel suite good-bye. He'll be lucky if he can afford a tent after he sinks his funds into this lame duck."

Shaler was amazed at how quickly Tweed's mind switched gears. Once the older man's victorious laughter died down, he turned and frowned at Shaler.

"Now that our dealin's with Pendleton are settled and outta the way, I wanna know what you plan to do about Casity Crockett," Tweed demanded.

"I offered her the cabin and the claim in Bonanza Gulch when we return to Colorado," Shaler informed his father as he strode toward his mount. "She intends to find a remote location for a few more weeks."

"And you plan to leave her here?" Tweed stared incredulously at Shaler. "I had no idea I'd raised such a damned fool!"

Scowling and muttering under his breath, Tweed struggled onto his mule. The ride back to Bonanza Gulch was anything but pleasant for Shaler. At regular intervals, Tweed hissed and cursed, flashing Shaler glares and grimaces.

"I shoulda convinced Cas to marry *me*, even if she wasn't my mail-order bride," Tweed griped three miles later. "At least she wouldn't be wanderin' around the Black Hills, tanglin' with the likes of *you* and Reece Pendleton."

"Cas isn't looking for security or love or anything

else," Shaler assured him tartly. "She doesn't expec
those things from a man. She told me so herself."

"Gee, I wonder why?" Tweed smirked caustically
"You and the other ruttin' stags who've been runnin
around loose in Dakota Territory haven't given her
anythin' to believe in and that's a fact! Nobody trust
a snake what's bit him twice!"

If it was Tweed's intention to make Shaler feel guilty
he had succeeded. Shaler had long been a cynic and
skeptic, looking for the worst in women and usually
finding it. He had projected those failings on tha
auburn-haired beauty and she, in turn, had adapted
his philosophies to suit her situation. As reluctant a
Shaler was to admit it, Tweed was right. The men in
Casity Crockett's life had done nothing to earn her
trust or affection. But even if Shaler did decide to d
the honorable thing and ask Casity to marry him, she
would reject him for pure spite.

And what the devil would he do with a wife anyway
Shaler had grown up wild and free, traveling whereve
the wind took him. And as James Hickok had said, i
was hard for some men to settle down when they had
so much tumbleweed in their blood. Shaler would
make a horrible husband and Casity would probabl
make a waspish wife. The passion they sparked in each
other wasn't nearly enough to last a lifetime . . .

Shaler exhaled a frustrated breath while he listened
to Tweed snort and growl inarticulately. No doubt i
would be a good long while before Tweed allowed
Shaler to live this reckless affair down. Months, mayb
even years! Tweed would keep Casity's bittersweet
memories alive until he drove Shaler mad. Well, Reec
Pendleton had been served his just deserts and maybe
Shaler deserved his, too. With each passing day, he had
come to regret his rocky relationship with that blue
eyed enchantress. But he couldn't bring himself to re

gret the splendorous passion he had discovered in her arms. For those magical moments, life had stood still and he had experienced sensations he never believed possible . . .

Don't start getting sentimental, McCain, Shaler scolded himself when the sweet memories sent a warm throb through his loins. Passion lost its potency after a time. It always had in the past and it always would. The attraction would have dwindled in a few months. He and Casity were too much alike in some ways and drastically different in others. Despite what Tweed thought, it would be best if Shaler and Casity went their separate ways. He had already made the mistake of allowing his hungry desire to rule his head. He wasn't about to make another error by letting noble intention dictate to him. A man was never truly satisfied by doing what he felt he *ought* to do. When it came to a man's feelings for a woman, he had to be compelled by the stirrings in his heart.

No, Shaler decided. A man had to be bound by the velvet chains of love, if there truly was such a thing. Shaler didn't love that headstrong, stubborn, fascinating female. And she didn't love him, either. Nor did he want to have anything more to do with him. So that was that.

After having this heart to heart talk with himself, Shaler was convinced that he knew what was best, even if Tweed didn't agree. But then, Tweed never agreed with Shaler on much of anything anyway. The old geezer was argumentative and opinionated by nature and by habit. Shaler supposed that was why he and Tweed usually got along so well. Tweed had raised his adopted son to be as contrary as his father!

Twenty-one

Casity didn't waste any time gathering her belong
ings from the cabin. As soon as Shaler and Twee
disappeared into the thicket of pines and headed to
ward Mule's Ear Gulch, she hiked off with her satchel
clutched in each hand. It wasn't difficult to locate
Lard Pail Bill Raddick's mining camp since she had
stopped there to ask directions to Bonanza Gulch
when she first arrived in Deadwood.

After tramping up and down the hills and valley
for more than an hour, Casity encountered two pros
pectors hauling a wagonload of supplies to the mining
camp. When she announced her destination, she was
offered a ride and readily accepted to save wear and
tear on her feet and give her mending leg a rest. After
a half hour of bumping along the rugged trail, Casit
spotted the colony of tents, shacks, and cabins nestled
in the steep-walled valley. Gathering her satchels, she
clambered down from the wagon to seek directions to
Wild Bill Hickok's cabin.

Before she had taken a dozen steps, a swarm of men
buzzed around her with wide smiles and enthusiastic
greetings. It still amazed Casity that men were such
primitive creatures. The opportunity to see a woman
had them stumbling all over each other and trotting
after her like kittens on the trail of fresh milk. No
one man in the congregation cared *who* she was, only

that she was *female*. Casity was sure she'd never been ogled quite so thoroughly for such an extended period of time. It was unnerving to have so many masculine eyes roving over her, and she felt the need to cover herself, even though she was fully clothed.

James Butler Hickok surveyed the pert auburn-haired beauty and her entourage of male admirers. So this was the most sought-after female in the Black Hills! The young lady had made quite a reputation for herself because of her beauty and spirit. Although Casity had yet to introduce herself, James recognized her after listening to Tweed's description, combined with that of the miners who had feasted their eyes on her the past two weeks. Casity was indeed stunning. That cloud of dark hair that danced with red-gold highlights and crystal clear blue eyes drew a man's gaze and held it fast.

Although most women would have soaked up all the attention like a sponge, this pretty female considered masculine interest a personal insult. She didn't flaunt her good looks or demand special consideration because she was a female. She was what she was. And what she was, James mused with a sigh of appreciation, was a lovely sight to behold, whether she preferred to be or not.

No wonder she had captured the fascination of every male between the ages of eighteen and eighty. She had it all—the poise, the delicate bone structure, and a beautiful face to match her body. She was definitely the kind of female who inspired dreams.

When Casity ambled toward him, James drew himself up to full stature and politely touched the brim of his hat. After nodding a silent greeting, Casity pirouetted to dismiss her ardent followers.

"If you don't mind, I'd like a private word with Mister Hickok," she declared in a businesslike tone.

Dejectedly, the crowd dispersed, leaving James alone with the lovely lass.

A curious smile played about James's mouth, making his blond mustache curl upward at the corners. "What brings you here, Miss—?" He regarded her for a moment, his blue eyes twinkling with amusement. "What shall I call you besides exceptionally lovely? Do you prefer to be known as Miss Crockett or Miss Lambert?"

Casity was caught off guard by Hickok's teasing question. She didn't have the faintest idea that Tweed had given James a detailed account of her life story. Nor was she aware that she had become a celebrity in Deadwood and its surrounding camps.

Hickok's good-natured smile put Casity at ease. She had heard conflicting reports about him during his years as marshal of the wildest cowtowns in Kansas. Some folks insisted that Hickok rode on both sides of law and order, breaking the rules as often as he enforced them. Others hailed him as a legendary gunfighting hero who helped pave the way for civilization in the rowdy cowtowns. Whether Hickok could shoot the cork out of a whiskey bottle at twenty paces, Casity didn't know. But she found him to be a quiet-mannered man with an engaging smile. Although the lines of his face testified to years of hard living, he was still a muscular, attractive man who towered over six feet in height. His blue eyes still held a spark of vitality and his perceptive gaze seemed to take in everything around him in one glance.

"You may call me Casity," she replied. "And what shall I call you, sir? James or Wild Bill?"

"What few friends I have call me James," he said as he gestured toward the homemade chair on the porch of his newly constructed cabin.

Casity took a load off her aching leg and sighed in

elief. "At least you have the luxury of a few friends, ames. I seem to collect enemies more readily." Casity urned her somber gaze on Hickok as he sank down n the chair beside her. "My enemies are the reason 've sought you out. My uncle was murdered by two nen who would have done the same to me weeks ago f I hadn't escaped—"

"I know. Tweed told me all about it. I'm sorry," ames said sincerely.

"He did?" Casity blinked in surprise.

James nodded. "I spent a few days with Shay and Tweed before starting construction on this cabin," he xplained. "They're *two* of my *few* friends. In fact, Shay helped me locate a mining site and file a claim. He's quite a man. Indeed, he turned out much better han expected, despite the three-year influence I had n him."

Casity had not come here to discuss Shaler McCain. n her opinion he leaned more toward *exasperating* han *extraordinary*. She was in no mood to hear his praises sung to high heaven. When she walked out of he cabin in Bonanza Gulch, she had closed that particular chapter of her life and was ready to get on to he next! Because of that rake, she'd been walking round with her leg in a splint and her heart in a ling. But her leg was mending and her bruised heart vould heal and she didn't care if she ever heard Shaler's name mentioned again!

"As I was saying, my life will be in jeopardy until hose two killers have been caught. I'd like to hire you o track them down and make sure they're punished or their vile crime. Although I don't know their names, I can give you an accurate description—and rom far closer range than I would have preferred," she dded emphatically. "I want to see justice served and

I'm willing to pay you a thousand dollars for your effort
If you want more, I'll find a way."

James shook his blond head. "I'm sorry, Casity, bu
I have no desire to be a bounty hunter or pin on an
other tin star. My eyesight isn't as good as it once wa
and my reflexes are slower," he admitted. "Since
don't shoot as fast or as straight as I used to, I'v
decided to leave marshaling to younger men."

Casity's shoulders sagged in disappointment. Whe
she learned that Hickok had arrived in Deadwood, he
hopes had soared, even though Tweed had warne
her away. Now she didn't know where to turn.

"I suggest you contact the U.S. and state marsha
in Nebraska," James advised. "I can give you the
names and the location of their offices. Since th
crime took place in Nebraska the law officials shoul
send out an all-points bulletin. You can have poster
distributed from here to Texas and west to Californi
By offering a sizable reward, you'll draw bounty hun
ers from far and wide . . . or you could hire Shay t
track the men down," he suggested. "He has a nos
like a bloodhound and lightning reflexes with a pisto
Although he usually keeps a low profile so he won
have to pin on a badge and tempt ne'er-do-wells t
take potshots at him for the sport of it, he's an exce
lent tracker and handy with weapons."

Casity would never consider the suggestion, not fo
a second. She wanted no further contact with Shale
McCain. She only wanted to forget what she wishe
she couldn't remember—the resonance of his voice a
it whispered across her responsive skin, the gentlene
of his touch, the crooked smile, that intriguing sparkl
in those amber eyes . . . Casity gave herself a mental sla
for being sidetracked.

"Well, if you're sure you won't change your minc
I won't take up more of your time." Casity rose, the

groaned when her leg threatened to buckle at the knee. Bracing herself against the outer wall of the cabin, she forced a smile. "It was an honor to meet you, James. I hope you'll find your fortune in the gold fields of Dakota."

"Where are you going?" he asked curiously.

"Into Deadwood to catch the stage. If I'm to make contact with state and federal marshals, I'll have to return to Cheyenne or travel to the territorial capital at Yankton. Sheriff Brown has his hands full trying to keep a lid on Deadwood and the entire county all by himself. I doubt he can spare the time to be of assistance in this matter."

"I'll accompany you to town," James volunteered.

"I can manage on my own, but thank you for the offer," Casity replied with an appreciative smile.

"I insist." James pivoted on his heel and strode into his cabin to gather a few essentials for his overnight stay in Deadwood. "Tweed would bite my head off if he knew I'd let you wander off alone in this wild country. He's quite fond of you."

"And I'm equally fond of him," Casity assured him.

"Maybe you should have married him." James flashed her a grin as he emerged from his cabin with a saddlebag slung over one broad shoulder.

"I probably should have," Casity agreed as James propelled her toward his steed.

"Or perhaps it was Shay whom you—"

Casity cut him off with a distasteful sniff. "I'd prefer that you don't mention that man's name around me more than is absolutely necessary. And if you must refer to him, please don't link my name to his in the same sentence!"

James chuckled at her sassiness. He was just beginning to realize how much spunk she had. The combination of beauty and vitality was irresistible.

"Very well then, if you don't wish to discuss you
know-who, shall we talk about the weather? It has been
unseasonably hot, hasn't it?" James questioned as h
assisted Casity into the saddle.

Tweed glanced around the quiet cabin. "Casity?"
When he received no response, he hobbled toward th
bedroom to find it empty. "She's gone." He wheele
around when he heard Shaler's hurried footsteps
"Where are you goin'?"

"To find Cas," Shaler threw over his shoulder.

Shaler hadn't given the matter much thought when
he realized Casity had sneaked away during their ab
sence. His actions were purely reflexive. She had lef
and he was going to bring her back before she go
herself in more trouble. That woman attracted it a
easily as she attracted men!

Tweed propped himself against the doorjamb an
watched his son leap into the saddle. "Just leave he
go, Shay," he said quietly. "It's what you wanted, afte
all."

Shaler gaped at the bushy-haired man in the ope
doorway. "I thought—"

"I've been givin' the situation some serious contem
plation durin' the ride back," Tweed interrupted
"I've decided yer right. What do either of us nee
with a woman anyhow? A purty girl like Casity won'
have no trouble latchin' onto a man if'n she want
one, for whatever reason. She don't stay put too goo
anyhow. She's always flitterin' off all over creatio
whenever it suits her."

Shaler couldn't believe what he was hearing! Fo
almost three weeks Tweed had been praising Casit
and he'd come unhinged when he realized Shaler ha

compromised her. Now, out of the blue, Tweed was shrugging her off. Why?

"Are you the same man who hammered me with his cane because of that female?" Shaler questioned.

"No, I'm the *sane* man who got over bein' furious to realize you was right all along. You and Casity Crockett mix as well as oil and water," Tweed declared with perfect assurance. "You ain't the right man for a woman like her and she's too much woman for a man like you."

Shaler's eyes narrowed into golden slits. "What the hell do you mean *a man like me?*"

"Yer a man who can't live without lonesome," Tweed said matter-of-factly. "You only want a woman around to satisfy yer urges. I was the same in my younger days. It's no wonder you turned out the way you did. You'll end up just like me—all used up and worn out with nobody to care. But to each his own."

He shrugged a thick-bladed shoulder and pulled his pipe from his pocket, calmly lighting it before he continued. "I made my choice and so have you. I shoulda known it was foolish to send for a mail-order bride in the first place. But I was sittin' around feelin' sorry for myself with this stiff leg, wonderin' if this was what it was gonna be like in my declinin' years. I got to thinkin' it would be nice to have someone to fuss over me, to share companionship." Tweed puffed on his pipe. "But I guess it wasn't meant to be. Casity Crockett came into my life and into yers by mistake and now we'll let her go. That's what you wanted and it's probably for the best."

"Damn it, Tweed. You change your mind faster than Indians change camps!" Shaler muttered sourly. "First you threw a tantrum when I wanted to let her go and now you don't care."

"I always did pride myself in adaptin' without too

much fuss," Tweed said proudly. "We came here to get Amos Grant's money back. In a couple of days the deed'll be signed and the job'll be done. We'll go on with our lives and put Deadwood behind us."

When Shaler scowled and reined his steed to thunder off, Tweed snickered wryly. Shaler had been so anxious to find Casity that he could barely sit still in the saddle. Tweed doubted Shaler even knew what compelled him to search. That young buck only knew he *had* to get going, there and then.

It was damned amusing to watch love sneak up on a man when he was so skeptical about it. Oh, Shaler had been fighting it like a wild mustang battling harness, but he cared about Casity Crockett more than he realized. And if it wasn't love then it was something damned near like it, Tweed decided. Something sure as hell had a hold on Shaler McCain.

By taking the opposing view, Tweed had attacked the blind side of Shaler's contrariness. If Tweed had ranted and raved as he had done when he learned Casity and Shaler had been as close as two people could get, that mule-headed son of his would have balked—again.

Tweed mentally patted himself on the back for letting Shaler think it was his idea to track Casity down. "Well, Shay, it looks as if Reece Pendleton ain't the only one in this neck of the woods who's been out smarted!"

Johnny Varnes flung his business partner a curious glance when a rap resounded on their office door. Since Wild Bill Hickok's arrival in Deadwood, both men had been walking on pins and needles, wondering if the ex-marshal who had run them out of Abilene was plotting to rout them from Dakota.

With his pistol poised and ready, Tim Brady answered the door. Johnny kept his six-shooter concealed beneath the desk. To their relief, it wasn't Hickok's face that appeared. Two haggard-looking cowboys greeted them.

"We're looking for Reece Pendleton," Ned Johnson declared as he watched Tim slide his pistol back into its holster. "The bartender said you might know where he is."

Johnny scrutinized the two hard-bitten hombres who filed through the door. "What do you want with Pendleton?"

"We used to work for him in Texas," Russel Bassett explained. "He sent for us. We would've been here two weeks ago, but we had to detour to Denver to see to some unfinished business. It turned out to be a wild-goose chase," he grumbled. "But we did happen onto a tidbit of information we need to convey to Reece—the sooner the better."

After Johnson and Bassett sank into their chairs, Johnny discreetly set his pistol aside and braced his forearms on the desk. "Reece rode out of town this morning to check on a claim he's planning to purchase. He should be back later this afternoon."

"We thought we better pass along the information as quickly as possible," Ned said between chomps on his wad of tobacco. "If you see Reece before we do, tell him we overheard a conversation in a Denver saloon that'll be mighty interesting to him."

"What information?" Tim Brady asked.

Russel looked over at Ned, who glanced warily back at him.

"Reece is our business associate," Johnny explained to his wary companions. "He told us he'd sent for you. What concerns him concerns us."

"Well, it happens that one of Reece's stockholders

by the name of Amos Grant isn't too happy about the
lack of dividends from Pendleton Mining Company,"
Russel reported. "Amos was boasting to his friends
that he'd hired somebody to get his money out of
Reece."

Johnny and Tim winced. "Who?" they chorused.

"Grant didn't mention any names," Ned replied.
"All he said was that Reece Pendleton wouldn't be
cheating anybody else out of investments in his
crooked company."

"Hickok," Johnny muttered grimly.

"No wonder Hickok didn't want to pin on a badge,"
Tim muttered back. "He must have some other
scheme in mind to break Pendleton, and us with him."

Russel hoisted himself out of the chair and raked
his blunt fingers through his unkempt mop of greasy
hair. "If you can point us in the right direction—" he
requested, "—we're going to treat ourselves to a bath, a
hot meal, and the company of some warm, willing females. Tell Reece we'll be in touch with him tomorrow
morning."

When the cowboys trooped out, Johnny stared apprehensively at Tim. "Hickok must have decided he
could make better money as a private investigator than
riding herd over cattle towns. Go fetch Jack McCall,"
he ordered. "We've got to convince Jack that now's
the time to dispose of Hickok. If Hickok has discovered that we're in cahoots with Pendleton, you can bet
he'll come after us next."

Tim nodded bleakly. "If McCall isn't half-soused
I'll make sure he is before I tote him in here. He's a
lot bolder when he has a few drinks under his belt."

"Just make sure he isn't too drunk to shoot
straight," Johnny insisted. "And keep bolstering his
confidence with praise while you're pouring whiskey
down his gullet. We want him just drunk enough."

When Tim sailed out of the office to locate Broken-Nose Jack McCall, Johnny paced from wall to wall. Reece Pendleton had obviously tried to bamboozle an investor assertive enough to seek retribution in a cunning way. If Tim and Johnny didn't protect themselves, their own investments would be in jeopardy. What they didn't need was Hickok pounding answers out of Pendleton that would incriminate them!

Damn, they should have pressed McCall harder when Hickok first showed up in Deadwood. If that drunken gunslinger didn't come through for them, they were going to have to take the risk of facing Hickok themselves.

Johnny poured himself a drink. He was feeling all the frustration he had felt the last time he and Tim had tangled with Hickok. The man had always been dangerous. Now he was more so, considering the information Bassett and Johnson had acquired in Denver. Hickok could ruin them all and Johnny wasn't looking forward to starting all over again elsewhere. But for damned sure, he wasn't going down with Pendleton. Reece was on his own from this day forward!

Twenty-two

It didn't take Shaler long to reach Lard Pail Bil Raddick's mining camp. He had ridden out of pure instinct after watching Casity's eyes light up at the mention of Wild Bill Hickok's name early that morning. Unless Shaler missed his guess—and he couldn' imagine that he had—Casity intended to hire Hickok to hunt her uncle's murderers down, despite what Tweed had said.

Shaler silently cursed Tweed for mentioning James' name at all. Knowing how determined that auburn haired hellion could be when she set her mind to something, she would approach James with a proposition. Damn that woman. Why couldn't she stay put She never seemed to be where Shaler left her!

After inquiring about Casity at the mining camp Shaler learned she had been there and gone. He mut tered a string of curses when he was told that Casit and James had left together several hours earlier From all indications, Casity had somehow managed to convince James to do her bidding. But that came a no surprise to Shaler. No man, not even James Butle Hickok, was immune to that woman. Hell's fire, Shale intended to chew James up one side and down the other the first chance he got. James should have hauled Casity back to the cabin at gunpoint, if need be, instead of riding off toward Deadwood with her

A look of surprise captured Shaler's features when he glanced up to see Tweed on his mule, waiting for him on the edge of camp.

"What are you doing here?" Shaler demanded as he reined his sorrel gelding to a halt. "I thought you were tired of being out in the blistering sun and aching from the hip down."

Tweed shrugged casually. "I thought I better come along to make sure you didn't do somethin' crazy— like drag Casity back to our cabin."

"Dragging her back is the least of my concerns now," Shaler muttered irascibly. "That firebrand came here to speak with James. Ten to one, she convinced him to hunt her uncle's killers down. The two of them rode off to Deadwood together."

"What!" Tweed hooted. "Surely James has more sense than to pack up and tear off to find those two men. Maybe he was just doin' the gentlemanly thing by escortin' her to town."

"Maybe," Shaler mumbled. "And then again, maybe not . . ."

The amusement Tweed had enjoyed while trailing along behind Shaler the past hour evaporated. He had hoped that bullheaded son of his would find Casity and convince her to return because he was afraid of losing her.

Lord, surely James wouldn't go tramping off on a manhunt. Why, he had just purchased his claim and built a cabin to share with Colorado Charley Utter who had come north with him from Cheyenne! But then, Tweed reminded himself, James always did have a restless streak in him. He couldn't stay put for any length of time, either. Even marriage hadn't slowed him down!

The thought of Casity tromping off with James soured Tweed's mood. He had wanted Shaler and

Casity to have the chance to let the fierce attraction between them grow into something strong and lasting. Obviously, Casity Crockett was as blind and stubborn as Shaler was. To distract herself from their unconventional courtship, she had attempted to enlist James's services and had struck out on her mission of revenge. Tweed hoped James was only doing the polite thing by accompanying her to Deadwood . . . and no farther. Otherwise, Tweed may never have the chance to see Casity or James again!

James opened the hotel room door and glanced around the modestly furnished quarters before he set Casity's satchels in the corner. He had rented them rooms side by side so he could keep an eye on her. Knowing how fond Tweed and Shaler had become of this lively beauty, James felt a certain obligation to keep her out of trouble—if that was within the realm of possibility. Considering Casity's track record, he would probably have his work cut out for him.

"I told the proprietor to send up a tub and hot water," James informed Casity. "While you're freshening up, I'm going down to the Number Ten Saloon to quench my thirst and enjoy a few games of poker. After you've rested, come fetch me from the saloon and we'll have lunch together."

"You're very kind, James," Casity murmured as she sank down on the end of the bed to rest her aching knee.

Laughter reverberated in James's broad chest. "I've been called a lot of things in my life, but *kind* wasn't on the list."

"I think you're very much the gentleman," Casity said with conviction. "I certainly know a gentleman when I meet one because there are so few around."

James leaned against the wall and crossed his arms over his chest. "You don't consider Tweed and Shay gentlemen?" he quizzed with a wry smile.

"Tweed, yes. Shaler McCain? Never!" Casity said disdainfully.

"Just exactly what is it that you find so offensive about Shay?" James asked curiously. "I think he's a very likable sort. Since I helped raise him for three years, are you implying that I failed to teach him proper manners?"

Casity glanced up to note the teasing twinkle in James's blue eyes and grinned in spite of herself. "No, I'm suggesting that three years wasn't ample time for what's-his-name's instruction in gentlemanly behavior. Some men never learn it at all, and he's one of them."

James pushed away from the wall and ambled in front of her, noting that the excessive heat and the traveling had taken their toll. "Don't be so quick to judge Shay," he murmured. "Those of us who came up through life the hard way never learn to expect much from other folks. Shay had as many tragedies to overcome as you have. When he lost his family in the Indian massacre, it devastated him. He was hard to handle because he didn't care about much of anything while he was trying to deal with his loss. For the first year he was bitter and withdrawn and he wouldn't even mention his family. In fact, he did very little talking at all. He wanted to take Tweed's name as his own, but Tweed wouldn't let him shut out his natural family as if they never existed."

His fingers curled beneath her chin, lifting her flushed face to his smile. "You know what it's like to lose someone you love. The pain fades in time, but the memories never die . . ."

James sank down beside her on the foot of the bed

and heaved an audible sigh. "I have a few ghost
haunting me, too," he quietly confessed. "When I wa
the marshal in Abilene I found myself in a showdow
with a hard-nosed Texas gambler, Phil Coe, and hi
infamous friends. When pistols started barking I wa
attacked from all directions at once. My deputy cam
rushing out of nowhere to assist me. I wheeled aroun
to fire, thinking one of Coe's henchman was tryin
to attack my blind side."

Casity studied the bleak expression on James's rug
ged features. She was seeing a vulnerable side of thi
legendary shootist.

"I shot a good and loyal friend by mistake." Hi
voice was no more than a pained whisper. "Mike Wil
liams had risked his life to save mine and I . . . sho
him . . ." James fought for hard-won composure. "Af
ter that, nothing mattered much anymore. I took of
my badge and started drifting wherever the wind too
me. I just couldn't forgive myself."

Casity laid her hand over James's wrist, giving it
compassionate squeeze. "I'm so very sorry, James."

"I don't ordinarily discuss the incident and I don'
even like to think about it," he confessed. "What tor
ments me to this day is that I never had the chanc
to tell Mike how much I valued his friendship. We ha
been to hell and back together many times. When
man risks his life for you and you don't have the op
portunity to thank him, you never forget it, especiall
when *you're* the reason there was no time left . . ."

Casity didn't know what to say to console him. Bu
his quiet admission made her realize the true reaso
she'd been distraught over her uncle's death. Sh
hadn't had the chance to tell Daniel farewell, to than
him for all he had done for her, and to beg forgivenes
for making the noise that had cost him his life. The
Daniel's murderers had sent her fleeing to save he

own life. She had been harboring overwhelming resentment and guilt. Her dealings with Shaler had only tied her emotions even more in knots.

"My point is, Casity, that we all have our crosses to bear. You have yours, Shay has his, and I have mine. Don't be so quick to judge a man unless you understand him completely. Shay came to Dakota at Tweed's request. They both have a mission, just as you have yours. But when times get tough, Tweed and Shay are the kind of men you want on your side."

He clasped Casity's dainty hands in his own and smiled gently down at her. "You may not want any free advice, but I'm offering it to you nonetheless. Go back to the cabin in Bonanza Gulch before you ride off to Yankton or Cheyenne. Tell Tweed and Shay good-bye, good and proper. They took you in when you had nowhere to go, just as they took me in when my restless streak led me to the mountains. You may not have a high opinion of men in general, but they don't come any better than Tweed and Shay. They care about you in their own special ways."

"Well, I—"

"Promise me," James insisted.

Casity sighed. She hadn't wanted to see Shaler McCain again—ever. He was the temptation she had never been able to refuse, the haunting memory that wouldn't die.

"All right," she obliged reluctantly.

"Good. I'm glad that's settled." James rose to his feet. "After you've rested a bit, come to the saloon. We'll send off a few letters to the law officials I know in Nebraska and then we'll enjoy a good meal." He handed her the derringer he carried in his belt. "Take this for your protection. If anybody bothers you, at least let them know you have a weapon. Sometimes a bluff is as good as a bullet."

When James winked, smiled, and closed the doo behind him, Casity found herself lost in thought. He eyes fell on the cold metal object in her hand. Sh couldn't help but wonder what she would have don the night her uncle had been killed if she had had weapon. Would she have fired? Could she pull th trigger in self-defense if she met with trouble this af ternoon? Casity hoped she wouldn't have to find out As James had said, there were times when a bluff wa effective. She would tuck the derringer in her purs for safety's sake, but she would only use it as a las resort. Besides, who would bother her in Deadwood– except perhaps Reece Pendleton, who held a grudge af ter she'd thwarted his attempt to seduce her. Most of th miners treated her with respect; her only complaint wa that they paid her attention when she simply preferre to be left alone.

No, Casity convinced herself, she wasn't going ou to meet trouble for once in her life. She would bathe change, and send off the letters for legal assistance– then enjoy her meal with Hickok as her companion.

Casity grinned at the thought. Imagine being es corted around town by the country's most famous pis tolero. It was definitely better than battling th emotions that hounded her when she was anywher near Shaler McCain!

Perhaps James considered Shaler a gentleman, bu Casity didn't and she never would. He was the onl man on the planet who made her feel vulnerable, th only man who pushed her willpower to the very limits And yet, James was probably right. She should retur to Bonanza Gulch to say her last good-bye, and t thank Tweed for being her friend when she had n one to turn to. As for Shay . . .

Casity gave herself a mental pinch when a flood o erotic sensations washed through her body. The mer

hought of that rogue triggered emotions she didn't
vant to feel. There was nothing between them except
n irrational physical attraction, she told herself real-
tically. She wanted that man out of her mind and
ut of her life, once and for all. She would bid him
dieu, just as James made her promise to do. Then
he would shake the dust of Deadwood off her heels
nd never look back.

That was the only way she was ever going to forget
hat exasperating man. And she *had* to forget him if
he wanted to salvage her sanity. These mixed emo-
ions had played havoc with her mind and body far
oo long already. Perhaps she had been too judgmental
nd critical, as James implied, but the painful truth
vas that she was afraid of Shaler McCain. She was
fraid she cared more for him than she should have,
fraid this riptide of feeling would bring more pain
han it already had.

But under no circumstances would she fall in love
vith him, despite the quiet whispers of her heart. No
natter how hot the sweet fires had burned, she would
ever surrender to the illusion of love. What she and
hay had shared only existed in a mystical paradise.
Those splendorous moments were like a fantastic
lream.

After giving herself that silent pep talk and watch-
ng the hotel attendant fill her tub, Casity stripped
nd sank into her bath.

"These are the most promising samples I've seen in
long time," Corbin Dunster enthused as he glanced
p at Reece. "The tracers indicate good color in a
earby vein."

Reece mentally rubbed his hands together in raff-
sh glee. The assayer who worked for the Pendleton

Mining Company had just confirmed what Reec had thought to be true. Reece had wasted no tim in taking the samples to Corbin the instant he r turned from Mule's Ear Gulch. And sure enoug Reece was going to be rich beyond his wilde dreams. Of course, he wasn't about to let Varnes an Brady know about this strike—they'd demand equ shares of the profit. Even though it would take all Reece's cash reserve to pay for the claim, hire a cre and move equipment to the mine, he wasn't going borrow money from Varnes and Brady. He would muc prefer to take a loan at the bank and cut a few corne for the next few months than let his business partne in on this juicy stake!

A wry smile pursed his lips when he thought Casity's rejection. She would change her tune whe she realized he was worth millions. And when she cam crawling back to him, he'd treat her as she deserved be treated, taking his pleasure without offering the e pensive trinkets she probably expected. Reece had a ready spent a great deal of time and money trying woo her into his bed. Now he could take what h wanted. Next time she wouldn't escape. When he mad her his possession, he would finally discover if she w everything he imagined she would be . . .

"If I were you, I'd get that claim deeded over soon as possible," Corbin advised after he checke the particles under a microscope. "If word leaks o about this strike, someone else might try to top you offer. George Hearst wouldn't bat an eyelash at pa ing seventy-five thousand for this claim—not after h took a gander at these samples."

The assayer's remarks snapped Reece out of h spiteful musings. He reached into his pocket to fis out a pouch of gold dust and handed it to Corbin. '

don't want any competition for this purchase. You make damned sure no one knows about this claim."

With a conspiratory smile, Corbin pocketed the pouch. "What purchase? What samples are you referring to, boss?"

Reece grinned devilishly. "What claim indeed?"

Still gloating over his success, Reece scurried out of his office and made a beeline to his hotel suite. After he washed away the dust and sweat, he was going to celebrate his good fortune. It was a shame he couldn't celebrate with that shapely beauty. For certain, the next time he tried to take what he wanted from her, he would be sure he relieved her of her weapons! As a precautionary measure, he had thoroughly checked her belongings before he had entered her room that fateful night. And still Reece had found himself staring down the barrel of a Colt .45. To this day, he didn't know how that weapon had magically appeared in her hand. But it wasn't going to happen again, he vowed. Nothing was going to make him happier than becoming stinking rich *and* seducing that sassy sprite!

Twenty-three

Shaler glanced in every direction at once while he and Tweed trotted down the main street of Deadwood. The oppressive heat and stale wind had brought a multitude of miners from their digs to wander from one watering hole to another. The streets were jam-packed with individuals in various degrees of intoxication. Although Shaler's astute gaze made a thorough sweep of the crowd, he saw nothing of the auburn-haired beauty who had dominated his thoughts since she left his cabin without a word.

"Where do you suppose that she-male is?" Shaler mused aloud.

"I don't rightly know," Tweed admitted as he studied the faces of the people ambling down the board walks. "But I can guess where James is. He has a taste for whiskey and poker— he's probably lounging in one of the saloons. I only hope he had the good sense to stash Casity in a safe place before he wandered off to enjoy his vices."

"Well, I'm absolutely certain she didn't room over there—" Shaler gestured toward the most expensive hotel in town—the one in which Reece Pendleton owned a suite. "After her last encounter with Pendleton, she'll stay as far away from him as she can get."

"It seems she's applyin' that same theory to you

too." Tweed sent Shaler a pointed glance. "Not that I blame her, you understand."

"Don't start with me again, Tweed," Shaler warned. "I'm not in the mood."

"Not in the mood for a lecture," Tweed clarified. "But it seems you were *in the mood* too often when it came to Casity. That's why she—"

"Enough!" Shaler growled. "Whether she wants to see me again or not, I have to be sure she doesn't do something rash . . . and that James doesn't help her do it!"

"I really don't know why you should care one way or the other," Tweed replied, refusing to keep the silence. "Casity's makin' it easy on you by gettin' out of yer life without demandin' a commitment after what you did. I still say you should let her go, if'n that's what she wants."

"And I still say you talk too damned much," Shaler muttered crankily. His gaze drifted down the street and settled speculatively on the stage depot. "I'm going to check with the ticket agent to see if Cas reserved a seat. At least I'll know where she's headed, even if I can't find her before she leaves."

"What do you wanna know that for if you want her outta yer life?" Tweed questioned. "For a man who claims he don't want no ties, yer sure takin' great pains to track that girl down."

Muttering inarticulate curses, Shaler nudged his steed forward. The gelding had only taken four steps—with Tweed's swaybacked mule at its heels—before Reece Pendleton appeared in the doorway of the hotel to flag him down. Delays. Hell's fire, that was exactly what Shaler didn't need as long as he had this uneasy premonition that had tormented him since he left the cabin earlier. He had felt the same sensation the last time he saw Casity and the feeling hadn't gone away as

the day progressed. It had only gotten worse after he
returned to Bonanza Gulch to find her gone.

"I'm glad you rode into town," Reece declared as
he strode into the street to block Shaler's path. "I'd
like to take care of the legal transaction for the claim
as soon as possible. I'll stop by the bank to collect the
cash while you transfer the deed at the claim office."

Before Shaler could postpone the meeting Reece
spun on his heels and scampered off, his coattails flap-
ping behind him.

"The report from the assayer must've been a
doozie," Tweed speculated with a snicker. "Pendleton
is so anxious to get his greedy hands on the claim that
he's practically hoppin' up and down."

Frustrated by the detour he was forced to make,
Shaler dismounted and led his horse toward the claim
office. Although he was anxious to have Reece Pendleton in his trap, he was far more eager to catch up with
Casity. Shaler had never been at ease when she was
out of his sight. Since the moment he met her, it had
seemed natural to have her by his side. Since she had
come and gone like the wind, he had felt an unac-
countable restlessness that nothing else could satisfy.

"Can I help you?"

Shaler shook himself loose from his thoughts to find
the claim agent staring at him bemusedly. No doubt
the bald-headed man thought Shaler was a little short
on sense—he was standing there looking through the
man as if he were invisible!

"Snap out of it, Shay," Tweed teased as he poked
his distracted son in the ribs. He flashed the claim
agent a playful grin. "Sorry, friend, my boy don't have
these mental lapses very often. Woman trouble."

"That'll do it every time," the clerk readily agreed.
"I was married once, but it only took once to cure me.
In fact, I—"

"I want to register a new deed for the buyer of our claim," Shaler interrupted before the rotund man went off on a lengthy tangent about the failure of his love life.

"Yes . . . er . . . of course," the clerk replied awkwardly. "Don't ever get me started on my ex-wife. Lord, the stories I could tell would curl your hair."

"Or make it fall out." Tweed added with a mischievous snicker.

The clerk made a swipe over his bald head with a stubby hand. "That's a fact. I'm living proof that a bad marriage can make a man pull his hair out."

"Can we get on with this?" Shaler prompted impatiently.

"Sure, sure, let me fetch the document and we'll have the deed transferred in a jiffy," the clerk assured him.

A *jiffy* turned out to be a quarter of an hour. By the time the ink dried, Reece had arrived upon the scene, anxious to scribble his signature on the document and tuck it protectively in his vest pocket.

Shaler didn't have the patience to gloat over hornswaggling the shady mining entrepreneur. The cloud of impending doom kept settling lower with each passing second. He knew he wouldn't be able to relax until he located Casity and assured himself that she was all right.

"It was a pleasure doin' business with you, Pendleton," Tweed said as he tucked the roll of bank notes in his pocket. "Thanks for takin' that claim off our hands."

"I hope it turns out to be profitable so I can recover my expenses." Reece silently scoffed at these foolish prospectors who didn't have the sense to know pure gold when they saw it.

"Oh, by the way," Reece added offhandedly, "have you any idea where Miss Lambert is?"

"What do you want with her?" Shaler questioned, trying to sound less agitated than he felt.

Reece smoothed his thick mustache into place and lifted an expensively-clad shoulder. "I haven't seen her for several days. I only wondered what had become of her."

Reece wasn't the only one! "I haven't seen her," Shaler replied brusquely before he spun on his heel and zoomed out the door.

Shaler had completed his obligation to Amos Grant as requested. The deed was in Reece's hands and the cash was in Tweed's pocket. Now Shaler could focus all of his attention on chasing Casity down.

"Will you slow down!" Tweed grumbled as he hobbled along on his cane. "I ain't ready for a foot race just yet. When we get home, I'm peelin' this dad-blamed splint off for good. It's been six weeks. If the break hasn't healed by now it never will."

"You start checking the saloons to find James," Shaler demanded, ignoring Tweed's grievances. "I'll speak to the stage agent and then look over the hotel registers. Cas has to be around here somewhere."

"I still don't see what all the fuss is about," Tweed called after him. "Chances are she ain't plannin' to leave town until tomorrow. She'll be exhausted since she had to walk part of the way from our cabin to Deadwood."

Shaler didn't know why a sense of urgency was pushing him so hard. It just was. He couldn't breathe easy until he found Casity. Of course, he didn't have the faintest idea what in the hell he was going to say when he found her, but he *had* to find her!

* * *

Tim Brady and Johnny Varnes paced the office like restless tigers while Jack McCall sipped a whiskey.

"Now's the time to dispose of Hickok," Johnny said as he came to stand directly in front of Jack. "You'll be famous overnight and we'll see to it that you walk out of the showdown scot-free."

When Jack looked as if he was about to object, Tim flung up a hand. "You're as fast on the draw as Hickok, probably faster. And you're a lot younger. Hickok never was anything but a blowhard who toted a sawed-off shotgun to back him up. Who could miss with a weapon like that? But he isn't carrying a shotgun now and that puts the odds in your favor."

Jack stared at the contents of his glass and took another sip. "I told you I'd think about it," he mumbled.

Muttering at Jack's hesitation, Johnny circled the desk to retrieve a chamois-skin poke. He let the glittering granules pouring from the pouch hold Jack's rapt fascination for a long moment. "Here's a generous twenty-five dollars worth," he declared as he measured the granules in the scale. "After you dispose of Hickok, there'll be another seventy-five waiting for you. Don't you think it's about time you avenged your brother's death?"

"And Phil Coe's," Jack added as he reached over to pour the gold dust into the tobacco box he kept in his pocket.

Tim frowned puzzledly at the unexpected remark. "What does Phil Coe have to do with it? Was he a friend of yours?"

"Cousin," Jack replied.

"Hickok killed your brother *and* your cousin and you haven't retaliated yet?" Johnny questioned, striving for an incredulous tone to prompt Jack into action. "Now's your chance to even the score and get paid for doing

it. Hickok has been in the Number Ten Saloon for ove
an hour, pouring down whiskey and playing poker
The timing is perfect."

Jack thrust out his empty glass. "Gimme anothe
drink."

"Just a short one," Johnny advised. "You need t
keep your wits about you. Hickok's vision may b
blurred, but yours damned well better not be. Whei
you beat him to the draw, you don't want to be to
drunk to enjoy it."

Pensively, Jack pulled his revolver from its holste
to make sure all six chambers were loaded. "I'll se
you in a few minutes," he murmured as he got up
from his chair and paced deliberately across the room

When the door clanked shut behind him, Johnn
grinned in triumph. "Now all we have to do is wait . . .

Revived and refreshed, Casity stepped onto th
street to find the town teeming with activity. Th
sound of tinkling pianos wafted through the saloo
doors. Laughter warbled through the open window
of the dance halls that lined the street. It seemed a
if the entire population of Dakota had converged o
Deadwood and that the prospectors were gearing u
for a wild night that would take their minds off th
oppressive heat.

Glancing this way and that, Casity tried to locate th
Number Ten Saloon. Anticipating a meal and inter
esting company, she made her way down the stree
dodging drunken miners and leering gamblers wh
made no attempt whatsoever to conceal their leche
ousness. What rude heathens men could be, sh
fumed silently.

Tossing her cynicism aside, Casity zigzagged dow
the boardwalk toward her destination. When sh

peeked inside the Number Ten Saloon, she saw James
playing poker with three men. He had forgone his
legendary habit of sitting with his back to the wall in
case trouble tried to sneak up on him. A man whom
Casity heard referred to as Charley Rich had taken
James's usual seat and was studying his cards.

"Mister Hickok?" she called from the door.

James half-turned to see Casity garbed in a stunning blue gown. He nodded toward the cards he held
and winked at her. "I'll be out as soon as we finish
this hand," he promised.

Casity surveyed the aces and eights James held, wondering if the other three players could beat such a hand.
After Reece Pendleton had insisted she learn to play
poker, Casity knew a good hand when she saw one . . .

A scraggly cowboy reeking of whiskey and sweat
bumped her broadside, so Casity stepped out of his
way. After casting a fleeting glance at the table, Jack
McCall swaggered over to order a drink at the bar.
Casity studied the bearded man's profile, noting the
crook in his nose and the odd way he kept staring
at the gambling table. When Jack glanced in her direction, Casity looked the other way. She heard the
click of boots on the planked floor and watched the
somber-faced hombre amble toward the table to
watch the four men bet on the strength of their cards.

Without warning, the scraggly ruffian stepped directly behind Hickok and drew his gun. Casity stared
in total disbelief when she realized what the man was
about. Before she could shout a warning, Jack McCall
took a step closer and fired.

Casity's throat constricted in horror when she saw
Hickok slump forward and then tumble from his
chair. The cards he held in his hand scattered across
the floor as he collapsed in a lifeless heap.

A startled squawk erupted from the table when the

bullet which killed Hickok plowed into the arm of Cap
tain Massey, who'd been sitting directly across from
him.

Casity covered her mouth to muffle her terrifie
scream and sagged against the outer wall of the saloo
in dazed disbelief. The scene she had just witnesse
paralyzed her body and her brain. Flashbacks of an
other horrifying moment leaped at her. Suddenly she
was reliving both tragedies as if they were happenin
at once!

The men at the table bounded to their feet, but Jac
McCall held them at gunpoint and backed cautiousl
toward the door. While Casity was trying to recove
from her shock, McCall wheeled around and dashe
onto the street. She fumbled to retrieve the derringe
from her purse, but Hickok's assassin ducked into th
butcher shop before she could force her tremblin
fingers around the weapon.

"Hickok's dead!" someone bellowed from inside th
Number Ten Saloon.

The sickening scene flashed before Casity's eyes lik
another recurring nightmare. Over and over again
Cavity had seen her uncle collapse on the floor, an
now Hickok . . . A choked sob gurgled in her throa
as she stumbled blindly along the boardwalk, battlin
the nausea that engulfed her.

When a surge of humanity rushed down the stree
toward the Number Ten Saloon, Casity swore she ha
somehow been transported straight to hell. There be
fore her, moving with the flow of curious bystander
were the two men who had chased her out of Ogallal
She had come all the way to Deadwood, Dakota, t
avoid these two killers—and here they were, dashin
directly toward her!

As luck would have it, Ned Johnson and Russel Ba
sett recognized Casity at the same instant she recog

nized them. Her survival instincts sprang to life in less than a heartbeat. She wheeled around to beat a hasty retreat, but Johnson and Bassett elbowed their way through the human barricade in an attempt to overtake her.

"Shay!" Casity heard the name tumble off her lips in a terrified screech. She would have given anything if he would appear and save her! Now that she felt the need to run for her life, she longed to run *toward* Shaler, as if he were her port in this most recent storm. He was the only man she wanted to turn to when her life was in jeopardy. It was strange but true. Hell's fire! Where was that man when she needed him?

Blinking back the tears, Casity cut through the oncoming crowd and scurried toward the drug store. Her heart was hammering so hard she was afraid it would beat her to death before those two cutthroats could get their hands on her.

Casity barged through the store, bumping into everything in her path, looking for the back door. When she stepped outside, she glanced warily around her, expecting to see her would-be killers. Pushing away from the building, she charged down the alley toward her hotel as fast as her tender leg would carry her.

Tears boiled down her cheeks, blurring her vision. Twice she stumbled over the crates that littered the alleyway and twice she regained her balance before she fell flat on her face.

She didn't even know why she was trying to escape, except that natural instinct always seemed to put her to flight when her life was at risk. It seemed that no matter where she went and what she did, she couldn't outrun her nightmares. Now she had yet another bad dream to haunt her. It was her fault that Hickok had fallen beneath an assassin's bullet. *Her fault!* If she hadn't gone to James, requesting his assistance, he

would still be lounging in his cabin in Lard Pail Bill
Raddick's mining camp. The only reason he had come
into town was because of her. And now he had died
because of her!

Well, no one else was going to die because of her,
Casity promised herself fiercely. Whatever happened
would happen to her alone. She wasn't about to dash
back to Bonanza Gulch and risk involving Shaler and
Tweed. She was a jinx. Her uncle had taken her in
when she had nowhere to go and he had lost his life
to those murdering scoundrels who were breathing
down her neck at this very moment. Then, James Butler Hickok had befriended her and she had cost him
his life, too.

Silently Casity called out Shaler's name, wishing he
could be there to comfort her, to chase the cruel world
away just as he had the night he had rescued her from
Indians.

She would give most anything to recapture those precious moments they shared beyond the limits of reality.
When she had been soaring in Shaler's arms, there had
been no past, present, or future. There had been only
those brief moments of bliss. And when she died from
her assassins' bullets, she would cherish those moments
and the memory of the sweet fires of summer . . .

A lump formed in Casity's throat as she plastered
herself against a wall to catch her breath. Sweet mercy,
it *had* happened, she realized with a start. Despite her
torment, nightmares, and anguish, she *had* fallen in
love with Shaler McCain!

Why else would the thought of him bring the only
comfort she could find? Why else would she have surrendered to him and to no other man?

From the moment she had awakened to find him
hovering over her, she had been utterly fascinated. He
had been gentle and compassionate as he tried to tease

her into good humor. He had loved away her grief and sorrow. She had seen the tender side of his nature before he turned his harshness on her. And although she had protested loud and long, nothing had eclipsed the memory of him. She had valiantly fought the feelings that tugged at her heartstrings, but the tender emotions had taken root. Even her fierce determination hadn't been enough to counter the love she felt for him.

The realization that she was in love—for the first and the last time in her life—brought Casity very little in the way of consolation. The knowledge of a love that had crept up on her while she was trying so hard to avoid it had come too late. Shaler would never know that he alone had touched that secret place in her heart that she had protected from the rest of the world . . .

The sound of muffled footsteps jostled Casity from her thoughts. In the distance she could see her would-be assassins barreling toward her, their pistols cocked and ready to fire. Her only option was to dash back into the street, hoping to lose herself in the crowd. Surely those two barbarians wouldn't drop her in her tracks with plenty of witnesses.

Bitter laughter broke from Casity when she realized that men like the ones following her wouldn't blink an eyelash at disposing of her whenever the opportunity presented itself. James Butler Hickok hadn't been safe sitting at a table in a saloon. The coward had shot him where he sat! At least when the bullets barked behind Casity, she would know the identity of her assassins.

That wasn't a particularly comforting thought, she realized bleakly. When those murderers caught up with her she would still be just as dead . . .

Twenty-four

When the news of Hickok's murder spread through
town like wildfire, Shaler felt as though a fist had hit
him in the midsection. Tweed was having as much difficulty dealing with the tragic news as Shaler was. The
blow had knocked them to their knees; they were
stunned and distraught over the loss of a long-time
friend.

The pathetic irony of Hickok's murder had Shaler
swearing under his breath as he and Tweed scurried
toward the Number Ten Saloon. James had faced far
better men than the drunken gambler who'd shot him
in the back. And why James had broken tradition to
take a chair that left his back to the door was truly
baffling. The one and only time James had made that
careless mistake had cost him his life . . .

Shaler's gloomy thoughts evaporated when he spied
Casity elbowing her way through the crowd like a fish
swimming upstream. Tears streamed from her eyes as
she glanced wildly around her. When she breezed past
him, Shaler snaked out an arm to catch her, despite
the two men who stood between them. To his bemuse-
ment, Casity recoiled as if she had been snakebit. But
the instant she realized who had grabbed hold of her,
a cry of relief broke from her throat. To Shaler's
amazement, Casity flew into him arms like a pigeon

eturning to roost and proceeded to squeeze the stuff-
ng out of him.

The unprecedented display of affection surprised
Shaler. It seemed to have the same effect on Tweed,
who gaped at Casity. She was clinging fiercely to
Shaler, burying her head against his chest and shaking
ike a leaf in a windstorm. Reflexively, Shaler's arms
nfolded her protectively against him.

"Cas?" he whispered as his lips grazed her pulsating
emple. "Are you all right?"

All right? How could she possibly be all right after
he had witnessed a second murder in a month and
ound herself chased by the very same men who had
ent her running for her life? Casity was sure she was
n the verge of losing her sanity. Her life was com-
letely out of control and she was near hysteria!

How precious were Shaler's brawny arms sheltering
er from the storm her life had become! She needed
im as she needed nothing else. He gave her strength
when there was none. He gave her courage when she
elt alone and terrified . . .

When Casity finally snapped to her senses and real-
zed she had tarried long enough to give her pursuers
chance to catch up with her, she launched herself
way from Shaler as abruptly as she had latched onto
im. She had to keep running before her would-be
ssassins spotted her in the crowd. She had to put some
istance between herself and Shaler, too, or his life
ould also be at risk. She couldn't lose Shaler, too!
Casity couldn't bear the thought!

"Cas?" Shaler stared bewilderedly after her as she
lew off, bouncing off bodies in her haste.

When Shaler ran to catch up with her, Tweed
lutched at his arm. "Let her go, Shay" he ordered
ravely. "We have other business to tend right now.

We have to say good-bye to a dear friend and mak
sure his killer is in jail."

Shaler stared after Casity until he lost sight of he
in the crowd. He was torn by feelings of obligation–
to James and to Casity. Hickok's death had obvious
hit her hard. The tragedy had come too closely on th
heels of her uncle's murder and she was having diff
culty coping. Shaler sorely wished he could be in tw
places at once. Casity's impulsive display alerted him t
the fact that she needed him, just as she had the nigl
he had found her unconscious in the stream. B
Tweed's grim expression indicated that he also neede
moral support.

Hell's fire, the feeling of impending doom that ha
haunted him throughout the day had been devasta
ing. And catastrophe had indeed struck. Emotio
compelled Shaler to reach out to the one pure, swe
memory in his mind. A pair of beguiling blue ey
haunted him as he allowed Tweed to shepherd hi
down the boardwalk. The look on Casity's face r
flected the same vulnerability he had witnessed th
first night they met. He longed to ease her pain, t
comfort and protect her.

Shaler glanced over his shoulder at regular interval
trying to determine where Casity was going. When h
finally saw her dart inside the hotel at the end of th
block, he glanced up at the sign to be sure that he kne
where to search for her when he had time. He coul
only hope she would stay put until he returned, b
considering the precedent she'd set, she could be t
hell and gone before Shaler could track her down.

Curse the woman! She was like a cyclone that ble
in and out of his life! How could that mere wisp of
female cause such an upheaval of emotion inside hir
Before Shaler could answer his own question, his foo
steps stalled at the scene of the hideous crime. Anoth

low of emotion twisted in his gut and he swore under ‌his breath. Anger, outrage, and grief hammered at him ‌while he listened to the three men who had been play‌ing poker with Hickok relate their bleak story.

When Shaler pivoted to see Sheriff Brown leading ‌Broken-Nose Jack McCall to jail, he had to fight the ‌urge to draw his pistol and send that cowardly bastard ‌to hell where he belonged!

"They say Hickok killed McCall's brother back in ‌Kansas. That's why McCall fired the shot," somebody ‌murmured close by.

"I heard McCall was paid to murder Hickok," some‌one else reported. "McCall admitted it himself when ‌Sheriff Brown and Calamity Jane caught up with him ‌in the butcher shop."

Shaler's gaze swung back to the sheriff and his pris‌oner to survey the stout, course-featured woman who ‌marched somberly behind the procession.

"I overheard two fellas talking earlier in the bath‌house," a third party spoke up. "They said somebody ‌hired a detective to look into Pendleton's operations. ‌It must've been Hickok. That's why he didn't want to ‌pin on a marshal's badge. He was probably being paid ‌a helluva lot more money to investigate Pendleton ‌Mining Company."

Shaler felt a knot coil in his belly. He had the sick‌ning feeling that he and Tweed were indirectly re‌sponsible for Hickok's death. Some fool had leaped ‌to the erroneous conclusion that Hickok had come to ‌investigate Pendleton. Had it been Pendleton himself ‌who hired an assassin? Or was it his ruthless associ‌ates? And how had word leaked out about the inves‌tigation? Shaler had told no one except James and ‌Casity . . .

Surely Casity hadn't . . . Outrage bubbled up inside ‌Shaler. Casity hadn't set James up, had she? She

couldn't have. Why would she? No, Shaler reassure
himself. It was wild conjecture—he was trying to mak
sense of this senseless murder—one for which he fe
responsible!

"Tweed, find out everything you can about Jac
McCall and his association with Pendleton, Varne
and Brady," Shaler instructed before he stalked off

"What are you gonna be doin' while I'm posin
questions?" Tweed demanded to know.

"I'm going to pose a few questions of my own," h
replied before he cut through the crowd like a knif

In frustration and torment, Shaler stormed dow
the street. He had lost an old friend and he wante
to know why! He also wanted to know if Casity ha
been involved. She'd damned well better not hav
been. The thought of being betrayed by that woma
cut deeper than anything else could!

Casity Crockett had damned well better be in th
hotel. If she wasn't he was sure as hell going to tur
this town inside out to find her! She had some e
plaining to do!

Casity didn't give a second thought to swiping th
bottle of whiskey beside the miner sprawled in a cha
inside the hotel lobby. He was sleeping off his drunke
stupor and Casity was sorely in need of a drink to calr
her nerves. Although she'd been a teetotaler unt
Tweed had introduced her to the taste of brandy whe
she first arrived in Deadwood, she was anxious to di
cover if one could truly drown one's troubles in a bottl

When her would-be assassins found her—and the
inevitably would—she wanted to be numb. She could ru
to the ends of the earth, but it would be wasted effor
Her uncle's killers seemed to track her wherever sh
went.

Perhaps Hickok was the lucky one, she mused as she eased open the door to her room. He had never seen the bullet coming. The dastardly deed had been over as quickly as it had begun. Casity, on the other hand, had to await her untimely end with nervous dread. Well, at least the whiskey would take the edge off, she assured herself.

When she sank down on the end of her bed, the tears she had valiantly tried to hold in check boiled down her cheeks like a river. She tipped the bottle to her lips and took a swallow. Fire seared her throat and burned its way to her empty stomach. Casity sucked in her breath and choked on a sob. This was even more potent than Tweed's brandy! It would take at least four drinks to numb her throat to the sharp taste. How she could get past those first four drinks she didn't know, but she was determined to try. Perhaps the fact that she had skipped a meal would cause the liquor to take effect almost at once.

After collapsing on the bed, Casity forced herself to take another drink. The liquor blazed through her throat and set fire to her vocal cords. She wheezed and sputtered for breath, but nothing helped. That being the case, she chugged another swallow of liquid fire.

Self-imposed torture, she concluded. Why men felt the need to pollute their bodies with whiskey she would never know. If this pain reliever was a sure-cure, it had yet to take effect. Casity felt worse rather than better. Its only advantage was the fact that forcing down the foul-tasting stuff distracted her from the reason she felt compelled to ingest it . . .

It didn't taste so bad after all, she decided after doing hand-to-glass combat for a few minutes. In fact, she could no longer taste the whiskey at all. It had suddenly lost its zing.

Casity frowned curiously at the peculiar tingle in

her nose and on her tongue. She took another drink to make the tingle go away. When she tried to focus on the door through which her assassins would come, it became fuzzy and shifted on its hinges. Casity tilted her head, trying to realign the suddenly sagging door. But it remained off balance as far as she could tell. And by that time only one of her eyes seemed to be functioning properly.

"My, it's getting hot in here," Casity declared to the empty room.

She reached behind her to unfasten the stays of her gown, but her fingers turned to thumbs. In desperation to peel off the excessive clothing, Casity opted to wiggle her arms through the neckline to disentangle herself from the garment. Even after she'd done so, the room still seemed like a furnace.

Propping herself up, Casity wobbled to the window and opened it wide. On her way back to the bed, she trampled on the expensive blue gown Reece had given her, disregarding the wrinkled heap. After she shucked her pantaloons and petticoats, she was better prepared for the afternoon heat. Plopping back on the bed in her skimpy chemise, Casity helped herself to another drink . . . or three.

Now this was more like it, she mused with a sigh. She was beginning to feel like a rag doll. Her innards had adjusted to the whiskey, even if her eyes hadn't. But no matter, she wasn't going anywhere. She was simply awaiting her destiny.

She thought of the derringer James had given her before he left the hotel. After rolling off the edge of the bed—quite by accident—Casity picked herself up off the floor and stumbled over to retrieve the handgun from her purse. Pistol in hand, she weaved back to the bed and positioned herself with her back to the wall. Perhaps if she still had her wits about her, she could get off one or two shots before her killers launched her into the hereafter . . .

The rap at the door brought Casity's head up in alarm. Damn, disaster had arrived much sooner than she had anticipated. Swallowing hard, Casity clutched the pistol in both hands and aimed it at the door.

"Cas? Are you in there?"

Casity frowned. Or at least she thought she did. Her facial muscles weren't cooperating as well as they usually did. It felt as if the left side of her face had slid down her neck. What an odd sensation!

"Cas, damn it, if you're in there, answer me!"

Whose voice was that? She should have recognized it. It did have a familiar ring, even though it sounded as if it was echoing down a long winding tunnel. If she could only recall where . . .

"Shay?" she slurred out when the voice finally registered.

He wasn't supposed to be here. She was the one who was going to get killed and he was supposed to be safely out of the way.

Grumbling at the unexpected interruption, Casity rolled off the bed and staggered toward the door. When her foot caught on her satchels, she had to grasp the metal rail at the bottom of the bed to maintain her balance. Although the floor kept shifting beneath her, Casity managed to navigate her way to the door and open it without hitting herself in the face.

Shaler gaped in stunned amazement at the half-naked imp. Her bloodshot eyes were glazed over and the coil of dark red hair pinned atop her head jutted above her left ear like a loose spring. This proud beauty, who was usually the epitome of elegance, looked downright comical. Too bad Shaler didn't feel like laughing.

"You're drunk!" he realized and said so.

"And you're not supposed to be here," Casity declared sluggishly. "Go 'way."

When she waved her hands, one of which pointed a derringer while the other held a whiskey bottle, Shaler moved sideways to avoid being accidentally shot. His befuddled gaze circled the room to see the window flung open wide and her clothes strewn everywhere. Hell's fire, what was the matter with this female? First she had squeezed him in two on the street and now here she was, drunk as a skunk, demanding that he leave. Well, Shaler wasn't leaving without a few answers and that was all there was to it!

After kicking the door shut with his boot heel, he grabbed Casity's arm and guided her back to the bed. When he shoved her down, she fell off balance and careened backward. Scowling, he clutched her by the shoulders and propped her upright.

"Go 'way," Casity insisted slurrishly and then frowned. "Did I say that already? I can't remember."

"I'm not surprised," Shaler grumbled sourly. "And come morning, your head will feel it's the size of a pumpkin."

Casity watched his lips move and tried to decipher his mumblings. Odd, it seemed as if English had suddenly become a foreign language.

"Cas, listen to me very carefully," Shaler growled as he grabbed her forearms and gave her a shake, hoping to bring her to her senses. It didn't help. Her head rolled on her shoulders and he had to cup her chin in his hand to prop it up. "Did you say anything to anyone about my reasons for being in Deadwood?"

It took several moments for Casity to process the question, especially since it sounded as if it were rebounding off the walls of a canyon.

"No, was I supposed to?" she replied with a blank stare.

Shaler rolled his eyes heavenward. "Of course not." When her head drooped, he tilted her chin up again, forcing her to focus on him. "Did you set James up?"

The pointed question caused Casity to reel sideways as if he had struck her a mighty blow. "James," she whispered brokenly. "I jinxed him." Tears shimmered in her eyes and trickled down her flushed cheeks. "You have to leave before I jinx you, too. Go away and don't come back—ever." Casity swiped at the drops streaming down her chin.

"What do you mean, you jinxed James?" Shaler prodded, wishing she had better command of her faculties.

Muffling a sniff, Casity tried to formulate her thoughts. "I'm bad luck. Everyone who comes near me eventually meets with disaster."

"Nonsense," Shaler scoffed.

"Then you 'splain it," she challenged.

Shaler didn't bother trying. He was too busy being relieved that his horrible suspicions couldn't have been further from the truth. Casity wasn't responsible for Hickok's death. Shaler was. He was the one who was to have been assassinated, not Hickok. Pendleton and his crooked partners had somehow discovered that Amos Grant had sent someone to expose the fraudulent activities of the mining company. Hickok had been the innocent victim of a careless assumption and a long-standing feud.

His thoughts trailed off when Casity burst into a sob and collapsed on the bed. Shaler gathered her in his arms and laid her head on his shoulder, only to have his shirt soaked by a flood of tears. Lord, he never realized this pint-size female had so much water in her!

"He's gone and it's all my fault," Casity blubbered against Shaler's shoulder. "I saw it happen and I couldn't stop it in time. I couldn't believe what I was

seeing, and when it registered in my mind it was to
late . . ."

Shaler closed his eyes and grimaced at the though
of what Casity had witnessed. No wonder she was s
haunted that she had turned to liquor.

"James wouldn't have been there at all if not fo
me," Casity told him in a quivering voice. "He accom
panied me into town for my safety, and it cost him hi
life!"

The torturous thought provoked another round c
hysteria. The pent-up tension spilled out as Shale
cradled her against him, just as he had done the firs
night they met. Again, he was privy to the vulnerabi
ity Casity fought so hard to conceal from the rest c
the world, and from herself.

"I was to meet James at the saloon and he was goin
to take me to lunch," Casity sniffled. "Jack McCa
bumped into me on his way inside to commit his ho
rible crime. If I had only known—"

The dreadful thought broke Casity's composure a
together. She sagged limply in Shaler's arms and l
the tears flow, making no effort to restrain them. F
the longest time, he simply held her. He knew Casit
felt personally responsible for Hickok's presence i
town this fateful day and he harbored the guilt tha
he was supposed to have been the target of the brut
murder.

When Shaler tipped the bottle to his lips and gu
zled it like a thirsty camel, Casity frowned in disa
proval. "Gimme that," she ordered sluggishly. "I pla
to drink until I can't see and you're draining my su
ply . . ." A muddled expression claimed her featur
as she peered up at Shaler. "Which one of those tw
heads is really yours?"

Shaler choked on his drink. Mercy, she was farth
gone than he'd thought. "If you're seeing doub

ou've already had enough," he assured her. "If you
drink much more, it'll kill you."

Casity shrugged carelessly. "It doesn't matter." The
thought of the two men who were undoubtedly searching for her at this very moment flashed through her
mind, putting her back on alert. "You have to leave!"

Shaler stared at her quizzically. The last thing he
wanted to do was leave her alone in her condition.
The last thing he wanted was to leave her—period!
Hell's fire, this was not the time for her to start fussing
over propriety and the attraction between them. She always did that. He hated it when she did that!

When Shaler helped himself to another swig of liquor, Casity tried to pry the bottle from his fingertips.
"I want you to go before it's too late."

"Too late for what?" Shaler questioned. "And don't
tell me it's because you're afraid we'll wind up in bed
together." He poured another drink down his gullet
before Casity could swipe the bottle away from him.
"We know each other pretty well—so quit pretending
it never happened. I'm staying with you so you might
as well get used to it."

He didn't comprehend the danger and Casity didn't
dare explain it to him. She wasn't about to risk his life
in a futile attempt to save hers. If he knew about her
would-be assassins, he might intervene and she would
have another death on her overloaded conscience.

It wasn't that she wanted him to go. Indeed, she
longed for him to stay, to chase the cruelties of the
world away once more before she met her doom. But
if his life was the price she had to pay for a few moments
of splendor, Casity couldn't take the risk. She loved
this man. In order to protect him she had to rout him
from her room and that was exactly what she was going
to do!

Twenty-five

"I want you out of my room . . . NOW!" Casit
shouted as she twisted out of his restraining embrac
and staggered to her feet. Her arm shot toward th
door, as if he didn't know where it was. "Get out o
here, Shay. I mean it!"

He calmly ignored the command and took anothe
swallow of whiskey.

"Curse it," Casity muttered as she clumsily lunge
forward to grab the bottle. "Gimme that whiskey an
get out!"

When she tripped over his feet, her momentur
landed her on top of him, knocking him off balance
Although Shaler sprawled on the bed, he did manag
to hold the bottle upright. But what was infinitel
worse than trying to dodge her flailing arms and re
tain his hold on the bottle was the titillating feel o
her body wriggling against his. Instant and tota
awareness engulfed him. Shaler longed to lose himsel
in this lovely lady, to forget everything that had an
semblance to reality. How could he even consider leav
ing her when he wanted her so badly that he ache
all over?

His arm came around her waist to hold her in plac
while he set the bottle on the nightstand. When hi
leg glided between hers and he half-twisted so tha
his body partially covered hers, the old familiar ser

sations ran rampant through him. He lowered his head, yearning to taste her petal-soft lips, to rediscover every curve of her body, to forget the tragedy that haunted him.

"No . . ." Casity whimpered, trying to dodge his kiss. If he touched her she'd become a fatal curse on his life. "No, Shay . . ."

Shaler's kiss had already stolen her breath and his masterful caresses had already glided up her bare leg, leaving a trail of fire in their wake. Casity didn't even try to blame her shameless surrender on her overindulgence of whiskey. She knew beyond all doubt why she had never been able to resist this handsome rake. She had fallen in love with him the first night he'd taught her the meaning of passion. From that moment she'd become addicted to the scent of him, the rich, velvety sound of his voice, and the feel of his sinewy body pressed against hers. He had a special way about him that buckled her defenses and made her body respond wildly.

Shaler McCain was more man than any man she'd ever met, and Casity found it impossible to resist him. He was forceful and yet gentle. He could be amusing and sometimes infuriating. He had earned her admiration with his amazing courage in the face of danger. He had drawn her respect with his fierce devotion to his father—misdirected though it was on occasion.

Casity adored that ornery, crooked smile that tugged at the corner of his lips, that sparkle that danced in his eyes. She cherished the comforting, and yet wildly exciting, feel of his arms embracing her. Shaler had touched each and every one of her emotions until he had become a living, breathing part of her life.

When his lips slanted over hers, Casity could think of nothing but loving him as she had never loved him before. This would be their last precious moment together and she longed to revel in each wondrous instant, to absorb his strength and courage to help her endure what was to come. When her arms slid over the muscles of his chest and she glided her fingers through the wavy hair at the nape of his neck, her defenses dissolved completely. Her body arched toward his, yearning to feel every powerful inch of him meshed familiarly to her. She wanted to touch his heart and mind, to leave her memory imprinted on his soul.

Although she'd be gone forever, a part of her would remain with this golden-eyed rogue who had introduced her to a splendorous passion that defied description. The love she was hesitant to acknowledge would be conveyed by the reverent way she touched him. Somehow Shaler would know that he alone had taught her the meaning of unconditional love.

Shaler felt the world shrink to fill a space no larger than Casity occupied when she came to life in his arms. Her pleasure was his own. Touching her was like a long-awaited feast for his deprived senses. She was a unique gift that thrilled and satisfied as no other could. He needed her to the point of desperation, craved her with an urgency beyond reason. She was the fire and he wanted to burn alive in her arms.

It was as if he had been born for this wondrous moment, lived to recapture these sensations that made life worth living. When he was in the magic circle of her arms he knew paradise. This lovely angel was his heaven on earth. She supplied the special emotions that had been missing from his life.

These were the feelings that Shaler had tried to sort out throughout this long, difficult day. Now that Casity was in his arms, he had all he wanted and needed. Her kiss and caresses could feed the gnawing hunger eating him alive. Casity was the air he breathed. He lived through her, with her, making her a vital part of his existence.

He cherished every bit of her shapely body with his hands and lips. He couldn't seem to get enough of her. Each touch satisfied and yet heightened the fierce needs boiling inside him.

Shaler resented the garments that separated them. He couldn't peel them away fast enough. He needed to lie flesh to flesh and heart to heart with this enchanting siren, to feel her pulse beating as if it were his own.

Casity returned each touch—bold caress for bold caress. The feel of her voluptuous body pressed familiarly against his drove him wild with wanting. Her fervent responses excited and aroused him by such maddening degrees that Shaler was sure the sensations bubbling inside him were about to erupt. Desire— like molten lava—raced through every fiber of his being.

Casity was consumed by the same wild sensations that engulfed Shaler, except it was ten times worse. She knew this would be the very last time she skyrocketed past the distant stars in his sinewy arms. This would be the last time she experienced life and love in its purest, sweetest form. There would be no tomorrow, no yesterday. There was only now, for as long as it would last. Knowing that, she cherished each sensation, savored the feel of his body beneath her hands and lips.

All her inhibitions abandoned her when she realized how brief was life, how precious each moment. Only love, burning like the sweet fires of summer, could turn each moment into an eternity. The pleasures of love made her life worthwhile. At least she could go to her grave knowing a love that had encompassed all emotion. Feelings this pure and profound transcended all measures of time and life itself. These intangible feelings were the priceless legacy handed down from one generation to another.

With the deliberation of a woman who had come to realize that she was totally and hopelessly in love, Casity set out to cherish every muscular inch of Shaler's brawny body, memorizing each lean plane. Her lips feathered over his nipples and glided over the muscles of his belly, evoking his muffled groan. Her hand slid provocatively over the column of his thigh, making him tremble beneath her adventurous touch. Casity felt his virile body clench when her lips and hands converged on the place where he was most a man. The brush of her fingertips and the flick of her tongue had him gasping for breath. When her lips enfolded him and her moist tongue trailed over the pulsating length of him, Shaler shuddered uncontrollably.

"God, woman . . . You're going to be the death of me—"

He fell silent the instant she took him into her mouth and teased him until he arched up to her in shameless surrender. Her hands and lips were making a meal of him, and he reveled in her bold intimacies— sweet, maddening torture.

Although Casity would have been content to taste and touch him for hours on end, Shaler hooked his arm around her waist and drew her to her knees in front of him; his hands shook so badly with barely restrained desire that she could almost feel the need she had summoned from him. She could see the hot flames of passion flicker in his amber eyes, detect the firm set of his jaw as he fought for some measure of control. She had made him need her in all the wild, hungry ways a man needed a woman who had brought him to the edge of infinity and left him teetering there.

Shaler bent over her, his lips taking hers, tasting his own need, inhaling his own desire. The thought of how intimately she had touched him drove him wild. With a groan, he laid her down and hooked his elbows beneath her knees to lift her to him. The instant she accepted the length of him and he felt her soft flesh surrounding him, Shaler came another step closer to dying of pure pleasure. He was like a wild man besieged by overwhelming need, clutching Casity ever closer, longing to bury himself so deeply inside her that they were one entity.

When Shaler's muscular body drove into hers, Casity gave herself up in flesh and spirit. She moved upon command, meeting each hard thrust, aching to capture all the wild emotion that fulfilled her as nothing else could. She and Shaler had become one body and soul. The love she felt for him streamed out of her body to whisper through him.

A gasp of ecstasy escaped Casity's lips when the tumultuous sensations exploded inside her. She clung to him, inhaling his masculine scent, worshiping the feel of him, the sight of him. Her body shuddered in uncontrollable release as Shaler held her close as if the world were about to end. And it would—all too soon. Casity knew that as surely as she knew she loved this magnificent man with every part of her being.

A ragged sigh drifted from Shaler when he felt the last pulsating throb leave him. As always, the passion he experienced in this woman's arms very nearly killed him. It satisfied and devastated, demanding every ounce of his strength and emotion . . .

The impatient rap at the door shattered the moment like a rock crashing through a window pane. Reality struck Casity a terrifying blow. Her assassins had arrived all too quickly, leaving no time to revel in the aftermath of a love that had come too late.

"Curse it, where'd I put that damned thing?" Casity

mumbled as she twisted out of Shaler's arms to locat
the derringer.

Another firm rap at the door caused her to curs
her inability to move quickly. When she finally spie
the handgun amid the garments on the floor, sh
dived headfirst off the bed to retrieve it.

In stupefied astonishment, Shaler watched Casit
clutch the hem of the sheet and drape it over her whil
she fumbled to grasp the weapon and aim it at th
door.

"Damn, but you're paranoid," Shaler grumbled.

He watched Casity brace herself against the wall a
if she were expecting an Indian war party. There wa
grim acceptance in her posture and her expression
as if she were preparing to stare death in the face an
defy it to the bitter end.

"I have every right to be paranoid," Casity whis
pered without taking her eyes off the door. Sh
groped for Shaler's breeches and tossed them in hi
general direction. "I knew they would come eventu
ally. I'll cover you while you sneak out the windov
Now hurry," she ordered urgently.

Shaler gaped at her for a long moment. He didn'
call her crazy but his look indicated he thought sh
was. What was it that she thought she knew that h
didn't know? Whatever it was, Shaler was prepare
for a confrontation. He had been forced to hide unde
her bed and then scramble out the window to escap
an encounter with Reece before the trap had bee
sprung. But Shaler no longer gave a whit what Pendle
ton or anyone else thought. Casity Crockett belonge
to him and he didn't give a damn who knew it. H
wasn't letting her out of his sight again. He wasn'
himself when she was gone and he wasn't going any
where without her!

Shaler scowled at the closed door. "Who the hell is it?"

"Sh . . . sh . . . You imbecile!" Casity hissed. "Keep your mouth shut!"

"It's me. Who the hell did you think it would be?" Tweed grumbled impatiently.

Casity slumped back on her elbow. Thank the Lord—she'd been granted a little more time. If she could send Shaler and Tweed on their way, she might even be able to escape, drawing her would-be murderers along with her. She could spare Shaler's life if she moved quickly.

"Give us a moment," Shaler insisted as he hurriedly stabbed his legs into his breeches—backward—and then had to start the procedure all over again.

"I ain't got all day," Tweed grunted. "Besides that, my leg's killin' me. I've been all over this damned town!"

While Shaler gathered Casity's garments and fastened her into them, Tweed propped himself against the door with a weary sigh. He listened to the scurrying sounds for a few minutes, then the door finally creaked open and he hobbled inside. His gaze fell to the rumpled bed and he glared at his son. While Tweed had been doing all the leg work, Shaler had been on his back. That hot-blooded scamp's sense of timing was terrible!

Shaler was thinking the exact same thing about Tweed's timing!

Tweed's annoyance faded when he noted Casity's bloodshot eyes and the protective way Shaler had his arm around her. Tweed's observant gaze drifted to the empty bottle on the nightstand.

"You okay, Casity?" Tweed questioned in concern.

"No, she's not okay," Shaler answered for her. "She was an eyewitness at the saloon."

"Good God," Tweed groaned sickly.

"I killed him, you know," Casity mumbled over her thick tongue.

"No, Broken-Nose Jack McCall did," Tweed assured her.

He frowned worriedly at the haunted expression on her lovely face. Tweed suddenly remembered how Casity felt obliged to shoulder the blame for her parents' deaths, and that of her uncle as well. She seemed to have a fierce sense of responsibility to those she loved and admired, including James Hickok.

"What happened to James ain't yer fault," Tweed insisted. "I refuse to let you blame yerself."

Casity pushed away from Shaler and balanced on her own two feet as best she could. "I would like to be alone, if you don't mind."

"I do mind," Shaler growled. "Quite a lot, actually. You're in no condition to be left alone."

"Come on, Shay," Tweed insisted as he pivoted toward the door. "You heard what she said. Let her be if 'n that's what she wants."

"I'm staying," Shaler shot back in a tone that allowed for no argument.

"Go away," Casity urged emphatically.

Tweed clutched Shaler's arm and pulled him toward the door. "She wants us out. Show a little respect for her wishes for once!"

With tremendous reluctance, Shaler allowed his father to propel him into the hall. Maybe Casity did need to sleep off the whiskey, but he detested the thought of leaving the premises. Every time he turned his back on her she disappeared and he had to chase her down.

"Quit draggin' yer feet, boy," Tweed muttered grouchily. "I found out plenty after talkin' to Sheriff Brown and some of the patrons in the saloons. It seems Varnes and Brady clashed with James when he was marshal in Abilene. He ran them outta town and cost them a lot of money in their gamblin' operation. They've borne a grudge against him for years. Now Varnes and Brady are demandin' a hasty trial and insistin' McCall had good reason to even the score with Hickok because of his old feud. I swear they're plannin' to bribe the jury and McCall is gonna walk, sure as hell!''

The unsettling information prompted Shaler to follow along behind his father. But Shaler took time to spare one last glance at the closed door. What he wanted was a written guarantee that Casity would be there when he got back.

Reluctantly, Shaler descended the steps. He still couldn't shake this uneasiness about leaving Casity alone. Although disaster had already struck, Shaler was still plagued by the premonition that something wasn't quite right. Casity's reaction to the knock at the door worried him no end. He had seen that terrified expression in her eyes while she was dashing down the street, and again when she dived off the bed to retrieve her derringer.

Casity was definitely expecting trouble. But why? He was determined to find out just as soon as Tweed told him all the information. One thing was for damned certain—Shaler had no intention of going any farther than the hotel lobby. If Casity went flying off, he was going to be one step behind her!

Ned Johnson elbowed his way to the hotel desk. He and Russel had grown impatient with their frantic search to locate the one woman who knew too much. They had already checked the registers in three boardinghouses and had turned up nothing for their efforts.

"Did you find her name?" Russel inquired as he glanced around Ned's broad shoulder.

"Not yet . . ." His index finger stalled on the familiar name on the ledger. "Lambert. Ain't that the name of that babbling blonde we questioned on the train to Cheyenne? She's the one who said that Crockett girl was headed to Denver."

"Looks to me like the two of them bamboozled us," Russel snorted.

"Let's have a look at this Priscilla Lambert. Unless I miss my guess, we'll find the woman we're looking for in room seven."

While Johnson and Bassett were ascending the steps, Shaler and Tweed were descending them. When Johnson plowed into Tweed, practically knocking his splinted leg out from under him without bothering to apologize, Shaler grabbed the discourteous hooligan by the collar of his shirt and shoved him against the wall.

"You got any manners, mister?" Shaler growled into Ned's clean-shaven face.

"Yeah, I got 'em," Ned smarted off. "Now get the hell out of my way before I—" His breath came out in a pained grunt when he felt the barrel of a Colt jab him in the belly.

"Before you *what*?" Tweed smirked when he noticed the startled expression on Johnson's face and spied the pistol Shaler had rammed into the rude ruffian, fist and all.

When Russel Bassett tried to knock Shaler's arm out of the way, he couldn't believe the astonishing speed with which the second pistol cleared its holster—and with his challenger's left hand, no less! Russel felt cold steel stab into *his* ribs. Damn, lightning didn't even strike that fast!

"Hey, friend, we don't want any trouble," Russe

drawled as he held up his arms in a gesture of surrender. "We were just in too big of a hurry, that's all."

Shaler glided his pistols into their holsters and
moved down a step so that he and the two bullying
hombres stood eye-to-eye. "Next time you find your-
selves in an all-fired rush, spare the time for a little
common courtesy," he advised with deadly menace.

"Bastard," Ned muttered under his breath before
he stalked off.

"Texans," Tweed scowled as he eased down the staircase. "I'd recognize that drawl anywhere." He shook
his head in dismay. "There's enough trouble in this
rowdy town without importin' more. It's gettin' to the
place a man can't even walk down the steps around
here."

Tweed limped across the lobby and plunked himself
down in the nearest chair. His leg was aching something fierce and he had gone as far as he cared to go
before taking a load off it. That suited Shaler just fine
since he had every intention of standing guard in case
Casity decided to flit off again.

"I've been hearin' all sorts of unnervin' rumors
around town," Tweed said without preamble. "The
worst part is Jack McCall don't seem the least bit worried about his upcomin' trial. I came right out and
asked that scoundrel why he didn't have the guts to
face Hickok in a fair fight. You know what that
drunken sot said?" Tweed snorted derisively. "McCall
just shrugged and said he didn't want to commit sui-
cide. It looks like he was definitely paid to do somebody's dirty work. Sheriff Brown found a tobacco box
full of gold dust in his pocket and everybody in town
knows McCall's reputation. He never has a cent because he buys a bottle every chance he gets."

"Did anybody notice where McCall was before he

entered the Number Ten Saloon?'' Shaler questioned
gravely before he cast another glance at the stairway.

Tweed nodded his bushy red head. "He was seen
comin' out of Varnes and Brady's office. O' course,
they're the ones who've been the most vocal about
shruggin' off the murder charge as if it was nothin'.
I'll bet they're in cahoots with McCall and paid him
in gold to do the killin','' he muttered resentfully. "I
tell ya, this so-called trial they're tryin' to set up is
gonna be the biggest farce in the territory. I'm also
willin' to bet Varnes and Brady are greasin' palms
right and left to be sure McCall walks away without
swingin' from a rope . . ."

A befuddled frown puckered Tweed's wrinkled face
when he noticed Shaler's thoughtful expression and
the odd way he kept staring at the stairwell. "What's
botherin' you, Shay?''

Fragments of conversation were ricocheting around
Shaler's brain and distinct images were haunting him.
He saw Casity scrambling for her weapon when the
unexpected rap resounded on the door. *They're coming,*
she had said. Who? Shaler hadn't been able to figure
out who she was talking about and had shrugged it off
since she had been tipsy. But he kept remembering her
bleak expression while she sat there waiting, as if expecting a cruel fate. She'd kept insisting that he leave.
Why? She had refused to tell him what was bothering
her. What had she anticipated . . . ?

Without warning, Shaler bounded out of his chair,
startling his father. Tweed's words echoed in his ear
and fear constricted his throat. "Texans . . ." Shaler
repeated half-aloud. "Two of them. Both in a great
hurry, going up the steps."

Lord have mercy! It couldn't have been, could it?
Had the two men Casity had planned to have arrested
for her uncle's murder found their way to Deadwood

Vas that who she had been running from when he
aw her rushing down the street, when she flew into
is arms and clung desperately?

Stark, pounding terror ripped through Shaler as he
ounded up the staircase to Casity's room. Although
'weed had hoisted himself out of his chair and was
houting questions, Shaler heard not a word.

Murderous fury propelled Shaler down the hall.
Vithout bothering to knock, he shoved a shoulder
nto the door and burst inside with two pistols ready
o fire. But to his disbelief, the room was empty.
Casity's belongings were gone and so was she. The
wo men he'd assumed to be her would-be killers had
isappeared as mysteriously as she had. But Shaler
ad the inescapable feeling that when he found Casity,
e would also find the two bullies.

"What the blazes is goin' on now?" Tweed de-
nanded as he huffed and puffed into the room.

Shaler wheeled back into the hall. "I think we just
net the two men who killed Casity's uncle," he re-
orted grimly. "The Texans . . ."

The color seeped from Tweed's ruddy cheek as he
ratched Shaler storm toward the back stairs. Damn,
' he hadn't been so insistent about drawing Shaler
side, they would have been with Casity. If anything
appened to that girl, Tweed would never be able to
orgive himself. Scowling at his gimpy leg, he scam-
ered down the hall to catch up with his son. Damn,
hat a terrible day this had turned out to be—and it
asn't over yet . . . !

Twenty-six

Casity veered around the corner of the hotel an[d] took off in a dead run, her luggage in each hand. Th[e] instant Shaler and Tweed had exited from her room she had collected her belongings and garbed herse[lf] in the men's clothes she had swiped a month earlie[r.] History seemed about to repeat itself. Again, she w[as] running for her life, chased by the two ruthless des[s]peradoes who wanted to silence her—permanently.

Although Casity had managed to scurry down th[e] hall toward the back steps, the two men had spotte[d] her before she could tuck the tangled mass of aubur[n] curls under her hat and make her escape. Damn th[e] luck! If they had appeared just a few seconds late[r] they wouldn't have seen her at all.

Casity would have remained in her room to awa[it] the inevitable, but she'd been afraid Shaler would r[e]turn and she feared for his life. Knowing how persi[s]tent her pursuers were about disposing of witnesse[s,] they would then take after Shaler—and maybe eve[n] Tweed. Hell's fire, she thought to herself, unconscious[ly] borrowing Shaler's favorite expression a second tim[e.] She really *was* a jinx to everyone whose life she h[ad] touched!

Casity had found no other alternative, considerin[g] Shaler's and Tweed's presence in the hotel, except

eat a hasty retreat. She had not, however, planned
n having those two hooligans hot on her heels.

She burst from the alley and dashed between two
uildings to reach the street. Frantic, she surveyed her
urroundings. When she spied an unattended wagon
eside a hitching post, she raced toward it to drop her
atchels in the bed before pulling herself onto the seat.
er eyes widened in alarm when Johnson and Bassett
ppeared on the boardwalk and dashed toward her.
nstinctively, she popped the reins over the mules,
nding the wagon lunging off.

"Hey, you, come back here with my wagon!" the
wner demanded in a loud voice.

Johnson and Bassett saw the wagon zoom off in a
oud of dust. They didn't even hesitate to confiscate
e nearest horses, and came thundering after her!

Casity sent a hasty prayer heavenward as she urged
e mules into their swiftest pace. She could hear the
atter of hooves behind her, but she refused to give
. Her natural instinct always put her to flight when
saster struck. If nothing else, her flight would save
aaler's life. Of course, he would never know she
d spared him. He wouldn't know a lot of things—
ke how much she loved him. Perhaps she should have
id the words when she had the chance. Perhaps . . .

Casity ducked away when a pistol barked in the twi-
ght. The reflexes she had developed after living in
rowdy cowtown came in handy the instant she heard
nfire. Ha! Missed her by a mile, she gloated as she
ced over the bumpy road. Casity didn't have the
ghtest idea where she was going—and she had to
ust the mules to find their way as darkness descended
 the Black Hills.

If she were lucky—and she certainly couldn't count
 that—she could leap from the wagon into a thicket

of trees to elude her pursuers. And if she were u
lucky . . .

Another shot echoed through the hills and Casi
dropped to her knees, using the wooden seat to prote
her. Her wild-eyed gaze scanned the broken terrain
searching for a place to make her leap without breakin
any more bones than necessary. As the breeze swishe
past her face, Casity focused on a grove of aspen
pines, and thick underbrush on the path ahead of he
A horseshoe bend of the road would give her th
chance to dive for cover without being spotted. Whil
her assailants were chasing down the runaway wago
she could scramble into the bushes—providedshecoul
still move after making the leap at high speed.

Like a cat poised to pounce, Casity awaited her o
portunity. Just as the wagon skidded around th
curve, she lunged sideways. The ground flew up an
hit her much sooner than expected, knocking th
breath clean out of her. By sheer will alone, sh
hauled herself up and plunged into the thicket.

Casity remained as still as a statue until dang
passed. Her injured knee had suffered a serious se
back, but all in all, she'd managed better than she
expected. She was still in one piece—for the moment
least.

All too soon Johnson and Bassett overtook th
wagon. The mules had slowed their breakneck pa
and Casity soundly cursed their lack of cooperatio
Weren't those contrary creatures supposed to run fr
forever?

"Damn it, she must have jumped off," Johnso
muttered as he wheeled his steed around.

To Casity's dismay, both men started blasting hol
in the underbrush along the road. She was forced
slither like a snake to keep from being blown to smit
ereens.

A frightened shriek betrayed her as an unidentified creature leaped up in front of her. Casity swore under her breath when she spied a jackrabbit bounding off to safety. She'd been exposed because of that confounded rabbit!

The crackle of twigs in the near distance caused her breath to stop in her throat. Casity had the unshakable feeling that catastrophe was closing in—she didn't know if she should leap to her feet or remain where she was.

"Cas?" Shaler's booming voice echoed in the night.

Casity lay sprawled facedown in the grass. How had he known where to find her? He truly must have a nose like a bloodhound, just as James Hickok claimed. Well, this was one time Casity wished he hadn't been so skillful. He was going to get himself shot, even after she had gone to such lengths to protect him!

When Johnson and Bassett wheeled to fire at the approaching rider, Casity cursed Shaler but good. If she hadn't known better, she would have sworn he had purposely drawn their attention. This was no time for heroics. She would never forgive Shaler if he got himself killed trying to save her! She'd been managing just fine until he showed up to complicate matters.

Shaler had seen the two renegades charge out of town and he had instantly given chase. Tweed hadn't been far behind. The instant Shaler realized the men had dismounted and were blasting holes in the underbrush he guessed the reason why. By drawing their attention, Shaler could tell their location in the darkness by the sparks flying from the barrels of their pistols.

With deadly intent, Shaler raised his revolver. An abrupt yelp indicated he had found his first mark. After his second shot, however, he heard only the sound of thrashing in the underbrush.

Casity screamed when Russel Bassett tripped ov[er]
her in his attempt to dodge the oncoming bullet. Befor[e]
she could roll away and dash to safety, Russel clawe[d]
at her in desperation. She found herself hauled to he[r]
feet and slammed against his heaving chest as a shiel[d.]

"Back off, you bastard, or I'll kill her," Russel be[l-]
lowed as he rammed the barrel of his revolver in[to]
Casity's neck.

A muffled curse rumbled from Shaler's directio[n.]
From all indications, he had dropped one desperad[o]
in his tracks, but the other had managed to latch on[to]
Casity for protection. Where the hell was Tweed? H[e]
was sure his father had been behind him a few minut[es]
earlier.

Holding Casity at gunpoint, Russel trompe[d]
through the brush toward the open road. When h[e]
could see Shaler's silhouette looming in the moonligh[t]
he swore vehemently. One encounter with this quic[k-]
draw hombre was enough. Ned Johnson could ha[ve]
testified to that if the bullet hadn't laid him low, nev[er]
to rise again.

"Throw down your pistol nice and easy-like," Russe[l]
demanded.

Shaler put a stranglehold on his revolver, defyin[g]
the command. If he tossed his weapon aside, he an[d]
Casity could both wind up dead. If he didn't, Casi[ty]
would be the first to go. Shaler would have one chanc[e]
at revenge—which would avenge Casity but it wouldn[']
do her one damned bit of good if she were lying in [a]
lifeless heap at this bastard's feet.

Where the hell was Tweed? If he'd show up abou[t]
now it would certainly simplify matters. Tweed coul[d]
get the drop on Casity's captor and Shaler would b[e]
the happiest man alive.

"I said *drop it*," Russel sneered.

By the dim light of the moon, Casity could see th[e]

ngerous glitter in Shaler's eyes. Sure as the world,
e was about to strike! Damn him! Why couldn't he
ve been long on sense and short on courage? She
d to do something—and quickly!

Despite the deadly peril, Casity's arm shot upward
d shoved the pistol away from her throat. Russel
as too busy monitoring Shaler's every move to react
Casity's counterattack until it was too late. When
e flung herself sideways, Russel was left facing
aler without a shield. Snarling viciously, Russel
med at his target, but he was up against one of the
stest guns in the West. Shaler's well-aimed bullet
ught Russel in the shoulder, spinning him around
e a top. Before he hit the ground a second shot
rked in the night, sending Russel's pistol tumbling
er the back of his hand. The third shot flipped the
at off his head and left him gaping at his challenger
stunned disbelief.

"Don't kill me!" Russel croaked when Shaler
ought his pistol into firing position and focused
ose steel-hard eyes on his wounded target.

"Why not?" Shaler growled poisonously. "You took
aniel Crockett's life without sparing him a thought.
hy should I show you the slightest mercy?"

"I didn't kill the old man," Russel bleated. "Ned
hnson did it."

Shaler snorted in disgust. "That's easy to say since
e isn't in any condition to contest you."

"It's the truth!" Russel crowed. "You can ask *her*.
he saw the whole thing!"

Shaler grimaced inwardly at the thought of Casity
itnessing not one but two murders. He was again re-
inded of how much she had endured and how cruel
nd insulting he had been to her. When he glanced at
asity for confirmation of Russel's story, the strange
xpression on her face startled him. But he didn't have

time to question her now. He took a threatening st
forward, causing his victim to shrink away.

"What are you doing in Deadwood?" he demand
gruffly.

"We came to work for Reece Pendleton," Russel
sponded when he heard the purposeful click of t
trigger and watched the gleaming barrel of the C
zero in on him. "He sent for us—we used to work f
him in Texas. We were hired to make sure Pendleton g
the claims he wanted, even if it meant roughing up
few prospectors."

Once Russell's tongue had loosened up, he sang li
a bird. "While we were chasing the Crockett girl
heard one of Reece's stockholders claim he sent son
body to investigate Pendleton. And I didn't have ar
thing to do with Hickok's murder, if that's what you'
thinking," Russel add hastily. "That was Varnes ar
Brady."

That's what Shaler appreciated most about wort
less desperadoes—their utter commitment to protecti
their own hides. They were eager to point an accusi
finger if they thought it would save them from a neckt
party or a bullet through the heart.

"Cas, can you fetch the wagon?" Shaler question
without taking his eyes off his prisoner.

Casity clambered to her feet and limped forwar
but her footsteps halted beside the man who had sav
her life a third time. She gazed at Shaler's craggy fe
tures in the moonlight and felt a hot rush of admir
tion and affection that nothing could contain.

"Thank you for saving my life again. I love yo
Shay. I just wanted you to know . . ."

Without awaiting Shaler's reaction, Casity hobble
off to do as she was ordered. Shaler blinked in bew
derment at the simple yet eloquent confession. It to
tremendous effort to keep his eyes pinned on his ca

ve rather than following Casity until she disappeared
ito the darkness.

After a few moments, she returned. Holding Bassett
gunpoint, Shaler marched him to the back of the
agon and cursed loudly when he found nothing to
se as improvised handcuffs.

"Here," Casity offered as she produced her petti-
ats from her satchel. "Tear these up."

When Shaler attempted to hold her gaze, Casity
ooked the other way. Although a rush of heartfelt
motion had compelled her to whisper her confession,
ie felt awkward now that the moment had passed.
he really shouldn't be embarrassed about telling
haler how she felt, she told herself. She had been
onest and she had given Shaler what he had once
id he had always wanted from a woman—a love that
as unconditional and unbinding. She expected nothing
return because a man like Shaler McCain cherished
is freedom. For him, it was enough to know that he was
ved because of the man he was—with no strings at-
ched.

After Shaler had bound his prisoner, he went in
earch of his earlier victim. Ned Johnson was not in
eed of medical attention. Only an undertaker could
ive the murderer what he needed—a pine box and a
lot in Mount Moriah Cemetery.

"You drive," Shaler requested as he loaded Johnson
the wagon bed and hopped onto the seat beside
asity. "I'm not turning my back on him." He sighed
egretfully. "I wish Hickok had stuck to that policy."

Grimly, Casity took control of the mules, keeping
iem at a trot as the wagon bumped along. She had
one only a mile before she spied the riderless steed
razing beside the road. When she stamped on the
rake, Shaler half-twisted to see Tweed's limp form
ing beneath the limb of an overhanging tree.

Shaler gestured toward their prisoner as he hand[ed] his pistol to Casity. "Keep an eye on him. If he mov[es] shoot him. If he opens his mouth, shoot him."

"Don't give her any ideas," Russel muttered. "She['d] like to see me dead!"

"That's what you had planned for her, wasn't it[?"] Shaler smirked sardonically as he hopped to t[he] ground.

In three long strides, Shaler closed the distance b[e]tween himself and his father. Squatting down on h[is] haunches, he rolled Tweed to his back to inspect t[he] goose egg on his forehead. After Shaler gave him [a] few insistent shakes, Tweed's head rolled to one si[de] and a pained groan tripped from his lips.

"Damned tree limb anyway," he mumbled as [he] propped himself up on a wobbly elbow.

Tweed shook his head to clear his senses. Wh[en] Shaler helped him to his feet, he swayed momentar[ily] before he recovered his balance.

"What happened?" Tweed wanted to kno[w.] "Where's Casity?"

"Nothing much happened," Shaler informed his f[a]ther as he shepherded him toward the wagon. "Casity[']s fine."

Nothing much happened? Casity rolled her eyes. Shal[er] shrugged off his heroics as if they were an everyd[ay] occurrence. He had invited the gunfire of two know[n] killers to spare her life and dropped one desperado [in] his tracks before outdrawing the other one. And [he] claimed nothing much happened? If Casity had be[en] able to shoot that straight, that fast, she would ha[ve] bragged about it to anyone who cared to listen!

Tweed slowly hauled himself onto the wagon se[at] while Shaler again took charge of their prisone[r.] Casity urged the mules toward Deadwood. Her fier[ce] need for revenge against her uncle's murderers ha[d]

nally been satisfied. After she gave her statement to
heriff Brown, she had little reason to remain in Da-
ota Territory.

The time had come for her to return to Ogallala.
here was still the matter of the dry goods store.
asity supposed it was only fitting that she take over
er uncle's business. Where else did she have to go?
he had to begin her life again somewhere. Ogallala
as the most practical place, since it had been her
ome for eight years.

Ah, she was going to miss Shaler McCain more than
e would ever know! But sometimes, it seemed love
eant letting go and facing reality. In Shaler's case,
nowing he was loved just for himself was enough to
tisfy him. He didn't want commitment, and Casity
asn't about to demand anything of him. She already
wed him her life. It would have been ungrateful to
xpect more than that!

Resolved to turn her back and walk away from the
nly man she would ever love, Casity stared ahead to-
ard the lights of Deadwood. This town definitely
asn't for her, she assured herself sensibly. It held too
any memories—some good but a lot of them bad. She
ad once considered retreating into the Black Hills and
ving like a hermit, but the pine-covered mountains
ould only remind her of a man who had come and gone
om her life, taking her heart with him. She would be
uch better off in Ogallala where nothing could trigger
ose memories. That was for the best, Casity told herself.
nd it was also her only practical option . . .

Twenty-seven

When Shaler volunteered to tend the tasks th
awaited them upon their return to Deadwood, Casi
hadn't argued. She had simply trudged up the ste
to her hotel room and collapsed in bed. The whisk
she had consumed, combined with the exhausting ta
of staying alive the previous afternoon and evenin
had drained every ounce of her energy. She had fall
asleep the minute her head hit the pillow.

Casity had been sleeping soundly until the do
burst open and Shaler appeared. He was scowling
her as if she had committed some terrible sin.

"I didn't have the chance to say this last night, b
I'm here to say it this morning," he boomed. "Nev
ever leave again without telling me where you're g
ing." He shook a lean finger in her face as she l
abed, watching him puff up in frustration. "And dor
ever refuse to tell me what the hell's going on, eithe
You could have gotten yourself killed last night ar
you probably deserved it—stubborn woman that yc
are!

"You knew Bassett and Johnson had arrived in tow
and you refused to tell me. Hell's fire, Cas," he rag
furiously. "If you had spoken up while we were in th
room together, we could have avoided that wild cha
all over creation and I would have been here to stc
what happened in town!"

Casity didn't take time to question what Shaler meant by his last remark. She was too busy defending herself—while enduring a horrendous hangover.

"I didn't want your life at risk," she snapped. "If you had left when I told you to, I would have handled them myself."

"With that pint-size derringer that only fires two shots in the hand of someone who doesn't know how to use it?" Shaler crowed sarcastically. "You wouldn't have had a chance, princess."

"I already thanked you for saving my life again," Casity muttered crabbily. "Now what is it you want? My apology for refusing to handle the situation as Shaler—God Almighty—McCain would have? Well, I'm sorry. I did what I thought was best."

Shaler had been harboring his frustration all through the night and hadn't had a wink of sleep. He was dead tired and taking it out on Casity, whether she deserved it or not. To make matters worse, he had a long ride ahead of him. The thought of leaving this high-strung hellion alone again was turning him wrong side out!

Scowling, he stalked over to brace his arms on either side of Casity's shoulders.

"I want you to stay out of trouble. Do you hear me, Cas?"

Who couldn't? He had probably awakened every patron in the hotel!

"I have to ride to Custer City and you damned well better be at the cabin with Tweed when I get back," he ordered gruffly. "Johnny Varnes and Tim Brady bribed the jury in the kangaroo trial they held while I was off chasing you and your would-be assassins. Now Jack McCall has been set free. After I told the judge what I knew about Brady and Varnes, he demanded another trial to be held in Yankton.

"Tweed's going to bring official charges against Va
nes and Brady for their part in Hickok's assassination
Shaler hurriedly continued. "After completing the p
perwork to have Russel Bassett extradited to Nebras
you and Tweed are going to the cabin and wait for me

How dare he sit there telling her where she had
be! She may love him but love didn't imply blind ob
dience! She wasn't his slave. Besides, he hadn't ev
mentioned her words of love. Apparently he had
ready assumed she cared for him and that was the e
of it.

Men! Who could understand them? Shaler was b
having as if it were her duty in life to fall in love wi
him. If he didn't love her, too, he could have let h
down gently instead of ignoring her confession a
demanding that she wait for him obediently while
went galloping off.

Well, she was *not* going to remain in Deadwood
be in love all by herself! She could certainly do it lo
distance and it would be better for both of them. T
insensitive cad. He could have said something, but
had ignored her statement completely!

"Every time I turn around you're gone and I
damned tired of chasing you," Shaler muttered cra
ily. "Now for once, do as you're told. Do you und
stand me, princess? I'm not asking you, I'm *tell*
you!"

"I understand you perfectly."

"Good!"

On impulse, his mouth came down hard on h
parted lips, kissing the breath out of her. It was a lo
moment before Shaler found the will to pull hims
away and rise to his full stature. He battled the co
flicting urges that warred inside him. Although
had to track Jack McCall down, he was filled w
overwhelming urge to climb into bed with this g

eous female. But if he didn't apprehend McCall—
nd quickly—it could take months to bind him over for
new trial.

Still muttering and growling, Shaler turned on his
eel and stalked out of the room, leaving Casity star-
g after him. Damn that man! If he felt anything
ecial for her he had just missed his last opportunity
 say so before he tramped off. She had waited with
ated breath, hoping . . .

"Well, what did you expect?" Casity asked herself
oud.

There was no law that guaranteed a man would love
 woman back. Shaler McCain certainly didn't need
er. He liked things just the way they were—no ties to
nd, no commitments to slow him down. His affection
r her was only passion-deep. She was no more than a
orsel to feed his lust and that was all she'd ever be. So
hy was she lying here living on hope? Nothing was
ing to change—not now or ever.

Despite her hangover, Casity flipped back the sheet,
sed from bed, and resigned herself to facing the
rst day of the rest of her life. After she notified Sher-
f Brown that she would be willing to testify against
ussel Bassett when he was bound over for trial in
ebraska, she had every intention of catching the next
age. If all Shaler wanted was occasional physical sat-
faction, he could find himself some willing harlot in
e "Badland" district when he returned to Dead-
ood.

Love had its limits, after all. Casity would never be
y man's private whore, no matter how deeply she
ved him. She had confessed her love for Shaler and
at was that. He had no right to expect more from
r. She had to preserve her self-respect and dignity.
 She had been a fool for falling in love with that
possible man in the first place. Nothing prompted

him to *ask* her to stay. No, Shaler had *ordered* her
wait for him in Deadwood. There was a differen
and, if he didn't know what that difference was, the
he didn't care enough!

Grumbling at her own emotional turmoil, Casi
took pen in hand and jotted a note to leave on h
pillow. After gathering her belongings she marche
out the door.

This ill-fated affair was truly over. She was leavin
her love for Shaler McCain in this room, in this tow
in this territory! This is where it had begun and,
damn, this is where it would end. There seemed
be a fine line between love and hate anyway.
shouldn't be all that difficult to fall back to the oth
side.

Casity clutched her satchels tightly and braced h
self for what she knew would be an unpleasant e
counter with Reece Pendleton. She had hoped
make a quiet departure from Deadwood, but as lu
would have it, Reece stood between her and the sta
depot. When his gray eyes narrowed at the sight
her, Casity tilted her chin to look down her nose
him.

"Going somewhere?" he inquired with his custo
ary haughtiness.

"Farther than you are, I expect," Casity countere

"And what is that supposed to mean?"

Reece had learned of Russel Bassett's and N
Johnson's arrival in Deadwood, as well as their ens
ing fate, but he hadn't yet contacted Bassett in jail
inquire about the details. The look on Casity's fa
suggested she held him responsible for the fact th
his henchman had taken after her, but Reece did
hold himself accountable for their actions. He d

however, carry a grudge after this sassy beauty had escaped his clutches before he could enjoy her. Considering the amount of money he had spent on her, he still thought she owed him a tumble in bed.

Casity felt his hungry gaze consume her. She knew what he was thinking. Unfortunately, she had a stage to catch and that left no time to give him the dressing-down he deserved. Eventually he would pay for his swindling tactics—Shaler and Tweed would see to that. Too bad she wouldn't be around to watch this arrogant lout get his comeuppance.

"Excuse me, Reece," Casity said as she stepped around him on the boardwalk. "I really don't have the time—"

His hand clamped around her elbow and he flashed her a menacing smile. "You really don't think I'll let you leave town until you've repaid me for all those costly trinkets, do you, Priscilla?"

Casity stared at the hand that held her captive before meeting his venomous stare. "Actually, the name is Casity Crockett, and surely you don't think I ever had any intention of giving you more than a few days of my time, do you?"

She had always wanted to tell this cocky bastard off. Now that she knew she'd never see him again, she could speak her mind without fearing repercussions.

"I allowed you to think your meager charm was getting to me, but I was never fooled by your phony gallantry," she hurled at him with great pleasure. "All I wanted was the money. Surely you can identify with that, Reece."

Her snide remarks put a vicious sneer on his thin lips, making them disappear beneath his blond mustache. "You little bitch—"

When he tried to backhand her, Casity swung one of her satchels sideways, catching him in the most sen-

sitive area of his anatomy. As he doubled over to catc
his breath, she clubbed him in the chin with the othe
satchel. Reece slammed against the wall of the pastr
shop and Casity beamed in spiteful satisfaction.

"Let's not stoop to name-calling, shall we? Instead
let me place a well-deserved curse on you. I hope you
business endeavors crumble to dust. I also hope a
the investors you've tried to cheat get all the gold an
you get the shaft."

"And what is *that* supposed to mean?" Reec
scowled as he propped himself upright, itching
pounce but hesitant to do so after suffering a deva
tating one-two blow from this feisty hellion.

Mischief danced in Casity's eyes as she spun aroun
to continue on her way. "I'm sure you'll find out wh
I mean soon enough . . ." *Or too late, as the case happe
to be,* she silently added as she whizzed on her way.

Casity sailed into the stage depot to purchase h
ticket. Thirty minutes later, the coach rolled out
Deadwood, and Casity settled back against the sea
The moment the stage crossed the boundary line
Dakota Territory, she vowed to leave every painf
memory buried in the Black Hills. She was strikir
the past five weeks and four days from her life, as
they never happened. She was returning to Ogalla
to put her uncle's estate in order and start a new lif

If there was one thing Casity had learned durir
that long month which didn't exist, it was that th
farther one ran from one's troubles, the longer th
way back. She realized now that if she had simp
dashed to Clint Lake's office and demanded prote
tion, she might have saved herself a harried cros
country chase plus a variety of other torment
including a sprained knee and a broken heart. But
that terrifying moment when Johnson and Bassett ha

een hot on her heels, her natural instinct had bade
er to run as far and as fast as possible.

And wasn't she doing the same thing now? Casity
ghed and peered out the window to watch the tow-
ring pines darken in the fading sunlight. She had
efused to stay put as Shaler had commanded because
e'd been afraid he'd hurt her more than he already
ad. Curse that impossible man! He could have spared
e time to say *something* to her before he stamped off!

Well, that was the first and last time Casity Crockett
ould humiliate herself by telling a man she loved
im. She had learned her lesson and she would never
ave herself that vulnerable again. She might accept
lint Lake's attention if he was still interested, but
er heart would never really be involved. Too bad
asity hadn't been listening to herself when she of-
ered Priscilla Lambert advice about trusting her
eart!

Two hours after Casity had shaken the dust of Dead-
ood off her heels, Tweed returned to the hotel to
nd her room empty and all her belongings gone.
Vhen he spied the folded note lying on the pillow, he
lucked it up and read the short but profound state-
ent.

A deep skirl of laughter rumbled Tweed's chest as
e ambled back into the hall. "Serves him right, it
oes."

Tweed returned to his room to rest his aching leg
hile Shaler rode off in search of Jack McCall. Tweed
asn't sure how long it would take Shaler to appre-
end Hickok's killer and serve him up to the territo-
al judge in Yankton. However long it took, it would
e ample time for the smoke to clear after Casity left
eadwood, burning her bridges behind her.

This fiery courtship between his bullheaded so
and that auburn-haired spitfire had become Tweed
favorite source of amusement. He liked Casity's fierc
determination and independence. Only time woul
tell how strong this love-hate relationship really was

Tweed was looking forward to the day he could giv
Shaler Casity's note. And in the meantime, Tweed in
tended to make some future plans of his own. He sa
down to compose his own letter—a long, detailed mi
sive which left no question as to his specific requests.
was his best effort, a masterpiece that was destined t
get results!

A look of disbelief claimed Casity's weary feature
as she veered around the corner of the train platfor
to take her seat in the first-class passenger car boun
for Ogallala. There before her sat the same chatterin
blonde she had encountered during her first rail rid
to Cheyenne almost two months earlier. Beside Pri
cilla was a tall, reasonably handsome young man o
about twenty-five, who seemed capable of matchin
Priscilla's penchant for conversation. When Priscill
glanced up and recognized Casity, she squealed wit
delight.

"You're alive! I wondered what had become of you,
Priscilla babbled. "I did as you requested by sendin
your pursuers to Denver on a wild-goose chase. Hav
they been apprehended? Did you deliver my letter
Was Tweed angry?"

Casity sank down beside Priscilla, who had shifte
sideways to make room. "I no longer have to run fo
my life," Casity summed up. "Everything turned ou
for the best."

Odd, wasn't it, how she had adopted Shaler's sty
by making each event sound as commonplace as th

ext. It really shouldn't have offended her, she sup-
osed, that he had also taken her declaration of love
1 stride.

"Well, that's certainly a relief," Priscilla said with
n audible sigh. "Oh my goodness, how inconsiderate
f me!" She twined her fingers in her husband's and
atted her eyes apologetically. "I'm sorry, my love. In
1y excitement, I forgot. This is the young lady I told
ou about who boarded the train in Ogallala and—"

"I remember her," Jacob Warner said politely. "I
as very sorry to hear about your plight. Priscilla told
1e all about it, Miss—" He waited for her to say her
ame.

Priscilla probably went to *great lengths* to explain her
light, Casity mused with a faint smile. "Crockett.
:asity Crockett," she supplied.

"Jacob Warner," he returned with an engaging
mile.

"As you can see, I took your advice and bet against
1e gambler," Priscilla said as she focused her wor-
hipping gaze on Jacob. "My new husband is every-
1ing I ever wanted in a man and so much more. He
wns a big ranch outside of Cheyenne. We're on our
'ay to Ogallala to sell our crop of calves. Jacob was
eturning from Nebraska to gather the replacements
or the cows he lost in the winter blizzard when I met
im. Since then, it's been pure heaven!"

Casity was glad to know that at least one woman in
er acquaintance had found fate smiling on her. Pris-
illa seemed genuinely happy and Jacob appeared
opelessly devoted.

While Priscilla babbled in extensive detail about her
ncounter with Ned Johnson and Russel Bassett at the
oundhouse en route to Cheyenne, Casity settled back
) listen. She thanked her lucky stars that Priscilla had
1anaged to sidetrack those two devils for a few weeks.

Even though they had still turned up in Deadwood t
scare another ten years off her life, she had emerge
unscathed.

During the hours she spent with the Warners, Casit
wondered what it would have been like if Shaler ha
returned her love. Why was she sparing him a thoug
anyway? She had resolved to close the door on yester
day and here she was, pining away for a love that woul
never be.

Enough of that, Casity told herself sensibly. If sh
didn't put McCain out of her mind she would driv
herself crazy. And considering all the torment she ha
suffered the past two months, she didn't need to ad
insanity to the list!

Twenty-eight

Shaler had been frustrated when he had ridden out of Deadwood with a warrant for Jack McCall's arrest. Now it was a month later and he was just as frustrated because of the amount of time required for due process to take effect. Throughout the ordeal, Shaler realized how great his need was to see justice served. He also began to understand Casity's fierce determination to see her uncle's murderers punished for their vile crime. *Casity . . .*

A sigh escaped Shaler's lips as he urged his steed into a trot and topped the rise overlooking Bonanza Gulch. Lord, he had missed her even more than he thought he would! Nothing had seemed the same without her. He hoped she would be as anxious to see him as he was to see her. Surely she would be, he encouraged himself. She had said she loved him—pure and simple. She would be at the cabin waiting for him.

In eager anticipation, Shaler burst through the door to find Tweed preparing his afternoon meal. The bulky splints that had once slowed Tweed down had been removed and he bore only a slight limp. Shaler's gaze swung toward the closed door of the bedroom and he impulsively headed toward it, only to have Tweed gesture for him to take a seat at the table.

"Glad yer back," Tweed enthused. "Take a load off, boy. I've got dinner ready."

"Where's—?"

Before Shaler could pose a question as to Casity whereabouts, Tweed butted in. "Tell me everythi that happened while you was gone," he demande "You did catch up with Jack McCall, didn't you?"

Shaler sank into his chair, but not without castir another expectant glance at the closed door. "I four Broken-Nose McCall in a saloon in Custer City," h reported. "He was carrying the hundred dollars blood money Varnes and Brady had paid him to di pose of Hickok and he had already gotten himse rip-roaring drunk by the time I arrived."

"That sounds like McCall," Tweed muttered as h turned back to the stove to stir the fried potatoes.

After Tweed limped to the table with a cup of coffe Shaler took a sip to lubricate his vocal cords and near choked. As usual, Tweed's coffee was as strong as t. and tasted the same.

"While Jack was enjoying his drinking spree, parked myself in the corner to listen to him boast th he had purposely set out to kill Hickok," Shaler co tinued. "He also bragged that the evidence which s him free in the trial in Deadwood was a crock of lie He assured everyone in the saloon who cared to liste that Tim Brady and Johnny Varnes had paid him gold dust to remove Hickok from Deadwood—perm nently."

"Those bastards," Tweed snarled in disgust. "The didn't have the guts to face James in a fair fight."

"After I listened to as much as I could stand, dragged McCall to the marshal's office," Shaler wer on between sips of coffee. "When McCall realized h had boasted in front of the wrong man, he put up fight. It gave me the perfect chance to take some my frustration out on him."

"I hope you broke his nose again," Tweed said spite-
ully.

"He spit a few teeth before I finished with him,"
haler assured his father. "I also thought I had fulfilled
ny obligation by presenting the town marshal with the
arrant. But he asked me to transport McCall to Yank-
on and make sure the evidence was presented in court
s it should have been during the first trial. And the
econd time, away from Varnes, Brady, and Pendleton's
noney, Jack McCall was found guilty of murder and
entenced to hang."

"Good." Tweed got himself up to check on their
neal. "I hope that bastard hangs high."

"He will," Shaler affirmed before taking another
ip. "No one's buying Jack's way out of the hangman's
oose this time."

"I wish I could say the same for Varnes and Brady,"
weed grumbled as he divided his midday meal onto
wo plates. "I think they must've discovered you were
he one sent here to investigate Pendleton, though I
on't rightly know how yet."

Shaler wondered if someone had passed along the
nformation that he and James had shared a bottle of
vhiskey in the Bella Union Saloon before leaving to-
ether. He hadn't given the incident much thought at
he time because he had been so preoccupied with
Casity, but his link with Hickok had turned out to be
lisastrous.

"Varnes and Brady lit outta Deadwood as soon as
hey found out you'd been deputized to hunt McCall
lown. Apparently they didn't bother tellin' Pendleton
ecause he's still around," Tweed went on to say. "I
uess they planned on lettin' him take the fall by his-
elf."

The news had Shaler scowling sourly. He wished he
ad gotten McCall's confession before he left Dead-

wood so he could have locked Brady and Varnes awa
Damn, another flaw in the justice system that allowe
criminals a headstart when they began to feel the hea

"What about Pendleton?" Shaler asked. His ga;
automatically darted to the closed bedroom door fc
the umpteenth time. Surely if Casity had been in ther
she would have emerged by now. Well, maybe she wa
down at the stream washing clothes and hadn't notice
his approach. That must have been it, Shaler decidec

Tweed chuckled mischievously as he set another cu
of coffee under Shaler's nose. "Reece has had a he
luva time with his mine in Mule's Ear Gulch. Whe
his men couldn't find much color, except in the san
ples we planted, he hauled his Blake jaw-crusher 1
the canyon. For two weeks he's been totin' hug
chunks of rock outta the shaft and crushin' it in h
fancy machine. He's been tellin' the crews to d
deeper, even if it was costin' him an arm and leg :
manpower and explosives."

Shaler grinned wryly. He could picture Reece scu
rying around, getting his fashionable garments co
ered with dust and all for naught.

"Reece ran clean outta money and went crawli
back to the bank for another loan, but he couldn't g
no more credit. His stockholders have refused to carr
him because I sneaked into his office while he was ;
the mine to swipe the list of investors and sent ther
a very informative letter—"

When the door suddenly burst open, Shaler swivele
around in his chair, expecting to meet a pair of cryst
blue eyes in a flawless face surrounded by a cloud (
curly auburn hair. Unfortunately, his gaze locked wit
a pair of smoldering gray eyes. A snarl thinned Reec
Pendleton's lips—and in his hand was a sawed-off sho
gun.

"You!" Reece growled in murderous fury. "You s(

ne up, didn't you? Those placer samples came from
his mine in Bonanza Gulch, didn't they? *This* is the
ich vein and you sold me a pile of rock!"

Shaler had been caught off guard. There was noth-
ng but the table between him and the outraged min-
ng entrepreneur who had arrived with vengeance on
iis mind and a murder weapon in his hands.

"What the hell are you rantin' about, Pendleton?"
Tweed responded while his wary gaze darted back and
orth between Shaler and Reece. If he could divert
his madman's attention long enough for Shaler to
each his pistols, they would have a sporting chance
gainst the loaded shotgun. "You look like you could
ise a decent meal. Why dontcha set that gun aside
nd join us? I just served up lunch."

"I'm not falling for any more of your manipulative
actics," Reece hissed furiously. "You salted that mine
o bleed me dry." His flashing gray eyes drilled into
5haler, who hadn't moved a muscle since Reece aimed
he shotgun at his chest. "You're the one Amos Grant
iired to recover his investments, aren't you? And you
ent that little bitch into town to dig up information.
t was a setup from the very beginning and she was
n it with you all along."

"Aw, hell, Pendleton," Tweed snorted as he calmly
icked up a bowl of beans and ambled across the
oom. "You've been out in the sun too long. Yer mind
s playin' tricks on you. If you ain't struck gold in
Mule's Ear Gulch yet, just dig a little deeper."

"That's what *she* said!" Reece snarled. "That bitch!
5he stood right there and told me she hoped my stock-
1olders got the gold and I got the shaft. I should have
known she—"

Tweed took full advantage of Reece's preoccupation
with his conversation with Casity. He hurled the bowl
of beans at Reece's face, splattering juice in his eyes.

That was all the time Shaler needed to kick over th table and use it as a shield. When Reece shook his hea to clear his eyes, his finger closed around the firin mechanism. But Shaler's reflexes were twice as fas Before Reece could squeeze the trigger, the barkin Colt sent a plug of lead zinging against the barrel the shotgun, knocking it off target. The instant aft the upturned barrel belched smoke, dust dribble from new holes in the roof. Shaler's second shot winge Reece in the shoulder, sending him reeling out th door.

"Cas! Stay put!" Shaler bellowed in warning.

He bounded to his feet to chase after Reece, wh had headed for his steed as if the devil himself wer hot on his heels.

"She ain't here so you don't have to fret about Reec takin' his vengeance out on her," Tweed informe Shaler.

Shaler wheeled around to stare at his father whil Reece raced off to safety. "Where the hell is she?" h demanded impatiently.

"Well, I was just gettin' to that before Reece showe up to spoil our lunch." Tweed glanced up at the sprin kles of sunlight that speared through the damage roof. "Damn, this cabin will be leakin' like a siev thanks to that scoundrel."

"Where's Cas?" Shaler prodded in exasperatio "In town?"

"In some town or another," Tweed answered as h reached down to pick up the table. "Not Deadwoo though. But she did leave a note on her pillow in th hotel before she left. I'll fetch it for you."

When Tweed scurried off, Shaler sighed in despera tion. "Hell's fire . . ."

His gaze drifted to the window—Reece had just di appeared over the hill. Shaler had intended to give chas but not until after he knew what had become of Casity and why. Curse it, he had told her to be here when he got back. He had given her explicit orders. Didn't that female ever listen?

"Here it is." Tweed produced the folded paper and then ambled to the stove to fetch their meal. In mischievous glee, he waited for Shaler to explode. His son didn't disappoint him.

"Damnation!" Shaler roared as he glared at the message a second time.

This is my last good-bye,
Casity Crockett

That was it? Good-bye? No explanation? No mention of the words she had murmured to him the night before she wrote this. Helplessly, Shaler focused his bewildered gaze on his father, who was having a devil of a time keeping a straight face.

"She said she loved me," Shaler growled.

"So?" Tweed sank down at the table to whittle off a piece of ham and chewed vigorously upon it.

"So? *So!*" Shaler boomed. "So if she loves me, then why did she leave a note with her last good-bye? Obviously she didn't love me at all or she would have been here when I got back!"

Tweed shoveled fried potatoes into his mouth and shrugged nonchalantly while Shaler circumnavigated the room. "Leavin' ain't got nothin' to do with lovin'," he pointed out, as if that explained everything—which it didn't. Not to Shaler's satisfaction, anyway. "Did you ask her to stay?"

"I *told* her to stay," Shaler muttered grouchily.

"Well, there you go." Tweed chuckled as he eased back in his chair to survey his scowling son. "I swear, hay, I must've overlooked part of yer learnin' when

it came to social graces and such. I never claimed t
be an expert on women, but I know for a fact that yo
don't *tell* them anything. You *ask* them, especiall
when yer dealin' with a woman like Casity Crocket
She was born contrary.'' He gestured toward the chai
"Sit down and eat yer lunch. You always were crank
when you missed a meal.''

Shaler did as he was told, but he didn't taste a singl
morsel of the food that he crammed down his gulle

"I don't rightly know why yer takin' the news s
hard,'' Tweed said as he polished off the last of h
meal. "You've been sayin' all along that you didn't war
no ties to bind, even if Cas ended up havin' yer bab
I admit I was a mite put out with you over this affai
but . . .'' He shrugged. "Yer right. You wouldn't mak
much of a daddy the way you like to pick up and tram
all over creation when the mood strikes you.''

"You think she's carrying my child?'' Shaler near
choked on his tasteless food.

Tweed leaned his elbows on the table and stare
directly at Shaler. "You'd know more about that tha
I would, now wouldn't you? Near as I can tell, yo
spent plenty of time practicin' what makes babies. S
there's always a possibility. But Cas certainly didn
confide nothin' to me 'fore she lit outta town. But
gotta give her credit for bein' realistic. I always di
think she was purty damned smart. She knew lov
wasn't enough to hold a man like you. And obvious
she wasn't askin' for somethin' she knew you couldn
give—like commitment, for instance. Why, you'd withe
and die in a week if'n you was confined like a cage
tiger—changin' dirty diapers and holdin' little tyk
on yer lap. That'd clip yer wings so short yo
couldn't fly.''

Tweed stifled a grin when Shaler's face contorte
in a wordless scowl. "Nope, settlin' down with a wi

nd kids ain't for you. Cas knew that, I s'pect. She let
ou off the hook, just like you wanted. When you stop
o think how badly you treated her, I'd say she was
ein' mighty generous about the whole thing."

His eyes darted discreetly toward Shaler to gauge his
eaction. Shaler's face was red and he was steaming
ike a clam.

"Cas will probably find herself a nice, respectable,
lependable man one day," Tweed continued casually.
'Knowin' the way Cas is—and I'm proud to say I came
o know her purty well—I don't think she's one to fold
er tent just because of her dealin's with you. She's got
oo much spunk for that. And there's plenty of men
vho'd leap at the chance to take yer place. Why, she
an have any man she wants at the bat of those long,
urly eyelashes. Before you know it, some conscien-
ious, carin' gentleman will be courtin' her nice and
roper, and they'll wind up married with babies of
heir own . . ."

"Damn her!" Shaler muttered as he slammed his
ork against the table.

"She knew she couldn't hold you so she let you go.
)amned sensible of her, if'n you ask me." He pushed
way from the table and got up from his chair. "Now
 you'll excuse me, I gotta stage to catch."

Shaler gaped in astonishment when Tweed entered
is bedroom and returned with his satchels. "Where
ne blazes are you going?" Shaler asked impatiently.

"Well, I sent off for another mail-order bride, but
nis time I was more specific— " Tweed paused when
haler howled like a wounded coyote. "But this time I
in't takin' the risk of havin' some other man snatch
ny bride before she gets to me. I'm going to *her* this
me. Her name is Cora Michaels. She lives in Denver
nd she responded to my ad in the *Rocky Mountain
Jews*. She's been widowed for five years and she was

growin' tired of lonesome. She loves to cook all sor
of mouth-waterin' recipes and she don't mind a ma
who enjoys puffin' on his pipe every now and ther
Cora just turned forty last spring and she sounds lil
just the kind of woman for me. Since I can afford
few of the luxuries I've lived without in the mountain
I'm movin' to Denver so I can visit with Amos wheneve
it meets my whim. Me and Amos are gonna invest i
a couple of gold mines. But this time we're gonna mal
damned sure the business is legitimate."

Shaler couldn't believe his ears! After twenty year
Tweed was walking out on him, too?

"Yer welcome to come along if'n you want," Twee
added generously. "Cora has her own house and sl
says she's got plenty of room for my boy if'n he wan
to come, too."

Now wouldn't they make a fine family, Shal
thought disgustedly. He and his pa and his stepmam
Well, at least this time Tweed wouldn't be robbing th
cradle . . .

The thought of a cradle caused Shaler to wince. F
never considered himself father or husband materi;
He had relished his freedom for so long that he kne
nothing else. But every time he thought of Casity lea
ing with only a brief message of good-bye it burne
him to the quick. How could she do that to him?

"Come visit any time," Tweed offered as he breeze
out the door. He paused on the stoop and peered u
at the vents Reece's shotgun had left in the ceilin
"Oh, by the way, Shay, if'n I was you, I'd repair th
roof first chance you get. Yer liable to get all wet whe
the rainy season sets in."

With that parting piece of advice, Tweed walke
away, grinning devilishly to himself. Whatever ha
pened now was totally and completely up to that mul
headed son of his who couldn't recognize love, eve

fter it hit him squarely between the eyes. Tweed had
oted Shaler's anger, shock, and disbelief. The cocky
ascal couldn't understand why Casity had left him if
he loved him.

Let Shay sit there and stew awhile. Time would de-
ermine what he really wanted. He had his options.
Ie could follow his heart or he could listen to that
ool head of his. The choice was up to him.

That was the way it had to be with Shaler McCain,
Tweed reminded himself. For too long Shaler had
ved by his own rules. No one could hog-tie him. He
vould just have to sit there and decide what he really
vanted from life. Now there would be no one to dis-
ract or influence Shaler. He could ponder while he
at alone in the cabin with its leaky roof, letting his
nemories float around him.

When all was said and done, Shaler wouldn't be able
o complain that he had been forced to do anything he
idn't want to do. Whatever he chose to do, he would
ave to accept full responsibility for his actions.

Of course, Tweed thought as he trotted his mule
oward Deadwood, if that boy had a lick of sense, he
vouldn't sit brooding in that empty cabin for very
ong. But he would have his work cut out for him if
e tried to win back Casity's love. Shaler always did
njoy a good fight and he thrived on challenges. To
weed's way of thinking, Casity Crockett was the great-
st challenge Shaler McCain had ever encountered.
he gave as good as she got—and she was every bit as
tubborn as Shaler.

"Like two peas in a pod," Tweed mused aloud and
nen grinned broadly when the thought of sampling
Cora's home-cooked creamed peas and new potatoes
rifted through his mind, tantalizing his taste buds.
Mmm . . ." he said with a sigh. "I can almost taste
m from here . . ."

Twenty-nine

Ogallala, Nebraska

Casity buzzed around the Crockett Dry Goods Stor putting the new inventory in its place. After she ha entertained Priscilla and Jacob, she had thrown he self into reorganizing her uncle's business and tallyir the ledgers.

Thanks to the conscientious town marshal who patrolled the abandoned building to prevent lootir and vandalism, Casity had returned to find the sto intact. She had thanked Clint Lake kindly for his e forts in her absence and had given him a full accou of the incident that had sent her fleeing from towr

With Clint's help, Russel Bassett had been a raigned for trial, and Casity had testified the previo week. To her relief, Russel had been sent to the sta penitentiary to serve a long sentence, which satisfie Casity's need to see justice done.

While Casity was dusting the shelves, the tinklir bell above the door announced the arrival of a cu tomer. She pivoted to find Clint Lake's bulky fran filling the entrance. Casity scolded herself for makir the same comparisons she had made for over a mont Against her will she found herself sizing the braw town marshal up against What's-his-name.

"Just thought I'd let you know there's a cattle he

...mped south of town," Clint informed her as he re-
spectfully removed his hat and flashed her a smile.
"It looks as if it'll be another wild night in Ogallala."

"Thank you for the warning," Casity murmured appreciatively.

"After all your difficulties during the spring season,
plan to keep a close watch on you," Clint assured her.
He approached her in long, swaggering strides. "I wish
you had come to me when trouble broke out. I worried
about you before and after I received your letter from
Deadwood." His hand traced her finely etched features. "You know how I feel about you, don't you?"

Casity tried hard not to make comparisons. And
Clint had made an effort to strengthen the relationship between them. She knew he held a certain affection for her, but he hadn't been open in admitting it
until after she returned to Ogallala.

"There's something I've been wanting to ask you
for a long time now," Clint declared. "I know most
women have serious reservations about getting involved with lawmen because of the risks."

Clint shifted awkwardly from one foot to the other,
struggling to formulate his thoughts—he always got
tongue-tied when he peered into those luminous blue
eyes. "We haven't had much time to really get to know
each other as well as I would like. My job prevents me
from escorting you out on the town in the normal manner, but—"

"What is it you wanted to ask me, Clint?" Casity
quizzed after he had hemmed and hawed for a full
minute.

Clint was so unlike McCain, who was blunt and to
the point, Casity noted. As adept as Clint was at keeping the lid on this rowdy cowtown, he was extremely
courteous and bashful around women—the proper
ones, at any rate. It was time she started encouraging

him after her month of self-imposed seclusion. Sh
needed a distraction to take her mind off this infuriati
preoccupation with What's-his-name.

When she left Dakota, she had vowed never to l
another man hurt her again. But after Casity ha
passed through the bitter stage of rejection, she re
ized she would only be giving What's-his-name sat
faction by shutting herself off from the world. The
were kind, decent men on this planet—a few, at lea
Clint Lake was one of them. It was high time that sh
sought the simple pleasures of companionship agai
Casity thought sensibly. What's-his-name had left su
an emptiness inside her. Now that she was aware of
the hole in her heart ached to be filled. She would a
complish nothing by pining away for a man who ha
never treated her with the respect and courtesy that Cli
had. She was lucky to have a man like Clint show
interest in her.

Clint wrapped his hand around Casity's, giving i
fond squeeze. "I thought we might have lunch t
gether . . . and I was hoping maybe you would
my . . ."

Casity smiled in amusement when he shifted se
consciously again. "Your girl?"

"Yes," he breathed in a rush.

"I would like that very much," Casity declared
mite more emphatically than necessary.

She wondered who she was trying to convince—Cl
or herself. But by damn, she was going to make a de
cated effort in this relationship. If she gave herself ha
a chance, she might even come to love Clint. He w
good *to* her and good *for* her and not the least
threatening. If anything, he was almost *too* nice. Wi
Clint, she always felt as if she were in control. But
was much safer than being involved with a dominati
force like What's-his-name.

"I'll come back about noon, if that's all right with
u." Clint's beaming smile could have lit a lost trav-
r's way. "And when this herd is loaded in the cattle
rs and the trail hands turn south, I'll delegate some
my responsibility to Deputy Rogers so we can spend
re time together."

"I'll be looking forward to that," Casity assured
m.

She wondered if she would recognize a proper
urtship if she were involved in one. Pensively, she
tched Clint amble out the door, his Stetson at a
nty angle. This relationship was going to be abso-
ely nothing like the one she'd had with What's-his-
me. No matter how long it lasted or what direction
took, Casity promised to give it a sporting chance.
She had been lonely the past month. That was a
nple fact. All her previous vows that she needed no
e in her life had been because of frustration and
jection. She did need someone and Clint was that
meone. He had shown real respect for her. He as-
med nothing and never took her for granted the
y What's-his-name did.

Casity Crockett was turning over a new leaf! There
s nothing here to remind her of the month she had
ent in Deadwood, clashing with an impossible man.
en if Clint Lake didn't set off any sparks, she was
mfortable with him. All Casity wanted was *comfort-
le* and *normal* and *predictable* after her frustrating
air with that difficult man in the Black Hills.

Things would be different this time because Clint
s nothing like McCain. Clint's eyes were pale green,
t glittering gold. His hair was blond and straight,
t wavy black. He stood six-feet-one, not six-foot-two.
int treated her with courtesy and respect, never
cking cynicism.

Clint and Shaler were completely different in every

way, Casity assured herself. Clint could help resto
her faith in men. She was going to ignore that wa
voice inside her for a change and give Clint a chanc
She'd meet him halfway. This was her opportunity fi
a new beginning and she planned to make the most
it.

And where What's-his-name was or what he was d
ing with whom, Casity didn't care! She was wasting i
more emotion on the man!

As Clint predicted, the trail herd from San Anton
blew the lid off Ogallala for four days. Casity had ke
off the streets as much as possible, especially at nigl
while the cowboys shot the place up and drank ther
selves blind. Clint had his hands full—the jail was teer
ing with trail hands recovering from hellish hangovers

Casity had encountered only one awkward sit
ation—a drunken cowboy who demanded credit for su
plies he wanted to purchase. But after the tragic orde
in the spring, she had become extremely cautious. Whe
the man became belligerent, she whipped out the pist
she had stashed under the counter and showed him tl
door. Thankfully, he had retreated without further i
cident, and Clint had made certain the scalawag didr
bother her again.

When things simmered down in Ogallala, Clii
came calling, leaving the nightly rounds to Depu
Rogers. Casity dressed in her elegant gold gown
compliments of Reece Pendleton, whom she hoped w
dirt-poor by now. When she met Clint at the back doc
he stumbled over his feet and stared at her in open a
miration.

"You look absolutely lovely," he said.

Shaler had never been generous with his prais

.sity reminded herself. Another point in Clint's fa-
r.

"I've been wanting to do this for a long time," Clint
.hispered as his arm glided around Casity's waist and
drew her close.

When his head moved slowly toward hers, focusing
. her lips as if they were the first he'd ever seen,
.sity gave herself up wholeheartedly to their first
.ss. Things would be better the second time around,
.e promised herself. She'd be less cynical and more
'ectionate.

Her arms moved up to Clint's broad shoulders and
.e yielded to the tender pressure of his lips playing
.on hers. She almost willed herself to feel the warm
.gles of desire sweeping through her body, assuring
r that Clint could take McCain's place in every
.y . . .

"What the hell's going on?" came a low growl from
.e shadowed alleyway.

Casity pulled herself away when the hauntingly fa-
.iliar voice rolled over her like thunder. To her dis-
.ay, the last man she ever wanted or expected to see
.ain appeared out of the darkness. Clint, bless him,
.apped a supporting arm around her, pulling her
.ossessively to his side.

"The dry goods store is closed," Clint growled in
.e same fierce tone the visitor had used. "If you need
.pplies, come back tomorrow. And use the main en-
.ance next time. I don't take kindly to strangers
.eaking around alleys."

Shaler's brows rose in response to Clint's remark
.d the way he held Casity to him. He had ridden
.ll-for-leather after he had sobered up from the
.irst binge of his life—prompted by Casity's abrupt
.rewell note. Shaler had sat in that empty cabin for
.ree endless days, listening to the silence, fighting

the memories that rose to haunt him. He had dru[nk]
himself blind before collapsing in a senseless stupo[r],
then regained consciousness to begin the process [all]
over again.

Unfortunately, liquor hadn't been the answer. A[nd]
he had discovered what hell must be like— an achi[ng]
emptiness that echoed with the sound of that blu[e-]
eyed siren's melodic voice. Suddenly, his life w[as]
empty, without meaning and purpose, and freedo[m]
was a curse. He had come to terms with his feelin[gs]
for that auburn-haired hellion and admitted to hi[m-]
self that he was absolutely crazy about her, that [he]
couldn't let her go without losing a vital part of hi[m-]
self. He loved and needed her.

Having come to the profound realization that li[fe]
after Casity Crockett was no life at all, Shaler had pil[ed]
on his horse and beat a hasty path to Nebraska. A[nd]
for what? To catch this infuriating female snuggl[ed]
up in another man's arms! Damn her gorgeous hid[e!]
She had said she loved him and here she was, kissi[ng]
the lips off the town marshal! Shaler wanted to sho[ot]
her where she stood!

Composing herself as best she could, Casity sa[id]
calmly, "As the marshal pointed out, the store is clos[ed]
for the night. If you need supplies, you can colle[ct]
them in the morning or leave without them *now*."

How dare she treat him like a stranger! He h[ad]
ridden hundreds of miles to see her and here she w[as]
lollygagging with this blond baboon. Shaler had to[ld]
Cas to be in the cabin when he got back and she h[ad]
defied him. Now here she was, letting this cowto[wn]
lawman squeeze the stuffing out of her. Women! Wh[o]
could understand them? Who in the hell cared to tr[y?]

With a mutter and a growl, Shaler wheeled arou[nd]
to stalk down the alley to return to the spot whe[re]
he'd had been standing when he heard a haunting

iliar voice echoing in the darkness. Annoyed
ugh he was with Casity and her curt dismissal, he
d his gaze following the couple as they strolled
in arm down the street. Part of him wanted to
off in a huff and another part wanted retribution.
t little imp wasn't going to sail off, gloating and
oying her night on the town, while he wallowed in
ery! He'd stay one step behind her, watching her
y move—or rather the moves of that love-starved
shal. Didn't he have rounds to make after dark? Who
patrolling the streets while Don Juan Lawman was
ting the town red with Casity?

he steady click of boots on the boardwalk caused
ity's back to stiffen. She didn't have the slightest
what Shaler McCain was doing in Ogallala and
didn't care, so long as he stayed out of her life.
was a closed chapter. That's the way she wanted
nd obviously the way he preferred it since he'd
nothing to say to her. So what the devil was he
g here? And why was he following her? Just to
oy her, no doubt. That was one of his favorite pas-
es.

hen Casity and Clint ambled into the restaurant,
er followed them and parked at a corner table.
h time Casity dared to glance in his direction,
e golden eyes bored into her with fierce intensity.
couldn't concentrate on conversation or enjoy her
l. In fact, the night she had so happily anticipated
become an exercise in frustration.

urse the man! Why wouldn't he leave her alone?
n't he done enough already? He was the only man
d ever professed to love—mistake though it had
. Now he behaved as if he had no intention of
g her forget it! And worse, he probably intended
ll Clint about their reckless affair and spoil her
ace for happiness. She knew perfectly well that

Shaler could interfere in another person's life wh
he chose to do so. Hadn't he barged in to rout Twee
mail-order bride and made her life a living hell in
process?

"Casity?" Clint frowned in concern when she re
ranged the food on her plate for the umpteenth ti
without taking a bite. "Are you feeling all right?"

"I'm fine," she snapped and then sighed apolog
cally. "I'm sorry, Clint. My nerves seem to be on edg

Clint's gaze swung to the sinewy giant in bucksk
who lounged at his corner table with his back to
wall, puffing on a cigar until he had surrounded h
self in a cloud of smoke. When Clint threw hin
stony stare, Shaler glared right back. Since staring
stranger down didn't prove the least bit effective, C
decided to ignore him and see how that worked.
focused absolute attention on his companion, not
the pinched expression that bracketed Casity's mou

"The school is having a box supper to raise mo
tomorrow evening," Clint informed her between bi
"Would you like to go?"

"Very much so," she replied as she shoved
boiled potatoes aside and separated kernels of c
with her fork.

Confound it, she couldn't conjure up a smidger
interesting conversation with Shaler sitting in the c
ner like a lookout. Her shoulders sagged in re
when he finally got up and swaggered out the do
Obviously he had tired of his irritating games a
had decided to seek out some willing female wh
be more appreciative of his attention. He could f
himself a woman in any of the dance halls or brotl
and she didn't care a jot or a tittle!

The instant Shaler was out of sight, Casity sho
him out of her mind and concentrated on Clint.
was going to enjoy herself this evening, even if it kil

Shaler McCain was not going to spoil her blos-
ing romance. That brawny galoot had had his
ce. Now it was over, done, finished!

y the time Clint had walked Casity back to the
lest home behind the dry goods store, she had
red herself that she didn't care where Shaler had
e as long as he didn't come back. And when Clint
ered her in his arms to kiss her good night, she
ployed every seductive tactic she'd learned from
er. That was all Shaler McCain had been—*experi-
. . .*

espite her attempt to force Shaler from her mind,
ity had the inescapable feeling that something was
ng and that it was never going to be right. The
s that encircled her didn't hold her the same way
was accustomed to being held. The lips that
shed against hers were gentle, but there wasn't the
e spark of pleasure that sent her senses reeling.
n the kiss *she* offered seemed to be meant for some-
y else.

ell's fire! Her feelings for that tawny-eyed giant
en't going to go away no matter how hard she tried.
hen Casity heard the haunted whispers of her
rt and felt disappointment stealing through her,
wanted to grab Clint's pistol and tear off to find
midnight-haired rascal so she could blow him to
gdom come! She had embraced Clint, but it had
n Shaler she'd been trying to kiss. That rake had
ght her to respond only to *his* unique brand of pas-
and there was simply no substitute.

amn him for making it impossible for her to love
one else!

Will I see you tomorrow at lunch?" Clint mured after he pried himself away from soft, sweet
ptation.

"I'll be waiting," Casity promised with feigned
thusiasm.

When Clint disappeared into the shadows, Ca
unlocked the door and breezed inside. She gasped
shock when an unidentified hand stole around
waist. Curse Shaler's ornery hide! She should h
known he'd be waiting to torment her . . .

Casity's eyes widened in terror when grimy fing
clamped over the lower portion of her face, mak
it impossible for her to shout to Clint. She found h
self hauled up against a bulky body—no matter wh
way she wiggled and squirmed she couldn't escape.
one thing was for certain—it wasn't Shaler. She so
wished it had been when a familiar voice hissed in
ear.

"You didn't expect to see me again, did you, bitc

Casity couldn't respond while the restraining h
mashed her lips against her teeth.

"Now that I've tracked you all the way to Nebra
I expect a proper welcome. This time you're goin
give me what I've always wanted."

Thirty

Chuckling fiendishly, Reece Pendleton herded Casity toward her bedroom. He had waited a long time to have his revenge on this conniving little bitch. He was sure she'd made use of the days they'd spent together in Deadwood to distract him from the cunning scheme that had sent him plunging into financial disaster. She had obviously sneaked into his office to steal the files that contained the names and addresses of his stockholders. She was responsible for alerting his investors to his business dealings. Because of her and her crafty partners, Reece had poured all his cash into a worthless mine and his investors had pulled out. He had accomplished nothing by confronting Shaler and Tweed, except getting himself shot in the arm.

After his last encounter with this sassy firebrand, Reece had interrogated Russel Bassett. Before Russel was carted away for trial, Reece had learned of the incident in Nebraska. When Reece's attempt to take his revenge against McCain fell through, he plotted to set a trap with Casity as the bait. And when he finished taking this feisty minx for his long-awaited pleasure, he intended to use her to extort money from her wily partners.

The time of reckoning had come, Reece mused as he grabbed at the drapery cords to use as shackles.

This haughty bitch was about to pay his price for hood-winking him. He was going to enjoy hearing her beg for mercy while he plundered her body and made her his possession.

When Reece shoved Casity facedown on the bed and plunked on top of her to hold her in place while he tied her up, she bit his finger and began to scream. Since there was no weapon at her disposal, Casity clutched at the pillow and shoved it back in Reece's face. While he blindly struggled to retain his grasp on her, she swung her arm backward to knock him off balance. When she felt his weight shift, she bucked like a bronc to unseat him.

A murderous growl exploded from Reece's lips when he tumbled off and landed on his face. To further infuriate him, Casity bounded off the bed, using his prone body as a springboard to propel her out of the room.

Casity prayed she could reach the back door to shout for assistance before Reece caught up with her. Unfortunately, she had only made it halfway across the parlor before he leaped at her. When his arms clamped around her knees, she pitched forward onto the floor. Her loud screech became a dull groan when the butt of Reece's pistol smacked against her head. The world went black and Casity slumped on the floor, oblivious to everything except the blinding pain that pulsated through her skull . . .

Reece cackled in sinister delight as he scooped Casity up and carried her back to the bedroom. By the time she roused he would have her tied spread-eagle to the bed posts. Once he had satisfied his lust, he would send a message to Shaler and Tweed and demand that the ransom money be left at a location he named.

The creak of the back door caused Reece to flinch.

He cursed at himself for neglecting to lock it. Who the devil had made himself at home? Hopefully, it wasn't the brawny marshal who had escorted this witch back to her house while Reece was lying in wait. Damn, he didn't need complications after he had schemed and plotted to enjoy his personal vendetta against this spitfire!

Quick as a wink, Reece snaked an arm around Casity's waist and tugged her limp body against him. Laying the barrel of his pistol to her head, he waited, hoping the intruder would leave as quickly as he had come.

"Cas?"

The familiar voice caused Reece to stiffen in disbelief. He had expected to keep this troublesome witch in captivity for a couple of weeks while his ransom note was being delivered. But from the sound of things Reece was going to have the wicked pleasure of demanding his ransom in person—here and now.

"Cas, damn it, I want to talk to you," Shaler growled impatiently. "I know you're here. I just saw lover boy swaggering down the street—"

When the moonlight filtered through the window to illuminate the female body draped over Reece Pendleton's arm, Shaler cursed the air blue. He never dreamed this swindling scoundrel would hotfoot it to Nebraska to attack Casity! Obviously Pendleton had come to seek his revenge after his attempt had been thwarted in Bonanza Gulch.

Hell's fire! If Shaler had sent that lovesick marshal packing and demanded to speak with Casity the instant he arrived in town, this never would have happened. And yet, considering the way this infuriating female had treated him, he should let Pendleton have her. That's what she deserved for tramping all over his heart.

"Well, well," Reece sniggered sarcastically. "I wasn't expecting to make contact with you quite so quickly. But all the better." He pressed the pistol barrel against Casity's temple when Shaler took a bold step toward him. "Easy, McCain. You won't get your hands on this bitch until I have my ransom money."

Shaler's eyes glowed with suppressed fury as he watched Pendleton stuff his pistol under Casity's chin, forcing her head back to an awkward angle. Pendleton was a desperate man who resorted to desperate means to save himself from ruin. If Shaler didn't watch his step, he was likely to get himself and Casity killed.

"How much do you want, Pendleton?" Shaler growled.

Reece was relishing every second of his triumph over this mountain man who had bamboozled him. "For starters, I want the deed to the mine in Bonanza Gulch and the full amount I paid you for the claim in Mule's Ear Gulch," he demanded.

Shaler didn't bat an eyelash. "Done. Now let Casity go. She had nothing to do with the scheme."

Reece snorted derisively. "Don't lie to me, McCain. She sneaked into my office and stole the list of investors while I was busy buying her costly trinkets."

"That was Tweed's doing," Shaler corrected. "While you were digging for gold all day and half the night, he rummaged through your files. Casity was caught in the middle of my investigation without taking part in it."

"It makes no difference one way or another," Reece declared. "I'll do whatever I want with her until you pay up."

Shaler didn't like the sound of that. He knew perfectly well what Pendleton had wanted from Casity since the day he bid a thousand dollars for the pleasure of her company. The thought of Pendleton or

nat Casanova marshal touching Casity turned his
nood pitch black.

"You lay a hand on her, Pendleton, and I promise
ou that you won't live to enjoy your ransom money,"
haler hissed between clenched teeth. "I'll track you
own and send you to hell where you belong."

Damnation, how he wished Casity would wake up
nd use the same tactic she had used against Russel
assett. But no such luck. The blow Pendleton had de-
vered had left her dead to the world. Pendleton had
ropped her against him in such a way that Shaler
ould have to shoot *through* her to get to that scoundrel!

"Now back out of here nice and easy," Reece in-
ructed as he shuffled around the side of the bed,
eeping Casity in front of him. "You hightail it over
o the banker's house and make the necessary arrange-
ents. I'll be in contact with you at midnight."

Shaler swore under his breath. He despised being
acked into corners. In this instance, it wasn't just his
fe at risk. Although he had entertained spiteful
noughts of shooting this feisty female a couple of
mes after finding her with her latest beau, he wasn't
oout to let Reece Pendleton do it! Shaler had to wait
ntil Reece let his guard down before he pounced,
ving himself that precious edge. In frustrated dis-
ast, Shaler backed across the bedroom and through
e parlor before easing out the door.

"Now get going," Pendleton snapped. "I don't have
l night."

Still using Casity as his shield, Reece eased over to
ck the door. Hurriedly, he squatted down to wrap
e drapery cords around Casity's wrists.

Shaler peeked around the edge of the drapes to
onitor Reece's activities, anxiously awaiting his op-
ortunity. While Reece was still bent over Casity's un-

conscious body, tying her up, Shaler charged through
the locked door like a crazed bull.

With a squawk of surprise, Reece stumbled over
Casity's limp body to retrieve his pistol. Shaler lowered
his shoulder and took him into the wall. A strangled
yelp erupted from Reece's lips when his belly slammed
into his backbone and the air gushed from his chest
as if he'd sprung a leak.

Using his forearm like a club, Shaler knocked
Reece's head into the wall, causing his victim to bite
his tongue. Before Reece could shove his opponent
away and give himself a fighting chance, Shaler buried
a steely fist in Reece's jawbone. The world shrank and
expanded before Reece's eyes as he struggled to maintain his balance. Another brain-scrambling blow
caused his eyes to cross and his knees to buckle.

It was Reece's misfortune to be the recipient of
Shaler's pent-up fury. One meaty punch after another
connected with Reece's face and soft underbelly.
Reece tried to fling up an arm to deflect the attacks
but nothing kept the bone-jarring blows from coming
at him in rapid-fire succession.

When Reece's pulverized body threatened to dri
down the wall like molasses, Shaler grabbed the front
of Reece's tattered shirt and jerked him upright. He
had just reared back to give Reece another taste of his
fist when he heard the click of a trigger behind him.

Shaler swiveled around to see Clint Lake standing
with his feet wide apart, flanked by Deputy Rogers and
two men who had heard the racket and had raced off
to summon assistance.

Reece was as desperate as one man could get! Although Shaler had beaten him black and blue, he still
had the presence of mind to attempt to maneuver the
situation to his advantage.

"Stop him!" Reece wailed through his puffy lips. He was trying to kidnap Casity!"

Clint wasn't certain what to believe, but he knew all well that this man had been following Casity all evening. When Shaler growled furiously and raised his arm to shut Reece up once and for all, Clint flipped his pistol and clanked Shaler over the head.

To Clint's amazement, the man only staggered momentarily. Clint was forced to hammer Shaler over the head a second time to knock him to the floor in an unconscious heap.

When Shaler collapsed, Reece had been struggling to come up with a reasonable explanation that would convince the marshal. If he played his cards right, he could take full advantage of this unexpected development and by the time Shaler woke up to tell his side of the story, Reece and his captive would be long gone.

"Thank God you got here in time, marshal," Reece said with an enormous sigh of relief.

Clint surveyed the battered man and frowned curiously. "Who the devil are you?"

"I'm the man who took Casity in when she fled to Deadwood," Reece explained, biting back a gloating grin. He was adept in twisting truths to persuade stockholders to invest in his company. Now he could utilize that well-developed skill to escape another disaster. "This scoundrel pestered Casity while she was in Dakota and he also stole thirty thousand dollars from me in a swindling scheme for a mining site."

When Clint frowned warily, Reece hurried on. "Although I was practicing medicine in Deadwood, I let gold fever get to me and I bought a claim from this wily rascal. It turned out to be a pile of rock that he had salted to make it appear highly profitable."

Clint hesitated again, glancing from Casity's unconscious form to Reece's bruised face. Since Casity had told him nothing about the month she had spent in Deadwood, Clint knew very little about her activities. She had behaved as if that month of her life hadn' happened.

"I'm the one who bought Casity the gold gown she' wearing because she arrived in town with very little money and no place to stay," Reece elaborated, pleased with himself for conjuring up such a believ able tale. "I also bought her several other garments— blue satin gown with a matching bonnet, a yellow dress with white lace and—"

"All right," Clint interrupted. "I believe you."

Why shouldn't he? Clint asked himself logically. He had seen Casity wearing the garments Reece had de scribed. Apparently, he was telling the truth. Why would he lie? The brawny galoot lying on the floor was the one who had followed Casity and made her nervous. She had obviously been afraid when this hoo ligan showed up to spoil their evening.

"I traveled down from Dakota to check on Casity," Reece continued before one or the other of his un conscious enemies awoke to dispute his story. "I crashed through the door when I heard Casity's wail and McCain's snarling threats. He tied her up and struck her on the back of the head before I could stop him. That's when he turned on me."

Reece wobbled over to sink down beside Casity, pre tending to examine her like any self-respecting phy sician would do. "Haul that ruthless scoundrel to jail and lock him up," Reece instructed while he inspected the knot on the back of Casity's head. "I'll get her settled comfortably in bed and fetch my medical bag from the hotel. When she wakes up, I'll come by your office to file charges and you can come back here to take Casity's testimony."

Clint found himself following the doctor's orders

efore he even realized it. With the help of Deputy
ogers and the two men who had flagged him down
n the street, Clint toted Shaler's limp body out of
ne parlor and headed for the jail.

A bubble of laughter rose in Reece's throat after the
our men disappeared from sight. By the time Shaler
egained command of his senses, it would be too late.
Congratulating himself on his quick thinking, Reece
ossed Casity over his shoulder and tiptoed out the
oor to steal two horses for his hasty flight. That done,
e reversed direction and scurried inside the dry
oods store to execute the second phase of his scheme.

After Reece gathered supplies for his journey, he
lanned to be on his way. Before he was through,
haler McCain would know that he was no match for
.eece Pendleton. By damn, he'd have the last laugh
n Shaler and enjoy his wicked satisfaction with Casity
rockett!

Thirty-one

With a dull groan, Shaler fought his way through the cloudy darkness. Disoriented, he propped himself up on an elbow to study his inky-black surroundings. When his fuzzy gaze landed on the barred window through which moonlight streamed like silver, Shaler jerked upright then moaned loudly. His skull felt as if it had been pounded with a sledgehammer and his brain throbbed in rhythm with his pulse. Obviously that damnfool marshal had clubbed the wrong man. Reece had somehow convinced Clint that Shaler was the one who needed to be carted off to jail. Hell's fire!

Hauling himself unsteadily to his feet, Shaler staggered toward the cell door. Fearing his head would explode if he dared to shout at the marshal, Shaler searched the meagerly furnished quarters for an object that would make some racket. He snatched up the chamber pot and raked it against the iron bars for what seemed like ten minutes before the door to the outer office opened and Clint Lake's lean form appeared.

"Open this damn cell," Shaler commanded harshly. "You arrested the wrong man."

"That's what they all say." Clint moseyed toward his prisoner, smirking as he approached. "But the doctor told me the whole story after I knocked you out."

"What doctor?" Shaler demanded impatiently.

"The one you were beating the tar out of after you ·ied to kidnap Casity," Clint replied in a tone that ·ndicated Shaler ought to know without being told.

"You imbecile!" Shaler erupted at the expense of ·is throbbing head. "Reece Pendleton is no more a ·hysician than you are. *He* was the one trying to kid-·ap Casity when *I* stopped him. All Reece *doctored* was ·e story he fed to you."

Clint frowned suspiciously. Now he wasn't sure who ·· believe.

"And you call yourself a lawman," Shaler scoffed ·austically. "That two-bit swindler came to Ogallala to ·bduct Casity and hold her for ransom. Reece de-·anded money from me in return for Casity's life, ·en ordered me back outside. While he was tying ·asity up, I crashed through the door. That's when ··u showed up and ruined everything." He glared at ·lint in disdain. "If you aren't man enough to keep ·n eye on that female then maybe you should court ·n ordinary woman—one you might be able to keep up ·ith, though I seriously doubt it!"

"I'm perfectly capable of taking care of Casity!" ·lint blared.

"Like hell!" Shaler snorted. "*I* had to ride all the ·ay down from Deadwood to save her from disaster ·nd *you* live in the same town! All you did was botch ·ings up so Reece could accomplish his fiendish re-·enge and extortion."

"Reece said *you* were the one up to no good and ·at you cheated *him* out of the claim," Clint flung ·ack at him.

"Pendleton owned a mining company in Dead-·ood," Shaler explained hurriedly, infuriated that ·very second he had to waste convincing this clown ·as costing him precious time that might save Casity.

"He was cheating his stockholders out of their divi
dends. One of his investors sent me to Dakota to in
vestigate him."

"I suppose you can prove that," Clint retorted, eye
ing Shaler warily.

"The whole reason for my conning that con man
was because no one was able to obtain enough evi
dence to shut Pendleton down," Shaler said sharply.
"Some of Reece's other investors had tried to take him
to court to get their money back, but Reece is shrewd
and can be very persuasive, as you ought to know by
now. The only way I had to recover any money was to
lure Reece into buying a worthless mine and using
the cash to reimburse my client."

Clint still wasn't convinced. This rascal was every
bit as persuasive as Pendleton. "If all that is true then
how did Pendleton know about Casity's wardrobe. He
described every dress and claimed he purchased them
when he took her in. Answer that if you can!"

Damn, Reece had really done a job on this marshal,
Shaler realized. Reece had twisted the truth to such
incredible extremes that Shaler barely recognized it
himself.

"Reece showered Casity with costly trinkets in his
effort to buy her affection," Shaler informed him.
"And if I hadn't showed up the night he decided to
have his way with her, he would have taken what he
wanted by force." Shaler looked Clint up and down
with obvious disgust. "Now let me out of here—
pronto! There's no telling what Reece has done with
Casity after you left him alone with her!"

Clint still hesitated and Shaler muttered under his
breath. "Curse it, *Flake,* if you don't believe me, high
tail it over to Casity's house and see if she's where you
left her. I can guarantee Reece has—"

"The name is *Lake,*" Clint growled.

haler shrugged him off. "Just go check on Reece
 you'll discover what a fool you've made of your-
. And if Casity doesn't survive this latest ordeal,
 holding you personally accountable—"

Marshal Lake!" Deputy Rogers called urgently as
scurried through the outer office and whizzed past
 row of cells. "The Crockett Dry Goods Store is on
!"

error froze Shaler's breath in his chest as his gaze
ked with Clint's.

Let me out of here, damn you!" Shaler roared.

lint fumbled with his keys—before he could swing
 door open and move out of the way, Shaler burst
ugh like a freight train, knocking Clint into the iron
s. In a flash, Shaler dashed through the office with
t scuttling after him. Both men stopped in their
ks when they saw the rolling smoke and leaping
nes engulfing the store.

God, Pendleton must have left Casity inside!" Clint
rled as he charged toward the burning building.

haler was afraid to second-guess Reece after his
uction plan had been interrupted. If Reece feared
ng apprehended, he might have decided to steal
money from the cash register, skip town, and leave
ity tied up in the flames. But, on the other hand,
ce may have deliberately set the fire to throw his
suers off while he carted Casity off to parts un-
wn, just as he had originally planned. Whatever
case happened to be, Shaler didn't dare *assume*
thing. He had to make sure Casity hadn't been left
lie in that raging inferno.

While the men from the volunteer fire department
d to contain the fire before it spread to adjacent
ldings, Shaler and Clint rushed to the alley and
ered through the back door. Unfortunately, they

met shoulder to shoulder and stuck there, each tryi to barrel through first

"Get out of my way," Shaler sneered as he jabb Clint in the midsection with an elbow.

"She's my girl and I'll save her without any he from you!" Clint growled, returning the jab with equ force.

"Your girl?" Shaler scoffed. *"My woman!"* His eel-li agility allowed him to squeeze through the openi first and surge into the cloud of smoke that fogged t parlor.

"What do you mean by that remark?" Clint dropp to his knees and scurried into the thick smoke, hopi to find Casity lying in the same place he had last se her.

"You think you're so damned smart," Shaler blar over the sound of crackling timbers. "You figure out for yourself, Marshal *Flake.*"

"Lake," Clint yelled. "And damn you, Mc*Pain,* you dare to—" His voice trailed off into a gasp whe flaming rafter snapped above him and plunged towa the floor.

Shaler moved with lightning speed, though why bothered trying to save this idiotic marshal who mig have already cost Casity her life, he didn't know! I cause of Clint's gullibility Reece had been allowed indulge his sinister need for revenge.

A pained grunt erupted from Clint when Sha slammed into him broadside, knocking him out of t way before the burning rafter crashed down.

"Thanks, Mc*Pain,*" Clint muttered, his voice mc resentful than grateful.

"You're welcome, *Flake.*" Shaler rolled to his kne and crawled toward the bedroom in search of Casi

"Lake," Clint called after him.

"Check the kitchen," Shaler ordered before

lled the collar of his shirt over his face to ward off
e suffocating wall of smoke closing in around him.
While Clint was scrambling across the floor to do
he was told, Shaler felt his way around the bed and
rned up nothing. He had just crawled back into the
rlor, choking for breath when he bumped into
int.

It was that damnfool marshal's fault that Shaler
uldn't breathe, that the building was ablaze, and
at Casity was nowhere to be found. Curse the man!
rst chance he got, Shaler vowed to beat some sense
o that moron marshal and repay him for the knot
 the back of his head.

'She wasn't in the kitchen," Clint muttered.

'She wasn't in the bedroom, either," Shaler replied,
spite the burning in his lungs.

'We better get the hell out of here while we still
1," Clint advised. "I can't see—"

Buckets of water splashed through the door, drench-
; both men. Shaler had been caught with his mouth
en and he spluttered to catch his breath after being
used by a well-meaning fireman.

'Marshal Lake, are you all right?" one of the fire-
hters called before another tidal wave of water
attered over the occupants of the burning building.
Like drowned rats, Shaler and Clint crawled toward
 back door on their hands and knees. The instant
y appeared beneath the cloud of black smoke, they
e jerked upright and propelled a safe distance
ay.

You saved my life," Clint wheezed begrudgingly.

My mistake, *Flake*" Shaler croaked before gasping
a deep breath of clean air. "I won't let it happen
in. I should have let you burn to a crisp. Casity's
sing and it's all your fault."

How the hell was I to know who to believe?" Clint

retorted before coughing and wheezing. He propp
himself against the wall of the pastry shop and tr
to recover from inhaling so much smoke. "Casity ne
mentioned you or even admitted that she knew y
when you showed up here tonight."

Shaler cursed silently. From all indications, Cas
had planned to write him out of her life so she co
court this blundering marshal. Well, thanks to hi
she was in the clutches of a desperate man with
personal vendetta against her and Shaler. And unl
Shaler missed his guess, Reece had kidnapped Cas
and was holding her for ransom. Reece had set u
smokescreen—literally—to give himself plenty of ti
to get away.

While Shaler and Clint were recovering from th
ordeal, firefighters converged on the dry goods st
to bring the blaze under control. Within a few m
utes, the flaming embers hissed beneath an avalan
of water.

When Shaler could breathe without choking,
hurried around to the front of the store to make s
Casity's body hadn't been left among the charred ru
of what had once been a prosperous business. To
relief, he found nothing.

"Pendleton must have taken Casity hostage, just
he originally planned," Shaler announced with gr
conviction.

Clint wiped the soot from his face and stared gri
at Shaler. "He could be anywhere."

"And whose fault is that, I wonder." Shaler snor
sarcastically.

"Damn it, Mc*Pain!*" Clint exploded. "I've had j
about enough of you and your snide remarks!"

"The name is *McCain* as you well know, and l
had plenty of you and your idiotic blunders," Sh
growled insultingly. "There's no accounting for so

people's tastes. Why Casity let you near her I'll never know. You're a helluva lot more trouble than you're worth."

"And why Casity had anything to do with the likes of you *I* can't imagine," Clint sneered in the same ridiculing tone. "If the truth be known, your intentions toward her were probably just as disgusting as Reece Pendleton's."

"She said she loved me!" Shaler countered testily.

"Of course she did and still does," Clint smirked sardonically. "That's why she returned to Ogallala and never even bothered to mention your name when I asked her to be my girl. It sounds like wishful thinking on your part, Mc*Pain.*"

"*McCain,*" Shaler corrected with a sneer. "And you can go jump in a lake, *Flake.* From here on out, this is a one-man rescue brigade. You create more problems than you could ever hope to solve!"

That said, Shaler tramped off to retrieve his steed. He didn't have the slightest idea which way in the hell to go first. Reece could have headed in any direction with his captive in tow. Tracking them at night wasn't going to be easy, either. So far, there was no ransom note. Shaler could only guess that Reece would return to the familiar terrain through which he had reached Ogallala. If Shaler were in Reece's shoes, he'd head for the cottonwood-lined creek to keep from being spotted until he could hide in an abandoned shack. The plains of Nebraska didn't offer as much protective cover as the trees and mountains of Dakota. If Shaler kept his wits about him, he might be able to pick up Reece's trail and overtake him before he disposed of Casity.

When Shaler heard the clatter of hooves behind him, he twisted in the saddle. He scowled when he saw Clint Lake atop his roan gelding, surrounded with provisions.

"I'm going with you," Clint declared in a voice that invited no argument. "I know this country better than you do."

"I've spent my life hunting and tracking in the Rockies," Shaler assured him tartly. "I hardly need your assistance. I'm not sure you could track your way out of a gunny sack!"

Clint jerked up his head and glared daggers at the infuriating man who could fire insults faster than bullets. "I'll have you know I was a scout for the Army of the West before I turned to marshaling. If I can track renegade Indians then I can damn sure trail Reece Pendleton!"

"I wintered with several tribes in the mountains," Shaler countered the boast—something he had never done until he found himself in competition for Casity's affection . . . if she had any left to give by the time he found her.

Clint took up his reins and nudged his steed ahead. "Good for you, Mc*Pain*. Just don't get in my way. I don't want your horse disturbing any hoof prints."

Shaler rammed his steed into Clint's, knocking him out of the way to take the lead. He wondered if he might have liked Clint if they hadn't found themselves rivals for Casity's affection. But Shaler hadn't come all this way to be bested by a cowtown marshal!

As far as Shaler was concerned, Clint Lake had displayed no talent at *anything*. The next few hours would determine how much assistance he could be. If there was one thing Shaler had gotten good at the past few months it was rescuing Casity from one calamity after another. He only hoped this most recent pitfall wouldn't turn out to be her last!

Thirty-two

Casity awoke to find herself staring at the world upside down, strapped over the back of a horse along with the supplies stolen from the dry goods store—enough to keep Reece from going hungry for two weeks. She was unaware of the events that had transpired since her unsuccessful escape attempt—and oblivious to Shaler's and Clint's efforts to save her. Neither did she know that Reece had set the store afire, depriving her of a livelihood in case he allowed her to live.

All that Casity really knew for certain was that if she didn't make another effort to save herself she wasn't long for this world. Pensively, she studied the various supplies encircling her. She would have given anything for a sharp knife to cut the ropes and dive for cover in the bushes that lined the stream along which they passed.

Casity tilted her head upward to survey the rope that bound her wrists. In Reece's haste to make his departure, he hadn't tightly secured the knot around the saddle horn. If Casity could discreetly contort her body and lift her arms she could possibly slip the knot off and free herself.

Gritting her teeth in determination, Casity laid her head against the saddle and dug her knees into the other side of the steed to shift her weight sideways.

She lifted her arms, holding her wrists directly above the pommel, and gave a quick tug. When she received nothing for her efforts except strained muscles, she tried again . . . and again . . . and again . . .

Casity was elated when she finally felt the knot glide over the saddle horn and sag against her back. Arching upward, she hurled herself away from the horse and rolled over in the grass. Struggling to her feet, she had only taken two jackrabbit hops before Reece realized she had escaped. A furious growl rumbled in his chest as he swung to the ground to give chase.

"Damn you, bitch," he seethed as he stalked after her. "I ought to dispose of you here and now. You're more trouble than you're worth . . . argh!"

Reece doubled over in pain when Casity wheeled around and bounded toward him like a butting ram. To her delight, she watched Reece stumble backward over fallen logs and splash into the creek. But before she could pivot around to lose herself in the underbrush, Reece leaped to his feet and charged after her, cursing her with every step. Casity tried to duck under the low-hanging limbs, but Reece snaked out a hand and yanked her hair painfully, forcing her off balance. When she fell back into his waiting arms, his sneering face hovered over hers.

"You asked for this, damn you," he snarled hatefully. "This time I'm going to make *sure* you don't escape again!"

Tweed Cramer stood beside Cora, his new bride, in the middle of Ogallala's main street, staring incredulously at the charred remains of the Crockett Dry Goods Store. He had been in high spirits when he stepped from the train and had rented a hotel room for the night. But his mood had nose-dived when he realized another calamity had befallen Casity. He also wanted to know if that stubborn son of his had followed his heart instead of his foolish head. Tweed's eyes drifted to his attractive wife and he found himself counting his blessings while poor Casity had nothing left to count.

When Deputy Rogers ambled past the demolished building, Tweed latched onto his arm. "Can you tell me where I can find Casity?"

Deputy Rogers eyed the fashionably-attired man who stood beside his petite, well-dressed wife. With a curious frown, he said, "You don't know? Where were you when the fire broke out?"

"My wife and I just arrived by train," Tweed informed him. "I met Casity while she was in Dakota and I came to see how she is."

Suspicion filled the deputy's mind. This influx of folks from Dakota had brought disaster for Casity Crockett. Reece Pendleton had also claimed he had come to visit Casity and now she was missing! The deputy reminded himself that he might very well be staring at another potential catastrophe.

"Now listen here, mister, that girl has had her share of trouble the past few months. You better not be in cahoots with Reece Pendleton or I'll haul you off to jail before you know where you went!"

"Reece Pendleton!" Tweed squawked in disbelief and then gaped at the pistol that had suddenly been turned on him. "Good God, don't tell me that scoundrel is responsible for puttin' Casity outta business!"

The shocked expression on Tweed's clean-shaven face and the genuine concern in his voice convinced Deputy Rogers that the newcomer was not another threat. He slid his pistol back into its holster and nodded somberly. "Because of Reece Pendleton this town has been jumping tonight," he reported. "Casity had

just returned from her date with Marshal Lake when
a man named McCain showed up and—"

"McCain?" Cora spoke up, only to be waved to silence by her new husband.

"You folks know him?" Deputy Rogers questioned

"Yes, I'm acquainted with him," Tweed acknowl-
edged without going into detail. "Go on, deputy
What happened after McCain showed up?"

"Well, according to McCain, that Pendleton fellow
sneaked in to kidnap Casity and hold her for ransom."

Tweed groaned in dismay, but he managed to hold
his tongue.

"The marshal and I thought McCain was the one
trying to abduct Casity so we stuffed him in jail."

Tweed muttered a series of hisses and curses without interrupting the deputy.

"But come to find out, it was Pendleton who had
knocked Casity on the head and then blamed McCain
While McCain was trying to explain, Pendleton se
fire to the store and hauled Casity away. Marshal Lake
and McCain are out searching for her at this very mo
ment."

A feeling of sickening dread swept over Tweed when
he remembered the encounter he and Shaler had wit
Reece before leaving Deadwood. It was glaringly ap
parent that Reece held Casity responsible for his woe
and that he had come to collect what he spiteful
considered his due. And it was Tweed's fault tha
Casity had received part of the blame. Damn it,
anything happened to that girl because of him, Twee
would never be able to live with himself!

"Which way did McCain and Lake ride out?" Twee
asked anxiously.

"Northwest," Rogers reported.

"Where's the blacksmith shop?" Cora inquire
"We need two mounts."

"Surely you aren't planning to take your wife with
u. It could be dangerous and she might get caught
crossfire," Rogers said confidentially to Tweed.

Cora's head snapped up when she overheard the
mments. "I do most certainly intend to accompany
y husband," she assured him in no uncertain terms.
Vhere Tweed goes, I go!"

That was one of the many things Tweed adored
out his new bride. She was full of spunk and devo-
n and was always ready and willing to accompany
m wherever he decided to go. In fact, her spirit re-
nded him of Casity. They were two of a kind, and
veed thanked his lucky stars he had found Cora!

Tweed broke into a smile when Cora reached up on
toe to place a quick kiss to his lips before she pivoted
her heel. "I'll be right back with your pistols and
munition."

Deputy Rogers grinned curiously. "If you don't
nd my asking, just how long have the two of you
en married? My wife hasn't treated me like that in
ars."

"Two glorious weeks," Tweed informed him
udly.

"That explains it," Deputy Rogers grunted as he
stured to Tweed to follow him to the blacksmith
op.

Perhaps that explained everything to the deputy, but
veed had waited overly long to wed and he intended
see that the sparkle never fizzled out of his marriage.
ra made him feel like a young man again. She was
en and caring and demonstrative and Tweed soaked
up like a sponge.

His thoughts trailed off when the grimness of
sity's situation struck him like a physical blow. He
s ashamed to be feeling so content while she was
 deep in turmoil. Knowing Shaler had finally ar-

rived in Ogallala was encouraging—he had hope
Shaler would come to his senses before it was too late . .
But considering the gravity of the situation, Twee
hoped to hell it wasn't too late already . . .

Shaler swung down from his mount to survey th
tracks they had picked up northwest of town. Usin
the glow from his cigar, he studied the prints tha
revealed the trail of two horses—one of which wa
carrying an excessive load, judging by the depth c
the tracks. The animal was taking shorter strides t
bear the heavy weight.

"I suspect Reece has Casity strapped on the bac
of the horse that's also carrying supplies," Shaler pr
dicted.

"Brilliant deduction," Clint smirked. "What did yo
think the man would do? Load *his* mount down, ju
in case we overtook him and he had to make a ma
dash for his life?"

Flinging Clint a poisonous glare, Shaler steppe
into the stirrup and urged his steed forward. "Loo
Flake, the last thing I need is your wisecracks. In fac
the last thing I need is *you*—period!"

Clint gave Shaler the once-over twice. "Honest t
God, Casity must have been in dire straits to let herse
get mixed up with you. I'd like to shoot you whe
you sit after that remark about Casity being yo
woman. I want you out of her life for good. Obvious
that's what she wants, too, since she never bothere
to mention you to me or anyone else when she cam
back. I've seen your kind before—born under a wa
dering star. Casity deserves better."

"I happen to love her!" Shaler exploded, amaze
at his own words.

McCain knew it was a damn shame he hadn't con

that realization sooner. But hell's fire, he'd been
ry after so much humiliation a decade ago.

alling in love with Casity Crockett had been much
rse than the first time, that was for sure! She had
ven Shaler crazy! She was so stubborn and inde-
dent and damn near impossible to predict. And
, her feisty spirit lured him to her like a moth to
: proverbial flame. Shaler couldn't walk all over
sity because her fiery nature matched his own. For
t he admired her, in a frustrated sort of way.

Casity had continued to haunt him night and day.
en she was in his arms, responding in wild aban-
n, nothing else mattered. It was more than desire
t drew Shaler to her and kept him there. If all he
d felt was passion, he wouldn't have drunk himself
nd trying to forget her and then ridden hell-for-
ther to get her back. He wouldn't have suffered so
ch jealousy when he saw Clint kissing her. She trig-
ed every possessive and protective instinct he had.

"You love her?" Clint asked sarcastically. "Don't
ke me laugh, Mc*Pain*. Men like you don't fall in
e, you fall in *lust*."

haler was sorely tempted to determine if Clint was
quick on the draw as he was with his tongue. It
uld also alleviate the competition for Casity's affec-
n—*if* she had any left to give by the time they caught
with her.

"And what do you think you have to offer a woman
e Casity?" Shaler sniped.

"At least I could give her devotion, stability, and all
: affection she could ever want!" Clint said with
eat confidence. "Why don't you let go of this ridicu-
s notion that Casity cares for you. I'm the one she
eds. She must have realized that, too, or she
uldn't have walked out on you in Deadwood."

"She didn't walk out on me because I wasn't th
for her to walk out on. I was—"

"So you walked out on her, did you? And you
surprised she pretended not to know you?" he scof
disdainfully. "Give it up, Mc*Pain*. You had yo
chance."

Before Shaler could say a word on his own beh
Clint rushed on. "I could make her happy if you'd r
out of here the same way you rode in. I've been sw
on her for almost a year. She was standoffish until
returned from Dakota. I think whatever dealings
had with you convinced her that she belonged w
me. And just when things were beginning to show d
nite possibilities, here you came out of nowhere!"

"She said she loved me," Shaler told Clint or
again. Unfortunately this stubborn ox still refused
believe it.

"If she said it at all, it was in a moment of madn
no doubt," Clint countered flippantly.

"It was immediately after I had saved her life
the *third* time," Shaler defended hotly. "At least I
tried to save her from disaster. You threw her to
wolves!"

"I didn't know what was going on," Clint protest
"But the point is you shouldn't expect to hold Ca
to her confession. People are prone to say crazy thi
when their emotions are running high. She obviou
confused love with gratitude."

"Maybe she did mistake love for gratitude," Sha
contended before his lips curved into a smile. "I
has it occurred to you that she may have come to y
only on the *rebound*?"

Before Clint could open his mouth to respond
the cutting comment, Shaler flung up a hand to
mand silence. He cocked his head to listen to
sounds of the night as his probing gaze circled

ve that lined the creek. As far as Shaler could tell,
s was the prime hiding place for miles, with its
nse underbrush. It wasn't so much that Shaler *heard*
thing that alerted him to Reece's presence, but
her he *sensed* danger lurking in the darkness.

Clint had apparently come to the same conclusion
ause he hadn't moved a muscle, either. They set
de their personal conflict and dismounted simulta-
usly, gliding their pistols from their holsters. Like
king tigers, they followed the winding creek that
tered like a ribbon of silver in the moonlight.

All his senses were on full alert as Shaler inched over
fallen limbs in his path. He cautioned himself not
take Reece for granted, even for a second. He had
ostage as leverage, and Shaler had no doubt the
undrel would play this situation to his greatest ad-
tage.

And it was all Clint's fault that Reece had any advan-
e whatsoever, Shaler thought sourly. If things didn't
n out as well as he hoped, Shaler had every intention
seeing that Clint paid dearly for his mistake!

Casity glowered at the despicable excuse for a man
o had bound her and left her sitting atop her steed
h a hangman's noose around her neck. Warily, she
nced up at the rope that had been tossed over an
erhanging limb. She had found herself in several
ht scrapes of late, but this was positively the worst!
l Reece had to do was snap the tree branch that
ved as his makeshift whip against the horse's rump
d she'd be off to the pearly gates. And to infuriate
r all the more, he had gagged her.

Reece snickered in fiendish amusement after Casity
ed to glare him down from her perch. He had
nted to take possession of this feisty female's body

just once before he disposed of her, but she'd b[e]
so difficult to handle that he couldn't risk letting [h]
escape again. Knowing that Shaler and that fool
marshal would be tracking him sooner or later, Re[ece]
had decided to make his stand. The tree-laden cr[eek]
was the perfect place to let his pursuers come to h[im.]
When they realized the precariousness of Casi[ty's]
plight, they would skedaddle back to town to fetch [the]
ransom money.

Of course, Reece had cleaned out the cash regis[ter]
in the dry goods store before setting the build[ing]
afire, but that wasn't enough money to support h[im]
in the manner to which he had grown accustomed[.]

Reece flinched when he heard the snap of twigs [in]
the near distance. It appeared that the moment [of]
reckoning had come.

Shaler muttered several epithets when the mars[hal]
stepped on a dry limb, accidentally announcing th[eir]
arrival. Damn the man! He wouldn't last a day in [the]
mountains, dealing with Indians. He'd be scalped [be]-
fore he knew what hit him.

"I know you're out there," Reece called as he p[osi]-
tioned himself beside the horse's rump, using Cas[ity]
and her horse as his shield. "Come out in the op[en]
so I can see you, McCain. And bring that marshal w[ith]
you. I know he's here, too, since he's sweet on t[he]
bitch."

Shaler sent Clint a glower that could have mel[ted]
metal. "I swear, *Flake*, you couldn't sneak up on sta[m]-
peding elephants."

"Hurry up," Reece snapped impatiently. "If y[ou]
dally another minute, I'll send Casity's horse off [at]
full gallop."

Shaler didn't understand the meaning of Ree[ce's]
threat until he stepped around the bend of the cre[ek]
to see the predicament Casity was in. There she [was,]

ith her arms tied behind her back and her chin tilted
p at an uncomfortable angle to prevent the noose
om rubbing her throat raw. One false move and
asity's life was over!

When Shaler and Clint revealed themselves, Reece
rinned in sinister delight. "I've been expecting the
vo of you," he said in mock greeting. "I hope one
f you had the foresight to bring the ransom money."

"We—" Clint started to speak the truth, but Shaler
eat him to the punch without batting an eyelash.

"I left the money in the saddlebags," Shaler declared
 he discreetly surveyed the situation. "Of course, I
n't have the deed to the mine with me, but I'm sure
e cash will tide you over until the claim can be trans-
rred."

"We can quibble over those details later," Reece as-
red him haughtily. "Now fetch my money."

"We left our horses half a mile away," Clint in-
rmed him.

Reece smiled sarcastically. "Then I suggest you start
alking, marshal. I'm running short on patience. It
ppens every time I'm deprived of a good night's
eep."

Casity peered at the two men standing in the moon-
ht that speared down onto the clearing beside the
eek bed. Her eyes absorbed every detail of Shaler's
owerful body, wondering why it had to be *this* impos-
le man that her heart desired instead of the man
o treated her with respect. It was a shame she
uldn't make herself love Clint Lake. It was that
lden-eyed rake's memory that she would cherish for
 eternity—into which she would soon arrive if Reece
d his way, and it looked as though he would!

When Clint pivoted to fetch the saddlebag—which
ntained nothing but beef jerky and canned beans,
ow warning growl froze him in his tracks.

"The marshal isn't going anywhere until you m[
away from Casity's horse," Shaler insisted.

"You're in no position to make demands, McCai[
Reece scoffed. "I'm not budging until I have [
money. You can risk this bitch's life if you wish. Af[
all, it isn't your neck or mine. As for me, I coul[
care less what happens to her."

Shaler seethed silently. Reece had no regard for a[
one but himself and was willing to make any sa[
fice—human or otherwise—to ensure his own safe[

"Get going, marshal," Reece demanded gruffly.

Casity had seen that deadly gleam in Shaler's e[
before. Sure enough, he was going to defy Reece. S[
had often heard it said that no creature alive was m[
dangerous or unpredictable than a renegade Indi[
who'd been cornered. The same held true for Sha[
McCain.

The last time she and Shaler had found themsel[
in a similar crisis, Casity had thrown herself sidew[
so he could get a shot at her captor. But this time, s[
could do nothing—short of hanging herself!

When Shaler became as still as stone, Casity brac[
herself, knowing full well that something drastic v[
about to happen. An unnerving calmness settled o[
him—one that Clint couldn't begin to emulate, thou[
he had stared death in the face several times himse[
But Clint's self-control couldn't hold a candle to t[
foreboding presence beside him. The truth was t[
Shaler McCain was quick-witted, lightning-fast and [
ferocious as a panther.

Right there and then, Casity placed her trust, fai[
and her life in Shaler's hands, just as she had plac[
her love—unrequited though it had been.

When Clint kissed her earlier that evening, she h[
known for certain that no man could ever take Shale[
place in her heart. No matter how hard she had tr[

forget the past, Shaler's memory burned like a bea-
n in the night. No man could set fire to her soul after
aler McCain had ignited those sweet fires with a for-
dden kiss. Casity would go to her grave loving that
ven-haired giant who stood his ground, refusing to
ll any man his master, refusing to be cowed by this
indling sidewinder who was, at this moment, hiding
hind a woman's skirts.

Shaler's penetrating gaze shifted momentarily to
sity. There was no fear in those luminous blue eyes.
e really hadn't expected to see any. Casity had flirted
th death so often the past few months that she had
rned to adapt to it. But what stunned Shaler to the
ne was her look of faith and trust. No matter what
d transpired between them, this fiery beauty had
aced herself at his mercy, prepared to accept what-
er fate he designed for her.

Her expression also held a hint of curiosity, as if
e were silently inquiring as to his plan of action.
though her gag prevented her from uttering a word,
aler knew she expected something unusual from
m. Shaler doubted Reece Pendleton did, however.
e was too busy gloating over the seeming success of
s scheme.

Without so much as moving a muscle, Shaler's at-
ntion settled on Reece's smug smile. "There's only
e thing I don't understand about these arrange-
ents, Pendleton," Shaler said in a carefully con-
olled voice.

Clint slowly pivoted back to his original position be-
le Shaler. His wary glance bounced from Reece to
sity. He didn't have the faintest notion what tactic
is daredevil intended to employ. Indeed, the tone
 Shaler's voice was so devoid of feeling that he could
ve been concealing killing fury or utter boredom
d Clint wouldn't have known the difference. But the

aura of deadly calm that surrounded him warr
Clint not to make any abrupt moves.

"Just what is it that has you befuddled, McCai
Reece questioned with an arrogant smirk. "I
whether this bitch will come out of this ordeal al
Surely you realize her chances are getting slimr
with every moment you delay."

"No," Shaler replied with a cold smile. "I told
I had every intention of seeing you deep in hell. T
wasn't a threat. That was a promise. I never m
promises I don't keep—just as I promised Amos Gr
I would get his money back from you." The fro
smile on Shaler's lips disappeared in less than a he
beat as his golden eyes riveted on Reece's face. "N
just how in the hell can you think you're going to
out of here alive— *no matter what else happens . . .*

Reece hadn't expected a counterthreat. He wa
quite as adept at concealing his emotions as Sh
was. His gray eyes narrowed to murderous slits.

Shaler's remark had assured Reece that the rans
money wasn't forthcoming, no matter what lever
Reece held over him. How he despised dealing v
this imposing lout who had hornswoggled him ou
his fortune, shot him in the arm, and beaten the
out of him. Reece would show this bastard no me
and he certainly wasn't cutting this haughty bitch
slack, either!

With a growling snarl, Reece exploded in co
blooded vengeance and popped his switch popp
against the horse's rump. He had every intention
distracting these two men by hanging Casity, giv
himself time to dive for cover and scramble off to saf

"The rope!" Shaler blared at Clint as he drew
Colt and fired with lightning speed.

Clint reacted immediately. Two pistols barked
instant the startled steed lunged away. The thr

and rope tied around Casity's neck frayed beneath
e onslaught of bullets, but it didn't snap in two when
e horse bolted out from under her. Shaler swore
hemently when Casity was left hanging in midair
a single strand.

The excessive strain on the single strand would have
apped it, sending the body crashing to the ground
fore too much damage had been done— *if* it had
en bearing the weight of a man. But that wasn't true
Casity's case. Shaler had made a critical miscalcu-
ion—one he knew would haunt him all the days of
life. Casity didn't weigh more than a hundred pounds
d that one strand of rope continued to hold her aloft
what seemed to Shaler like an eternity.

God have mercy! This was the only time Casity had
t her complete faith and trust in his hands and he
d killed her! She was swinging by her neck and he
uldn't reach her fast enough!

"Cas . . . ! ! !"

Shaler's haunted voice echoed in the night like the
wling wind before it died into the kind of silence
t knew no equal—not on this side of heaven . . . or
ll . . .

Thirty-three

Shaler suffered for every sin he had ever committ[ed] plus a few he had never even considered, as he dash[ed] forward to grab Casity. For those horrible mome[nts] while she was hanging by that one strand of ro[pe] Shaler wondered if *he* would ever be able to brea[the] again. Before he could reach Casity, the rope fin[ally] snapped and she dropped like a rock on the mu[ddy] creek bank. His heart seemed to plunge to his st[om]ach, refusing to beat.

His pistol swung toward the clump of bushes wh[ere] Reece had disappeared. Vengeance churned ins[ide] Shaler like a boiling thundercloud. The instant he [saw] the gleam of the silver barrel protruding from [the] underbrush, he fired two consecutive shots. A blas[t of] gunfire exploded from the bushes and Shaler di[ved] to the ground, only a few inches away from Casi[ty's] crumpled form. Reece's wild shot hit the tree a[nd] Shaler waited, wondering if he had found his ma[rk.] But it was difficult to tell since Clint proceeded [to] blast two more holes in the bushes for good m[ea]sure . . .

Although Shaler knew he should check to see w[hat] condition Reece was in, his foremost concern [was] Casity. Her lips were deathly pale and her lashes [lay] against her wan cheeks as if they never meant to f[lut]ter open again. As if he were handling fragile crys[tal]

Shaler drew her onto his lap and pressed the heel of his hand against her chest.

"Breathe, damn you, princess," he muttered in frustration. "Don't you dare give Pendleton one ounce of satisfaction!"

Frantic, Shaler touched his fingertips to her throat, willing himself to find her pulse. He wondered if he felt a faint breath of life stirring inside her or if he had only imagined it.

"Curse your hide, McPain," Clint roared furiously. "You and your heroics! You killed her. You were afraid she was going to choose me over you and so you let her die!"

Shaler spared the near-hysterical marshal a withering glance before he forced air in and out of Casity's lungs with the heel of his hand. "Did you think Pendleton planned to let her live, even if we did hand over the ransom?" His derisive snort assured Clint that he had been entertaining false hope if he harbored any such assumption. "Besides, I didn't see you coming up with any better ideas."

"You didn't give me time to think of any options," Clint huffed as he squatted down to brush the back of his hand over Casity's ashen cheek.

"Yeah, right," Shaler scoffed sarcastically. "There wasn't time for your slow-acting brain to come up with a solution. Hell would have frozen over . . ."

His voice trailed off when Casity stirred slightly. Hope soared inside Shaler when he felt her shudder in his arms.

"Don't just stand there, Flake. Go see if you can find Pendleton," Shaler ordered brusquely. "Damn, who tells you what to do in Ogallala? Deputy Rogers?"

Clint drew himself up. Oh, how he would love to smash his fist into this rascal's face. "The name is Flake, damn it."

"Fine, go check on Pendleton, *Lake damn it,*" Sha
demanded.

Clint stamped angrily toward the bushes, his pis
aimed and ready. But since Reece hadn't tried
bushwhack them the past few minutes, Clint was
expecting to find the man in any condition to fig
back.

"Dead," Clint pronounced without the slight
hint of pity.

Shaler didn't waste any time mourning Pendleto
passing, either. The man had been without a c
science or a heart. He'd had a black soul.

When Clint stomped back, his green eyes narrow
menacingly. "Now that the worst is over, I want y
out of my town, Mc*Pain.*"

Just to get Clint's goat, Shaler bent to press a ten
kiss to Casity's forehead. "Wake up, princess. Mars
Flake wants us to get out of *his* town."

"Not *her!* Just *you!*" Clint muttered. "And keep y
hands off her. She's still my girl."

Shaler ignored him. He pulled Casity's limp b
between his bent legs and reached around to un
her wrists before giving her a shake.

"Quit that!" Clint blared. "She barely escap
hanging, for crissakes. You'll jerk her head off—"

His voice trailed off when Casity moaned grogg
and nuzzled against Shaler's chest as if she belong
there. Despite Clint's objections, Shaler propp
Casity against him as if he were her human armch:
patiently waiting for her to fight her way through
cobwebs that tangled her mind. And all the wh
Shaler sat there grinning devilishly, despite Cli
hostile glare. He had taken on better men than t
love-starved marshal on his bad days.

Still dazed from her near-brush with death, Ca
curled into the warm strength that surrounded h

is familiar scent caused her malfunctioning brain to
over between dream and reality. When her arm
oped over Shaler's shoulders in a reflexive display
' familiarity, he grinned at the murderous scowl that
:cupied Clint's features.

"Why don't you haul Pendleton off?" Shaler sug-
:sted. "I can take care of Cas. No need for you to
et about that."

To further infuriate Clint, Shaler dropped another
ss to her brow and snickered inwardly when she nuz-
ed closer. Even if Casity's stubborn mind refused to
lmit there was still a powerful chemistry between
em, her body remembered his touch and responded
stinctively. Her reaction gave him hope that they
uld make a new beginning . . . if this pesky marshal
uld go away and leave them alone!

"I'd be crazy to even consider leaving Casity in your
utches," Clint growled sourly.

"You said it, *Flake*. I didn't." Shaler flashed him an
nery smile that displayed pearly white teeth.

"Get your damn hands off her!" Clint exploded in
utrage.

When Clint reached down to draw Casity into his
ms, Shaler refused to release her. Casity was stung
' the odd sensation that she was a wishbone about
be snapped in two. When her eyes fluttered open,
e saw two fuzzy faces swimming above her.

She felt as if every ounce of strength had been
ained from her. Besides the raw flesh on her throat,
r head was still pounding from the blow Reece had
:livered when she had tried to escape from her room
rlier that evening. But despite her exhaustion,
asity was content to nestle in Shaler's protective
ms. That was where she wanted to be, whether he
.lly wanted her there or not.

When her vision cleared, her gaze focused on

Shaler's face, memorizing each feature that she h
feared she would never see again. When her hand rc
reflexively to limn his cheekbones, a faint smile hc
ered on her mouth.

"There for a moment, I wasn't sure your aim w
true," she rasped through collapsed vocal cords.

"It was *my* bullet that snapped the rope," Clint i
sisted, grasping at any attempt to earn Casity's adr
ration—and most of all, her love. "This darede
played your life as his wild card and he very nea
lost!"

"*Your* bullet?" Shaler scoffed insultingly. "Consid
ing your accuracy, your bullet more than likely kill
yonder tree!"

Casity didn't care whose bullet hit its mark. She v
simply relieved that someone's had!

"I don't have to stand here and endure any mc
of your insults, Mc*Pain*," Clint muttered testily.

"No, you don't," Shaler agreed, his eyes danci
with mischief. "You'd probably have more fun if y
trotted off to arrest somebody. And you'd undou
edly enjoy it even more if you took an innocent vict
into custody by mistake."

Shaler's gaze returned to Casity. "This clov
clubbed me over the head and stashed me in jail, thir
ing I was the one who tried to kidnap you. If not 1
Marshal *Flake* here, you'd still be safely tucked in bec
Shaler didn't have the heart to tell her that she did
have a bed—or a home— left.

"Damn it, Mc*Pain!*" Clint roared. "Do you plan
hold that over my head for the rest of my life?"

Casity couldn't suppress a grin. Shaler was givi
Clint fits. How well she knew that feeling, but it v
more amusing when she wasn't on the receiving er
Shaler McCain could be pretty devilish when

anted to be. She had always loved and hated that
out him.

Since Clint was having no luck whatsoever dealing
ith Shaler, he turned his attention to Casity and tried
different approach—a far bolder one.

"Casity?" Clint carefully curled his fingers beneath
r chin, tilting her face to his. He ignored Shaler as
he weren't there—and Clint sorely wished he wasn't.
want you to come back to town with me right now.
hatever happened in Deadwood is of no consequence
me," he assured her. "All I care about is you and
."

How noble of him, Shaler thought to himself. Hell's
e, what was it going to take to rout this man? Shaler
dn't spent three days in a drunken stupor, endured
horrendous hangover, and ridden all this way just
r his health! He had come to confess what was in his
art, even if he had to say it in front of Sir Galahad
ake!

"I'm sorry you had to put up with this brute," Clint
ntinued as he traced the delicate curve of her jaw.
He doesn't know how to treat a woman like a lady."

No, he didn't, Casity silently agreed. But Shaler
cCain had a most intriguing way of treating a lady
e a woman. And who was Clint to pass judgment
Shaler? Criticizing Shaler's shortcomings was a
ivilege she reserved for herself and she took offense
Clint's remark. Never mind that she had been guilty
insulting Shaler a time or ten herself!

"Marry me, Casity," Clint proposed on the spot.
'll treat you right and I—"

"I rode all the way down from Dakota to talk to
r," Shaler butted in. "You can wait your turn."

Casity was touched by Clint's proposal, and by the
ct that he seemed willing to put the past months in
eadwood behind them forever, no matter what had

happened there. Although Casity had tried to preten
the time she had spent with Shaler didn't exist, ther
was simply no getting around it. She had fallen in lov
with Shaler and Clint couldn't take his place, no mat
ter how desperately she tried to make it happen.

For a long moment, Casity stared up at the sinew
giant who constantly turned her emotions wrong si(
out. The taste of his kisses had lingered on her li;
and his masculine scent clung to her skin. Casity ha
spent a month trying to forget everything about th
exasperating man. She had progressed through all tl
appropriate stages of heartbreak—spitefulness, ange
rejection, and indifference. She had mouthed all tl
customary platitudes. But the very sight of him ha
unfurled invisible tentacles that unlocked the precio
memories she had tried to bury in her heart. Shal
had colored every thought, feeling, and sensation th
made her who and what she had become.

Casity simply couldn't promise Clint something sl
would never be able to give. He was a kind, carir
man and he deserved more from a wife. Shal
McCain, rascal though he could be when he felt lil
it—and he felt like it quite often—was the only m;
her heart desired. Nothing Casity had done could ;
ter that fact. The sweet fires of summer burned in h
soul. Loving this ruggedly handsome frontiersm;
was a habit she hadn't been able to break.

Stubborn pride be damned, Casity decided. Aft
what she had just endured, she wanted to recaptu
those forbidden moments of indefinable pleasure
the ones she had discovered that first night Shaler h;
rescued her from certain death and taught her tl
meaning of passion. She was prepared to accept wh;
ever terms he offered, if only for a few precious m
ments that could compensate for all the turmoil . .

'I don't want to leave you here alone with him,"
int insisted, jolting Casity from her musings.

'It's all right, Clint," Casity assured him. "The least
an do is pay Shay the courtesy of listening to what
came all this way to say."

Progress! Shaler thought in satisfaction. At least
sity hadn't told him to go to hell—which was where
had been while he waited and wondered if she
uld survive.

'If this scoundrel had something so important to
to you, why did it take him over a month to ride
Nebraska to say it?" Clint quizzed, hoping to make
r see the foolishness of letting herself become in-
lved with this reckless tumbleweed all over again!

'I was expecting Casity to be in Deadwood when I
t back from tracking Jack McCall to Custer City,"
aler began. "It took me a full month to fulfill my
ligation to a good friend who helped to raise me
ring one of the worst times in my life. I wanted to
two places at once, but I couldn't. So I had to wait
til I got back to say what I wanted to say to Casity."

Clint hesitated, stung by the uneasy feeling that he
s about to lose the woman he loved to this ornery
pscallion. When Clint saw the way Casity was staring
at this brawny rogue, he felt a desperate need to
eak the wicked spell Shaler seemed to cast over her.

"Casity, this is madness! You're not the kind of
man to follow a whim. You're sensible and practi-
l—and I can give you all the things a woman needs!"

"You heard her, *Flake*, get lost," Shaler said impa-
ntly. "I'll bring her back to town when she feels up
traveling."

"But—"

"Hell's fire!" Shaler muttered, his patience de-
eted. "You're harder to get rid of than the plague!"

"I'll be fine, really," Casity reassured Clint.

Muttering under his breath, Clint stormed off
retrieve Reece's horse and see to hauling their vict
back to town. He hated to admit defeat, but Clint h
the unshakable feeling he had fought a difficult bat
and lost. If he hadn't been able to convince Casity
come with him now, he would never have anoth
chance. Shaler McCain wasn't a man who gave up e
ily, no matter the odds. He had proved that in h
dealings with Reece Pendleton.

Mulling over that depressing thought, Clint head
back to town, wishing that neither he nor Casity h
ever laid eyes on Shaler McCain. All his plans for
future with Casity crumbled around Clint like sa
castles eroding in the wind. He had lost her forev
And he wasn't feeling noble or generous enough
pretend to be a good sport about it, either!

Thirty-four

When they were finally alone, Shaler's head dipped
wn to take Casity's soft lips beneath his, savoring
d devouring her in the same moment. Lord, he'd
arly starved to death for this kiss! He'd gone hungry
ce the day Casity had walked out of his life more
an six weeks earlier. When she kissed him back, he
braced his feelings joyfully.

'Was there something you wanted to say to me?"
sity prompted when she finally came up for air.

She waited, hoping the tender kiss indicated the be-
ning of something long and lasting between them.

Shaler inhaled a deep breath, wrestling with the un-
niliar words he had uttered to no other woman in
his thirty years. It was like prying apart the shell
at surrounded his heart, exposing a vulnerability he
d spent years concealing from the world. But know-
g Clint Lake was waiting his chance made Shaler
termined to see that he and this bewitching nymph
me to an understanding—here, now, and forever-
re.

'I love you, princess," he murmured with genuine
ection. "I did then and I still do. I don't even re-
ember what it felt like not to want you with every
er of my being. I was afraid to trust the feelings
at you stirred inside me, afraid to let them show for
ir they would overwhelm me. And I know I'm not

as well-mannered and proper as your Prince Char
ing of a marshal. But just because I love you i
different way doesn't mean I love you any less."

His head moved toward hers, his amber eyes hold
her hostage until his lips brushed over her quiveri
mouth in the gentlest kind of kiss. "Honest to G
Cas, I never knew how love could be until there
you."

Casity felt the earth move beneath her when Sha
stole the breath from her lungs with another seari
kiss. His words echoed in her ears and filled her he
with such incredible joy that she was afraid she wo
explode. Shaler loved her? He honestly loved h
Casity never thought she would hear those words fr
his lips . . .

Before she was prepared to end the splendorous k
Shaler withdrew to trace her enchanting features.
hate to admit it, but I think I made a mistake,"
confessed—and that took some doing because Sha
hated being wrong about anything.

Casity winced as if she had been stabbed strai
through the heart. Now what was he going to do? T
man was making her crazy!

"If this is going to turn out like the night of
storm when I thought we were going make a new
ginning, then I don't want to hear it!" Casity mutte
as she attempted—unsuccessfully— to wriggle out
his arms. "I suppose Tweed will show up and tell
all over again that he sent you to find a way back to
good graces, no matter what you have to say or do!

Shaler blinked in surprise and then groaned in
may. So that was why Casity had given him the c
shoulder when they returned to the cabin. "You
wrong, princess," he said simply.

"Are you denying that was your ultimate purp

en and now?" Casity quizzed him, her eyes probing
eply into his.

Shaler reached out to trail his index finger over
ose dewy lips that had become more addicting than
ne, more satisfying than the gallon of whiskey he
d drunk to forget the anguish of Casity's farewell
ote. Just holding her again, drinking in the taste of
r, brought back those sweet memories of paradise.
aler couldn't remember another time in his life
en emotions hit him so hard or left such a lasting
pression. This bewitching firebrand forced him to
al with each and every one of them.

"Well?" Casity prodded when he refused to answer
mediately.

"No, I'm not denying that Tweed ordered me to
deem myself," he admitted and then hurried on.
But what I said and did *that* night came from the
art. There was no pretense then or now. Nor have
forgotten anything about the first night we spent
gether or that evening we were waylaid by the storm.
hose memories are more precious to me than any
her moments in my life."

When Casity relaxed against him, Shaler smiled in
lief, thankful they had leaped that hurdle without
argument.

"What I regret most of all is making the foolish
mment that just once in my life I wanted to hear a
oman say she loved me without expecting anything
return. But when you gave me your love, as well as
the freedom a man could possibly want, I never
lt as if I had everything and yet nothing at all. When
lost you, I suddenly lost my reason for being."

His lean fingers tunneled through the wispy cloud
auburn hair. Reverently, he tilted her face up to his
ss and sighed when her lips melted beneath his.

"I suffered the torments of the damned each time

your life was in jeopardy," he admitted huskily. "
cursed you each time you walked away, knowing y
took another part of me with you when you le
You've come to mean everything to me, Cas," Sha
assured her. "Without you I could barely stand n
self. Don't ever leave me again. I can't face the thoug
of letting you go."

When his strong arms embraced her, Casity forg
all the turmoil of the past. She was simply drifting
this wondrous eternal present, reveling in the exq
site pleasure of knowing she was loved.

"Marry me, princess," he whispered against h
lips. "Come to the mountains with me and be my lo
my life . . ."

When his masterful caresses glided beneath h
gown to dissolve her bones and turn her flesh to fi
Casity couldn't formulate a single thought, much le
a reply. All she wanted was to relive each and eve
magical moment she had spent in his arms, saili
over rainbows and soaring beyond stars. Shaler's lo
was the most precious gift life had to offer. Tho
agonizing weeks they had spent apart had only assur
her that life without this wonderful man was no mo
than a meaningless existence.

"Well, princess?" Shaler murmured as his kiss
drifted over her shoulder and his hand glided ov
the garments that deprived him of seeing and tou
ing her silky flesh. "Are you going to marry me,
must I kidnap you?" A quiet skirl of laughter rumbl
in his chest as he smiled against the roseate bud
had unveiled with his bold caresses. "Maybe y
would prefer abduction, since it's become such a
miliar occurrence in your life."

"Abduction? No," Casity breathed raggedly as h
tongue flicked at the throbbing peak, causing flam

o dance down her spine. "Seduction? Yes. That hasn't
)een common enough to suit my tastes."

Shaler raised his ruffled head and grinned roguishly.
Now that all their inhibitions and insecurities had
allen away, there was a new dimension to this fierce
attraction between them. Casity was playing the saucy
siren, and she played it exceptionally well! He adored
he way she was peeking up at him from beneath that
an of thick lashes, the way her delicate brows arched
o a provocative angle.

"Casity Crockett, you can be a full-fledged tempt-
ess when you want to be," he teased playfully.

"If that's so, why aren't I getting the results I want?"
he tossed back at him, her blue eyes dancing with
nischief.

"Because, princess, you haven't said the magic
vords."

His forefinger scaled the full swell of her breast and
lowly circled the dusky peak. His tantalizing caress
rced a soft moan from her throat.

"Please, Shay . . ." she whispered, her voice convey-
ng the frustrated passion that rippled inside her.

"Wrong words," he murmured against her quiver-
ng flesh. "I need to hear you say you love me in all
e ways I love you."

Casity framed his ruggedly handsome face in he
ands and drew his moist lips back to hers and gazed
ulfully into those amber pools. "I want you any way
can get you, Shaler McCain, and that's a fact," she
ssured him. "I'll do whatever it takes to keep you
ith me from now until forever. I love you, Shay, as I
ave loved no other. You're in my blood like a fever
can't cure and no longer want to try. You're all I'll
ver need . . ."

"Do you mean that? Truly?" Shaler prodded, his
xpression somber.

Casity couldn't fathom why he seemed so intent o
hearing her admit that she would sacrifice anythin
to be with him. But she didn't hesitate to assure hin
"I mean it with all my heart, Shay."

As much as Shaler yearned to strip away every la
article of clothing that separated them and expre
his love for Casity in ways no words could convey, l
had to tell her what had happened in town after sl
had been kidnapped. Shaler had wanted to hea
Casity say she would walk away from her life in th
cowtown to share their love, but he hadn't wanted h
to turn to him because she had nowhere else to g
He shouldn't have pressed her for unconditional cor
mitment, but he had to know that what she felt f
him couldn't be altered by outside influences.

Deep-abiding love did demand commitment, aft
all. It was such a simple and yet such a profound em
tion—far more complicated than Shaler had ev
imagined. But when it came to his love for Casity, l
knew it had to be all or nothing. There couldn't
anything in between. This gorgeous woman meant t
much to him, and he refused to settle for less th
everything she had to give because he wanted to gi
her everything within his power in return.

When Shaler became silent, Casity frowned cu
ously. "What's the matter?"

"Because of Pendleton's fiendish need for reveng
he set fire to your store, hoping to distract Clint a
me from following him out of town," Shaler inform
her as gently as possible. "At first I feared Pendlet
had left you in that blazing inferno. I walked throu
flames to find you." Shaler swallowed hard and forc
himself to finish. "There's nothing left, Cas. I
sorry."

Casity stared blankly up at him. Every worldly p
session she owned was gone? For a brief mome

panic clutched at her chest. But when her wide gaze locked with Shaler's, she reminded herself of those terror-filled moments when she had been hanging by her neck, feeling life's breath seeping out of her. All she had really wanted from this world, while she literally hung between life and death, was Shaler's love. Losing her keepsakes and trinkets had never even crossed her mind when she had come so close to dying. Material possessions held no value when one was forced to identify the true treasures of one's life.

Casity could tell by Shaler's expectant expression that he regretted having to report her catastrophic losses. He was holding his breath, unsure of how she was going to react. Now she understood why he had been so insistent on knowing the nature of her commitment to him. Shaler had once claimed that he wanted to be loved for himself, not as a means of security and protection.

After all they had been through together, did he think she would trade his love for all the riches in this life? He obviously didn't realize how just strong her affection for him was. Perhaps she would have to *show* him. It was a most intriguing prospect!

"You have no need to worry about money," Shaler assured her when she continued to stare up at him without uttering a word. "I put the deed to the mine in Bonanza Gulch in your name. Fact is, you've been filthy rich for a month and you didn't even know it."

"Thank you kindly, but I don't want your money," he replied with an impish smile.

"What about the cabin in Dakota? It's yours to dispose of as you see fit," he offered generously. "I want to make up for all the misery you've been through."

"Give it to someone else," she requested as her fingertips dived beneath his buckskin shirt to brush her hand over his chest.

The silly man! Didn't he know that his love was all
she needed? When he had confessed his affection for
her, he had given her the world.

"Then what is it that you want, princess?" he murmured huskily as her caresses sizzled through him like
lightning, causing a white-hot throb of desire to pul-
sate in his loins.

"What I want is for you to clam up and kiss me,"
Casity replied in a seductive purr that vibrated down
Shaler's backbone and sent tingles of anticipation rico-
cheting through every nerve ending.

"So what you're really saying is that all you've ever
wanted from me was my body?" Shaler chuckled at the
devilish twinkle in her eyes and the exaggerated nod
of her auburn head. "Damn, princess, I think I'm insulted."

"You'll get over it," Casity whispered as her adventurous fingers explored the muscles of his belly. "In
fact, I'll be right here to see that you *enjoy* getting over
it . . ."

The thunder of approaching hooves and a thrashing
in the underbrush caused Shaler to growl like an ill-
tempered grizzly bear. "Hell's fire, if that's Marshal
Flake coming to pester me again, I swear I'll rearrange
his face with my fist. I have yet to repay him for hammering me over the head and carting me off to jail . . ."

His voice trailed off when the lead rider burst
through the bushes, shouting at the top of his lungs
and waving his arms like a windmill.

"Well, I'll be damned!" Shaler croaked.

Shaler wasn't the only one astounded by Tweed's unexpected arrival. "What the devil is he doing here?"
Casity questioned. "And who is that woman with him?"

"Whatever Tweed is doing here, it is *not* to make sure
I've come to weasel my way back into your good graces.

Shaler told her firmly. His golden gaze locked with hers. "I love you. *Know* it and *believe* it because it's true."

Her understanding smile prompted an audible sigh of relief. He never wanted to live with so much torment between them again!

While Shaler and Casity were frantically pulling their clothes back on, Tweed swung down from his exhausted mount and spun around to lift Cora from the saddle. Casity assessed the dramatic changes that had taken place in Tweed's appearance since the last time she had seen him. Gone was the wooly beard and shaggy mane. His buckskin clothes had been replaced by a tailor-made jacket and matching breeches that complimented his sturdy physique. Tweed looked ten years younger without his beard, mustache, and the splint that left him hobbling around like a man twice his age.

"What the blazes are you doing in Ogallala?" Shaler asked without a polite greeting. His gaze darted from his elegantly dressed father to the attractive middle-aged woman who apparently had no problem charging off cross-country on a rescue mission in the middle of the night.

"Cora and I are on our honeymoon," Tweed explained as he proudly drew his bride up beside him and curled a possessive arm around her.

"Honeymoon?" Casity chirped.

"I didn't have time to tell you that Tweed ordered himself a new bride," Shaler murmured quietly. "It looks as if she's brought out the best in him, doesn't it?" A wry smile quirked his lips as he surveyed his father. "I never realized you could clean up so nicely."

After Tweed made the introductions, he demanded to know the details of the encounter that had left Pendleton draped over the back of a horse.

"There isn't all that much to tell," Shaler replied

with his customary nonchalance. "Casity is safe and
sound and that's all that matters to me." Then he
asked, "Just how did you find us?"

"We met Marshal Lake trotting across the meadow,"
Cora answered. "He seemed like a rather nice young
man until Tweed asked if he knew where to find you.
Then he started muttering and growling like a rabid
dog before galloping off."

"I see yer still makin' friends as easily as you always
did, Shay," Tweed snickered as he glanced speculatively
at Casity. "From what I learned in town, the marshal
is mighty sweet on you. Are there weddin' bells clanging
in yer future, Cas?"

"For Casity and me," Shaler responded. *"Not for
Marshal Flake!"*

Tweed grinned broadly at the announcement.
Shaler had finally followed his heart. It had certainly
taken him long enough!

"What splendid news," Cora enthused. "I'll be
happy to help you with the arrangements. I'm delighted with the idea of having a new son *and* daugh-
ter-in-law!"

Casity liked Cora on sight and every moment thereafter. Cora and Tweed seemed a perfect match, even
if the marriage had been arranged by mail. Cora's
warm brown eyes were filled with spirit and vitality.
Tweed Cramer had been blessed with incredible luck.

"We welcome the offer," Shaler assured his new
stepmother before glancing meaningfully at Tweed.
"Casity and I were just getting around to discussing
a wedding date when you arrived."

Tweed muffled a snicker behind an artificial cough.
If this hot-blooded rake had been involved in nothing
more than a discussion, Tweed would eat his newly
purchased plug hat, brim and all! It was also apparent
that Shaler had a few more . . . er . . . arrangements

he wanted to make in private before he rode back to town. Tweed took his cue after Shaler sent him at least a half-dozen pointed glances that requested the late arrivals make themselves scarce, leaving the social amenities until later.

"Well, I s'pose Cora and I should get back to town," Tweed declared as he assisted his new bride into the saddle. "We had a long rail ride and a frantic trip here to make sure Casity was all right. We'll see the two of you in the mornin'."

Shaler watched his father and Cora disappear into the trees. Perhaps it had been impolite to hurry Tweed on his way, but Shaler wanted Casity all to himself. A man could only stand so much society before the hunger that had plagued him for weeks got the better of him.

"Now, where were we before we were interrupted?" Shaler questioned seductively as he pulled Casity against him.

"We were just a kiss away from heaven," Casity whispered as she raised parted lips in eager invitation.

"Take me there again," Shaler rasped, his voice thick with longing. "It's been so long . . ."

Shaler groaned deep in his throat when Casity plied him with kisses and caresses. Her touch was like sunshine and summer wind. Never before had he known such inner peace, such sublime pleasure. It was as if his protective shell had fallen completely away, and he gained strength with each moment that they loved—body, heart, and soul. What a shame he had wasted precious days that he could never recapture. His stubborn pride had cost him priceless minutes and hours that were lost forever.

When he had told Casity that he had made a mistake, he had spoken the truth. It wasn't enough just to be loved unless forever was part of the bargain. He

couldn't turn back the hands of time and savor those
lost moments, but he could reap the most from the
years to come. This blue-eyed siren made him want
all those intangible blessings from life that he had
never even considered until she filled his world to
overflowing . . .

When Casity's inventive caresses teased and tor
mented him, over and over again, Shaler forgot how
to think, how to breathe. Her hands and lips were
everywhere at once, weaving a tapestry of indescrib
able pleasure. The wildfire they ignited in each other
had become a raging blaze of inextinguishable passion
that consumed and demanded all Shaler had to give

This spirited beauty had changed all his cynical
theories and made a true believer out of him. He lived
for her love; he fed upon it. Casity fanned the flame
with her tender touch and her whispered devotion.
She branded her initials on his heart and left him to
wonder how he had fought these fierce feelings as
long as he had. One look into those sapphire pool
that sparkled with love and he was drowning in the
fathomless depths, never to rise again and not caring
if he ever did.

"God, I love you, Cas," Shaler rasped as he twisted
to draw her body beneath his. "I want you . . . I need
you . . . I love you so much it scares me to death . .

Casity peered up into the shadowed face that formed
the perimeters of all her dreams. Shaler McCain fright
ened? The man had never been afraid of anything
far as she knew. Casity had seen him in every situation
imaginable, watching him defy all odds and test h
amazing talents. But the techniques he displayed when
he made wild, sweet love to her were the ones she loved
best of all.

Her hands glided up the ladder of his ribs and along
his powerful shoulder to frame his bronzed face. "I

longer afraid to care so much. But what frightens
e most is that I won't be granted time enough to show
u how much you mean to me," Casity whispered as
r body instinctively arched to meet the powerful
ngth of his, absorbing his strength as if it were her
vn, cherishing him with every part of her being. "I
nt to love you forever and beyond."

Shaler gathered her tightly to him, shuddering with
e intensity of the emotion that engulfed him. "This
the way love should be, princess," he murmured
fore he kissed her with all the passionate affection
possessed. "This invisible bond is so tender and
t so tough that nothing can tear it apart. Where
ere is love this pure and sweet there will always be
ever for the two of us . . ."

When he became a living, breathing part of her,
aring each breath, each frantic heartbeat, Casity
ew she had discovered the secret of blissful eternity.
aler took her beyond life's physical limitations,
nding her skyrocketing into a dimension of exis-
nce beyond time.

"Those sweet fires of summer we created together
ll burn through all the seasons of all the years to
me because they are the eternal flames of this love
eel for you," he whispered ever so softly, so sincerely.
And then, Shaler took her into his heart, his body,
d his soul. Love, with its sweet promise of eternity
Casity's silken arms, spread through him like a glo-
us, delicious warmth that left nothing unclaimed or
touched by its shimmering essence . . .